'Moyes again proves herself a worthy successor to Maeve Binchy and Rosamund Pilcher with her second novel . . . [she] deftly handles her involved plot, skillfully exploring the different family dynamics; her thoughtful tone and light touch makes this a delightful read' – *Publishers Weekly* on *Foreign Fruit*

'Moyes evokes the strictures of time beautifully, as well as the enervating charms of a sleepy resort'
– *Good Housekeeping* on *Foreign Fruit*

'Blissful, romantic reading' – *Company* on *Foreign Fruit*

'A very beautiful and very moving story' – Lesley Pearce on *Sheltering Rain*

'The characters are strong, believable and endearing – and will evoke recognition and sympathy from all ages . . . An enjoyable read – and a promising debut novel' – *Sunday Express* on *Sheltering Rain*

'Wonderful full-blooded traditional storytelling, but with a fresh slant' – Sarah Harrison on *Sheltering Rain*

'Believable characters, faithfully described scenery, horses and hounds, mud and mould, this is good, old-fashioned storytelling at its best . . . it is almost impossible to stop reading' – *North Shore Times*, Australia on *Sheltering Rain*

Also by Jojo Moyes:

Sheltering Rain
The Peacock Emporium

About the author

Jojo Moyes was born in 1969 and was brought up in London. A journalist and writer, she worked for the *Independent* newspaper until 2001. She lives in East Anglia with her husband and two children.

JOJO MOYES

FOREIGN FRUIT

CORONET BOOKS

Hodder & Stoughton

First published in Great Britain in 2003 by Hodder & Stoughton
This paperback edition published in 2004 by Hodder & Stoughton
A division of Hodder Headline

A Coronet paperback

1 3 5 7 9 10 8 6 4 2

A CIP catalogue record for this title is
available from the British Library

ISBN 0 340 83414 5

Typeset in Plantin Light by
Palimpsest Book Production Limited,
Polmont, Stirlingshire

Printed and bound in Great Britain by
Clays Ltd, St Ives plc

Hodder & Stoughton
A division of Hodder Headline
338 Euston Road
London NW1 3BH

To Charles Arthur
and Cathy Runciman

Acknowledgements

I would like to thank a number of people who in their various ways helped make this book possible, most importantly Nell Crosby of the Saffron Walden Women's Institute, and her husband Frederick, for providing me with their memories and mementos of life in a 1950s seaside town.

Likewise Neil Carter, General Manager of Moonfleet Manor in Dorset, for his insights into the renovation and running of a country house hotel. And Moonfleet's beauty therapist Tracie Storey for, among other things, explaining what pickling is.

Heartfelt thanks again to Jo Frank at AP Watt for hand-holding, motivating and occasional whip-cracking services to writing. And to Carolyn Mays of Hodder and Stoughton and Carolyn Marino of HarperCollins US for not just tactfully spotting the wrinkles, but allowing me the time and space to iron them out. Thanks also to Hazel Orme for her forensic line editing skills, and for teaching me more about grammar than I ever learned at school . . . I'll raise a metaphorical glass to Sheila Crowley for being an unstoppable force and also for showing me the interior of some of the best pubs and restaurants in London. And to Louise Wener for being a sounding board, partner in crime, and reminding me periodically that cocktails are of course an essential element of the whole publishing process.

Thanks to Emma Longhurst for persuading an old hack that publicity can be fun and to Vicky Cubitt for being endlessly prepared to indulge those of us who work from home with an ear. Closer to home, I must thank Julia Carmichael and the staff of Harts for their support, Lucy Vincent without whom I would have never got any work done, and to Saskia and Harry for sleeping occasionally and thus allowing me to do it. To Mum, and Dad, as ever. And most of all to Charles. Who puts up with it. And me. Not necessarily in that order. One day we'll talk about something else in the evenings . . . honest . . .

'Each has his past shut in him like the leaves of a book known to him by heart and his friends can only read the title.'

Virginia Woolf

Prologue

My mother once told me you could discover the identity of the man you were going to marry by peeling an apple and throwing the skin, in one piece, over your shoulder. It formed a letter, you see. Or, at least, sometimes it did: Mummy wanted things to work so desperately that she simply refused to admit that it looked like a seven, or a two, and dredged up all sorts of Bs and Ds from nowhere. Even if I didn't know a B or a D.

But I didn't need apples with Guy. I knew from the first moment I saw him; knew his face as clearly as I knew my own name. His was the face that would take me away from my family, that would love me, adore me, have beautiful little babies with me. His was the face I would gaze at, wordlessly, as he repeated his wedding vows. His face was the first thing I would see in the morning and the last in the sweet breath of night.

Did he know it? Of course he did. He rescued me, you see. Like a knight, with mud-spattered clothes in place of shining armour. A knight who appeared out of the darkness and brought me into the light. Well, the station waiting room, anyway. These soldiers had been bothering me, while I waited for the late train. I had been to a dance with my boss and his wife, and missed my train. They had had an awful lot to drink, and they kept talking and talking to me and just wouldn't take no for an answer, even though I knew jolly well not to talk to squaddies, turned as far away from them as I could and sat down on a bench in the corner. And then they got closer and closer until one of them started grabbing at me, trying to make out that it was some sort

1

of joke, and I got terribly afraid as it was late and I couldn't see a porter or anyone anywhere. And I kept telling them to leave me alone, but they wouldn't. They just wouldn't. And then the biggest one – who looked brutish – pushed himself against me, with his horrible bristly face and his stinking breath, and told me that he would have me, whether I liked it or not. And of course I wanted to scream but, you see, I couldn't because I was absolutely frozen with fear.

And then Guy was there. He came bursting into the waiting room and demanded to know what the man thought he was doing and said he was going to give him a real hiding. Then he squared up to the three of them, and they swore at him a bit, and one of them lifted his fists back, but after a moment or two, like the cowards they were, they just swore a bit more and ran.

And I was shaking, and terribly weepy, and he sat me down on a chair and offered to get me a glass of water so that I would feel a bit better. He was so kind. So sweet to me. And then he said he would wait with me until the train came. And he did.

And it was there, under the yellow station lights, that I first looked at his face. I mean, really looked. And I knew that it was him. It was really him.

After I told Mummy, she peeled an apple just to see, and threw it over my shoulder. To me, it came up looking like a D. Mummy swears to this day that it was clearly a G. But by then we were way beyond apples.

PART ONE

One

Freddie had been ill again. Grass, this time, apparently. It sat in a foaming, emerald pool in the corner by the tallboy, some of the blades still intact.

'How many times do I have to tell you, you dolt?' shrieked Celia, who had just trodden in it wearing her summer sandals. 'You are *not* a horse.'

'Or a cow,' added Sylvia, helpfully, from the kitchen table, where she was sticking pictures of domestic appliances laboriously into a scrapbook.

'Or any bloody animal. You should be eating bread, not grass. Cake. Normal things.' Celia picked her shoe from her foot and held it, between finger and thumb, over the kitchen sink. 'Ugh. You're *disgusting*. Why do you keep doing this? Mummy, tell him. He should at least clean it up.'

'Do wipe it up, Frederick dear.' Mrs Holden, seated in the high-backed chair by the fire, was checking the newspaper for the timing of the next broadcast of *Dixon of Dock Green*. It had provided one of her few compensations since the resignation of Mr Churchill. And that latest business with her husband. Although, of course, she only mentioned Mr Churchill. Both she and Mrs Antrobus, she told Lottie, had watched all the episodes so far, and thought the programme simply marvellous. Then again, she and Mrs Antrobus were the only people in Woodbridge Avenue with televisions, and took some delight in telling their neighbours quite how marvellous nearly all the programmes were.

5

'Clean it *up*, Freddie. Ugh. Why do I have to have a brother who eats animal food?'

Freddie sat on the floor by the unlit fire, pushing a small blue truck backwards and forwards along the rug, lifting the corners as he did so. 'It's not animal food,' he muttered contentedly. 'God said to eat it.'

'Mummy, now he's taking the name of the Lord in vain.'

'You shouldn't say God,' said Sylvia, firmly, as she stuck a food mixer on to mauve sugar paper. 'He'll strike you down.'

'I'm sure God didn't actually say grass, Freddie dear,' said Mrs Holden, distractedly. 'Celie darling, could you pass me my glasses before you leave? I'm sure they're making the print smaller in these newspapers.'

Lottie stood patiently by the door. It had been rather a wearing afternoon and she was desperate to get out. Mrs Holden had insisted that she and Celia help her prepare some meringues for the Church sale, even though both girls loathed baking, and Celia had somehow managed to extricate herself after just ten minutes by pleading a headache. So Lottie had had to listen to Mrs Holden's fretting about egg whites and sugar, and pretend not to notice when she did that anxious fluttery thing with her hands and her eyes filled with tears. Now, finally, the horrid things were baked and safely in their tins, shrouded in greaseproof paper and, surprise, surprise, Celia's headache had miraculously disappeared. Celia placed her shoe back on her foot and motioned to Lottie that they should leave. She pulled her cardigan round her shoulders and straightened her hair briskly in the mirror.

'Now, girls, where are you going?'

'To the coffee house.'

'To the park.'

Celia and Lottie spoke at the same time, and stared at each other in mute accusatory alarm.

6

'We're going to both,' said Celia, firmly. 'Park first, then for a coffee.'

'They're going off to kiss boys,' said Sylvia, still bent over her sticking. She had pulled the end of one plait into her mouth. It emerged periodically, silkily wet.

'Mmmmmmwaahhh. Mwah. Mwah. Eeyuk. Kissing.'

'Well, don't drink too much of it. You know it makes you go all unnecessary. Lottie dear, make sure Celia doesn't drink too much of it. Two cups maximum. And be back by six thirty.'

'In Bible class, God says the earth will provide,' said Freddie, looking up.

'And look how sick you got when you ate that,' said Celia. 'I can't believe you're not making him clear it up, Mummy. He gets away with *everything*.'

Mrs Holden accepted her glasses and placed them slowly on her nose. She wore the look of someone who was just about managing to stay afloat in rough seas by insisting against all evidence that she was actually on dry land. 'Freddie, go and ask Virginia to bring a cloth, will you? There's a good boy. And, Celia dear, don't be horrid. Lottie, straighten your blouse, dear. You've gone peculiar. Now, girls, you're not going off to gawp at our new arrival, are you? We don't want her thinking the residents of Merham are some kind of peasants, standing there with their mouths hanging open.'

There was a brief silence, during which Lottie saw Celia's ears flush ever so slightly pink. Her own were not even warm: she had perfected her denials over many years and against tougher interrogators. 'We'll come straight home from the coffee house, Mrs Holden,' said Lottie, firmly. Which could, of course, have meant anything at all.

It was the day of the great changeover, of those arriving on

7

the Saturday trains from Liverpool Street, and those who, only marginally less pale, were reluctantly heading back to the city. On these days the pavements were criss-crossed by small boys hauling hastily constructed wooden trolleys piled high with bulging suitcases. Behind them exhausted men in their good summer suits linked arms with their wives, glad, for the sake of a few pennies, to begin their annual holiday like kings. Or at least without having to lug their own cases to their lodgings.

So the arrival was largely unseen, and unremarked upon. Except, that is, by Celia Holden and Lottie Swift. They sat on the bench of the municipal park, which overlooked Merham's two-and-a-half-mile seafront, and gazed, rapt, at the removals van, its dark green bonnet just visible beneath the Scots pines, glinting in the afternoon sun.

Below them the breakwaters stretched away to the left, like the dark teeth of a comb, the tide easing its way backwards across the damp sands, dotted with tiny figures braving the fierce, unseasonal winds. The arrival of Adeline Armand, the girls decided afterwards, had been an occasion to match the arrival of the Queen of Sheba. That is, it would have, had the Queen of Sheba chosen to do it on a Saturday, in the busiest week of Merham's summer season. This meant that all those people – the Mrs Colquhouns, the Alderman Elliotts, the landladies of the Parade and their like – who could normally be relied upon to pass judgement on the extravagant ways of newcomers who arrived with whole lorryloads of trunks, large paintings that featured not portraits of family members or scenes of horses galloping but huge splodges of colour in no particular pattern at all, inordinate numbers of books, and artefacts that were quite *clearly* foreign were not standing silently at their gates, noting the steady procession disappearing into the long-empty art-deco house on the seafront. They were queuing at Price's Butcher's on Marchant Street, or hurrying to the meeting of the Guesthouse Association.

'Mrs Hodges says she's minor royalty. Hungarian or something.'

'Rot.'

Celia looked at her friend, her eyes widening. 'She *is*. Mrs Hodges spoke to Mrs Ansty, who knows the solicitor or whoever it is was in charge of the house, and she *is* some kind of Hungarian princess.'

Below them a scattering of families had appropriated the little stretches of beach between them, and could be seen seated behind straining striped windbreaks, or sheltering in beach huts against the blustery sea breeze.

'Armand's not a Hungarian name.' Lottie put up her hand to stop her hair whipping into her mouth.

'Oh? And how would you know?'

'It's just rubbish, isn't it? What would a Hungarian princess be doing in Merham? She'd be up in London, no question. Or Windsor Castle. Not in a sleepy old dump like this.'

'Not your end of London, she wouldn't.' Celia's tone verged on the scornful.

'No,' Lottie conceded. 'Not my end of London.' No one exotic came from Lottie's end of London, an eastern suburb liberally dotted with hastily erected factories, which backed on to the gasworks in one direction and acres of unlovely marshes in the other. When she had first been evacuated to Merham, during the early years of the war, she had had to hide her incredulity when sympathetic villagers asked her if she missed it. She had looked equally nonplussed when they asked the same of her family. They tended to stop asking after that.

In fact, Lottie had returned home for the two years until the war ended, and then, after a series of fevered letters between

Lottie and Celia, and Mrs Holden's oft-stated belief that not only was it nice for Celia to have a little friend her own age but One Really Had To Do One's Bit for the Community, Didn't One?, she had been invited to return to Merham, initially for holidays, and gradually, as those holidays extended into schooltime, for good. Now Lottie was simply accepted as part of the Holden family; not blood perhaps, not exactly a social equal (you were never going to get rid of that East End accent entirely), but someone whose continued presence in the village was no longer to be remarked upon. Besides, Merham was used to people coming and not going home. The sea could get you like that.

'Shall we take something? Flowers? So that we have an excuse to go in?'

Lottie could tell Celia felt bad about her previous comments: she was now bestowing on her what she considered her Moira Shearer smile, the one that revealed her lower teeth. 'I haven't got any money.'

'Not shop-bought. You know where we can find pretty wild ones. You get enough for Mummy.' There had been, Lottie acknowledged, the faintest echo of resentment in the last sentence.

The two girls slid off the park bench and began to walk towards the edge of the park, where a single cast-iron railing signified the start of the cliff path. Lottie would often walk this route in summer evenings when the noise and suppressed hysteria of the Holden household became too much. She liked to listen to the gulls and the corncrakes skimming the air above her and remind herself who she was. This kind of introspection Mrs Holden would have considered unnatural, or at least overly indulgent, and Lottie's gathering of small bunches of flowers was a useful insurance. But almost ten years of living in someone else's house had also ingrained a certain canniness; a sensitivity to potential domestic turbulence that belied the fact that she was not quite out of her teens. It was important that Celia never regard her as competition, after all.

'Did you see the hatboxes going in? Must have been at least seven,' said Celia, stooping. 'What about this one?'

'No. Those wilt in minutes. Get some of the purple ones. There, by the big rock.'

'She must have a heap of money. Mummy said it needs loads doing to it. She spoke to the decorators and they said it was an absolute tip. No one's lived in there since the MacPhersons moved to Hampshire. Must be – what, nine years?'

'Don't know. Never met the MacPhersons.'

'Dull as ditchwater, the pair of them. She had size-nine feet. It hasn't got a single decent fireplace, according to Mrs Ansty. They all got looted.'

'The gardens are completely overgrown.'

Celia stopped. 'How do you know?'

'I've been up there a few times. On my walks.'

'You sly thing! Why didn't you bring me?'

'You never wanted to walk.' Lottie looked past her to the removals van, feeling a silent rush of excitement. They were well used to people coming – Merham was a seasonal town after all; its seasons punctuated by new visitors, their arrivals and departures ebbing and flowing like the tides themselves – but the prospect of having the big house occupied again had added a certain breathless anticipation to the last fortnight.

Celia turned back to her flowers. As she rearranged them in her palm her hair was lifted by the wind in a golden sheet. 'I think I hate my father,' she observed aloud, her eyes suddenly fixed on the horizon.

Lottie stood still. Henry Holden's dinners with his secretary were not something upon which she felt qualified to comment.

'Mummy's so stupid. She just pretends nothing's happening.' There was a brief silence, interrupted by the rude cry of the gulls hovering above them. 'God, I can't wait till I leave this place,' she said, finally.

'I like it.'

'Yes, but you don't have to watch your father making an ass of himself.' Celia turned back to Lottie, and thrust her hand at her. 'There. Do you think that's enough?'

Lottie peered at the flowers. 'You really want to go up there? Just to gawp at her things?'

'Oh, and you don't, Mother Superior?'

The two girls grinned at each other, then sprinted back towards the municipal park, cardigans and skirts flying out behind them.

The drive to Arcadia House had once been circular; its remaining neighbours could still remember processions of long, low cars that halted with a crisp bite of gravel before the front door, then continuing round its graceful sweep and exiting down the lane. It had been an important house, sited well inside the railway tracks (so important was this distinction that houses in Merham were advertised as either 'inside' or 'outside'). It had been built by Anthony Gresham, the eldest son of the Walton Greshams, when he returned from America having made his fortune creating an unremarkable piece of engine equipment that was bought by General Motors. He had wanted it, he said grandly, to look like a film star's house. He had seen a house in Santa Monica, owned by a famous actress of the silent screen, which was long and low and white, with great expanses of glass and smaller windows like portholes. It spoke to him of glamour, and new worlds and a brave, bright future (a future that, ironically, had not been his: he died aged forty-two after being hit by a car. A Rover). When the house had been finally completed, some of Merham's residents had been shocked by its modernity, and had complained privately that it was not, somehow, 'fitting'. So that when the next owners, the MacPhersons, moved out a few years later, and it was left empty, some of the older villagers felt curiously relieved, although they might not have said as much. Now the northern side of the drive had become completely overgrown, a tangle of brambles and elder prematurely ending it by the gate that had once led to the sea path. This caused a large amount of gear-crunching and swearing from the delivery-van drivers who, having offloaded the last of their cargo, were now trying to reverse around each other back to the lane, partially blocked by a car that had entered behind them.

Lottie and Celia stood for a while, watching the puce faces and sweaty efforts of those still carrying furniture, until a tall woman, with long chestnut hair pulled severely back into a bun, ran out waving a set of car keys and pleading, 'Just wait a moment. Hold on. I'll move it over to the kitchen garden.'

'Do you think that's her?' whispered Celia, who had inexplicably ducked behind one of the trees.

'How would I know?' Lottie held her breath, Celia's sudden reticence having prompted her own sense of awkwardness. They pressed close to each other, peering round the trunk, holding their full skirts tight behind them with their hands to stop them billowing out.

The woman sat in the car and looked at its instruments, as if considering which one she should use. Then, with an anguished bite of her lower lip, she started the ignition, wrestled with the gearstick, took a deep breath, and shot straight backwards with an almighty crunch into the front grille of a removal van.

There was a brief silence, followed by a loud expletive from one of the men, and the lengthy blast of a horn. Then the woman raised her head and the girls realised that she had likely broken her nose. Blood was everywhere – down her pale green blouse, over her hands, even on the steering-wheel. She sat straight upright in the driving seat seeming a little stunned, and then, looking down, began to search for something to stem the bleeding.

Lottie found herself running across the overgrown lawn, her handkerchief already in her hand. 'Here,' she said, reaching the woman at the same time as several exclaiming people began to congregate around the car. 'Take this. Put your head back.'

Celia, who had hurried behind Lottie, peered at the woman's spattered face. 'You've taken an awful crack,' she said.

The woman accepted the handkerchief. 'I'm so sorry,' she was saying to the lorry driver. 'I'm just no good with gears.'

'You shouldn't be driving,' said the man, his bulk barely contained by his dark green apron; he was clutching what remained of his front light. 'You didn't even look in the mirror.'

'I thought I was in first. It's awfully close to reverse.'

'Your bumper's fallen off,' said Celia, with some excitement.

'It isn't even my car. Oh dear.'

'Look at my light! I'll have to get a whole new unit for that. That's going to cost me time as well as money.'

'Of course.' She nodded sorrowfully.

'Look, leave the lady alone. She's taken quite a knock.' A dark-haired man in a pale linen suit had appeared at the car door. 'Just tell me what the damage is and I'll

14

see you right. Frances, are you hurt? Do you need a doctor?'

'She shouldn't be driving,' said the man, shaking his head.

'*You* shouldn't have been so close,' said Lottie, irritated by his lack of concern. The driver ignored her.

'I'm so sorry,' the woman muttered. 'Oh dear. Look at my skirt.'

'Come on, how much? Fifteen shillings? A pound?' The younger man was peeling off notes from a roll he had taken from his inside pocket. 'There, take that. And another five for your troubles.'

The driver looked mollified – he probably didn't even own the van, thought Lottie. 'Well,' he said. 'Well. I suppose that'll have to do.' He pocketed the money swiftly, his martyrdom apparently tempered by an astute determination not to push his luck. 'I suppose we'll be finishing up, then. C'mon, lads.'

'Look at her skirt,' whispered Celia, nudging her. Frances's skirt was almost down to her ankles. In a bold print of willows, it was curiously old-fashioned.

Lottie found herself studying the rest of the woman's clothes: her shoes, which looked almost Edwardian, her lengthy string of globular amber beads. 'Bohemians!' she hissed, gleefully.

'C'mon, Frances. Let's get you inside before you start bleeding all over the interior.' The young man stuck his cigarette into the side of his mouth, gently took the woman's elbow and helped her from the car.

As she walked towards the house, she turned suddenly. 'Oh, your lovely handkerchief. I've covered it with blood.' She paused, looking at it. 'Are you local? Do come and have some tea. We'll get Marnie to soak it. It's the least I

15

can do. George, do call Marnie for me. I'm afraid I might splutter.'

Lottie and Celia glanced at each other.

'That would be lovely,' said Celia. It was only after they shut the door behind them that Lottie realised they must have left the flowers on the drive.

Celia seemed less sure when she entered the main hallway. In fact, she came to such a juddering halt that Lottie, who hadn't been concentrating, smacked her own nose on the back of Celia's head. This was less to do with any natural tendency towards hesitation on Celia's part (her nickname among her younger siblings was Sharp Elbows) than her coming face to face with the large painting stacked against the curving banister opposite the front door. On it, in impasto oils, a naked woman reclined. She was not, Lottie observed from the positioning of her arms and legs, the modest sort.

'Marnie? Marnie, are you there?' George led the way, striding across the flagstone floor, past the packing cases. 'Marnie, can you get us some warm water? Frances has had a bit of a bump. And can you make some tea while you're there? We've got visitors.'

There was a muffled answer from an adjoining room and the sound of a door closing. The lack of rugs and furniture meant that sound was amplified, bouncing off the stone floors and into the largely empty space. Celia clutched Lottie's arm. 'Do you think we should stay?' she whispered. 'They seem a bit . . . *fast.*'

Lottie gazed around her at the house, at the racks of oversized paintings, at the stacked, rolled rugs slumped against the walls like stooping, elderly gentlemen, the African carving of a woman's bloated stomach. It was all so different from the houses she knew: her own mother's – cramped, dark, full of oak furniture and cheap china knick-knacks, permeated with the smell of coal dust and boiled vegetables, constantly interrupted by the noise of traffic or next-door's children playing outside; the Holdens', a sprawling, comfortable mock-Tudor family home, which seemed to be valued for what it communicated as much as what it housed. Their furniture was inherited, and had to be treated reverently – more so, it seemed, than its occupants. No cups were to be placed upon it, or children to knock against it. It was all, Mrs Holden announced, to be 'handed on', as if they were simply guardians of those pieces of wood. Their house was permanently arranged for other people, made nice 'for the ladies', made straight for Dr Holden 'when he comes home', with Mrs Holden a fragile little King Canute, desperately trying to push back the inevitable dirt and detritus.

And then there was this place – white, bright, alien; a strange angular shape, with long, low opaque windows, or portholes through which you could see the sea, and its elaborate, chaotically arranged treasure trove of exotica. A place where every item told a story, held a rich provenance from foreign lands. She breathed in the house's scent, the salt air that had permeated the walls over the years overlaid by the smell of fresh paint. It was strangely intoxicating. 'Tea can't hurt. Can it?'

Celia paused, scanning her face. 'Just don't tell Mummy. She'll fuss.'

They followed the mournful Frances into the main living room, which was flooded with light from the four windows that faced outward on to the bay, the two middle ones curved around a semi-circular wall. At the furthest window to the right, two men were struggling with a curtain pole and heavy drapery, while to their left a young woman was kneeling in the corner, placing lengths of books into a glass-fronted bookcase.

'It's Julian's new car. He's going to be absolutely furious. I should have let you move it.' Frances lowered herself on to a chair, checking her handkerchief for fresh blood.

George was pouring her a large glass of brandy. 'I'll sort Julian out. Now, how is your nose? You look like something by Picasso, dear girl. Do you think we need a doctor? Adeline? Do you know a doctor?'

'My father's a doctor,' said Celia. 'I could call him if you like.'

It was several seconds before Lottie noticed the third woman. She sat perfectly upright in the centre of a small sofa, her legs crossed at the ankle and her hands clasped in front of her, as if completely removed from the chaotic exertions around her. Her hair, which was the kind of blue-black seen on ravens' feathers, sat close to her head in sleek waves, and she wore a red dress of Oriental silk, cut unfashionably long and close, overlaid by an embroidered jacket upon which peacocks preened their iridescent plumage. She had huge dark eyes outlined in kohl, and tiny child's hands. She was so still that when she dipped her head in greeting, Lottie nearly jumped.

'Aren't you marvellous? There, George. You have found us some scouts already.' The woman smiled, the slow, sweet smile of the perennially charmed. Her accent was unfathomable; perhaps French, definitely foreign. It was low, and smoky, and held a sneaking lilt of amusement. As for her clothes and makeup – it was impossible. She was way beyond the realms of experience, even of someone whose upbringing stretched further than the twin poles of Merham and Walton-on-the-Naze. Lottie was transfixed. She looked at Celia, seeing her own gormless expression reflected back at her.

'Adeline. This is – oh, goodness, I didn't ask you your names.' Frances raised a hand to her mouth.

'Celia Holden. And Lottie Swift,' said Celia, who was doing something odd with her feet. 'We live behind the park. On Woodbridge Avenue.'

'The girls very kindly lent me their handkerchief,' said Frances. 'I've made rather a mess of it.'

'You poor darling.' Adeline took Frances's hand.

Lottie watched, waiting for her to offer some comforting squeeze, some reassuring pat. Instead, stroking it gently, she lifted it to her ruby mouth and there, in front of everyone, without even a hint of a blush, bent slowly and kissed it. 'How *awful* for you.'

There was a short silence.

'Oh, Adeline,' said Frances, sadly, and pulled her hand away.

Lottie, the air knocked from her lungs at this bizarre demonstration of intimacy, dared not look at Celia.

But then Adeline, after a momentary pause, turned back to the room, and her smile turned into a full-wattage beam. 'George, I didn't tell you. Isn't this sweet? Sebastian has sent down some artichokes and plovers' eggs from Suffolk. We can have them for supper.'

'Thank goodness.' George had walked over to the men by the window and was helping support the curtain pole. 'I wasn't in the mood for fish and chips.'

'Don't be such a snob, darling. I'm sure fish and chips here are absolutely wonderful – are they, girls?'

'We really wouldn't know,' said Celia hurriedly. 'We only eat at proper restaurants.'

Lottie bit her tongue, remembering the previous Saturday when they had sat on the sea wall with the Westerhouse brothers eating skate from greasy newspaper.

'Of course you do.' Her voice was low, languorous, and faintly accented. 'How very proper of you. Now, girls. You will tell me, what is the single best thing about living in Merham?'

Celia and Lottie stared at each other.

'There's not much,' Celia began. 'In fact, it's rather a bore. There's the tennis club, but that shuts in the winter. And the cinema, but the projectionist gets ill a lot and they don't have anyone else who can operate it. If you want to go somewhere smart, you really have to go to London. That's what most of us do. I mean, if we want a really good night – if you want to go to the theatre, or a really top restaurant—' She was speaking too fast, trying to look insouciant, yet stumbling over her own untruths.

Lottie looked at Adeline's face, its smile of interest becoming just slightly blank, and felt overwhelmed with fear that this woman was going to write them off. 'The sea,' she said, abruptly.

Adeline's face turned to meet her, her eyebrows lifting slightly.

'The sea,' Lottie said again, trying to ignore Celia's furious expression. 'Living right by it, I mean. It's the best thing. Hearing it in the background all the time, smelling it, walking along the shore and being able to see the curve of the earth . . . knowing when you look out that there is so much going on underneath it that we shan't ever see, or know about. Like this big mystery, right on our doorstep . . . And the storms. When the waves come right up over the wall and the wind blows the trees so hard that they bend over like grass, and being inside watching when you're all warm and cosy and dry . . .' She faltered, caught Celia's mutinous face. 'That's what I like, anyway.'

Her breathing seemed unnaturally loud in the silence.

'It sounds perfect,' said Adeline, lingering over the last word, her eyes fixed on Lottie's so that the girl blushed. 'I am so glad already that we came.'

'So how badly did she damage the van? Do you think they'll bring it to my dad's?' Joe pushed his empty coffee cup across the Formica bar, his expression serious. But, then, Joe didn't really have any other expressions. His grave eyes, always peering upwards as if in deferential concern, looked out of place on that freckled, ruddy face.

'I don't know, Joe. It was only a light or something.'

'Yes, but it will still need replacing.'

Behind him, sometimes swamped by the sound of scraping chairs and cheap crockery, Alma Cogan sang of her 'Dreamboat'. Lottie glared at the undreamy features of her companion, wishing she had never mentioned their visit to Adeline Armand's house. Joe always asked the wrong questions. And usually managed to bring the conversation round to his father's garage. Joe, as only son, would inherit the ramshackle business one day, and already this weighty inheritance hung as heavy on him as the succession on a prince regent. She had hoped that by bringing him into her confidence about their extraordinary visit he, too, might have been transported by the strange, exotic characters and the huge ocean-liner of a house. That he, too, might have found himself far away from the tight little world of Merham's social confines. But Joe just focused on the mundane, his imagination constrained by the domestic (How had their maid prepared tea if they'd only just delivered the trunks? Exactly which light was it that the woman broke? Wouldn't that fresh-paint smell have given them all a headache?) and Lottie found herself becoming both irritated that she had ever told him and sorely tempted to describe the painting

21

of the naked woman, just to make him blush. It was so easy to make Joe blush.

She would have discussed it all with Celia. But Celia was not talking to Lottie. She had not spoken to her since their walk home, during which Celia had spoken rather too much. 'Were you deliberately showing me up in front of those people? Lottie! I can't *believe* you started spouting all that stuff about the sea. As if you care about fish swimming about underneath it – you can't even swim!'

Lottie had wanted to talk to her about the provenance of Hungarian princesses and Adeline kissing Frances's hand like a suitor, and about what relation George was to either of them (he didn't behave like anyone's husband: he had paid both women far too much attention). She wanted to talk about how, with all that work to do and her house in absolute chaos, Adeline had just sat there in the middle of the sofa like she had nothing to do other than let the day go by.

But Celia was now deep in conversation with Betty Croft, discussing the possibilities for a trip to London before the end of summer. So Lottie just sat and waited for this particular summer storm to blow itself out.

Except Celia had evidently been more put out by Lottie's interruption than even she had said. As the afternoon drew on, and the blustery clouds outside grew darker, and loaded with rain, and the café filled with recalcitrant children and their exasperated parents, still clutching their damp, gritty beach towels, she ignored Lottie's attempts to join in the conversation and her offer of a slice of bread and butter pudding, so that even Betty, who normally loved a good row between friends, started to look a bit uncomfortable. Oh, Lord, thought Lottie, resignedly. I'm going to pay for this one. 'I think I'll go back,' she said aloud, staring at the murky dregs of instant coffee in the bottom of her cup. 'Weather's closing in.'

Joe stood up. 'Shall I walk you? I've got an umbrella.'

'If you like.'

Adeline Armand had had a portrait of herself propped up in what must have been the study. It hadn't been a proper painting – it had been loose and choppy, as if the artist hadn't been able to see properly and had had to guess where the marks were meant to go. But somehow you could see it was her. It was that jet-black hair. And that half-smile.

'They had a storm over at Clacton on Saturday. Snow in April, can you believe it?'

She hadn't even minded about the car. Hadn't even wanted to look at it to check on the damage. And that man – George – had just peeled off a roll of notes as if he were flicking through old bus tickets.

'Went from mild and sunny to hail and everything all in the space of a couple of hours. There were people on the beach, as well. I reckon some of them would have been swimming. You're getting wet, Lottie. Here, take my arm.'

Lottie threaded her arm through Joe's and turned back, craning to see the front of Arcadia House. It was the only house she had ever seen that had a front and back of equal magnificence. It was as if the architect couldn't bear to make one view inferior. 'Wouldn't you love to live in a house like that, Joe?' She stopped, heedless of the rain. She felt a little giddy, as if unbalanced by the afternoon's events.

Joe looked at her and then up at the house, leaning over slightly to make sure she was covered by the umbrella. 'Looks a bit too much like a ship.'

'That's the point, though, isn't it? It's next to the sea, after all.'

Joe looked worried, as if he were missing something.

'Imagine. You could pretend you were on a liner. Just sailing along the ocean.' She closed her eyes, briefly forgetting about her row with Celia, picturing herself on the upper floors of the house. How lucky that woman was to have all that space to herself, all that room to sit and dream. 'If I had that, I think I'd be the happiest girl alive.'

'I'd like a house that overlooked the bay.'

Lottie glanced at him, surprised. Joe never expressed a desire about anything. It was one of the things that made him such easy, if unchallenging, company. 'Would you? Well, I'd like a house that overlooked the bay and had windows like portholes and a great big garden.'

He half-smiled at her, catching something in her tone.

'And a great big pond where swans could live,' she added, encouragingly.

'And a monkey-puzzle tree,' he said.

'Oh, yes!' she said. 'A monkey-puzzle tree! And six bedrooms, with a closet you could walk into.' They were walking slower now, their faces pink from the fine rain blown in from the sea.

Joe furrowed his brow in thought. 'And outbuildings that you could put three cars in.'

'Oh, you and your cars. I'd like a big balcony where you could step out of your bedroom and be right on top of the sea.'

'And a swimming-pool underneath it. So you could just jump off the edge when you fancied a dip.'

Lottie started to laugh. 'First thing in the morning! In my nightie! Yes! And a kitchen underneath so that the maid could leave me my breakfast when I'd finished.'

'And a table, right by the pool, so I could sit there watching you.'

'And one of those umbrella things . . . What did you—'

24

Lottie slowed her pace. Her smile slid from her face and she regarded him warily from the corner of her eye. She thought she might have imagined it, but his grip on her arm grew a little lighter, as if he was already anticipating her withdrawal. 'Oh, Joe.' She sighed.

They trudged on up the cliff path in silence. A solitary gull flew ahead of them, pausing occasionally on the railing, convinced against all evidence of the imminent arrival of food.

Lottie waved a hand at it to make it go away, feeling suddenly furious. 'I have said to you before, Joe, I'm not interested in you that way.'

Joe looked straight ahead, his cheeks slightly flushed.

'I do like you. Heaps. But just not in that way. I do wish you wouldn't keep on.'

'I just thought – I thought, when you started talking about the house—'

'It was a game, Joe. A silly game. Neither one of us will ever own a house half the size of that one. C'mon. Don't sulk, please. Or I'll have to walk the rest of the way by myself.'

Joe stopped, letting go of her arm and turning to face her. He looked very young, and grimly determined. 'I promise I won't go on any more, then. But if you married me, Lottie, you'd never have to go back to London.'

She looked up at the umbrella, then thrust it back at him, letting the sea-spray and rain cover her head in a fine mist. 'I'm not getting married. And I've told you, I'm never going back, Joe. Ever.'

Two

Mrs Colquhoun took a deep breath, smoothed the front of her skirt and nodded at the pianist. Her reedy soprano rose like a young starling taking its first tentative flight across the crowded front room. Then crashed like a fat, shot pheasant, prompting Sylvia and Freddie, who were seeking sanctuary behind the kitchen door, to slide downwards clutching their mouths and each other to stop their screams of laughter escaping.

Lottie tried to stem the smile pulling at her own lips. 'I wouldn't laugh too hard,' she whispered, not without some relish. 'You're down to duet with her at the Widows and Orphans.'

In the six short months since their inception, Mrs Holden's 'salons' had achieved some degree of fame (or notoriety – no one was quite sure which) in the politer reaches of Merham society. Nearly everyone who considered themselves anyone attended the fortnightly Saturday gatherings, which Mrs Holden had initiated in the hope of introducing, as she put it, 'a little cultural perfume' into the seaside town. Ladies were invited to read a passage from a favoured book (*The Collected Works of George Herbert* was this month's choice), or play the piano or, if brave enough, to attempt a little song. There was no reason, after all, why their friends in the city should be able to suggest they were living in a vacuum, was there?

If there was just a hint of plaintiveness in Mrs Holden's

voice when she asked this question – which she did, frequently – then it should be blamed on her cousin Angela, who lived in Kensington, and had once suggested laughingly that Merham's cultural life might benefit greatly from the building of a pier. At this Mrs Holden's ever-present smile had gone distinctly wobbly at the corners, and it had been some months before she could bring herself to ask Angela to come again.

Attendance, however, was no guarantee of quality, as Mrs Colquhoun's vocal efforts were proving. Around the room, several of the women blinked hard, swallowed, and took slightly more sips from their teacups than strictly necessary. As Mrs Colquhoun drew to a painful close, a few cast surreptitious glances at each other. It was so difficult to know quite how honest one should be.

'Well, I can't say I've met her myself, but she *says* she's an actress,' said Mrs Ansty, when the tentative applause had died down. 'She spoke to my Arthur yesterday when she came in for some hand cream. Very . . . talkative, she was.' She managed to imbue the word with some disapproval.

This was what the ladies had really come for. The chatter evaporated, and several leaned forward over their cups.

'Is she Hungarian?'

'Didn't say,' said Mrs Ansty, relishing her role as appointed sage. 'In fact, my Arthur said that for a woman who talked so much, she said hardly a thing about herself.'

The ladies looked at each other, raising their eyebrows as if this were, in itself, a thing of suspicion.

'There's meant to be a husband. But I've not seen hide nor hair of him,' said Mrs Chilton.

'There is a man there, often,' said Mrs Colquhoun, still flushed from her vocal exertions. But, then, she was often quite flushed: she hadn't been the same since her husband

27

came back from Korea. 'My Judy asked the maid who he was, and she just said, "Oh, that's Mr George", as if that explained it all.'

'He wears linen. All the time.' In Mrs Chilton's eyes, this was extravagance indeed. Mrs Chilton, a widow, was the landlady of Uplands, one of the largest guest-houses on the Parade. That would normally have excluded her from such a gathering but, Mrs Holden had explained to Lottie, everyone knew that Sarah Chilton had married beneath her, and since her husband's death she had taken great pains to turn herself into a woman of some standing. And she ran a very respectable house.

'Ladies, can I get anyone some more tea?' Mrs Holden was leaning towards the kitchen door, trying not to bend over too much because of her girdle. She had bought it a size too small, Celia told Lottie scornfully. It left great red welts all around her thighs. 'Where is that girl? She's been all over the place this morning.'

'She told my Judy that she hadn't wanted to come. They had been in London, you see. I believe they left in rather a hurry.'

'Well, it doesn't surprise me that she's on the stage. She dresses very *extravagantly*.'

'That's a fine word for it,' snorted Mrs Chilton. 'Looks like she's been going through a child's dressing-up box.'

There was a faint ripple of laughter.

'Well, have you seen her? All silk and finery at eleven o'clock in the morning. She was wearing a man's trilby when she went into the baker's last week. A trilby! Mrs Hatton from the Promenade was so taken aback she came out with half a dozen cream horns she hadn't ordered.'

'Now, ladies,' said Mrs Holden, who disapproved of gossip. Lottie always suspected this to be down to her own

28

well-founded fear of becoming the subject. 'Who is next? Sarah, dear, weren't you going to read us something lovely from Wordsworth? Or was it Mr Herbert again? The one about the broom?'

Mrs Ansty placed her cup carefully back on her saucer. 'Well, all I can say is, she sounds a bit . . . *unconventional* for my liking. Call me old-fashioned, but I like things orderly. One husband. Children. No leaving places in a hurry.'

There was much nodding from various upholstered chairs.

'Let's have some George Herbert. "I struck the board and cry'd, No more." Is that it?' Mrs Holden cast around the low table for the book. 'I can never remember the exact words. Deirdre, do you have a copy?'

'Well, she's not invited anyone up to see the house. Although I've heard all sorts went in there with her.'

'You'd expect a small gathering. Even the MacPhersons put on a small gathering. It's only polite, really.'

'Perhaps some Byron?' said Mrs Holden, desperately. 'Shelley? I can't remember who it was you said. Now, where is that girl? Virginia? Virginia?'

Lottie slid silently back behind the door. She took pains to ensure that Mrs Holden didn't see her, having been told off repeatedly for being 'watchful'. She had an odd way of looking at people, Mrs Holden had said recently. It made people uncomfortable. Lottie retorted that she couldn't help it: she might just as well be accused of having hair too straight, or the wrong-shaped hands. She thought secretly that it probably only made Mrs Holden uncomfortable. But, then, everything seemed to make Mrs Holden uncomfortable lately.

She was trying to stop them talking about the actress because, Lottie knew, Adeline Armand made her uncomfortable too. When she had heard that Dr Holden had dropped in there to take a look at Frances's nose, her jaw had begun to tic in the same way as it did when he said he was going to be 'a little late home' for dinner.

In the next room, Virginia emerged through the hall door and collected the tray, her presence briefly quieting the visitors. Mrs Holden, expelling an almost audible sigh of relief, began to bustle about, shepherding her to and from her various visitors.

'The Guesthouse Association is having a meeting tomorrow,' Mrs Chilton announced, wiping non-existent crumbs from the sides of her mouth when the maid had gone. 'There's a view that we should all put our prices up.'

Adeline Armand was briefly forgotten. While the ladies of the salon were not among those whose families were dependent on the holiday trade – Mrs Chilton was the only one who actually worked – there were few whose income was not boosted by Merham's regular summer visitors. Mr Ansty's chemist shop, Mr Burton's tailor's just behind the Parade, even Mr Colquhoun, who let out his bottom field to caravanners, all did better business in the summer months, and subsequently paid great attention to the opinions and decisions of the all-female and immensely powerful Guest-house Association.

'There's some think ten pounds a week. That's what they're charging over in Frinton.'

'Ten pounds!' The whispered exclamation bounced around the room.

'They'll go to Walton instead, surely.' Mrs Colquhoun had gone quite pale. 'Walton has amusements, after all.'

'Well, I have to say, Deirdre, I'm with you,' said Sarah Chilton. 'I don't think they'll stand for it myself. And with the spring being as blowy as it's been so far, I don't think we should be pushing it. But as far as the Association goes, I seem to be in a minority.'

'But *ten pounds*.'

'The people who come here don't come for the amusements. They come for a more . . . genteel kind of holiday.'

'And they're the kind of people who can afford it.'

'No one can afford it at the moment, Alice. Who do you know with money to splash around?'

'Do let's not go on about money,' said Mrs Holden, as Virginia appeared with a refreshed teapot. 'It's a little . . . vulgar. Let's leave the good ladies of the Association to sort this one out. I'm sure they know best. So, Deirdre, what did you do with your ration books? Sarah, you must be relieved that your guests no longer have to bring them. I wanted to throw ours into the kitchen waste, but my daughter said we should frame it. Frame it! Can you imagine?'

Lottie Swift had dark, near-black eyes, and smooth brown hair of the type more normally found on those hailing from the Asian subcontinents. In summer, her skin tanned just a little too quickly and in winter had a tendency towards sallowness. The undesirability of such dark, if delicate colouring was one of the few things Lottie's mother and Susan Holden would have agreed upon, had they known each other. Where Celia, generously, saw a darker-skinned Vivien Leigh or Jean Simmonds, Lottie's mother had only ever seen 'a touch of the tar brush', or an ever-present reminder of the Portuguese sailor whom she had met briefly, but with long-standing consequences, when celebrating her eighteenth birthday near the docks in east Tilbury. 'You've got your father's blood,' she would mutter accusingly, as Lottie grew. 'Better for me if you'd disappeared with him.' Then she would pull Lottie fiercely to her in a strangulated hug, and push her away again just as abruptly, as if contact so close were only advisable in small measures.

31

Mrs Holden, while less blunt, wondered if Lottie couldn't pluck her eyebrows a bit more. And about the advisability of her spending so much time in the sun 'bearing in mind how dark you do go. You don't want people mistaking you for . . . well. A gypsy or something.' She had grown silent after this, as if fearful that she had said too much, her voice tinged with pity. But Lottie had not taken offence. It was hard to take it from someone you yourself pitied.

According to Adeline Armand, however, Lottie's colouring was not evidence of her inferior status or her lack of breeding. It was proof of an exoticism that she had not yet learned to feel, an illustration of a strange and unique beauty. 'Frances should paint you. Frances, you must paint her. Not in all these awful things, this serge and cotton. No, something bright. Something silky. Otherwise, Lottie darling, you over-power the things you wear. You – you smoulder, *non*?' Her accent had been so thick as she spoke that Lottie had had to struggle to make sure she wasn't being insulted.

'Moulder, more like,' said Celia, who was less than pleased by Adeline's comments. She was used to being the one who generated attention. All that Adeline had said about her appearance was that she was 'so charming, so typically English'. It had been the 'typically' that had really stung.

'She looks like Frida Kahlo. Don't you think, Frances? The eyes? Have you ever sat for anyone?'

Lottie looked blankly at Adeline. Sat where? she wanted to ask. The older woman waited.

'No,' Celia interrupted. 'I have. My family had one done when we were younger. It's in our parlour.'

'Ah. A family portrait. Very . . . respectable, I'm sure. And you, Lottie? Has your family ever sat for a portrait?'

Lottie glanced at Celia, toying with an image of her mother, fingers raw and stained from stitching shoe leather at the factory, seated like Susan Holden above the mantelpiece. Instead of posing elegantly, hands folded in her lap, she would be scowling, her mouth drawn into a thin line of dissatisfaction, her thin, dyed hair pulled back into two unflattering pins, and welded unsuccessfully around rollers. Lottie would be beside her, her face as expressionless, her dark eyes as apparently watchful as ever. Where Dr Holden had stood behind his family there would be a big, empty gap.

'Lottie hasn't seen her family for a while, have you, Lots?' Celia said protectively. 'Probably can't remember whether you've got a portrait or not.'

Celia knew very well that the nearest Lottie's mother had ever come to a portrait was when she had appeared in the local paper, standing in a row of factory girls when the Leather Emporium opened just after the war ended. Lottie's mother had cut out the photograph and Lottie had kept it, long after it had yellowed and become brittle, although her mother's face was so small and indistinct that it was impossible to tell whether it was her. 'I don't really go to London any more,' she said, slowly.

Adeline leaned towards her. 'Then we must make sure you have a painting done here, and you can give it to your family when you see them.' She touched Lottie's hand with her own, and Lottie, who had been transfixed by her elaborate eye makeup, jumped, half afraid that Adeline might try to kiss it.

It was the fifth visit that the girls had made to Arcadia House, during which time their initial reserve about the strange and possibly fast crowd who all seemed to stay there had gradually dissipated. It had been replaced by curiosity, and a growing recognition that whatever else went on there, nude painting and uncertain domestic situations notwithstanding, it was far more interesting than their traditional alternatives of walking to and from town, refereeing the children or treating themselves to ice-cream or coffee at the café.

No, like some kind of ongoing theatrical performance, there was always something happening at the house. Strange painted friezes appeared around doorways or over the range. Writings – usually about the work of artists or actors – were scribbled and pinned haphazardly to walls. Exotic foods appeared, sent from people in various grand estates around the country. New visitors metamorphosed and drifted away again, rarely – apart from a core group – staying long enough to introduce themselves.

The girls were always welcomed. Once they had arrived to find Adeline dressing Frances as an Indian princess, draping her in dark silks spotted with gold threads, and painting elaborate markings on her hands and face. She herself had dressed as a prince, with a headdress that, in its extravagant peacock adornments, and intricately interwoven fabrics, must have been genuine. Marnie, the maid, had stood looking mutinous as Adeline painted Frances's skin with cold tea, withdrawing in high dudgeon when she was instructed to bring flour to make Adeline's hair look grey. Then, while the girls watched silently, the two women had posed in a variety of arrangements while a thin young man who introduced himself rather pompously as 'School of Modotti' had taken their photograph.

'We must go somewhere dressed like this. To London, perhaps,' Adeline had crowed afterwards, as she examined her altered appearance in a mirror. 'It would be such fun.'

'Like the *Dreadnought* Hoax.'

'The what?' Celia had temporarily forgotten her manners. She frequently did when at Arcadia.

'A very good joke Virginia Woolf played. Many years ago.' George had stood and watched the whole proceedings. He only ever seemed to watch. 'She and her friends blacked up and travelled to Weymouth as the Emperor of Abyssinia and his "imperial entourage". A flag lieutenant or somesuch ended up giving them a royal salute and escorting them all around HMS *Dreadnought*. Caused a frightful stink.'

'But such fun!' said Adeline, clapping her hands together. 'Yes! We could become the Rajah of Rajasthan. And visit Walton-on-the-Naze.' She swirled around, laughing, so that her elaborate coat flew out around her. She could be like this, childlike, exuberant – as if she weren't an adult woman at all, weighed down by the responsibilities and worries that being female seemed to entail, but more like Freddie or Sylvia.

'Oh, Adeline. Nothing too dramatic.' Frances looked weary. 'Remember Calthorpe Street.'

She was like that. Half the time, Celia confided afterwards, she hardly understood a word that was said. It wasn't just the accent. They didn't talk about normal things – about what went on in the village, and the cost of things, and the weather. They would go off at tangents and talk about writers and people Lottie and she had never heard of, draping themselves over each other in a manner that the girls knew Mrs Holden would find scandalous. And they would argue. My God, they would argue. About Bertrand Russell saying they should ban the bomb. About poetry. About anything. The first time Lottie heard Frances and George 'in discussion' over someone called Giacometti, it had become so fierce and passionate she had been afraid that Frances would be struck. That had been the inevitable outcome at home when her mother argued with her boyfriends at that pitch. At the Holden house nobody ever argued. But Frances, normally subdued, melancholy Frances, had batted back every criticism of this Giacometti that George put forth, and then finally, having told him that his problem was that he needed to 'respond with instinct, not intellect', walked out of the room. And half an hour later had come back in, as if nothing had happened, to ask him if he would take her to town in his car.

They seemed to obey none of the normal social rules. There had been the time that Lottie had come by herself and Adeline had walked her round the house, showing her the dimensions and unique angles of each room, ignoring the piles of books and dusty rugs still unplaced in various corners. Mrs Holden would never have let someone see her house in this unfinished – often unclean – state. But Adeline didn't even seem to notice. When Lottie tentatively pointed out a missing banister in one of the stairwells, Adeline had looked mildly surprised, then observed in that impenetrable accent of hers that they would tell Marnie and she would take care of it. What about your husband? Lottie wanted to ask, but Adeline had already glided off to the next room.

And there was the way she was with Frances: less like sisters (they didn't argue like sisters) than a kind of old married couple, finishing each other's sentences, laughing at private jokes, breaking off into half-explained anecdotes about places they had been. Adeline told everything and revealed nothing. When Lottie thought back after each visit, which she did – each being filled with such colour and sensation that it had to be digested slowly afterwards – she realised that she knew no more about the actress than she had on their first visit. Her husband, whom she had yet to refer to by name, was 'working abroad'. 'Darling George' was something in economics – 'such a brilliant mind'. ('Such a brilliant beau, I bet,' said Celia, who was working up something of a crush on the linen-clad one.) Frances's tenancy of the house was never explained, although the girls noted that, unlike Adeline, she didn't wear a wedding ring. Neither had Adeline asked much about Lottie: having established only the details that she needed to relate to – whether she had been painted, whether she was interested in certain things – she displayed no interest in her history, her parents, her place in the world.

This was exceedingly odd to Lottie, who had grown up in two homes where, despite their myriad differences, one's history informed everything that was likely to happen to one. In Merham, her history within the house meant that she was accorded all the advantages given as a right to Celia – all the education, upbringing, clothes and food – while both parties were subtly aware that these gifts were not quite unconditional, especially now that Lottie was heading towards her coming of age. Outside the house, the Mrs Anstys and Chiltons, the Mrs Colquhouns would assess one immediately by history and associations and ascribe all sorts of characteristics simply by those virtues – as in 'He's a Thompson. They're all prone to laziness', or 'She was bound to leave. The aunt bolted two days after her confinement.' They were not interested in what one cared about, what one believed in. Celia would be held to their collective bosom for ever, for being the doctor's daughter, for being from one of Merham's best families, despite officially having become 'A Handful'. But if Lottie had turned to Mrs Chilton and asked her, as Adeline Armand once had, 'If you could wake up in someone else's body for just one day, who would it be?' Mrs Chilton would have suggested that they remove Lottie to the nice institution over at Braintree where they had doctors to deal with people like her . . . like poor Mrs McGrath, who had been there ever since her monthlies turned her funny.

They were definitely Bohemians, decided Lottie, who had just discovered the word. And it was only to be expected of Bohemians.

'Don't care what they are,' said Celia. 'But they're a

damn sight more interesting than the old bores around here.'

It was not often that Joe Bernard found himself the focus of attention from not one but two of Merham's more attractive young ladies. The longer Adeline Armand lived in the village, the more disquiet had been expressed about her unconventional way of living, so Lottie and Celia had had to become increasingly inventive in disguising their visits. And on the Saturday afternoon of the garden party they had been left with no option but to call on Joe. The presence of most of their friends' mothers in the house meant that they couldn't use visiting as an excuse, while Sylvia, feeling mutinous after Celia had reneged on a promise to let her use her new record-player, was threatening to follow them and tell if they went anywhere even remotely off-limits. So Joe, who had the afternoon off from the garage, had agreed to come and pick them up in his car and pretend to be taking them on a picnic up at Bardness Point. He hadn't been terribly keen (he didn't like lying – it made him blush even more than usual) but Lottie had employed what Celia now referred to sarcastically as her 'smouldering look' and that had been Joe in the bag.

Outside the filtered gloom of Mrs Holden's front room it was a glorious afternoon, the kind of May Saturday that hinted of simmering summer afternoons to come, that filled Merham's streets with dawdling families, and sent shop displays of beach-balls and postcards spilling out on to the pavements. The air was filled with the cries of overexcited children and the twin scents of candyfloss and sun oil. The fierce winds that had so far plagued the east coast had, for the last few days, dropped, lifting temperatures and moods so that it felt, prematurely, like the first true day of summer.

Lottie leaned out of the window and tipped her face up to the light. Even so many years on, she still got a faint thrill of excitement to be at the seaside.

'So what are you going to do, Joe, while we're inside?' Celia, in the back of the car, was applying lipstick.

Joe pulled out across the level-crossing that separated the two sides of the town. Although Arcadia House was, as the crow flies, less than a mile from Woodbridge Avenue, to get there by road one had to dip into the town, past the municipal park, and come out again on the winding coast road. 'I'll go to Bardness Point.'

'What, by yourself?' Celia snapped her compact shut. She was wearing little white gloves and a bright red dress with a circle skirt that nipped in almost painfully at the waist. She didn't need a girdle, although her mother was forever trying to persuade her to wear one. It would, apparently, hold her in 'properly'.

'It's just if your mother asks me anything about the weather when I drop you back. I shall need to know what it's been like up there, just so I can say so without messing up.'

Lottie felt a sudden pang of conscience at their using him in this way. 'I'm sure you don't have to do that, Joe,' she said. 'You could just drop us outside when we get back. She won't have a chance to ask you anything.'

Joe's jaw set, and he indicated to turn right into the high street. 'Yes, but if I do that my mother will want to know why I didn't pass on her good wishes and then she'll be in a stew.'

'Good thinking, Joe,' said Celia. 'And I'm sure Mummy will want to say hello to your mother.'

Lottie was pretty sure Mrs Holden would want to do nothing of the sort.

'So what's going on at this house after all? When do you need picking up?'

'If it's a garden party, I'd imagine they'll be doing tea, don't you, Lots?'

Lottie found it hard to picture sponge cakes and scones being laid on at Arcadia House. But she couldn't imagine what other form a garden party might take. 'I suppose so,' she said.

'So about half past five? Six o'clock?'

'Best make it half past five,' said Celia, waving at someone through the window before remembering that it was Joe's car she was in and sinking quietly down on the back seat. 'That way we'll be home before Mummy starts going on.'

'We won't forget this, Joe.'

There were only two cars on the drive when they arrived, a paltry total that, when Joe remarked upon it, prompted Celia, already snappy through overexcitement, to observe, 'Just as well you weren't invited, then.' He didn't snap back; he never did. But he didn't smile, even when Lottie squeezed his arm with as much apology as she could muster when they climbed out. And he drove off without waving.

'I do hate a man who sulks,' said Celia cheerfully, as they rang the doorbell. 'I hope they don't have coconut cakes. I do detest coconut.'

Lottie was feeling faintly sick. She had none of the appetite for social gatherings that Celia displayed, largely because she still felt uncomfortable explaining herself to those who didn't know her. People were never satisfied if she said she lived at the Holdens'. They wanted to know why, and then for how long, and whether she missed her mother. At Mrs Holden's last garden party (Poorly Children In Africa) she made the mistake of admitting that it had been over a year since they had last met and subsequently found herself, uncomfortably, an object of some pity.

'They're outside,' said Marnie, who looked, if it were possible, even more grim-faced than usual as she opened the door. 'You won't need your gloves,' she muttered, as she followed them down the hallway, gesturing towards the back.

'On or off, then?' whispered Celia, as they walked towards the light.

Lottie, her ears already trained on the voices outside, didn't answer.

It was not your standard garden party: that much was clear immediately. There was no marquee (Mrs Holden always insisted on a marquee, in case of rain), and no trestle tables. Where is the food going to go? thought Lottie absently, then cursed herself for sounding like Joe.

Instead they walked out across the patio area, and Marnie gestured towards the steps that led down to the small stretch of private beach, which ended at the water. It was on this, scattered around a variety of blankets, that the garden-party guests sat, some sprawled barefoot, some seated, deep in conversation.

Adeline Armand was seated on a mint-green wrap made from some fabric with a satin sheen. She was dressed in a shell-pink summer frock of crêpe-de-Chine, and a large, floppy white hat with a broad brim, the most conventional outfit Lottie had seen her wear so far. She was surrounded by three men, including George, who was peeling leaves from some peculiar plant (an artichoke, Adeline explained later) and handing them to her, one by one, from under the half-shelter of a large parasol. Frances was wearing a swimsuit, revealing a surprisingly lean, toned body. She stood more comfortably in her skin than in her clothes, her shoulders thrown back as she laughed heartily at something a neighbour had just said. There were at least four bottles of red wine open. There was no one else Lottie recognised. She stood still, feeling foolish and overdressed in her white gloves. Celia, beside her, was trying to remove hers behind her back.

George, suddenly looking up, spotted them. 'Welcome to our little *déjeuner sur l'herbe*, girls,' he called. 'Come and sit down.'

Celia had already kicked off her shoes. She was picking her way through the sand to where George was seated, her hips swinging in a manner Lottie had seen her practising at home when she thought no one was looking.

'Are you hungry?' said Frances, who looked unusually cheerful. 'We've got some trout and some delicious herb salad. Or there's cold duck. I think there's some left.'

'We've eaten, thanks,' said Celia, sitting down. Lottie sat slightly behind her, wishing that more people were standing up so that she didn't feel so conspicuous.

'What about some fruit? We've got some gorgeous strawberries. Has Marnie taken them in already?'

'They don't want food. They want a drink,' said George, who had already busied himself pouring two large goblets of red wine. 'Here,' he said, holding one up to the light. 'One for Little Red Riding Hood.'

Celia glanced down at her skirt and then up again, pleased by the attention.

'Here's to the fragile bloom of youth.'

'Oh, George.' A blonde woman in huge sunglasses leaned over and tapped his arm in a way that made Celia bristle.

'Well, they might as well enjoy it while they've got it.' He had the well-lubricated look and loosened vowels of someone who had been drinking all day. 'God knows, they won't look like that for long.'

Lottie stared at him.

'Frances knows. Give it five years and they'll be thick-hipped matrons, a couple of brats hanging on their skirts. Fine upholders of the moral majority of Merham.'

'I know nothing of the sort.' Frances, smiling, folded her long limbs on to a picnic blanket.

Something about George's tone made Lottie uneasy. Celia, however, took a glass from him and gulped down half of its contents as if accepting a challenge. 'Not me,' she said, grinning. 'You won't find me here in five years' time.'

'*Non*? And where will you be?' It was impossible to see Adeline's face under her hat. Only her neat little mouth was visible, curved up in its polite, inquisitive smile.

'Oh, I don't know. London, perhaps. Cambridge. Maybe even Paris.'

'Not if your mother has her way.' Something about Celia's determined ease in this company irritated Lottie. 'She wants you to stay here.'

'Oh, she'll come round in the end.'

'That's what you think.'

'What's the matter?' said George, dipping his handsome head to Celia's. 'Is Mater concerned for your moral welfare?'

Something about the way that Celia and George looked at each other made Lottie's chest tighten.

'Well . . .' said Celia, slyly. Her eyes held a sudden flash of promise. 'There are an awful lot of big bad wolves about, after all.'

Lottie eventually settled down on the edge of Adeline's wrap, fighting the urge, even as she sat, to sweep sand from its folds. She felt overdressed and suburban, and had trouble keeping up with the conversations around her, which made her feel stupid. Adeline, who normally took pains to make her feel at ease, was engrossed in conversation with a man Lottie hadn't seen before. She sipped her wine, trying not to grimace, and picked at a bowl of cherries.

'Fabulous house, Adeline darling. More moderne than deco, don't you think?'

'Of course Russell is an idiot. And if he thinks that Eden is going to pay the slightest attention to him and his bloody scientists, he's a deluded idiot.'

'Did I tell you Archie has finally got one into the Summer Exhibition? Hung so that it looks like a postage stamp, but you can't have everything . . .'

It was a long afternoon. There were no coconut cakes. Lottie, her cardigan pulled around her shoulders to stop herself tanning, watched the tide gradually ease away, lengthening the shore and turning an intricate sandcastle that must have been made early that morning into a swollen pimple. She could hear Celia giggling manically behind her and knew that she must be drinking. The girls only ever had wine at Christmas, and even the thimbleful of sherry they had been allowed before lunch last year had made Celia pink and her voice lift two pitches. Lottie had drunk half of her glass, before surreptitiously spilling it into the sand behind her. Even that had made her head ache, and her brain feel fuzzy and befugged.

When Marnie cleared away the last of the plates, Lottie moved round a little so that she could see Celia. She was telling George about 'the last time she had been to Paris'. The fact that she had never been to Paris seemed to have little impact on her elaborate tale, but Lottie, noticing the somewhat combative air between her and the blonde woman, thought it would be unsporting to undermine her now. From under her sunglasses, the blonde woman's smile had become more of a snarl and, scenting victory, Celia had become exuberant.

'Of course, the next time I go I'm going to have dinner at La Coupole. Have you had dinner at La Coupole? I'm told the lobster is absolutely superb.'

She stretched out her legs in front of her, letting her skirt ride up over her knees.

'I'm awfully hot, George,' said the blonde woman suddenly. 'Shall we go in?'

Oh, Celia, thought Lottie. You've met your match here.

Celia glanced at George, who was smoking a cigar, his head tilted back towards the sun. A flicker of something thunderous passed across her face.

'I suppose it is rather warm,' George said. He sat up, brushing sand from his shirtsleeves.

Then Frances stood up. 'I'm getting overheated here too. I think it's time for a swim,' she said. 'Are you coming, Adeline? Anyone?'

Adeline declined. 'Too, too sleepy, darling. I'll watch.'

But George, shaking his dark hair like a big shaggy dog, had started to undo his shirt, as if suddenly reanimated. 'That's what we need,' he said, tamping out his cigar. 'A nice refreshing dip. Irene?'

The blonde woman wrinkled her nose. 'I haven't my things.'

'You don't need swimming things, woman. Just go in your slip.'

'No, George, really. I'll watch from here.'

The other men were stripping off now, down to shorts or trousers. Lottie, who had wondered if she was about to fall asleep, had been jolted awake, and was watching the shedding of everyone's clothes with quiet alarm.

'C'mon, girls. Lottie? I bet you can swim.'

'Oh, she doesn't go in the water.'

Lottie now knew Celia had drunk too much. She would

45

never have so carelessly referred to Lottie's inability to swim (a deep embarrassment to a seaside-dweller) if she had been sober. She shot her friend a furious glance, but Celia wasn't paying attention. She was busy wrestling with her zip.

'What are you doing?'

'I'm swimming.' Celia grinned broadly. 'Don't look at me like that, Lots. I've got my slip on. It's no different from a swimsuit, really.'

And then she was off, whooping and squealing as she followed George and a handful of others to the water's edge. Frances ploughed in, pushing forth until she was up to her waist in the waves, then diving under like a porpoise, her swimsuit wet and shiny, like the pelt of a seal.

Celia, having reached the water, had gone in up to her knees and hesitated, until George reached for her arm and, laughing, swung her round so that she fell into the water. Around them, the other guests rose and fell boisterously in the waves, pushing and splashing each other, the men naked to the waist, the women in fine layers of lace undergarments. Not one of them, Lottie noted, was wearing a girdle.

When Celia first turned to wave at her, however, Lottie wished Mrs Holden had been more successful in trying to persuade her daughter to wear one: now that her slip and underwear were soaked with seawater, few parts of Celia's anatomy were protected from view. Get down, under the water, she tried to gesture at her, waving her hands ineffectually, but Celia, her head thrown back as she laughed, didn't seem to notice.

'Don't worry, darling.' Adeline's voice came low and intimate from beside her. 'No one will pay any attention. When we are in France, we are usually naked from the waist up.'

Lottie, trying not to think too hard about what such

holidays in France might comprise, gave a weak smile in reply, and reached for the wine bottle. She felt a distinct need for fortification. 'It's just Mrs Holden,' she said, quietly. 'I don't think she'd be terribly pleased.'

'Then here,' Adeline handed her a large, boldly patterned scarf, 'go and give her this. Tell her it's a sarong, and that I said all the finest people are wearing one.'

Lottie could have kissed her. She took the fabric and padded down to the beach, tying her cardigan around her waist as she did. It was late enough in the afternoon now: the risk of tanning was minimal.

'Here,' she shouted, bare feet lapped by the receding tide. 'Celia, try this.'

Celia didn't hear her. Or perhaps didn't want to hear her. She was squealing as George dived for her waist, lifting her into the air and dropping her back into the shallows.

'Celia!' It was hopeless. She felt like someone's aged, pernickety aunt.

Eventually George saw her. He came wading through the waves, his hair plastered to his head, his rolled-up trousers sticking to his thighs.

Lottie tried to keep her eyes above his waist. 'Can you give this to Celia? Adeline said it was a sarong, or something.'

'A sarong, eh?' George took it from her and looked behind him at Celia, who was launching herself backwards on the swell. 'Think she needs covering up, do you?'

Lottie looked back at him, her face straight. 'I don't think she realises quite how uncovered she is.'

'Oh, Lottie, Lottie, serious little guardian of morals . . . Look at you, all hot and bothered about your friend.' He looked back down at the cloth, a grin spreading across his face. 'I've got a better solution,' he said. Then: 'I think it's you who need cooling off.' And, without warning, he swept

47

his arms around her waist and threw her up and over his wet shoulder.

Lottie was aware of being bumped along as he began to jog, and panicked, tried to get her arm behind her to ensure that her skirt was still covering her knickers. Then she was falling down, a huge wave of salt water sweeping over her face so that, coughing and spluttering, she struggled to find the sea floor under her feet. She could hear muffled laughter above her, and then, gasping, found her head above water again.

She managed to stand and paused for a second, her eyes stinging, salt burning the back of her throat. She felt herself retch a couple of times, and made blindly for the shore. When she got there, she bent over, gasping. Her dress was stuck to her legs, her layers of petticoat melded together. Her top, which was a pale cotton, had become almost see-through, clearly revealing the outline of her brassière. On raising a hand to her hair, she discovered it was loose, that the tortoiseshell slide that had held it back off her face was no longer there.

She looked up and saw George, hands on hips, grinning. Celia, behind him, was wearing a look of appalled amusement.

'You bloody pig.' The words fell out of Lottie's mouth even before she knew she was going to say them. 'You bloody, bloody pig. That was *not on*.'

George looked briefly stunned. Behind her, the lull of conversation from the picnic blankets stalled.

'Oh, it's bloody funny for you,' she yelled, aware that there was a large lump in the back of her throat, threatening tears. 'You with handfuls of money and your linen bloody suits! Doesn't matter to you if your clothes get ruined. Look at my summer dress! Look! It's my best one! Mrs Holden will kill me! And you've lost my bloody comb.' And to her own horror, the tears came, hot tears of frustration and humiliation.

'Steady on, Lots.' Celia's face had fallen. Lottie knew she was embarrassing her, but didn't care.

'Come on, Lottie. It was only a joke.' George made towards her, looking both exasperated and apologetic.

'Well, it was a very stupid joke.' Lottie looked round to see Adeline beside her. She was holding up her wrap to place it around Lottie's shoulders. Her expression was one of mild rebuke. Lottie caught her spicy, jasmine scent as Adeline covered her.

'George, you must apologise. Lottie was our guest, and you had no right. Lottie, I am very sorry. I'm sure we can get Marnie to launder your lovely dress and make sure it is all right for you.'

But how will I get home? Lottie thought desperately, confronted by an image of herself tottering along the road in Adeline's feather boa and Chinese slippers. She was interrupted by a voice from up on the cliff path.

'Celia Jane Holden. What on *earth* do you think you're doing?'

Lottie spun round to find above her the horrified faces of Mrs Chilton and Mrs Colquhoun, who had been taking the scenic route home from Woodbridge Avenue. It had apparently proven rather more scenic than they had expected.

'You get out of that water and back into your clothes this instant. *Where* are your decency and decorum?'

Celia had gone quite white. She held her hands to her chest, as if suddenly aware of her state of undress. George lifted his hands in a placatory manner, but Mrs Chilton had pulled herself up to her full five feet four inches, so that her bosom appeared to be hoisted somewhere beneath her chin, and was not about to be pacified. 'And I don't know who you are, but you, young man, are old enough to know better. Persuading respectable girls out of their clothes in broad daylight . . . You are a disgrace.' She caught sight of the wine bottles on the sand. 'Celia Holden, you had better not have been drinking. Goodness gracious! Are you trying to earn yourself a reputation? I do not imagine for one minute that your mother is going to be pleased about this.'

Mrs Colquhoun, meanwhile, held both hands to her silent mouth, as shocked as if she had just witnessed some human sacrifice. 'Mrs Chilton – I really—'

'Lottie? Is that you?' Mrs Chilton's chin was pulled so far into her neck that they had become one huge pink trunk of disapproval. The fact that Lottie was dressed did not appear to placate her. 'You make your way up here this instant. Come on, girls, both of you, before anyone else sees you.' She hauled her handbag under her chest, both hands tightly gripping its clasp. 'Don't you look at me like that, Celia. I am not leaving you here with this disreputable rabble. I am going to take both you girls home personally. Goodness gracious, what your poor mother is going to make of this I don't know.'

Exactly three weeks later, Celia left for secretarial school in London. It was meant to be a punishment, and Mrs Holden was faintly put out that her daughter seemed not just unrepentant but rather indecently pleased to be going. She would stay with Mrs Holden's cousin in Kensington and, if she did well on her course, would have the chance to work at her husband's office in Bayswater. 'London, Lots! And not a charity coffee morning or hideous sibling in sight.' Celia had been in an uncommonly good mood for the entire run-up to her departure.

Lottie, meanwhile, had listened to Celia getting carpeted

by her father, and wondered from the silent safety of their room what it was likely to mean for her. Nothing had been said about her going to London. She didn't want to leave. But when she heard them muttering in lowered voices about 'bad influences', she knew it wasn't Celia they were talking about.

Three

It had to be said; she was not a girl one could warm to, even if she did try terribly hard. There was nothing wrong with her exactly; she was always helpful, and tidy, and usually polite (unlike Celia, she wasn't prone to what her husband called 'hysterics') – but she could be terribly short with people. Blunt enough to be considered rude.

When Mrs Chilton had brought them both back on that dreadful Saturday afternoon (she was still having nightmares about it) Celia had at least had the grace to look shamefaced. She had thrown her arms around her mother's waist and pleaded, 'Oh, Mummy, I know I was awful, but I'm really, really sorry. Honestly I am.' Furious as she was, she had been quite taken aback; even Mrs Chilton's granite expression had softened. It was very hard to resist Celia at the best of times.

Lottie, however, had failed to apologise at all. She had looked rather cross when told to say sorry for her behaviour, and retorted that she had not only kept all her clothes on but would never have entered the water of her own free will, as well they all knew. Except she said 'bloody knew', which immediately got Mrs Holden's back up. There was still something of the fishwife in that girl, despite all her best efforts.

No, said Lottie. She would not apologise for her behaviour. Yes, she was sorry that they hadn't been straightforward about where they were going. Yes, she had been there when

Celia had stripped to her underwear – and not done anything about it. But she personally had been far more sinned against than sinning.

Mrs Holden had become rather cross at this point, and told Lottie to go to her room. She hated losing her temper, and it made her feel even more resentful towards the girl. Then Sylvia had come in and said – right in front of Mrs Chilton, mind – that she had seen Celia practising kissing on the back of her hand, and that Celia had told her she had kissed 'simply loads' of nice men and that she knew of a way of doing it without getting pregnant. And even though it was plain to Mrs Holden that Sylvia had got carried away and was indulging in stories, she knew jolly well that Sarah Chilton would be unable to keep the child's comment to herself, and that had made her crosser with Lottie than ever. It had to be Lottie – there was no one else to be furious with.

'I don't want to see you anywhere near that house from now on, do you hear me, Lottie?' she said, making her way up the stairs after Sarah had left. 'I really am very cross with you both. Very cross. And I will not have you embarrassing the family in this way again. Goodness only knows what Dr Holden is going to say when he gets home.'

'So don't tell him,' said Lottie, emerging from their room, her face straight. 'He's not interested in women's gossip anyway.'

'Women's gossip? Is that what you call it?' Susan Holden stood on the stairs, clutching the banister. 'You both humiliate me in front of polite society and you think this is just women's gossip?'

From inside their room, she heard Celia mutter something.

'What was that? What did you say?'

After a moment, Celia stuck her head round the door. 'I

53

said we're terribly sorry, Mummy, and of course we'll stay well away from the "disreputable rabble", as Mrs Chilton so eloquently put it.'

Mrs Holden gave them both her longest, hardest look. But she swore she could see the faintest of smiles playing around Lottie's lips. Then, realising she was not about to get any more out of either of them, she mustered what little dignity she could and walked slowly back downstairs to where Freddie was building himself a rabbit hutch out of old crates. In the good parlour. To live in.

And now Celia had gone. And Lottie, although she had been careful to do all her chores, had been relentlessly polite and had helped with Sylvia's homework, had for weeks been mooning around like a sick puppy when she thought no one was looking. It was all rather wearing. And somehow Susan Holden felt rather less comfortable about Lottie's presence in the house than she once had. Not that she would have admitted it to anyone. Not after all the hard work she had been seen to put into the girl's upbringing. It was just that when it had been the two of them together, and she had fed them together, bought their clothes together, scolded them together, it had been somehow easier to consider Lottie part of the family. Now, with Celia gone, she felt unable to deal with her in quite the same way. If she admitted it to herself, she felt inexplicably resentful of her. Lottie seemed to sense this, and had behaved even more impeccably, which was peculiarly irritating too.

Worse, she had the distinct suspicion that, despite everything she said, Lottie was still going to that actress's house. She offered to help Virginia with the shopping, which she had never done before, then took several hours just to get a few mackerel. Or even half a day to pick up Dr Holden's newspaper. Twice she had come home smelling of scents that

54

you most definitely could not get in Mr Ansty's shop. And then, when one asked her, she would fix one with that rather too direct stare and say, in a tone that, frankly, Mrs Holden found rather aggressive, that No, She Had Not Been To The Actress's House Because Hadn't Mrs Holden Told Her Not To? She really was too much, sometimes.

She should have known, really. Lots of people had warned her against taking in an evacuee. She had disregarded those who said that all London children had nits and lice – although she had peered quite closely at the younger Lottie's hair when she arrived; and those who said she would steal, or that the parents would follow and camp in their house and they'd never be rid of any of them.

No, there was only the mother, and she had never visited so much as once. She had written Susan Holden two letters: once after the first long stay, thanking her in that awful handwriting of hers; the second a year later when Susan had invited the child to return. But she had seemed rather relieved to have the child off her hands.

And Lottie had never stolen anything, or run away, or got too forward with boys. No, if anything, she was forced to acknowledge, it was Celia who had been a little too *developed* in that direction. Lottie had done what she was told, and helped with the little ones, and kept herself nice and presentable.

Susan Holden felt suddenly guilty, picturing eight-year-old Lottie standing at Merham station, her arms wrapped protectively around her brown-paper-wrapped bundle of clothes. In the midst of all the chaos, she had looked at Mrs Holden silently, with those huge dark eyes, and as Susan began to chatter a welcome – even then the child was rather unnerving – she had slowly lifted her right hand and taken Susan's own. It had been a curiously moving gesture. And a rather

55

unbalancing one too, symptomatic of everything she had been since: polite, self-contained, watchful, affectionate in a rather reserved way. Perhaps it was unfair to be so hard on the girl. She had done nothing really wrong. She was just going to have to adjust to Celia's absence. The girl would be leaving them soon anyway, once she had sorted herself out with a good job. And Susan Holden prided herself on her Christian sense of charity. But then she thought about the way that Henry had looked at Lottie that time several weeks ago when she had hitched up her skirt to go into the paddling-pool with Frederick. And felt rather complicated about her houseguest again.

Celia had a boyfriend. It hadn't taken her long, Lottie thought wryly. There had been a substantial gap between letters and then she had written a breathless account of some awful trouble she had got into at a railway station and how this man, whom she was now stepping out with, had 'saved' her. Lottie hadn't taken much notice at first: Celia always had been prone to exaggeration. And he was not the first man Celia had sworn was the one for her. Not even in the short time she had been in London. There had been the man she had met on the train between Bishops Stortford and Broxbourne; the man who served her at the café on Baker Street who always gave her an extra coffee when his boss wasn't around; and there was Mr Grisham, her shorthand teacher, who had definitely examined her loops and abbreviations with more than teacherly interest. But then, gradually, the letters were less about these men, and the supposedly interminable evenings in with Aunt Angela and her awful brood, and the girls at secretarial school, and increasingly about dinners at fashionable restaurants, and walks on Hampstead Heath they had had together, and the general superiority of Guy in everything from conversational skills to kissing technique ('For God's sake burn this before Mummy sees it').

Lottie read, and tried to decipher what was definitely the truth. For 'monied family', she decided, one should read simply 'own house, with inside toilet'; for 'absolutely gorgeous', a face which didn't resemble that of a disgruntled bulldog; and for 'mad, simply passionate about me', Celia probably meant that Guy had turned up to meet her at the times and places that he had said he would. It was hard not to be a little cynical – Lottie had lived for many years with Celia by now, and had learned the hard way that Celia and veracity were not always the closest of bedfellows. Lottie, for example, had heard herself described by her friend as having been rescued from a burning building during the Blitz; as a mysterious *émigrée* of Middle European origin, and as an orphan whose parents had been killed by a doodlebug while celebrating their wedding anniversary with a dinner of smoked salmon and black-market vodka. She had not challenged Celia on any of these, despite becoming gradually aware of their provenance. No one ever challenged Celia: it was one of the things Lottie had learned at the Holden house. There was a feeling that doing so would be like opening Pandora's box. In fact, no one even mentioned that Celia told fibs. The one time she had mentioned one of these 'untruths' to Mrs Holden, Mrs Holden had got quite shirty and told her she was sure there had been some mistake and, really, Lottie was being rather rude going on and on about it. Perhaps Celia hadn't even got a boyfriend, Lottie thought. Perhaps all these men were figments of her imagination, and she was really spending her evenings practising her needlepoint and piano scales with Aunt Angela's children. The thought made her smile. Just to get Celia going, she had made no mention of Guy in her next letter, but she had asked lots of questions about Aunt Angela's children.

It had been an odd couple of months; only now was Lottie getting used to life without Celia. But with that increased comfort, she had become aware of an increased tension within the house, as if Celia's absence had removed some focus that, like invisible glue, had been holding the whole thing together. Dr Holden's absences had become more frequent, which had rather stretched Mrs Holden's brittle hold on everyday life. At the same time Freddie and Sylvia, as if responding to some unseen siren, had chosen this time to become more shrill and excitable, shredding what remained of her 'nerves', and giving Dr Holden an oft-spoken reason for not returning home. 'Is it impossible to get a moment's peace in this house?' he would ask, in his low, seemingly measured tones, and Mrs Holden would jump, like a dog about to be kicked outside on a cold night.

Lottie would watch him silently as he withdrew to his study, or on some unheralded night call, returning his 'Good night, Lottie' with equal civility. He was never rude to her, had never made her feel like a usurper within the house. Then again, half the time he had hardly seemed to notice her at all.

When she had first arrived in the house, he had been less reserved. He had been friendly, had smiled more. Or perhaps she just remembered it like that. On her first night in the house, when she had wept silent tears, unsure what exactly it was that she was crying for but paradoxically afraid that her hosts would hear and send her home again, he had let himself quietly into her room and sat down on the bed. 'You mustn't be afraid, Lottie,' he had said, placing a warm, dry hand on her head. 'I imagine life has been pretty difficult for you in London. You're safe now.'

Lottie had been stunned into silence. No adult had ever spoken to her as he had. With solemnity. And concern. And without some kind of threat or disparagement. Most of them hadn't even remembered her name.

'For as long as you are here, Lottie, we shall do everything we can to ensure your happiness. And when you are ready to leave, we shall hope that you remember your stay with fondness. For we are all sure that we shall be fond of you.'

With those words he had patted her and left, taking with him her eternal gratitude and what passed in her eight-year-old heart for devotion. Had he known that she had never had so much as a father-figure in her life before, let alone kind words from one, he might perhaps have tempered his attempt at affection. But no; Dr Holden had smiled, patted her comfortingly, and little Lottie had stopped crying and lain in her soft bed and wondered about the magical and unforeseen existence of men who didn't swear, demand that she fetch things from the corner shop, or smell of Old Holborn.

As she had grown older, she had developed a slightly less rosy view of Dr Holden. It was hard not to, when you witnessed at close hand the cruelty that could be inflicted by a man who simply refused to interact with his wife. In the mornings he would retreat behind his newspaper, emerging from behind his inky curtain only to chastise Freddie or Sylvia mildly for some reported misbehaviour, or to pick up his coffee cup. In the evenings he would come in late and distracted, would insist that it was impossible for him to talk until he had had a drink and 'a few minutes' peace', which usually managed to stretch far beyond his supper. And meanwhile Mrs Holden, who seemed unable to read the signs, would be twittering around him anxiously, trying to anticipate his needs, trying to engage him in conversation, trying to get him to notice her new hair-do/nail polish/cardigan without anything so crass as actually telling him about them.

It was at times like these that Lottie would feel vaguely cross with him. She could see that being married to someone like Mrs Holden would be rather irritating. But it did seem unnecessarily cruel to ignore her in this way, especially when she did so much to try to make his life better. As far as Lottie could see he did nothing to try to improve hers. And over the years Mrs Holden had grown more anxious, and more twittery, and Lottie had watched his attempts to hide his irritation with her become fewer, and his absences longer, and she had decided that, what with her mother and Dr and Mrs Holden, marriage was definitely A Bad Lot and something to be avoided, a bit like sewage outlets or chickenpox.

'I think here, don't you? It's too white, at the moment. Too vacuous. Too . . . spare.'

Lottie squinted, trying to see what Adeline apparently could. It just looked like a wall. She wasn't sure how a wall could be spare. But she nodded, and tried to look intelligent, and raised an eyebrow as if she understood when Adeline announced that Frances had plans for 'something figurative'.

'I have this idea,' Adeline said. 'For a mural. I don't want pictures of forests or lakes . . .'

'Or Palladian landscapes,' said Frances, who had appeared behind them. 'I can't bear temples and pillars. Or deer. Really can't stand those awful deer.'

'No. I have an idea.' Adeline paused, ran a finger down the wall. 'It will be a human landscape. We will all appear. All Arcadia's people.'

'Like a kind of Last Supper. But without the religion.'

'Or the symbolism.'

'Oh, no, we've got to have some symbolism. No good paintings without a bit of symbolism.'

They had lost Lottie completely. She stared at the white wall, its reflected light almost blinding in the afternoon sun. Below them, the beach stretched out, segregated by its break-water, packed with holidaymakers despite the approaching autumn. If it had been down to her, she would probably have put a few pots of plants in front of it. Or a bit of trellis.

'. . . and you, Lottie. We said we would paint your portrait, didn't we? You will feature. And Celia, in her absence.'

She tried to imagine how she would appear on the wall. But all she could picture was one of those cartoon doodles that had appeared everywhere in the war – saying 'Wot, no . . . ?'

'Will I have to pose?' she said.

'No,' said Frances, smiling. She had smiled a lot, lately. It sat awkwardly on her face, pulling its long sides up like old pantaloons on thin elastic. 'We know you now. I prefer something a little more . . . impressionistic.'

'Her hair. You must show her hair. Do you ever let it down, Lottie?' Adeline reached out a slender hand and stroked it.

Lottie flinched. She could not help herself. 'It gets a bit tangled. It's too fine.' She reached up to smooth it, pulling unconsciously away from Adeline.

'Stop putting yourself down, Lottie. Men find it so boring.'

Men? Lottie realigned her vision of herself: as someone in whom *men* might be interested. Up until now it had only been *boys*. Or, more specifically, Joe, who barely counted as that.

'One should always refer only to one's good points. If one only ever draws the eye to the good, people rarely noticed the bad.'

It was the closest she had come to revelation. But Lottie barely noticed.

'Perhaps we could get Lottie painting.'

'Oh, yes! What an idea, Frances. Would you like that, Lottie? Frances is the most fabulous teacher.'

Lottie shuffled her feet. 'I'm not very good at art. My bowls of fruit usually end up looking as if they're about to keel over.'

'Bowls of fruit . . .' Frances shook her head. 'How can you engender passion for art with bowls of fruit? Come on, Lottie. Come and draw what is in your head, your heart.'

Lottie stepped back, reluctant and self-conscious. Adeline's fingers found her back, propelled her gently forward. 'You need to learn to dream, Lottie. To express yourself.'

'But I don't even do art any more now we've finished school. Mrs Holden says I should do book-keeping, so that I can get a good job in a shop.'

'Oh, forget shops, Lottie. Look, it doesn't have to *be* anything. Just enjoy the feel of the pastels. Pastels are beautiful to work with. See . . .' Frances began drawing lines on the wall, smudging the colours with her paint-stained fingers, her movements confident and sure. Lottie watched, briefly forgetting herself.

'Don't forget to include yourself, Frances darling.' Adeline placed a hand on her shoulder. 'You never include yourself.'

Frances kept her eyes on the wall. 'I'm not good at painting myself.'

Marnie emerged at the back door. Her apron was covered in blood and feathers, and a half-plucked goose hung by its neck from her left hand. 'Excuse me, ma'am, Mr Armand has arrived.'

Lottie had been staring at the pastel marks. She glanced at Adeline, who smiled gently and nodded, dismissing Marnie. Lottie waited for her to rush to the door – to straighten herself, or race to put on some makeup, as Mrs Holden invariably did – feeling herself flush with excitement that she was finally going to meet Adeline's elusive husband.

But Adeline turned her attention back towards the white wall. 'Then we will have to get someone to paint you, Frances,' she said, seemingly unconcerned. 'You are, after all, an essential part of our picture, *non*?'

Marnie's face reappeared in the doorway. 'He's in the drawing room.'

Frances stepped away from the wall and looked at Adeline in a way that made Lottie feel furtive. 'I think I am more effective as an invisible presence,' she said slowly.

Adeline shrugged, as if relinquishing an oft-fought argument, raised a hand slightly, then turned and walked towards the house.

Lottie had not been sure what she had been expecting but Julian Armand was so far from anything she might have even considered that she had looked past him twice before realising that this was the man to whom Adeline was introducing her.

'So charmed,' he said, holding her hand and kissing it. 'Adeline has told me so much about you.'

Lottie didn't speak, staring in a manner that Mrs Holden would have found certifiable at the short, dapper man with slicked-down hair and an extraordinary curled moustache, like wrought ironwork on his face.

'Lottie,' she whispered. And he nodded, as if that were quite gracious enough.

It was not hard to see where Adeline got her extravagant tastes. He was dressed in fashions that might have been fitting several decades ago and even then only in certain esoteric circles; tweed knickerbockers with a matching waistcoat and jacket. He wore a tie of emerald green, and perfectly round tortoiseshell glasses. From his top pocket hung an extremely elaborate fob watch, while in his left hand he held a silver-topped cane. His highly polished brogues were the only conventional thing on him, and even those bore little resemblance to the brogues Lottie knew – the ten-shilling pairs on the high street.

'So this is Merham,' he said, looking around him at the view from the window. 'This is where you have decided to base us.'

'Now, Julian, you are not to make any judgements until you have lived here for a whole week.' Adeline reached for his hand, smiling at him.

'Why? You have plans for me?'

'I always have plans for you, dearest. But I don't want you to decide until you have woken to the sound of the sea, and drunk good wine while watching the sun set. Our new home is a little paradise, and its hidden charms all the better for their slow appreciation.'

'Ah. I am an expert at slow appreciation, as you know.'

'But, my dear Julian, I know you are also seduced by the bright and the new. And I, and this house, are neither. So we have to make sure that you view us with the right eyes. Isn't that so, Lottie?'

Lottie nodded dumbly. She was having trouble concentrating – she had never seen anyone behave towards her husband the way Adeline was, this excessive courtliness.

'Then I promise I shall say not a word. So – who is going to show me around? Frances? Are you well? You look like the sea air agrees with you.'

'I'm fine, thank you, Julian.'

'And who else is here?'

'George. Irene. And Minette has just left. She is writing again. And Stephen is coming at the end of the week. I told him you would be back.'

'Marvellous.' Julian patted his wife's hand. 'A home already. All I have to do is sit down in the midst of it all and pretend I have always been here.' He turned around slowly, pivoting on his stick as he examined the room. 'And this house? What is its history?'

'We know a little, thanks to Lottie and her friend. It was built by the son of a local family, and when he died it was owned by a couple . . . Who?'

'The MacPhersons,' said Lottie. He was wearing a great big fat ring on his little finger. Like a woman's dress ring, it was.

'Yes, the MacPhersons. But it is in art-moderne style, as you can see. Quite unusual, I think. And it has a wonderful light, *non*? Frances says it has a wonderful light.'

Julian turned to Frances. 'It certainly does, dear Frances. Your taste and judgement, as always, are impeccable.'

Frances gave him a slight, almost pained smile. 'And will you be returning to Cadogan Gardens soon?' she asked.

Julian sighed. 'No, I'm afraid we have slightly burnt our bridges as far as that's concerned. A little misunderstanding about money. But we will have a lovely time here, until things are entirely sorted out. I will be here until the Biennale. If that is not too much of an inconvenience.' He smiled as he said it, apparently secure in the knowledge that his presence was never an inconvenience.

'Then let us make you fully at home,' said Adeline. 'I will show you around.'

Lottie, jolted into movement, became aware of her manners. 'I'd better go,' she said, shuffling backwards towards the door. 'It's getting on a bit and I only said I was going for milk. It . . . it was nice to meet you.'

She waved, and moved to the door. Adeline, raising an arm in farewell, had already walked out on to the terrace, her arm draped around Julian's tweedy waist. As Lottie turned to close the door behind her, she saw Frances. Oblivious to Lottie's presence, and as still as one of her own compositions, she was staring after them.

She had been prepared to feel rather sad for Frances: she had looked rather left out. It must be difficult for her with Julian back; Lottie knew all about how easy it was to feel like a spare part. And George evidently didn't fancy her, or he wouldn't have flirted so much with Celia and the Awful Irene. But then, two nights later, Lottie saw her again.

It was nearly half past nine, and Lottie had offered to walk Mr Beans, the Holdens' elderly and irascible terrier. It was really Dr Holden's job, but he had been unavoidably detained at work, and Mrs Holden, who had gone all wobbly at the news, was having trouble getting Freddie and Sylvia to stay in their beds. Freddie said he had eaten her begonia, and kept running to the bathroom pretending to be sick, while Sylvia, reappearing at the top of the stairs in her slippers and an old gas mask, had demanded her eleventh glass of water. Joe was round, playing Scrabble, and when Lottie had offered to take the dog for his evening constitutional, Mrs Holden had been rather grateful and said that as long as Joe escorted her, she couldn't see why not. But they shouldn't be too long. And to stay on the roads. Lottie and Joe cut across the municipal park, watching the last rays of the sun disappear behind the Riviera Hotel, and the streetlights gradually blink and stutter their way into sodium light. A few feet away Mr Beans grunted and sniffed at unknown scents, weaving a drunken path along the grass verge. She had not taken Joe's arm and, walking beside her, he kept bumping her elbow gently, as if silently prompting her to.

'Have you heard from your mother at all?'

'No. She'll write nearer Christmas, I expect.'

'Isn't it a bit odd, never speaking to her? I should miss mine.'

'Your mother and mine are very different beasts, Joe.'

'I should hardly call my mother a beast.' He tried to laugh, as insurance in case she had meant some kind of a joke.

They walked on in silence, watching a few shadowy figures make their way, murmuring, along the seafront towards unseen baths and beds.

'When is Celia coming home? Saturday, you said?'

That had been part of the problem. Mrs Holden had wanted to tell her husband in person. She liked to bring good news: she would work unfeasibly hard for his smile.

'She's on the afternoon train. I've got to take Freddie to the barber's in the morning.'

'Doesn't seem like eight weeks already, does it? I'll take Freddie if you like. I've got to get mine done. Dad says I'm starting to look like a teddy-boy.'

'Listen,' said Lottie, standing.

Joe lifted his head, as if scenting the air. Below them, the steady rush and hiss of the sea told of an incoming tide. A dog barked, interrupting Mr Beans's scented reverie. And then she heard it again. Jazz music: strange, arrhythmic, almost out of tune. A horn, and something else underneath it. And laughter.

'Can you hear it?' She held Joe's arm, forgetting herself. It was coming from Arcadia House.

'What is it? Someone strangling a cat?'

'Listen, Joe.' She paused, trying to catch the melancholy sound. It wafted over, and then withdrew. 'Let's go closer.'

'Will Buford has got three new American rock-and-roll records at his house. I'm going over there in the week to listen. Do you want to come?'

But Lottie, her cardigan pulled around her shoulders, was running now, tripping down the steps to the best vantage-point. Mr Beans cantered happily behind, his claws clipping on the concrete. 'Mrs Holden said we should keep to the roads,' Joe called to her vanishing figure. Then, after a moment, he went after her.

Lottie was leaning over the railings towards Arcadia. In the near dark, its strips of glass windows glowed brightly, sending banks of light on to the paved terrace. Illuminated there was a small gathering of people; if she really squinted Lottie could just about make out Julian Armand, seated on the old iron bench, his feet resting up on a table. Across the terrace was someone taller, smoking. That was probably George. And there was another man Lottie didn't recognise, talking to him.

And then, bathed in a pool of light, there were Frances and Adeline, dancing together, their arms resting on each other's shoulders, Adeline's head tipped back as she laughed lazily at something Frances was saying. They swayed together, breaking off briefly to pick up glasses of wine, or to call across to the men.

Lottie wondered at the slight thrill that passed through her at the scene. Frances did not look mournful any more. Even at this distance she looked confident, radiant in the gloom. Like she was in control of something, if Lottie could have worked out what. What is it that can transform someone like that? she wondered. How could that be Frances? When she had last been there Frances had been wallpaper, a tepid, beige presence against the little glowing beacon that was Adeline. And now she overpowered her: she looked taller, more vital, an exaggeration of herself.

Lottie, transfixed, could hardly breathe. Arcadia kept having that effect on her. She felt herself drawn in, carried on the breath of the minor chords that blew tantalisingly towards her on the sea breeze. They whispered their secrets; suggested new places, new ways for her to be. You need to learn to dream, Adeline had told her.

'I think Mr Beans has done his business now,' said Joe, his voice cutting across the dark. 'We should really be getting you home.'

Dearest Lots [the last letter went],

You are perfectly mean not to ask me simply loads of questions about Guy. But I know it's just because you're madly jealous so I'll forgive you. The men of Merham are not quite in the same league as London after all!!! Seriously though, Lots, I have missed you loads. The girls in my course are a catty bunch. They had all grouped off before I got there, and do lots of whispering behind hands during our breaks. I got a bit upset about it at first, but now I have Guy I just think they are silly, and must have very boring, empty lives if they feel the need to indulge in schoolgirl games. (Guy said that.) He is taking me to dinner at Mirabel to celebrate the end of my shorthand and typing exams. Don't tell Mummy but it will be a miracle if I pass the shorthand. Mine looks like Chinese lettering. Guy said that too – he's been all over the world and has seen some of these things for real. I was going to send you a photograph of us both at Kempton Park races, but I only have the one and I'm frightened of losing it, so you'll just have to imagine him. Just picture Montgomery Clift with lighter hair and a suntan and somehow you're half-way there . . .

It was the third letter in which she *somehow* hadn't managed to include a picture of 'Guy'. Lottie was *somehow* not terribly surprised.

Lottie stood silently as Mrs Holden attacked her with

the clothes brush, brisk downward sweeps removing non-existent lint from her fitted jacket.

'You should wear your hairband. Where is your hairband?'

'It's upstairs. Do you want me to get it?'

Mrs Holden frowned at Lottie's hair. 'It would probably be a good idea. Yours does tend to fly away rather. Now, Frederick. What on earth have you done to your shoes?'

'He's polished them with black instead of brown,' said Sylvia, with some satisfaction. 'He says they look more real.'

'Real than what?'

'Feet. They're hoofs,' said Freddie, turning his toes in and out again with pride. 'Cow's hoofs.'

'Well, really, Frederick. Can I not leave you alone for one minute?'

'Cows don't have hoofs. They have feet.'

'No, they don't.'

'Yes, they do. Cows have cloven feet.'

'You've got cow's feet, then. Fat cow's feet. Ow.'

'Sylvia, Frederick, stop kicking each other. It's not nice. Lottie, go and get Virginia, and we'll see if we can rescue them in the five minutes before we leave. Now, Sylvia, where is your coat? I asked you ten minutes ago to put your coat on. It's quite cold today. And what have you done to your fingernails? You could grow potatoes in them.'

'That's because she's been picking her nose. Ow! You've got cow's feet! Big fat ugly cow's feet.'

'Sylvia, I've told you once, don't kick your brother. We'll get you a nailbrush. Where's the nailbrush? What on earth is your sister going to say when she sees the state of you all?'

'Oh, for God's sake, stop fussing, woman. It's only Celia. She wouldn't care if we met her wearing our bathing-suits.'

Mrs Holden flinched, not looking up at her husband, who

was seated on the stairs doing up his shoes. Only Lottie noticed her eyes fill with tears, and the surreptitious attempt she made to wipe them away with her sleeve. Then she ran down the corridor to find Virginia.

Sympathetic as she was, Lottie had other concerns. She and Joe were not speaking. On the way back from walking Mr Beans, he had said he wasn't sure she should be spending so much time at Arcadia. They were getting quite a reputation, that lot. And if Lottie was seen down there too often, well, it would rub off, wouldn't it? And because he cared about her, because he was her friend, well, he thought it only right to let her know. Lottie, already furious at his interruption, had demanded, in sneering tones that surprised even herself, exactly what business it was of his who she spent her time with? She could be spending it with Dickie bloody Valentine for all he had to do with it.

Joe had flushed. She could see it even in the dark, and that had made her feel guilty and irritated at the same time. And then, after a short silence, he had said rather solemnly that if she didn't know by now she never would but that no one would ever love her like he did and even if she didn't love him back he still felt the need to look out for her.

Lottie, enraged, had rounded on him. 'I told you, Joe, that I didn't want you to say that to me ever again. And now you've ruined it. You've ruined everything. We can't be friends. If you can't keep your damned feelings to yourself, then we can't be friends. So why don't you go home to your mother and keep your concerns about my reputation to yourself?'

And with that she had yanked poor old Mr Beans up on his lead and walked furiously home, leaving Joe standing silently by the park gates.

Normally, Joe would have called for her by now. He would have appeared at the door, asking if she wanted to have a coffee, or play board games, and made some joke about their falling-out. And Lottie, secretly pleased to see him, would be glad to smooth things over and have him as her friend again. He had become more important, with Celia away and everything. And, irritating as he was, he was the only other real friend she had. She had always known she was somehow too dark, too awkward for the Betty Crofts and her like from school; that she had been tolerated in their crowd simply because of Celia.

But this time, Joe was evidently stung. Four days had passed and still he hadn't come. And Lottie, thinking back to the harsh way in which she had spoken to him, was left wondering if she should approach him to apologise, or whether if she did Joe would convince himself that this was yet another invitation for him to love her again.

Mrs Holden's voice echoed down the hall. 'Lottie, come on. The train gets in at four fifteen. We don't want to be late, do we?'

Dr Holden brushed past her. 'Go and calm her down, Lottie, there's a good girl, or Celia will take one look at our little band on the platform and head straight back to London.' He smiled at her as he spoke, a smile of exasperation and tacit understanding. And Lottie responded in kind, feeling vaguely ashamed as she did so.

Perhaps mindful of another rebuke, Mrs Holden did not speak for the ten-minute journey to the station. Dr Holden didn't either, but that was nothing unusual. Sylvia and Freddie, however, overexcited simply by the prospect of being in the car, fought wildly and pressed their noses up at the windows, shouting at passers-by. Lottie, who had been told to sit between them, occasionally pulled one down, or scolded the other, but she was still preoccupied with the problem of Joe. She would go round there this evening, she decided. She would apologise. She could do it in a way that made it clear she didn't want any romantic stuff. Joe would come round. He always did, didn't he?

The train arrived at four sixteen and thirty-eight seconds. Freddie, who had been closely monitoring the station clock, informed them loudly of its lack of punctuality. For once, Mrs Holden failed to scold him – she was too busy craning her neck, trying to catch a glimpse of her daughter over the heads of the other arriving passengers, her voice lifting weakly over the sounds of slamming carriage doors.

'She's there! Third one down!' Sylvia had broken free of her mother's grasp and was running down the platform. Lottie watched her, then found herself half walking, half running too, followed closely behind by the Holdens who seemed to have temporarily forgotten their reserve.

'Celie! Celie!' Sylvia threw herself at her older sister, almost unbalancing her as she stepped down on to the ground. 'I've got new shoes! Look!'

'I've got new shoes too!' fibbed Freddie, pulling at Celia's hand. 'Did you go really fast on the train? Were there any spies in London? Did you go on a double-decker bus?'

Lottie stood back, feeling unaccountably awkward as Mrs Holden threw her arms uninhibitedly around her daughter's shoulders, her face beaming with maternal pride. 'Oh, I've missed you! We've all missed you!' she was saying.

'We certainly have,' said Dr Holden, waiting until his wife released Celia before enveloping her in his own bear-hug. 'It's lovely to have you home, darling.'

It wasn't just the bite of outsiderdom that was making Lottie feel shy. It was Celia herself. It had only been a matter of months yet Celia looked transformed. Her hair had been cut and moulded into glossy curves, and her lips were outlined in a bold, almost startling red. She was wearing a belted green woollen coat that Lottie had never seen before, and a pair of patent shoes with a matching handbag. The shoes had tapering heels that were at least three inches high. She looked like someone out of a magazine. She looked beautiful.

Lottie smoothed her own hair back under her hairband and glanced down at her buckled walking shoes with stout soles. Her legs were clad in cotton socks, instead of Celia's nylons. They were too hot already.

'God, it's nice to see you all,' Celia exclaimed, looking around at them. And Mrs Holden was so pleased to see her that she didn't even chastise her. 'Lots? Lottie. Don't hang back, I can hardly see you.'

Lottie stepped forward, and allowed herself to be kissed. A sweet perfume lingered as Celia stepped back. Lottie fought the urge to rub lipstick from her cheek.

'I've got loads of things for you from London. I can't wait to show you all. I went a bit mad with the money Aunt Angela gave me. Oh, Lots, I can't wait to show you what I've got you. I liked it so much I nearly decided not to give it to you at all.'

'Well, let's not stand here all day,' said Dr Holden, who had started to look at his watch. 'Come away from the train, Celie dear.'

'Yes, you must be exhausted. I must say, I didn't like the idea of you travelling all that way by yourself. I told your father he should have collected you.'

'But I wasn't by myself, Mummy.'

Dr Holden, who had grabbed her suitcase and was already half-way towards the ticket office, stopped and turned.

From behind Celia, a man stepped down from the train, stooping slightly, then straightened up behind Celia. Under one arm, he was clutching two huge pineapples.

74

Celia's smile was dazzling. 'Mummy, Daddy, I'd like you to meet Guy. And you'll never guess . . . we're engaged.'

Mrs Holden sat in front of her dressing-table pulling pins carefully from her hair, her gaze fixed unseeing on the reflection in front of her. She had always known it was going to be difficult for Lottie when Celia started to blossom. It was inevitable that Celia would show her pedigree at some point. And she had to admit, down in London her daughter had blossomed in a way even she couldn't have imagined. Her little girl had returned home looking like a fashion-plate.

Susan Holden put the pins carefully into a little china pot and replaced the lid. She didn't like to admit quite how relieved she was at Celia becoming engaged. To a chap of some standing, too. Whether it was out of happiness for Celia, or thankfulness that she was now 'taken care of', the whole family had, in their way, felt the urge to celebrate. (Henry had given her a quite uncharacteristic peck on the cheek. She still felt quite warm just thinking about it.)

But Lottie's response to Celia's news had been positively peculiar. When he had initially emerged from the train, she had stared at the young man in a manner that was almost rude. Oh, they had all stared – Celia had taken them by surprise, after all. Mrs Holden had to acknowledge she'd probably stared a little herself. She hadn't seen a pineapple for years. But Lottie didn't take her eyes off him. Mrs Holden had particularly noticed this, because the girl had stood right in her line of vision. It had been rather irritating. And then when Celia had announced their engagement, all the colour had drained from her face. Actually drained, like you could have watched it sliding down. She had looked quite pasty afterwards. Almost as if she were going to faint.

Celia hadn't noticed. She was too busy showing off her

ring and chattering on about weddings. But no, even in the midst of all the excitement, Mrs Holden had noted Lottie's strange response and felt the faintest fluttering of alarm. Even as she digested her daughter's news with a mixture of shock and joy, she had found herself eyeing her surrogate daughter with concern.

Perhaps it wasn't so surprising. After all, no one other than Joe would ever be interested in her, Mrs Holden thought, with a peculiar mix of pity and pride in her own daughter. Not with that colouring. And that history.

She reached for her cold cream and began methodically removing the rouge from her cheeks. Perhaps we have been unfair taking her in, after all, she thought. Perhaps we should have left well alone, left her with her London folk.

It is possible we have given her expectations.

Four

'Totally unclothed they were. I tell you, ladies, I felt quite faint.' Mrs Colquhoun raised a hand to her mouth, as if pained by the memory. 'Right by the sea path too. Anyone could have seen.'

This was possible, the ladies of the salon conceded, while privately acknowledging that it was debatable whether anyone other than Deirdre Colquhoun would have stumbled across George Bern and Julian Armand enjoying a bracing morning swim. In fact, most were well aware that Mrs Colquhoun had taken an unusual number of walks along the sea path in the past months, even in inclement weather. But, of course, no one wanted to suggest that it was down to anything other than a desire to see Merham's standards upheld.

'Weren't they a bit foolhardy, in this water?'

'I would imagine they were rather blue,' Mrs Ansty observed, smiling. Then stopped, when she realised no one else thought it amusing.

'And do you know he actually waved to me? The young one? Actually stood there and waved . . . as if . . . I could see . . .' Mrs Colquhoun's voice tailed away, her hand still lifted to her mouth as if recalling some horror.

'He was singing last week, that Mr Armand. Just stood on the terrace belting out some sort of opera, if you please. In broad daylight.'

The ladies tutted.

'Something German, I believe,' said Margaret Carew, who had a great passion for Gilbert and Sullivan.

There was a short silence.

'Well,' said Mrs Ansty. 'I do believe, ladies, that the inhabitants of that house are beginning to lower the tone of our town.'

Mrs Chilton put down her cup and saucer. 'I'm becoming increasingly concerned about next summer's visitors. What if word gets round about their antics? We've got a reputation to uphold. And we don't want their influence spreading among our young folk, do we? Heaven knows what could happen.'

There was a brief lull in the conversation. No one wanted to bring up the incident with Lottie and Celia on the beach. But Susan Holden was far too buoyed up by Celia's engagement to continue to feel cowed by it. 'Another piece of pineapple, anyone? Or perhaps a slice of melon?' She emerged through the door and bustled around the room, stooping to offer little slices of the fruit, which she had carefully placed on cocktail sticks, and arranged in attractive circles (*Good Housekeeping* magazine was very keen on attractive food arrangements).

'You know, it's amazing to think how far this fruit has travelled just to be here. I said to Henry last night, "There are probably more pineapples on aeroplanes these days than people!"' She laughed, pleased by her little joke. 'Go on, do try some.'

'It's quite different from the canned variety,' said Mrs Ansty, chewing meditatively. 'It's almost a little sharp for my taste.'

'Then have some melon, dear,' said Mrs Holden. 'It's got a lovely mild flavour. You know, Guy's father imports fruit from all sorts of amazing places. Honduras, Guatemala, Jerusalem. Last night he told us about fruits that we've never even heard of. Did you know there is a fruit shaped like a star?' She had gone quite pink with pride.

Mrs Ansty swallowed, and winced with pleasure. 'Ooh, that melon is lovely.'

'You must take a bit home for your Arthur. Guy has told us he'll get his father to send us some more from London. He's got ever such a big company. And Guy is the only child, so he'll have a very nice business to go into one day. More pineapple, Sarah? There are some napkins here, ladies, if you need them.'

Mrs Chilton smiled primly and refused a second piece. They were all pleased that Susan had got Celia safely betrothed, but it didn't do to get too full of oneself. 'You must be so relieved,' she said carefully.

Susan Holden looked up sharply.

'Well . . . girls can be such a worry, can't they? We're all very glad you've got your Celia taken care of. And we'll be keeping our fingers crossed for little Lottie. Although she's never been *quite* as much of a worry to you, has she, dear?' She accepted a proferred Nice biscuit from Virginia, who had just entered with a tea tray.

Mrs Holden's smile had gone all wobbly again.

Mrs Chilton settled back on her chair, and gave her an encouraging one of her own. 'Now, ladies, what are we going to do about Arcadia House? I've been thinking . . . perhaps someone should have a quiet word. Someone with weight, like Alderman Elliott. But I think they should be told, those Bohemians, or whatever they think they are. I don't think they understand quite how we do things in Merham.'

Lottie lay on her bed, pretending to read, trying not to listen to the sounds of laughter outside where Celia and Guy were playing tennis on the lawn, apparently oblivious to the blustering wind and Freddie's over-zealous ballboying.

She stared accusingly at the page in front of her, aware that she had been gazing at the same paragraph for nearly forty minutes. If anyone had asked her what it was about, she wouldn't have been able to answer. Then, if anyone had asked her what anything was about she wouldn't have been able to answer. Because nothing made sense. The universe had exploded, fragmented, and all the bits landed back in the wrong place. Except only Lottie had noticed. She heard Celia shriek accusingly, the cry dissolving into loud giggles, and underneath it Guy's voice, more measured, instructing her in something. His voice held a bubble of laughter too, but he hadn't let it out.

Lottie closed her eyes and tried to breathe. Any time now she knew Celia would send someone upstairs to see if she would come and join them. Perhaps make up a comedy four, if Freddie demanded to be allowed to play. How could she explain her sudden aversion to tennis? How could she explain her reluctance to go outside? How long before someone realised that it wasn't Lottie being 'unsociable', as Celia had laughingly accused her, that it wasn't just another of her foibles, this sudden reluctance to spend time with her best friend?

She stared at the new blouse hanging on the door handle. Mrs Holden had given her one of her 'looks' when she had thanked Celia for it. She knew she thought her graceless. Lottie should have been more grateful. It was a very nice blouse.

But Lottie hadn't said much at all. Because there was nothing Lottie was going to be able to say. How could she? How could she explain that the first moment she had set eyes on Guy everything she knew, everything she believed, had been sucked away from her like someone pulling a rug out from under her feet? How could she explain the searing pain of familiarity at his face, the bitter joy of recognition, the deeply held certainty that her very bones were already familiar with this man? They had to be – weren't they cast from the same human porcelain as his? How could she tell Celia she couldn't possibly marry the man she had brought home as her fiancé?

Because he belonged to Lottie.

'Lottie! Lots!' The voice drifted upwards, carried on the air. Just as she had known it would.

She waited until the second summons, then opened the window. Looked down. Tried to keep her gaze on Celia's upturned face.

'Don't be boring, Lots! You're not studying for exams now.'

'I've got a bit of a headache. I'll be down later,' she said. Even her voice sounded different.

'She's been in there all day,' said Freddie, who was throwing tennis balls against the side of the house.

'Oh, come on, do. We're going to head over to Bardness Point. You could fetch Joe. Make a four. Come on, Lots. I've hardly seen you.'

She wondered that Celia couldn't tell her smile was false. It hurt the sides of her mouth. 'You go on. I'll just wait for this headache to go. We'll do something tomorrow.'

'Boring, boring, boring. And I've been telling Guy what a bad influence on me you are . . . You'll think I'm fibbing, won't you, darling?'

'Tomorrow. Promise.'

Lottie pulled her head back into the bedroom, so that she wouldn't have to see their embrace. She lay face down on her bed. And tried to remember how to breathe.

Guy Parnell Olivier Bancroft had been born in Winchester,

which made him technically English. But that was the only English thing about him. Everything – from his tanned skin, so at odds with most of the pale English complexions around him, to his relaxed, diffident manner – marked him out as separate from the young men Lottie and Celia had known. Merham men, anyway. He was a self-contained, polite, reserved young man but he none the less carried the casually gilded air of the heir apparent, surprised by little, and prepared at all times for good things to happen. He seemed to suffer none of the tortured self-examination of Joe, or be driven by the bullish competitiveness of the other boys. He gazed a little wide-eyed around him, as if permanently amused at some unforeseen joke, occasionally letting out bursts of uninhibited and joyful laughter. (He was the kind of man you couldn't help smiling at, Mrs Holden confided to her husband. But then Guy made her smile a lot; once she had got over the shock of her daughter's swift engagement, she had viewed him as indulgently as a first-born son.) Guy seemed as unfazed by the man at the taxi rank as at the prospect of formally asking Dr Holden for his daughter's hand in marriage. (He hadn't, yet. But, then, he had only been there a couple of days and Dr Holden had been terribly busy.) If he was a little passive, a little less forthcoming than the Holdens would have liked, then they weren't going to judge him for it – gift horses and all that.

But none of this should have been a surprise. For Guy Bancroft had spent most of his life freed from the rigid social conventions of boys' public schools, or suburban social circles. An only child, he had grown up as the veritable apple (his joke) of his father's eye and, after a short unsuccessful spell at a British boarding-school, had been regathered to the family bosom and carted, along with their luggage, from tropic to subtropic, as Guy Bertrand Bancroft Senior, astutely recognising the appetite of deprived Britons for non-indigenous fruit, swiftly built up his import business finding channels to satisfy their increasing passion.

Guy had subsequently spent his childhood wandering the huge fruit estates of the Caribbean, where his father had initially based himself, exploring the deserted beaches, making friends with the black workers' children, educated sporadically by tutors when his father remembered to hire them. Guy didn't need formal education, he would exclaim. (He was very fond of exclaiming. It might explain why Guy was rather quiet.) What good had 1066 and all that ever done him? Who cared how many wives Henry VIII had had? (The King could hardly have kept track himself.) Everything *he*'d learned was at the School of Hard Knocks. Graduated (his mother used to raise her eyebrows comically at this point) from the University of Life. No, the boy would learn far more left free to roam wild. More about geography – compare and contrast the stepped crop fields of central China with the vast open agricultural acres of Honduras – more about politics, more about real people, their cultures and beliefs. Maths he could learn from the accounts. Biology – why, look at the insect life!

But they all knew the real reason. Guy Senior just liked having him around. Late and much longed-for, the boy was all he had ever wanted. He didn't understand those parents who wanted to pack their offspring off to stuffy old private schools where they would learn stiff upper lips and snobbishness and likely be bugger— 'Yes, darling,' Guy's mother would interrupt firmly at this point. 'I think you've made your point.'

Guy told them this over a succession of family meals. He left out the bit about buggery, but Celia had told her that when they lay in bed, talking in the darkness. Well, Celia talked. Lottie had pretended unsuccessfully to be asleep, believing her only hope of sanity lay in being unable to flesh out the vision of Guy into any kind of human reality.

They were not the only ones talking about Guy. Mrs Holden had been quite disconcerted by his casual mention of his black friends, and asked Dr Holden repeatedly afterwards whether he thought that was all right.

'What are you worried about, woman?' said Dr Holden irritably. 'That it'll rub off?' Things were different out there, he said, eventually, when Mrs Holden's face had stayed pinched and hurt beyond even its usual time frame for such things. The boy probably didn't have many opportunities to meet his own. And besides, Susan, times were changing. Look at the immigration. (He had rather wanted to read his newspaper in peace.)

'Well, I just wonder if it betrays a little . . . laxity on the part of his parents. How's a child supposed to grow up knowing what's what if they're only mixing with . . . staff?'

'So remind me to fire Virginia.'

'What?'

'Well, we can't have Freddie and Sylvia *talking* to the girl, can we?'

'Henry, you're being deliberately obtuse. I'm sure Guy's family are perfectly fine. I just think . . . his upbringing sounds . . . a little *unusual*, that's all.'

'Susan, he's a fine young man. He has no tics, no obvious deformities, his father is extremely wealthy, and he wants to take our troublesome young flibbertigibbet off our hands. As far as I'm concerned he could have been brought up playing the bongo drums and eating human heads.'

Mrs Holden hadn't known whether to laugh or be appalled. It was so hard to gauge Henry's sense of humour some-times.

Lottie was unaware of any of this. At mealtimes, she had spent most of the time focused intently on her soup, or praying that no one would bring her into conversation. Not that she really had to worry. Mrs Holden was too busy quizzing Guy about his family, and what his mother thought of life back in Britain, while Dr Holden asked the odd question about whether his father was likely to be affected by all that trouble over land reforms in Guatemala and whether the Cold War was really going to make a difference to overseas traders.

For it was too difficult to be near him. It was too hard to listen to his voice (when had she heard it before? She *must* have heard it before. Its timbre was etched on her very soul). His proximity sent her thoughts scrambling, to the point where she was sure she would betray herself. The scent of him, that barely detectable sweetness, as if he still carried the tropics on his very person, left her stumbling over once-familiar words. So it was safer not to look at him. Safer not to see his beautiful face. Safer not to have to watch Celia drape her hand possessively over his shoulder, or absentmindedly stroke his hair. Safer to stay away. Safer to stay away.

'Lottie? Lottie? I've asked you three times whether you want runner beans. Do you need your ears syringed?'

'No, thank you,' whispered Lottie, and tried to stop her heart from jumping out of her chest. He had looked at her once. Only once, when she had been frozen, standing on the platform, almost felled with shock at her own reaction to him. His eyes, when they had met hers, had borne into her like twin bullets.

'It's a D.'

'No, no, you're looking at it from the wrong angle. It could look like a G.'

'Oh, Mummy. Really. You can't cheat like that.'

'No, honestly, darling. Look. It really is a G. Isn't that lovely?'

Lottie had walked into the kitchen to fetch a glass of milk. She hadn't eaten properly for several days and, feeling nauseous, had hoped the milk might settle her stomach. She hadn't expected to find Celia and her mother peering over their shoulders on to the flagstoned kitchen floor. Mrs Holden had an uncharacteristic air of merriment about her. At the sound of Lottie's footfall, she looked up and gave her a rare, uninhibited smile.

'I – I just came for some milk.'

'Look, Lottie. Come here. It's very like a G from this angle, don't you think?'

'Oh, Mummy.' Celia was laughing hard now. Her hair had separated into golden ribbons, one of which was caught on her cheek.

Lottie peered over on to the kitchen floor. There lay a piece of apple peel, carved carefully in one elongated spiral, lying in an uneven curve.

'It's definitely a G.'

'I don't understand,' said Lottie, frowning. Mrs Holden scolded Virginia if she left bits of food on the floor. It would apparently encourage pests.

'G for Guy. I've never seen a clearer one,' said Mrs Holden determinedly, before stooping and picking it up. She winced slightly as she did this: she was still buying her girdles too small.

'I'm going to tell Guy it was a D. He'll be fearfully jealous. Who do we know who's a D, Lots?'

She hardly ever saw Celia and her mother laughing together. Celia had used to say her mother was the most irritating woman on earth. It made her feel like Celia had joined some new club, as if they had both moved on and left her behind.

'I'll get my milk.'

'Elvis the Pelvis,' said Freddie, who had walked in, holding the dissected innards of an old wristwatch.

'I said D, you little idiot.' But Celia said it fondly.

No wonder she's being nice to everyone, thought Lottie. I'd be nice to everyone.

'Do you know, Mummy? Guy says my lips are like petals.'

'Bicycle pedals,' said Freddie, screaming with laughter. '*Ow!*'

'D for Dreamboat. D for dreamy. He is a little dreamy, isn't he, Mummy? I wonder where he's gone sometimes. Shall we do one for you, Lottie? It might come out as a J . . . you never know . . .'

'I don't know what's got into that girl,' said Mrs Holden, at Lottie's bristling, departing back.

'Oh, Lottie's Lottie. She'll be all right. She's just got a bate on about something.' Celia smoothed her hair back and checked her reflection in the mirror over the fireplace. 'Tell you what, do me another one. With that green apple there. We'll use a sharper knife this time.'

She was offered a job in Shelford's Shoes, at the far end of the promenade. She took it, not because she had to – Dr Holden said she was welcome to wait a while and decide what she wanted to do – but because being out at the shoe shop three days a week was so much easier than being at the Holdens'. And it was almost impossible to get to Arcadia. There were spies all over the town, just waiting to warn off anyone who ventured up towards the House of Sin.

Guy had left for almost a week, and for that short period she had been able to breathe again, had just about managed to appear normal. (Luckily Celia was so locked into her little bubble of love that she hadn't really questioned what Mrs Holden was now referring to as Lottie's 'episodes'.) But then he had returned, and said his father had told him to 'have some fun, a little holiday' before starting his fledgling career in the family business. And Lottie, who had now become physically bowed by the weight of longing she carried around with her, had braced herself for yet more of the same.

Worse, he was now living with them. He had been about to search for lodgings, had asked the Holdens whether there was anywhere particular they would recommend – that Mrs Chilton's place, for example. But Mrs Holden wouldn't hear of it. She had made him up a room at Woodbridge Avenue. At the far end of the house, you understand. With a water-closet of his own. So there would be no need for any walking around the house in the middle of the night, would there? ('Very sage, dear,' Mrs Chilton had said. 'There's no accounting for hormones.') But there had been no question of not having him to stay. Mr Bancroft Senior would see that they were a welcoming family. With a large house. The kind of family one would positively aspire to marry into. And the huge crate of exotic fruit he sent up every week in lieu of housekeeping money didn't go amiss, admittedly. No point Sarah Chilton being on the receiving end of *that*.

And three days a week Lottie would walk resignedly down the hill and across the municipal park, bracing herself for a day of squeezing size-eight feet into size-seven Mary Janes, and wondering how long she was going to be able to live with this degree of pain and longing. Joe hadn't come.

It had taken her almost ten days to notice.

*   *   *

They decided on a letter. An invitation. There were ways of getting people to do what you wanted without confrontation, Mrs Holden said. And Mrs Holden was very keen on avoiding confrontation. The ladies of the salon wrote a polite letter to Mrs Julian Armand, asking if she would care to join them, partake of a few refreshments, and see a little of local society. It would be their pleasure, they said, to welcome a fellow aficionado of the arts. The inhabitants of Arcadia House had traditionally played a part in the town's social and cultural life. (That last bit wasn't strictly true but, as Mrs Chilton said, any women worth their salt would feel obliged to attend.) 'Nicely put,' said Mrs Colquhoun.

'More than one way to skin a cat,' said Mrs Chilton.

Lottie was on her way out when Mrs Holden caught her. She had decided to go to Joe's house. It had been too long and, locked in her own private purgatory, she had decided that any diversion would be a welcome one, even one involving Joe's repeated protestations of devotion. She had developed, perhaps, a little more sympathy for him now. She had had, after all, a rude and unexpected introduction to the pain of unrequited love.

'Lottie, is that you?'

Lottie halted in the hallway, sighing under her breath. There was little she wouldn't do to avoid being paraded in front of the salon. She hated that look of pitied understanding on their faces, their silent, sympathetic acknowledgement of her increasingly fragile place in the Holden household. She might like to get something more permanent soon, Mrs Holden had said, more than once now. Perhaps go for a nice department store. There was a lovely one in Colchester.

'Yes, Mrs Holden.'

'Can you come in, dear? I need to ask a favour of you.'

Lottie walked slowly into the parlour, smiling vaguely and insincerely at the expectant faces in front of her. The room, its temperature raised unnaturally by a newly fitted gas fire, seemed to swell with the overheated scents of slightly stale powder and Coty cream perfume. 'I was just going down to town,' she said.

'Yes, dear. But I'd just like you to deliver a letter for me on the way.'

So that was it. She relaxed, turned to go.

'To the actress's house. You know the one.'

Lottie turned back. 'Arcadia?'

'Yes, dear. It's an invitation.'

'But you said we weren't to go there. You said it was full of . . .' She paused, trying to remember Mrs Holden's exact phrase.

'Yes, yes, I'm quite aware of what I said. But things have moved on. And we have decided to appeal to Mrs Armand's better judgement.'

'Right,' said Lottie, taking the proffered envelope. 'See you later.'

'You're not going to let her go alone.' That was Deirdre Colquhoun.

Susan Holden glanced around. There was a brief silence as the ladies looked at each other.

'Well, she can't go by herself.'

'She's probably right, dear. After . . . everything. She'd be better to go with someone.'

'I'm sure I'll be perfectly safe,' said Lottie, not without some irritation.

'Yes, dear. But you have to accept that there are some things about which your elders know better. Where's Celia, Susan?'

'She's having her hair set,' said Mrs Holden, who was

beginning to look flustered. 'Then she's looking at some of the bridal books. It's best to be prepared for these things . . .'

'Well, she can't go alone,' said Mrs Colquhoun.

'There's Guy,' ventured Mrs Holden.

'Then send the boy with her. She'll be safe with him.' Mrs Chilton looked satisfied.

'G-Guy?' stammered Lottie, flushing.

'He's in the study. Go and get him, dear. The sooner you're there, the sooner you'll be home. Besides, it'll do Guy good to get out. He's been stuck indoors with Freddie all morning. Poor boy is very patient,' she said, in explanation.

'B-but I'll be fine by myself.'

'You're being terribly antisocial at the moment,' said Mrs Holden. 'Honestly, it's all I can do to drag her out of her room. Doesn't see her friend Joe any more, poor old Celia can hardly tempt her out . . . Come on, Lottie. Try to be a bit civil, will you?' Mrs Holden left the room to find Guy.

'How's the job, dear? Going well?'

Mrs Chilton had to ask twice.

'Fine,' said Lottie, struggling to pay attention, aware that this would become evidence of another example of her surliness.

'I must come in for winter boots. I'm definitely in need of some. Do you have any nice ones in yet, Lottie? Something with a bit of fleece in the lining?'

Oh, God, he was going to walk into the room. And she was going to have to talk to him.

'Lottie?'

'I think we're still on sandals,' she whispered.

Mrs Chilton raised an eyebrow at Mrs Ansty. 'I'll call in later in the week.'

She had managed to leave the room without looking at him. She had nodded a cursory greeting to his 'hello', then fixed her gaze resolutely on the floor, oblivious to the flickering glances of exasperation exchanged by the older women. But now that they were out of the house and walking briskly along the road, Lottie found herself in an acute dilemma, torn between the desperate desire to run from him, and the agony of him considering her ignorant and rude.

Thrusting her hands deep into her pockets, her face down against the wind, she concentrated on keeping her breathing regular. It was almost beyond her to consider anything else. Soon he will be gone, she told herself, like a mantra. And then I can force everything to be normal again.

So bent on her task was Lottie that it took her some minutes to hear him.

'Lottie? Lottie, hey, slow down—'

She stopped and glanced backwards, hoping that the wind whipping her hair would hide the flush that spread rapidly across her face.

He reached out an arm, as if to slow her. 'Are we in a hurry?'

His voice had a slight accent, as if those loose-speaking, easy-limbed countries of his youth had rubbed the corners off him. He moved fluidly, as if there were enjoyment in the act of motion alone, as if there were no physical full stops to him.

Lottie searched for an answer. 'No,' she said. 'Sorry.'

They walked on, more slowly this time, in silence. Lottie nodded a greeting at one of her neighbours, who raised his hat at them both, observing, 'Blowy.'

'Who was that?'

'Just Mr Hillguard.'

'He the one with the dog?'

'That's Mr Atkinson.' Her cheeks stung. 'He's got a moustache too.'

A moustache. A moustache, she scolded herself. Who the hell notices a person's moustache? She began to pick up her pace as they headed up the hill towards Arcadia. Please let this be over soon, she willed. Please let him remember some errand he had to do in town. Please just let me be.

'Lottie?'

She stopped, biting back tears. She was starting to feel slightly hysterical.

'Lottie, please wait.'

She turned. Looked at him fully for the second time. He stood before her, huge chestnut eyes set in a too-handsome face. Bewildered. Half smiling.

'Have I offended you?'

'What?'

'I'm not sure what I've done, but I'd like to know.'

How can you not know? she thought. How can you not see? Don't you see in me what I see in you? She waited, briefly, to answer. Just in case he did.

Wanted to weep with exasperation when he didn't.

'You haven't done anything,' she said, and began walking again, so that he couldn't see how hard she was biting her cheeks.

'Hey. *Hey*.' He had grabbed hold of her sleeve.

She pulled her arm away as if he had burnt her.

'You've been avoiding me since I got here. Is this some weird thing because of me and Celia? I know you've always been close.'

'Of course not,' she said crossly. 'Now, please, let's go on. I'm very busy today.'

'I don't see how,' came the voice behind her. 'You seem to spend most of your time stuck in your room.'

A big lump of nothing had swollen in the back of Lottie's throat. It was choking her. Her eyes were pricking with tears. Make him go away, God. Please. It's not fair to do this to me.

But Guy pulled level with her again. 'You know, you remind me of someone.' He didn't look at her this time. Just kept walking alongside her. 'I can't work out who just yet. But I will. Is this the house?'

Out of the wind, the sun flooded her back with its warmth. Lottie walked less briskly up the drive, the gravel crunching under her feet. She had got half-way to the house when she realised she could not hear his.

'Wow.' He was standing back, one hand lifted to his brow, squinting into the sunlight. 'Who lives here?'

'Adeline. And her husband, Julian. And some of their friends.'

'It's not like an English house. It's like the houses I grew up with. Oh, wow.' He was grinning now, walking towards the house, peering sideways up at the cubic windows, at the bleached white of its façade. 'You know, I'm not so keen on British houses. The traditional Victorian types, or all that mock-Tudor stuff. They feel kind of dark and poky to me. Even Celia's folks' house. This is much more my kind of thing.'

'I like it,' said Lottie.

'I didn't think there were houses like this over here.'

'How long is it since you lived here?'

He frowned thoughtfully. 'About twenty years. I was around six when we first left England. Are we going in?'

Lottie looked at the envelope in her hand. 'I'm not sure,' she said. 'I suppose we could just pop it through the letterbox . . .'

She looked longingly at the door. It had been almost two weeks since she had visited. Celia hadn't wanted to come with her. 'Oh, that crowd,' she had said dismissively. 'Bunch of boring misfits. You want to come to London, Lots. Have some real fun. You might meet someone.'

'I'm not meant to like them,' she explained. 'The people who live here. But I do.'

Guy looked at her. 'Then let's go in.'

It was Frances who opened the door, not Marnie. 'She's gone,' she explained, turning back down the corridor, wiping fish scales from her hands on to an ill-fitting white apron. 'Left us. Rather a pain, really. None of us is particularly good at domestic things. I'm meant to be preparing fish for supper. I've made the most awful mess of the kitchen.'

'This is Guy,' said Lottie. But Frances just waved a hand. There were too many visitors to Arcadia to make formal introductions really worthwhile.

'Adeline's out on the terrace. She's meant to be planning our mural.'

While Guy gazed around him at the house, Lottie stole furtive glances at his profile. Say something awful, she willed. Be dismissive about Frances. Make me go off you. Please. 'What's the fish?' he said.

'Trout. Awful slimy things. They've been flying all over the kitchen.'

'Want me to have a go? I'm pretty handy at gutting fish.'

Frances's relief was almost palpable. 'Oh, would you?' she said, and ushered him into the kitchen, where two rainbow trout bled silkily on to the bleached wooden table. 'I don't know why she left. But she was always cross with us about something. I was rather afraid of her by the end, moody old thing.'

'She disapproved of us. Our household.' Adeline had appeared in the doorway. She was wearing a long, finely pleated black skirt with a white blouse and black necktie. She smiled, her eyes on Guy. 'I think she would have been more comfortable with something . . . a little more traditional. Have you brought us a new guest, Lottie?'

'This is Guy,' Lottie said. Then forced herself to add: 'Celia's fiancé.'

Adeline's gaze flickered from Guy to Lottie and back again. She paused, as if considering something, then lifted a hand in greeting. 'It is lovely to meet you, Guy. And I should offer my congratulations.'

There was a short silence.

'We never seem to keep housekeepers for very long. Will this knife do? It's not terribly sharp.' Frances held up the bloodied knife.

Guy tested the blade on his thumb. 'No wonder you're having trouble. This is about as sharp as a butter-knife. Got a steel? I'll sharpen it for you.'

'I suppose we should get someone else in,' said Frances. 'We never think of things like sharpening knives.' She rubbed distractedly at her cheek, unwittingly leaving a bloody smear.

'Oh, it's such a bore finding staff.' Adeline looked briefly ill-tempered. She raised a hand to her forehead theatrically. 'I can never think of the right questions to ask. And I never check that they're doing the right things. I don't even know what it is they *should* be doing.'

'And they always end up getting cross with *us*,' said Frances.

'You need staff to manage your staff,' said Guy, who, with deft sweeping motions, was sharpening the blade along the upheld steel.

'You know, you're quite right,' said Adeline. She must like him, Lottie observed: she reserved that smile for people she felt relaxed with. She had known Adeline long enough now to recognise the other kind, where the corners of her mouth lifted, but not her eyes. Lottie, meanwhile, simply stared at Guy, hypnotised by the regular metronomic swoosh of metal against metal, the repetitive flash of his tanned arm under his shirt. He was so beautiful: his skin looked almost polished, the light from the windows reflected off the planes of his cheekbones. His hair, unfashionably long, fell in dark gold layers, darkening towards his collar as if harbouring rich secrets beneath. On his left eyebrow several hairs at the junction with his browbone were white, possibly the result of some accident. I bet Celia hasn't noticed that, thought Lottie, absently. I bet she doesn't see half the things I can see.

Adeline saw.

Lottie, lost in her reverie, felt the increasing heat of her stare, and, turning to meet her eyes, found herself blushing as if caught in the middle of some transgression.

'And where is Celia today?'

'Having her hair done. Mrs Holden asked Guy to come with me.' She hadn't meant it to sound so defensive. But Adeline just nodded.

'There!' Guy held up one of the trout: rinsed and gutted, it hung balefully by its tail. 'Want me to show you how to do the other one?'

'I'd rather you did it for me,' said Frances. 'It takes you about a tenth of the time.'

'Delighted,' said Guy. As Lottie watched him carefully slit the shimmering belly from throat to tail, she found she had begun to weep.

They had tea, which Lottie made, out on the terrace. Frances really was hopeless at domestic tasks. She had forgotten to strain the first pot she made so the milk was speckled with black tea-leaves. The second one she forgot to add the tea altogether, and had looked as if she was about to cry when this was gently pointed out. Adeline had thought it amusing, and offered them wine instead. But Lottie, anxious that Guy didn't think ill of them, had declined, and taken charge of the tea-making. She was glad of the time to herself. She felt as if she had started to fizz with electricity, unable to control the direction of its current.

When she emerged, carrying the tray and its odd assortment of crockery, Adeline was showing Guy the beginnings of their mural. In the time since Lottie had last visited strange lines had begun to appear on the white surface, silhouettes nudging each other along the wall. Guy, his back to her, was tracing one of the lines with a square-tipped finger. His open collar had dropped back from his neck, revealing a deeply tanned nape.

'You're here, Lottie. Look, I put you far away from George, as I didn't want you to be offended by him. He is a thoughtless man,' said Adeline. 'His brain is full of the Russian economy and suchlike. It seems to leave little room for sensitivity.'

His forearm had little blond hairs all over it; as fine as the down on a butterfly wing. Lottie could see every single one.

'I want to have you carrying something, Lottie. Maybe a basket. Because tipping you slightly will show that sinuous quality of yours. And I want to have your hair hanging loose, in a sheet.' Frances was staring at the sketchy image, as if it were nothing really to do with the real Lottie.

'And we will dress you in exotic colours. Something bright. Very unEnglish.'

'Something like a sari,' said Frances.

'The girls here dress in much more drab colours than those where I grew up.' said Guy, turning to include her in conversation. 'Here everyone seems to wear brown or black. When we lived in the Caribbean everyone wore red, or bright blue, or yellow. Even me.' He grinned. 'My favourite shirt had a bright yellow sun on the back. Huge it was, with rays stretching right up to my shoulders.' He stretched his arms across his chest, as if pointing them out.

Lottie placed the tray carefully on the table, to try to stop the crockery rattling.

'I think we should dress Lottie in red. Or perhaps emerald,' said Adeline. 'She is so exquisite, our little Lottie, and always hiding herself. Always making herself invisible. I am on a mission,' she confided to Guy, breathing almost intimately into his ear, 'to show this town that Lottie is one of its most precious jewels.'

Lottie felt a searing anger at Adeline, the prickling suspicion that she was being mocked.

But nobody appeared to be laughing.

Guy didn't even seem perturbed by Adeline's behaviour. He had grinned back at her, then turned slowly to Lottie. He really looked at her then, as if seeing her properly.

The two faces, his and Adeline's, staring intently at her, unbalanced Lottie to the point where she could no longer contain herself. 'No wonder you can't get any staff. This place is a pigsty! You need to tidy it! No one will come if you don't tidy it.' She leaped up and began moving empty wine bottles and newspapers across the terrace, gathering up long-empty wine glasses, refusing to meet anyone's eyes.

'Lottie!' She heard Adeline's soft exclamation.

'You don't have to do that, Lottie,' said Frances. 'Sit down, dearest. You've just made the tea.'

Lottie swept past her, pushing at her outstretched hand. 'But it's dirty. In some places it's actually *dirty*. Look, you need some carbolic. Or something.' The words were tumbling over themselves. She moved inside, became manic, sweeping piles of papers off tables, pulling at curtains. 'You won't get a new housekeeper otherwise. No one will come. You can't live like this. You can't *live* like this!'

Her voice broke on the last words, and suddenly, she was running down the corridor and out of the front door into the bright afternoon sunlight, heedless of the bemused cries of the people behind her.

Guy had found her in the garden. She was sitting by the little pond, miserably throwing tiny pieces of bread into its murky waters, her back to the weathered brick of the house. On his approach she glanced around, groaned, and buried her face in her too-tanned arms. But he didn't say anything. Wordlessly, he sat down beside her, handed her a plate and, as she sat looking up at him furtively from under her hair, pulled a large blushing fruit from the crook of his arm. As she stared at its unfamiliar shape, her curiosity battening down her embarrassment, he pulled a penknife from his pocket and began to score its flesh lengthways. Absorbed in his task, he peeled away the four regular sections of skin, forcing the knife down carefully along the fruit's innards, levering the flesh away from the stone. 'Mango,' he said, handing her a piece. 'Came today. Try it.'

She looked down at the moist, glowing flesh in front of her. 'Where's Celia?'

'Still at the hairdresser.'

Upstairs, Freddie was crying. They could hear his angry, childish sobs, punctuated by muffled protests.

She studied his face. 'What's it taste of?' She could smell the fruit on his fingers.

'Good things.' He lifted a piece from the plate. Held it towards her lips. 'Go on.'

She paused. Realised her mouth was already open. The flesh was smooth and sweet. It tasted perfumed. She let it melt slowly on her tongue, losing herself in the succulence of it, shutting her eyes better to imagine warm, foreign climes, places where people wore red and yellow and bright blue, places where they carried the sun on their backs.

When she opened her eyes, he was still looking at her. He had stopped smiling. 'I liked them,' he said.

Lottie was the first to break their gaze. It took some time. She stood, brushing non-existent earth from her skirt. Then she turned, and walked back towards the house, feeling deep within her the first easing of a long-endured storm.

She turned before she got to the back door.

'I knew you would,' she said.

Five

It might simply have been a way of keeping some semblance of sanity, but Lottie liked to believe there was a kind of inevitability to it from then on. Like she knew, after she discovered the Merham 'salon' invitation, unopened, still in her pocket, that it would be Guy who suggested they return, on the pretext that there was a gentleman who wanted to talk about his father's business. (Mrs Holden would never dare object to anything concerned with business, after all.) Like she had known, too, that Guy would somehow choose a time when Celia had gone off on some other beautifying mission: to look at shoes in Colchester, or new stockings in Manningtree – the kind of jobs a man, even a fiancé, couldn't possibly be expected to attend. Like she knew that he now saw her differently. She might not be wearing emerald, but she had taken on some of the qualities of Adeline's precious jewel; and in return she glowed from within, and drew his eye, like a brilliant catching the light.

None of this was acknowledged, of course. In the same way that Lottie had found ways to avoid Guy, now she simply found him walking alongside her towards the municipal park. Or that it was his arms holding the washing-basket as she pegged up the sheets. Or that he had already volunteered to walk Mr Beans as she left for some errand down at the Parade.

And more quickly than she could have predicted, Lottie lost her shyness around Guy; found the exquisite pain of being near him replaced by a flickering anticipation, an uncharacteristic desire to talk, a welling belief that she was in the place she was always meant to be. ('She's dropped some of that moodiness. Less mulish,' Mrs Holden observed. 'Susan, it'll be in the family,' said Mrs Chilton. 'I'll lay money the mother is a Grade A sourpuss.') She tried not to think about Celia. It was easy when she was with him: then she felt enclosed by invisible walls, sheltered by her belief that it was her right to be there. It was when she was alone with Celia that she felt naked, her actions exposed to a distinctly murky light.

Because she couldn't look at Celia in the same way. Where once she had seen an ally, now she saw a rival. Celia wasn't Celia any more, she was an amalgam of elements against which Lottie had to compare herself: a helmet of stylishly cut blonde hair against her straight, dark schoolgirl plait; a glowing, peachy complexion against her own honeyed skin; long, chorus-girl legs against her own. Were they shorter? Dumpier? Somehow less shapely?

And then there was the guilt: at night she blocked her ears to the sound of Celia breathing, wept silent tears at her desperate desire to betray the girl she thought of as her sister. No one had been closer to her. No one had been kinder to her. And this wretched sense of duplicity made her resent Celia even more.

Occasionally she got a glimpse of their old relationship, like clouds parting to reveal a stretch of endless blue, but then they regathered and Lottie couldn't view her without reference to Guy. If Celia blew him a kiss, she fought the urge to throw herself irrationally between them – a human block against his receiving it; a casual arm draped across his shoulder filled her with thoughts little short of murderous. She swung between guilt and a raging jealousy, the pendulum most often settling at a low depression between.

Celia didn't seem to notice. Mrs Holden, now in a frenzy about the prospective nuptials, had decided that none of her daughter's clothes were worthy of her impending position in society, and was determined to buy her a whole new wardrobe. Celia, after confiding to Lottie that she was sure she'd be able to sneak something new for her too, had thrown herself into the task with only the faintest backward glance at her less well-dressed friend. 'I'm going to pick up some brochures this afternoon for the honeymoon,' she said. 'I think a cruise would be just perfect. Don't you think a cruise would be perfect, Lottie? Can you imagine sitting up on deck in one of those bikinis? Guy is desperate to see me in a bikini – he thinks I'll look simply marvellous. All the Hollywood stars go on cruises these days – I heard in London . . . Lots? Oh, sorry, Lots. Thoughtless of me. Hey, look, I'm sure when you get married you'll go on a cruise too. I'll even keep the brochures for you if you like.'

But Lottie didn't feel envious: she was just grateful for the extra time with Guy. And tried to believe, as they strolled apparently coincidentally down the road again to Arcadia, that Guy felt that little swell of gratitude too.

The children saw Joe before he saw them. It wouldn't have been hard: he was thrust deep under the bonnet of an Austin Healey, wrestling with a distributor cap. Freddie, walking past on his way back from picking up groceries with Sylvia and Virginia, ran up behind him and shoved a hand still sticky with some unidentified sweet up under Joe's shirt. 'Celia's going to have a baby!'

Joe emerged, rubbing his head where it had impacted on the underside of the bonnet.

'Freddie!' Virginia cast an anxious look out on to the road, dived into the open-fronted garage and began hauling her charge away.

'She is! I heard her and Mummy talking about how to make one last night. And Mummy said she's got to get Guy to take care of his matters and then she won't have to have a new baby every year.'

'Freddie, I'll tell your mother you've been spouting nonsense! Sorry,' she mouthed at Joe, as Freddie wriggled free of her usually iron grasp.

'Why don't you come any more?' Sylvia stood in front of him, her head tilted to one side. 'You were going to show me how to do Monopoly and you didn't come the next day like you said.'

Joe rubbed at his hands with a rag.

'Sorry,' he said. 'I've been a bit busy.'

'Lottie says it's because you're cross with her.'

Joe stopped rubbing. 'Is that what she says?'

'She says you stopped coming because she's going out with Dickie Valentine.'

Joe chuckled despite himself.

'Is Lottie having a baby too?' Freddie was peering into the engine, reaching in an exploratory plump pink arm.

'Sylvia. Freddie. Come *on*.'

'If Lottie has a baby, will you teach it how to play Monopoly?'

'If you have an eraser, you only have to have one baby.'

Joe, retrieving Freddie's hand, had begun to shake his head. Virginia, beside him, was laughing.

Freddie, sensing their mirth, began to gather pace. 'Lottie is having a baby with Dickie Valentine. He's going to sing about it on the television.'

'You want to watch what you're saying, Freddie. Someone might believe you.' She turned to Joe, giggling. She liked Joe.

He was obviously wasting his time mooning over Lottie. The silly girl thought she was too good for him by the looks of it, too important, seeing as how she lived with the Holdens as one of their own. But she wasn't any better than Virginia. She had just got lucky.

'It'll be Elvis Presley she's stepping out with next, according to these two.' She smoothed her hair back, wishing she'd worn a bit of lipstick this morning, like she'd intended.

But Joe didn't seem to notice. He didn't even seem to think Elvis Presley was funny. He had gone all serious again.

'You out much lately, then, Joe? Been over to Clacton at all?' Virginia moved a little closer to him, positioning herself so that her slim legs were directly in his view.

Joe looked down, and shifted a little on his feet. 'No. Been a bit busy.'

'Freddie's right. We haven't seen you around much.'

'No. Well.'

'I got a thumbnail. Look.' Freddie thrust his hand at Joe.

'A hangnail, Freddie. I told you. And it'll go soon. Stop waving it around at people.'

'I can make a hydrogen bomb. You can buy hydrogen at the chemist. I heard Mr Ansty say.'

Joe glanced over at the clock, as if waiting for them to go. But Virginia pressed on: 'He means hydrogen peroxide. Look, Joe, there's a few of us going to the new dance-hall over on the Colchester Road on Saturday. If you wanted to come, I'm sure we could get you a ticket.' She paused. 'There's this band from London. They're meant to be really good. They do all the rock-and-roll numbers. We'd have a laugh.'

Joe looked at her, and wrung at his rag.

'Think about it, then.'

'Thanks, Virginia. Thanks. I'll – I'll, er, let you know.'

★   ★   ★

In the year of 1870 an American sea captain called Lorenzo Dow Baker docked at Port Antonio and, on taking a leisurely stroll through one of the local markets, discovered that the natives were particularly fond of eating a strangely shaped yellow fruit. Captain Baker, an enterprising soul, thought they looked and smelt inviting. He bought a hundred and sixty bunches of them for a shilling each, and stored them in the hold of his ship. When he returned to port in New Jersey, America, eleven days later, the local fruit merchants leaped upon the fruit, and paid him the grand sum of two dollars a bunch.

'Not a bad profit,' said Julian Armand.

'For a few bananas. The locals went mad for the new fruit. Those who could see past the strangeness to the sweetness . . . they were the ones who got the reward. And that was really the start of the fruit-importing industry. Old Baker became the Boston Fruit Company. And the company that grew from that company is one of the biggest exporters today. Dad used to tell me that as a bedtime story.' He grinned at Lottie. 'He doesn't like telling it any more as the company is so much bigger than his.'

'A competitive man,' said Julian, who was sitting with his bare feet up on a pile of books. He had a pile of lithographs on his lap and was sorting them into two piles, one on each side of him on the sofa cushions. Beside him Stephen, a pale, freckled young man who never seemed to speak, picked up those he had discarded and examined them closely too, as if it were a matter of courtesy. He was, apparently, a playwright. Lottie had added the 'apparently', in the manner of Mrs Holden, as it had recently occurred to her that none of them, except Frances, seemed to do anything at all.

'And his business is successful?'

'It is now. I mean, I don't know how much money he makes

or anything, but I do know that since I was a boy our houses have got bigger. And our cars.'

'Competitiveness has its rewards. And your father sounds very determined.'

'Can't bear to lose at anything. Even to me.'

'Do you play chess, Guy?'

'I haven't in a while. Do you fancy a game, Mr Armand?'

'No, not I. Useless, I am, as a tactical thinker. No, if you are any good, you should play George.'

'George's mind is pure mathematics. Pure logic. I often think he is half man, half machine,' said Adeline.

'You mean he's cold.'

'Not cold, exactly. George can be terrifically kind. But not a man to love.' The gentle conversation belied the fact that there was an edge to the air that afternoon that had little to do with the imminent onset of autumn. Lottie had not sensed it at first: a barely perceptible vibration between the people in the room, a charge. Adeline lifted a strand of Lottie's hair. 'No, not a man to fall in love with.'

Lottie sat silently at Adeline's feet, trying not to blush at Adeline's use of the word, roused from a reverie of cargo ships and exotic fruits. Adeline was dressing her hair with tiny, embroidered roses that she had rediscovered in a cushioned box. 'I had them sewn on my wedding dress,' she said. Lottie had been horrified. 'It was only a dress, Lottie. I like to keep only the best of the past.'

She had insisted on sewing them into Lottie's hair, 'just to see'. Lottie had refused at first; what would Adeline 'see' when she had a load of fabric buds in her hair? But then Guy had said yes, she should. That she should allow Adeline to untangle her long plait, that she should sit quietly while it was brushed and then ministered to. And the thought of having Guy's gaze upon her, no matter for how long, was so delicious that Lottie, with the requisite protestations, had finally acquiesced. 'I'll have to take it out before we go, though. Mrs H would have a fit.'

Adeline paused as Frances walked through from the terrace; Lottie felt her hands still on her hair, and Adeline's faint intake of breath as she passed. Frances had not said a word in the hour and a half that they had been there. Lottie hadn't noticed at first; all her senses were trained on Guy, and it was quite common for Frances to be outside, these days, working on her mural. But then she, too, had become aware of a certain *froideur*, the way that Frances refused to answer Adeline's repeated enquiries about whether she would like a drink, a new paintbrush, some of Guy's delicious fruit.

Lottie, glancing up as she passed, had seen Frances's long jaw tense and tighten, as if barely containing some violent response. Her square, bony shoulders were rigid, and she bent forward over her tray of paint as if daring anyone to obstruct her path. It would have looked almost aggressive, had it not been for the soft pink blur to her eyes, the way her eyelashes had separated wetly into the points of little stars.

Julian has upset her, Lottie thought. She was never like this before he arrived. Somehow Julian's mere presence had altered her demeanour; this was her discomfiture made explicit. 'Can I help with your painting, Frances?' she said.

But Frances, disappearing into the kitchen, did not respond.

There were four more days until Guy's parents arrived to meet the Holdens, and Lottie, conscious that this would likely spell an end to their time together, was intently memorising and storing up each moment of their time there, like a small child hoarding sweets. It was a problematic task, as often she became so determined to imprint it all on her memory that she appeared distracted and vacant to those around her. 'Lottie has left us again,' Adeline would say. And Lottie, several minutes later, would jump, suddenly aware that she was the focus of attention.

Guy said nothing. He seemed to accept those parts of her character that other people felt the need to remark upon. He didn't question them, anyway, and Lottie, who was heartily sick of having her character questioned, was grateful.

The Bancrofts were to arrive on Saturday, and would stay in the Riviera Hotel, where they had booked the best room, the one with a huge private terrace overlooking the bay. ('A little flashy,' said Mrs Chilton, who was rather put out that Uplands had not been called upon to accommodate the visitors. 'But, then, I suppose they are practically foreigners.') Since Guy had announced their imminent arrival, Mrs Holden had dissolved into a domestic frenzy, leaving the overworked Virginia puce and furious.

'I think I should like to meet your parents, Guy. Your father sounds a very interesting man.'

'He . . . I'd say he's a bit of an acquired taste,' said Guy. 'He's more direct than some British people are used to. I think some find him a bit American. A bit brash. Plus he's only really interested in business. Everything else he finds a bit of a bore.'

'And your mother? How does she cope with living with such a force of nature?'

'She laughs at him a lot. In fact, I think she's the only person who does laugh at him. He's a bit explosive, you see. It's quite easy to be . . . intimidated by him.'

'But you are not.'

'No.' He glanced sideways at Lottie. 'Then, I've never done anything to upset him.'

The unspoken 'yet' hung in the air. Lottie felt it, and was faintly chilled by it. She looked away from Guy to her shoes, which were scuffed from running around on the beach with Mr Beans. Dr Holden had remarked that he had never known the dog walked so often. Adeline, meanwhile, got up and left the room, apparently in search of Frances. There was a silence, while Julian continued to sort through his lithographs, occasionally holding one up to the light, and 'hmphing' in either an approving or a derogatory manner. Stephen had uncurled from beside him and stretched, his thin cotton shirt lifting to reveal a pale belly as his arms reached for the ceiling.

Lottie glanced at Guy, blushing as she met his eye. Wherever he was in a room (sometimes outside a room) she was acutely aware of his presence, as if she could pick up tiny vibrations on the air, and found herself quivering in response. As she looked back down, letting the weight of the rosebuds pull her hair in a sheet to hide her face, she was conscious that he did not look away.

They both jumped at the sound of shouting. It was Frances's voice, muffled, so that it was impossible to hear what she was saying. The tenor, however, was unmistakable. Adeline's voice could be heard underneath it, sweeter, reasoning, before Frances's exploded again, an exclamation that something was *impossible!* and then a loud crash as some piece of kitchen equipment hit the flagstone floor.

Lottie stole a look at Julian, but he seemed remarkably unconcerned: his head lifted for a moment, as if reaffirming something he already suspected, then he returned to his lithographs, muttering under his breath about print quality. Stephen glanced over, pointed something out on the surface of the paper, and they nodded together.

'No, you don't, because you choose not to. You have a choice, Adeline, a choice. Even if it is easier for you to pretend you do not.'

It was as if they couldn't hear. Lottie felt mortified. She

hated to hear people argue: it set her nerves jangling, made her feel five years old, vulnerable and impotent again.

'*I won't have it, Adeline. I won't. I have told you, so many times. No, I have begged you . . .*'

Go and stop them, Lottie willed. Someone. But Julian didn't look up.

'Want to go?' mouthed Guy, when she braved his eye.

Julian lifted a friendly hand in greeting as they exited. He was chuckling at something Stephen had said. In the kitchen, all was silent.

He took her hand as they walked down the gravel drive. Lottie, his touch burning all the way to the top of Woodbridge Avenue, forgot the sound of raised voices, the rosebuds still woven into her hair.

'What on earth have you done to yourself, Lottie?' said Mrs Holden. 'You look like you've been divebombed by seagulls!'

But Lottie didn't care. As he had let go of her hand, he had reached up to touch a bud. 'A force of nature,' he had murmured.

There were certain ways of doing things; certain standards that should be met. And Adeline's response to the ladies of the Merham salon had, it appeared, fallen a long way short.

'She is sorry that at present she is unable to attend? Why? Is she busy? Is she looking after children? Applying for the job of prime minister perhaps?' Mrs Chilton had taken it particularly badly.

'But she hopes we will find the time to drop in to her some day,' said Mrs Colquhoun, reading from the piece of ivory notepaper. 'That "some day" is not very specific, is it?'

'I'll say it's not,' said Mrs Chilton, waving away a piece of melon. 'No, thank you, Susan dear. That fruit played havoc with my insides last week. No, I find her whole response very inadequate. Very inadequate indeed.'

'She *has* invited you to drop in on her,' said Celia, who, her legs tucked under her on the sofa, was flicking through a magazine.

'That's not the point, dear. It wasn't her place. We had invited her, therefore she should have accepted. You can't just turn it round and invite us back.'

'Why not?' said Celia.

Mrs Chilton looked at Mrs Holden. 'Well, it's not done, is it?'

'But she's hardly being rude, is she? Not if she's inviting you?'

The women looked exasperated. Lottie, sitting on the floor doing a jigsaw with Sylvia, thought privately that Adeline had been rather clever. She had not wanted to visit the 'salon' on their terms but she understood that individually the ladies would not feel sufficiently confident to visit Arcadia. She had escaped, while also putting the onus on them.

'I can't see that she's been as rude as you think,' said Celia carelessly. 'Can't see why you're bothered about having her visit you anyway. You spend half your time trying to get everyone to stay away from her.'

'But that's the point,' said Mrs Holden, crossly.

'Yes,' said Mrs Colquhoun. She looked down. 'I think.'

Mrs Chilton was studying the rest of the letter, squinting at it through half-rimmed glasses. 'She wishes us well in our artistic endeavours. And hopes that a quote from that great poet Rainer Maria Rilke will provide some inspiration: "Art too is just a way of living, and however one lives, one can, without knowing, prepare for it; in everything real one is closer to it.'" She lowered the letter, and looked around the room. 'What on earth is that supposed to mean?'

He had been rather down for days, she'd thought. A bit preoccupied and serious. So Mrs Holden didn't know whether to be relieved or discomfited when she saw that Guy, sitting over by the gas fire on Dr Holden's good chair, was laughing silently behind his newspaper.

The first of the winter storms had hit Walton, pulling all the unsecured windowboxes on the promenade off their sills and dumping them and their remaining flowers in the road in small terracotta heaps. It would hit Merham within the hour, said Mrs Holden, coming off the telephone. 'Best secure the shutters. Virginia!'

'I'll run Mr Beans up the road now before it starts raining,' said Lottie, and Mrs Holden had given her a sharp look, apparently as confused as ever by Lottie's polar swings between moodiness and helpfulness. Celia had been upstairs, in the bath, and Guy offered to come with her, apparently in need of some fresh air. But now they had been out for almost ten minutes and Lottie realised he had said not a word to her. He had said barely a thing to anyone all day, and Lottie, knowing that it was their last walk before the arrival of his parents, felt desperate to have some thread drawn between them, some fine channel of communication secured.

The rain began to fall in thick, unwieldy blobs as they got to the far end of the municipal park, and Lottie, the wind in her ears, began to run towards the beach huts, their vibrant, random colours still bright under a smudged charcoal sky, motioning to Guy to do the same. She skipped along to those numbered from eighty to ninety, remembering that there were a couple of deserted huts where the locks had rusted away from the wood. She wrenched a door open and ducked inside just as the deluge proper began. Guy ducked in behind her, his shirt already wet, making half gasping, half laughing noises, pulling at his wet shirt, and Lottie, conscious of his proximity in the enclosed space, began to make a great fuss of drying an indifferent Mr Beans with a rag.

The hut had been unloved for a long time: speeding clouds could be glimpsed through slivers in the roof, while apart from a cracked cup and a rickety wooden bench, there was little to suggest it had ever sheltered happy holidaymakers. Most of the other huts also had names – Kennora (or other unbeautiful hybrids of their owners' names), Seabreeze, Wind Ho! – and damp cushions and deck-chairs that sat outside for seemingly the whole summer, while gritty families passed round pots of tea. During the war they had all been commandeered and buried, to form part of the coastal defences; when they were resurrected in their brightly coloured row Lottie, who had never seen a beach hut, had fallen in love with them, and spent many hours walking backwards and forwards reading the names to herself and imagining herself to be part of some family.

Mr Beans was undoubtedly dry. She perched on the bench, pushing back wet wisps of dark hair from her face.

'Some storm,' Guy said, peering through the open doorway as the blackened clouds raced across the horizon, darkening distant fathoms out at sea. Above them, gulls rode the winds, screeching and calling to each other above the noise of the rain. Lottie, looking up at him, suddenly thought of Joe, whose first comment would have been that they should have brought an umbrella.

'You know, the storms in the tropics are seriously wild. One minute you're sitting there in the sun, the next you can see this thing moving across the sky like a train.' He trailed his hand along in the air, his eyes trained upon it. 'And then *pow*! Rain like you wouldn't believe – the kind that comes right over your feet and runs down the road like a river. And the lightning! Forked lightning that just lights up the whole sky.'

Lottie, who just wanted to hear him speak, nodded dumbly.

'I saw a donkey killed by lightning once. When the storm came they just left it out in the field. No one thought to bring it in. I was just getting to our house and I turned round, because there was this huge crack, and the lightning hit, and the donkey didn't even move! It just jumped a little, like something had blown it off its feet, then landed on its side with its legs all stiff. Still had its little cart attached. I don't think it knew what hit it.'

She wasn't sure if it was anything to do with the donkey, but Lottie realised she was close to tears again. She rubbed at Mr Beans's hair with her hand, blinking furiously. When she sat up, Guy was still staring out at the sea. Far over to his left, she could see a patch of blue; the edge of the storm.

They sat in silence for a while. Guy, she noted, didn't look at his watch once.

'What will happen when you have to do your National Service?'

Guy kicked at the floor. 'Not doing it.'

Lottie frowned. 'I didn't think anyone got out of it. Not you being an only child and all.'

'Health reasons.'

'You're not ill, are you?' She had failed to keep the anxiety from her voice.

It was just possible that he blushed a little. 'No . . . I . . . I've got flat feet. My mother says it's from running around with no shoes on all my life.'

Lottie found herself gazing at his feet, feeling perversely

glad that he had some physical imperfection. It made him more human somehow, more accessible.

'Not quite as glamorous as "old shrapnel injury", is it?' He grinned ruefully, kicking at the sandy wooden floor, his restless leg testament to his discomfort.

Lottie didn't know what to say. The only person she knew to have done National Service was Joe, and his two-year posting to the tepid confines of the Payroll Corps had been such an embarrassment to his family that no one in the town ever talked about it. Not in front of them, anyway. She watched the sheets of rain fall, the frothing sea rising up to threaten the sea wall.

'You're not laughing,' he said, grinning at her.

'I'm sorry,' she said solemnly. 'I don't think I have much of a sense of humour.'

He raised an eyebrow, and she was smiling despite herself.

'What else don't you have?'

'What?'

'What else don't you have? What are you missing, Lottie?'

She looked up at him. 'Flat feet?'

They both laughed, nervously. Lottie felt she might burst into uncontrollable giggles. Except that they would ride too close to the surface; too close to something else.

'A family? Do you have one?'

'Not one that you'd recognise. I've got a mother. Although I suppose she might dispute that description of herself.'

He was looking at her steadily. 'Poor you.'

'Poor you nothing. I've been very lucky living with the Holdens.' She had said it so often.

'The perfect family.'

'The perfect mother.'

'God. I don't know how you survived *that* for ten years.'

'You haven't met mine.'

For some reason, they both found this hysterically funny.

'We should be very understanding. She has many crosses to bear.'

He was watching an oil tanker. It traversed the horizon at the exact point where sea and sky met. He let out a long breath, and lifted his legs on to the bench. Stretched out, they reached all the way to the door. She could just see a glimpse of his ankle; it was brown, the exact same shade as the inside of his wrists.

'How did you meet her?' she asked eventually.

'Celia?'

'Yes.'

He shuffled his feet, reached down to rub at some wet spray marks on his pale trousers.

'By chance, I suppose. We have this apartment in London, and I'd been staying there with my mother while my father went to the Caribbean to look at some farms. She likes to stay in London sometimes, catch up with my aunt, go shopping. You know the stuff.'

Lottie nodded, as if she did. Under her feet, Mr Beans strained at his lead, keen to continue his walk.

'I'm not a great one for towns, so I went to my cousin's place in Sussex for a few days. My uncle's got this farm, and I've stayed there ever since I was a child because my cousin and I – well, we're nearly the same age and he's probably the closest friend I've got. Anyway, so I'm meant to be back in London, but me and Rob, we go to the local pub, and one thing leads to another and it's a little later than I intended. So I'm sitting at the station waiting, because there's only one train left into London, and I see this girl walk past.'

Lottie's chest tightened. She wasn't convinced she wanted

to hear this any longer. But there seemed no safe way of stopping him. 'And you thought she was beautiful.'

Guy looked down at his feet, and half laughed. 'Beautiful. Yes, I thought she looked beautiful. Mostly I thought she looked drunk.'

Lottie's head shot up. Guy sat down beside her on the wooden bench and raised a finger to his lips. 'I promised I wouldn't tell . . . You've got to promise, Lottie . . . She was absolutely rotten. I saw her weave past the ticket office, where I was standing, and she was giggling to herself. I could see she'd been to some kind of party because she was all dressed up. But she had lost a shoe, and she was holding the other in her hand with her little bag or whatever it was.'

Above them the rain beat thunderously on the roof. Where it hit the ground, it splashed up into the hut, making Mr Beans jump.

'So I thought maybe I should just keep an eye on her. But then she went into the station waiting room and there were these lads in uniform, and she sits down with them and starts chatting away, and they're obviously loving it, so I just thought maybe she knew them. They all seemed like they knew each other. I thought maybe they'd all been to the dance together.'

Lottie's mind was reeling with the thought of what Mrs Holden would say at the picture of her daughter drunkenly engaging servicemen in conversation. It also explained why she hadn't brought her satin slingbacks home: she had told Mrs Holden that a girl from secretarial school had stolen them.

'And at one point she sits on one's lap, and she's laughing and laughing, so I thought she must know him, and I walked away, back to the ticket office. And then – it must have been about five minutes later – I hear this shouting, and then a woman's voice shouting, and after a few minutes I think I should probably take a look, and—'

'They were attacking her,' said Lottie, for whom this story was ringing some bells.

'Attacking her?' Guy looked puzzled. 'No, they weren't attacking her. They had her shoe.'

'What?'

'Her shoe. They had this pale pink shoe of hers and they were dancing around holding it up so that she couldn't get it.'

'Her shoe?'

'Yes. And she was so rotten that she kept bumping into things, and falling over. And I watched for a minute, but then I thought it was pretty unfair as she obviously didn't know what she was doing. So I stepped in and asked them to give her her shoe back.'

Lottie stared at him. 'And what did they do?'

'Oh, they were pretty sarky to begin with. One of them was asking me if I fancied my chances. Ironic, really, given the result. And between us, Lottie, I was pretty polite with them, because I didn't fancy my chances against three of them. But they were all right, really. Eventually they just threw the shoe at her and went off up the platform.'

'So they didn't try to grab her?'

'Grab her? No. I mean, they may have grabbed her a little when she sat on the fellow's lap. But not so as she got upset or anything.'

'And what happened?'

'Well, I just thought someone really needed to take her home. I thought she'd probably got off quite lightly actually. But she was in such a state that she could easily have fallen asleep on the train, and I didn't think it was a good idea for her to be alone . . . looking like that.'

'No . . .'

He shrugged. 'So I took her back to her aunt's place, and her aunt was pretty suspicious of me to begin with, but I left her my name and number so that she could call my mother, and check that I was . . . well, you know. And then Celia rang me the next day to apologise, and say thank you, and we went for a cup of coffee . . . and, well . . .'

Lottie was still too stunned by this version of events to absorb the implications of his last words. She shook her head. 'She was drunk? You looked after her because she was drunk?'

'Ah. But she told me the truth about that. She had thought she was only drinking ginger ale, but someone at this dance had evidently been slipping vodka or something into it, so before she knew it she was all over the place. Pretty bad behaviour, really.'

'She told you that.'

Guy frowned. 'Yes. I felt pretty sorry for her, to be honest.'

There was a long silence. The sky outside was now neatly bisected into blue and black, the sun already reflected in the wet road.

It was Lottie who broke the silence. She stood, so that Mr Beans leaped happily out on to the path, ears pricked at the departing storm. 'I think I'd better go back,' she said briskly, and began to walk.

'She's a nice girl.' His voice caught on the wind behind her.

Lottie turned briefly, her face tense and furious. 'You don't have to tell me that.'

The other ladies had definitely developed something of an air when she mentioned her morning walks, so Deirdre

Colquhoun felt rather disinclined to tell them about her latest discovery, compelling as it had been.

No, Sarah Chilton had been rather curt when she had mentioned Mr Armand on Tuesday, so there was no reason why she should tell them that for two mornings running now she had seen something she considered just as dramatic. The men didn't seem to come any more, so it had been rather a shock to see her, and Deirdre Colquhoun had had to pull her little opera glasses from her handbag to make sure it was the same woman. Wading into the waves, she had been, not seeming to notice the cold or anything, in that tight black swimsuit of hers, her hair scraped back into an unfashionable bun. And even as she waded in, in a manner that frankly Deirdre Colquhoun found a little mannish, you could see she was sobbing. Yes, sobbing, loudly in broad daylight, as if her heart would break.

Six

It was not the welcome Mrs Holden had planned. That welcome had involved her standing, pristine in her good wool dress with the matching belt, her two youngest children in front of her, as she opened the doors to welcome their visitors, the wealthy, cosmopolitan family to whom they were now going to be linked by marriage. That version had the Bancrofts pulling up in their gleaming Rover 90 four-door saloon (she knew it to be this model, as Mrs Ansty had heard it from Jim Farrelly who worked the desk of the Riviera Hotel) and her skipping out past an immaculate front lawn, and greeting them both like long-lost friends – perhaps even as Sarah Chilton and one or other of the ladies just happened to be passing by.

In that version, the preferred version, her husband emerged behind her, perhaps placed a proprietorial hand on her shoulder, the kind of simple gesture that spoke volumes about a marriage. The children, meanwhile, smiled sweetly, kept their good clothes clean, and held up their hands to shake those of the Bancrofts in a rather charming manner before offering to show them indoors.

They did not wait until two minutes before the guests were due to arrive to reveal that they had not only found a dead fox in the road down by the Methodist Church, but that they had scraped it up into a seaside bucket, laid it out on the floor in the living room and, with the help of Mrs Holden's best sewing scissors, planned to make a fox fur from it.

Neither, in the preferred version, did Dr Holden announce that he had been called out to a sick patient and didn't expect to be back before tea time, despite it being a Saturday and despite almost the whole of Merham being quite aware that his secretary, that red-headed girl who always managed to put a superior tone in her voice when she answered the telephone to Dr Holden's wife, was leaving town the following day to take up a position in Colchester. She closed her eyes briefly, and summoned an image of her rose garden. It was what she did when she didn't want to think too hard about that woman. It was important to think about nice things.

Perhaps most importantly, in the preferred version, Mrs Holden wasn't also faced with three of the most miserable young people she had ever had the misfortune to encounter. Celia and Guy, far from being bathed in the glow of the newly affianced, had been decidedly surly and barely spoken to each other all morning. Lottie had hovered silently in the background, brooding darkly in that way she had: it really made her look most unattractive. And none of them seemed to care that she had made so much effort to make the afternoon go smoothly: every time she jollied them up a bit, tried to get them to put a brave face on, or at least give her a hand keeping control of the children, they would variously shrug, look at the floor or, in Celia's case, look meaningfully at Guy, her eyes glittering with tears, and announce that she simply couldn't be expected to be cheerful every darned day. 'Now, I have really had enough of this, dears. Really. This place has an atmosphere like a mortuary. Lottie, you go and make the children clear up that blasted animal. Get Virginia to help. Guy, you go and wait outside for the car. And, Celia, go upstairs and brighten yourself up a bit. Put some makeup on. These are your in-laws you're meeting, for goodness' sake. It's your wedding.'

'That's if there's going to be a wedding,' said Celia, so miserably that Lottie's head whipped round.

'Don't be ridiculous. Of course there's going to be a wedding. Now, go and put on some makeup. You can borrow a bit of my scent if you like, perk yourself up a bit.'

'What, the Chanel?'

'If you like.'

Celia, momentarily cheered, raced upstairs. Lottie trudged mutinously to the drawing room, where Virginia was still shaking from her discovery of the dead animal, and Freddie was lying on the sofa clutching himself theatrically and complaining that he would never, ever, ever be able to sit down again, ever, thanks to his mother.

She knew what was making Celia so miserable, and it caused her equal measures of delight and self-loathing. Late the previous evening, as the storm receded, Celia had asked Lottie to come up to their room and, once there, seated on the side of the bed, had confided that she needed to talk to her. Lottie knew she had flushed. She sat very still. Stiller when Celia said: 'It's Guy. He's been really off with me for the past few days, Lots. Not himself at all.'

Lottie had been unable to speak. It was as if her tongue had swollen, filling the entire space within her mouth.

Celia studied her nails, and then, abruptly, lifted her hand to her mouth and bit one off. 'When he first came here he was like his London self, you know. He was so sweet, always asking me whether I was all right, whether I needed anything. He was so affectionate. He used to take me round to the back porch while you were all clearing up after tea and kiss me until I thought my head was going to spin right off . . .'

Lottie coughed. She had stopped breathing.

Celia, oblivious, stared at her hand, then looked up, her blue eyes brimming with tears. 'He hasn't kissed me properly for four whole days. I tried to get him to last night and he just dismissed me, muttered something about there being lots of time later. But how can he feel like that, Lots? How can he not care whether he kisses me or not? That's the kind of behaviour you expect from *married* men.'

Lottie fought to contain the swell of something uncomfortably like excitement leaping within her. Then flinched as Celia turned towards her and, in one swift movement, threw her arms around Lottie's neck and burst into sobs. 'I don't know what I've done, Lots. I don't know whether I've said something and he's just not telling me. It's possible – you know how I do chatter on about nothing and I don't always think about what it is I've said. Or perhaps I just haven't looked pretty enough lately. I do try. I've been wearing all sorts of nice things that Mummy bought me, but he just – he just doesn't seem to *like* me as much as he did before.'

Her chest heaved against Lottie's. Lottie stroked her back mechanically, feeling treacherously relieved that Celia couldn't see her face.

'I just can't work it out. What is it, Lots? You've spent enough time with him now. You must know what he's like.'

Lottie tried to keep her voice steady. 'I'm sure you're imagining it.'

'Oh, don't be such a cold fish, Lottie. You know I'd help you, if you asked. Come on, what do you think he's thinking?'

'I don't think I'm qualified to say.'

'But you must have *some* idea. What can I do? What am I supposed to do?'

Lottie closed her eyes. 'It might just be nerves,' she said, eventually. 'Perhaps men get nerves just like we do. I mean, with his parents coming and all. It's a big thing, isn't it, introducing one's parents?'

Celia pulled back, and stared intently at her.

'Perhaps he feels more tense about it than you know.'

'Perhaps you're right. I hadn't thought of that at all. Maybe he *is* nervous.' She smoothed back her hair, glancing towards the window. 'Because no man would want to admit he was nervous, would he? It's not really the kind of thing men do.'

Lottie wished with a kind of grim fervour that Celia would just go. She would say anything, do anything, if she could get Celia to leave her alone.

But Celia moved back to her and gave her a clinging hug. 'Oh, you are clever, Lots. I'm sure you're right. And I'm sorry if I've been a bit – well – distant lately. It's just I've been so wrapped up in Guy and weddings and everything. It can't have been much fun for you.'

Lottie winced. 'I've been fine,' she croaked.

'Right. Well. I'll go downstairs and see if I can get the rotten old pig to pay me some attention.' She laughed. It still sounded like a sob.

Lottie stared at her departing back, then sank slowly on to the bed.

It had all become real then. That Guy and Celia were getting married. That Lottie was in love with a man she genuinely couldn't have; a man who, more importantly, had done nothing to suggest that her feelings were reciprocated, other than to accompany her on a few walks to a house he liked, and to admire some silly childish flowers in her hair. Because that was it, wasn't it? When you boiled it down, there was nothing to say that Guy liked her any more than he liked – say – Freddie. Because he spent lots of time with Freddie too. And even if he did like her, there was no way they could do anything about it. Look at the state Celia had been in just because he had paid her slightly less attention over the past few days.

Oh God, why did you have to come here? Lottie groaned, resting her forehead on her knees. I was perfectly content until you came here. And then Mrs Holden called her down to give Virginia a hand rearranging the good silver.

Celia, despite her good intentions, had been unable to shake off her sense of dejection. And possibly with good reason. Lottie watched as she paraded her newest dress in front of Guy, as she pinched his arm playfully, and laid her head in a coquettish manner upon his shoulder. Lottie watched as Guy patted her with the comfortable detachment of a man patting his dog, and Celia's smile become rigid in response. And Lottie fought to control the simmering cauldron of emotions bubbling inside her. And went to help Sylvia lace up her good shoes.

For a man who hadn't seen his parents for almost a month, a man who professed to adore his mother, and thought his father one of the finest men he knew, Guy had seemed less than enthralled by the prospect of their imminent arrival. At first Lottie had put down to impatience his incessant pacing around outside; then she looked closer and saw that he was arguing with himself under his breath, like the mad lady down at the park who used to wave a pair of drawers at anyone who dared venture on to what she thought of as her bowling green. Guy's face did not look eager: it looked troubled, and ill-tempered, and when he shrugged off Freddie's persistent requests to play tennis again with an uncharacteristic expletive, Lottie watched silently from the drawing-room window and prayed passionately to whatever deity it was up there that it was she who was the cause of, and the remedy for, his misery.

Susan Holden looked at these three miserable young people and sighed. Not a stiff upper lip or an ounce of backbone among them. If she, with the troubles she had – Henry's wretched absences, Freddie's obsessions, and Sarah Chilton still making pointed comments about how lucky it was that they had got Celia betrothed *all things considered* – could face the world with a smile, then you'd think these ruddy children could just get hold of themselves and brighten up a bit.

She pursed her lips at her reflection, then reached into her bag and pulled out a lipstick. It was quite a bold one for her, not one she would have worn in front of the salon ladies, but applying it carefully (wincing as she bent forward), Mrs Holden told herself that some days one needed all the props one could get.

That red-headed girl wore lipstick the colour of Christmas candles. The first time she had called into Henry's office and seen her there she had been unable to take her eyes off it.

Perhaps that had been the point.

Virginia called up the stairs: 'Mrs Holden, your visitors are here.'

Mrs Holden checked her hair in the mirror and took a deep breath. Please let Henry come home in a good mood, she prayed. 'Let them in, dear, I'm coming down.'

'And Freddie is refusing to let go of that – that dead thing. He says he wants to keep it in his bedroom. It's made the rug smell awful.'

Mrs Holden thought, with some desperation, of roses.

'What a simply beautiful garden. How wonderfully clever you are.' Sweet words, to a nervous, under-appreciated potential mother-in-law. And Susan Holden, still knocked on to a back footing by Dee Dee Bancroft's broad American accent (Guy hadn't said anything!) found herself quite shaky in her gratitude.

'Are those Albertines? Do you know they're simply my favourite roses? Cannot grow them in the darned excuse for a garden we have in Port Antonio. The wrong soil, apparently. Or I had them too close to something else. Then, roses can be terribly tricky, can't they? Prickly in more ways than one.'

'Oh, yes,' said Susan Holden, trying not to look at Dee Dee's long brown legs. From here she could have sworn that the woman wasn't wearing any hosiery.

'Oh, you have no idea how I envy you this garden. Look, Guy honey, they've got hostas. Not a slug bite out of them. I don't know how you do it.'

Guyhoney, as Mr Bancroft Senior was apparently known to his wife, turned from the back gate, which looked down over the playing-fields, and began walking back up to where the ladies were sitting under a flapping parasol, sipping at warm tea.

'Which direction is the ocean?'

Guy, who had been sitting on the grass, stood and walked over to his father. He pointed over to the east, his words carried away on the brisk winds.

'I do hope you don't mind sitting outside. I know it's a bit blustery, but it might be the last beautiful afternoon of the year, and I like to enjoy the roses.' Mrs Holden had made frantic motions behind her back to get Virginia to bring out more chairs.

'Oh, no, we love to be outdoors.' Mrs Bancroft put a hand to her hair, to stop it whipping into her mouth as she drank some tea.

'Yes. Yes, one does miss the outdoors in the winter.'

'And Freddie put a dead fox on the drawing-room rug,' said Sylvia.

'Sylvia!'

'He did. It wasn't even me. And now Mummy says she won't let us in there ever again. That's why we have to sit in a freezing cold garden.'

'Sylvia, that is not true. I'm so sorry, Mrs Bancroft. We did – erm – have a little incident in the room just before you came, but we had always intended to have tea out here.'

'Dee Dee, please. And don't you worry on our account. Outside is fine. And I'm sure Freddie can't be as bad as our son. Guy Junior was just the most horrific child.' Dee Dee beamed at Susan Holden's shocked expression. 'Oh, awful. He used to bring back insects and put them in boxes and jars and then forget about them. I'd discover spiders the size of my fist in my flour bin. Ugh!'

'I don't know how you cope out there with all those insects. I'm sure I'd have spent half the time living in terror.'

'I'd like it,' said Freddie, who had spent the last ten minutes peering at the fresh leather and walnut interior of Mr Bancroft's brand new Rover. 'I'd like a spider as big as my fist. I'd call it Harold.'

Mrs Holden shuddered. It was somehow harder to think of one's rose garden when one was sitting in it.

'I would. It would be my friend.'

'Your only friend,' said Celia who, her mother noted, had recovered some of her tartness. She was seated on the edge of the picnic rug, her legs towards Lottie's, picking miserably at a plate of biscuits.

Lottie was hugging her knees, looking past everyone else

131

at the front gate, as if waiting for some signal to leave. She had not offered to hand the scones round, as Mrs Holden had requested before the Bancrofts arrived. She hadn't even changed into something pretty.

'So where's this house that you told us about, Junior? I bet it isn't half as pretty as Susan's house here.'

Mr Bancroft strode over to the table, his cigarette waving in his hand for emphasis. His voice, although English, was of indeterminate origin and had a definite transatlantic lilt, which Susan Holden found very *unconventional*. Mind you, there seemed to be little conventional about Guy Bancroft Senior. A large man, he was wearing a bright red shirt, a hue one might expect to see on a cabaret performer, and he spoke very loudly as if everyone else were at least fifty yards away. When he had arrived he had planted great wet kisses on both her cheeks in the French style. Even though he was quite clearly not French.

'It's over in that direction. Past the municipal park.' Guy steered his father towards the coast again and pointed.

In normal circumstances, one might have thought him rather . . . common. There was absolutely no refinement in his manners. His clothes, his loud voice, all pointed to a certain lack of upbringing. He had sworn twice in front of her, and Dee Dee had just laughed. But he did have a certain polish: that of money. It was apparent in his wristwatch, in his shining handmade shoes, in the very beautiful crocodile handbag they had bought Susan Holden from London. When she had pulled it from its tissue paper, she had fought an uncharacteristic urge to lower her head just to breathe in that delicious expensive smell.

She tore her mind from the handbag to check her watch again. It was nearly a quarter to four. Henry really should have called by now to say whether he would be home for supper. She didn't know how many to cook for. Did the Bancrofts think they were staying? The idea of making her broiler chickens stretch out to a meal for seven made her chest quite fluttery with anxiety.

'What – towards our hotel?'

'Yes. But it's on a promontory by itself. You wouldn't see it from the coast road.'

She could get Virginia to run down and get a joint of pork. Just in case. It wouldn't be wasted if they didn't stay: the children could have it in rissoles.

Dee Dee leaned over, her hand pinning her blonde hair to her head. 'My son has been telling us all about your fascinating neighbours. It must be lovely to have so many artists on your doorstep.'

Susan Holden sat up a little straighter, beckoning to Virginia through the window. 'Well, yes, it is rather nice. So many people assume that a seaside town has little to offer in the way of culture. But we do our best.'

'You know, I envy you that, too. There's no culture out on the fruit plantations. Just the radio. A few books. And the occasional newspaper.'

'Well, we do like to cultivate the spirit of the arts ourselves.'

'And the house sounds fantastic.'

'House?'

Susan Holden looked at her blankly.

'Yes, Mrs Holden?' Virginia stood in front of her, clutching a tray.

'Sorry, did you say house?'

'The art-deco house. Guy Junior says it is one of the most beautiful houses he's ever seen. I must say, in his letters he's had us fascinated.'

Virginia was staring at her.

133

Mrs Holden shook her head. 'Er – don't worry, Virginia. I'll come in and talk to you in a minute . . . I'm sorry, Mrs Bancroft, could you repeat what you just said?'

Virginia departed with an audible tut.

'Dee Dee, please. Yes, we're great fans of modern architecture. Mind you, where I grew up in the Midwest, everything's modern, you know? We call a house old if it was put up before the war!' She burst into peals of laughter.

Mr Bancroft tapped his cigarette into a flower-bed. 'We should take a walk down there later this afternoon. Take a look at it.'

'At Arcadia?' Lottie's head swung round.

'Is that its name? How glorious.' Dee Dee accepted another cup of tea.

'You want to go to Arcadia?' Mrs Holden's voice had risen several keys.

Lottie and Celia exchanged looks.

'I understand it's the most fabulous place, absolutely full of exotic types.'

'It is that,' said Celia who, for the first time that day, was smiling.

Dee Dee glanced at Celia and back at her mother. 'Oh. Maybe it's a little difficult. I'm sure they don't want us gawping at them. Guyhoney, let's leave it for another day.'

'But it's only five minutes down the road.'

'Honey—'

Mrs Holden caught the glance Dee Dee sent her husband. She straightened a little in her chair. Looked deliberately past her children. 'Well, of course I do have a standing invitation to visit Mrs Armand . . . I mean, only last week I received a letter . . .'

Mr Bancroft stubbed out his cigarette, and downed his tea

in a thirsty gulp. 'Then let's visit. C'mon, Guy, you show us what you've been talking about.'

Mrs Holden would be regretting those shoes. Lottie watched as, for the fifteenth time in the short walk, the woman in front of her turned an ankle on the uneven surface of the sea path, anxiously glancing behind her to see whether her visitors had noticed. She needn't have worried: Mr and Mrs Bancroft were arm in arm and oblivious, chatting companionably, pointing out to sea at distant vessels, or up above them to some late-flowering flora. Guy and Celia were at the front, Celia's arm threaded through his, but with none of the easy conversation of his parents. Celia talked, and Guy walked, his head down, his jaw set. It was impossible to know if he was listening. Lottie brought up the rear, half wishing that the fiercely protesting Freddie and Sylvia had been allowed to come, if only to give her something else to focus on other than that pair of golden heads, or to provide a lightning conductor for Mrs Holden's palpably increasing aura of tension.

Lottie didn't know why she'd suggested they come. She knew Mrs Holden must be regretting it already, even more than the high-heeled shoes: the closer they came to Arcadia, the more nervous looks she cast around her, as if afraid they might bump into someone she knew. She had adopted the halting, uneven gait of the incompetent criminal, and she refused to meet Lottie's eye, as if afraid she might be challenged on her *volte face*. Lottie wouldn't have bothered – she felt simply miserable: miserable at having to spend yet another hour faced with beaming parental pride in the would-be bride and groom, at having to look again upon the face of the man forbidden to her; at the idea that they were about to inflict all this upon Adeline, who wouldn't know how to put on an afternoon tea if it leaped up and buried her in Darjeeling.

Guy's mother was calling to Celia again. Celia had cheered up immeasurably: partly because of all the attention she was getting from Dee Dee and partly, Lottie suspected, because the thought of her mother at the actress's house filled her with mischievous delight. Lottie was glad she was a little happier, and wanted to quench that happiness with a raw and burning ferocity.

Guy's parents hadn't seemed to notice her.

They'll all be gone soon, she told herself, closing her eyes. And I'll do more shifts at the shoe shop. I'll make up with Joe. I'll make sure my mind is occupied. That it's so full I can't find any room to think of him. And then Guy, turning into the driveway, chose that moment to meet her eye, as if his very existence could make a mockery of any attempt she might make to control her feelings.

'This it?' Mr Bancroft was standing back on his heels, in much the same manner that his son had several weeks earlier.

Guy stopped, gazing at the low white house in front of them. 'That's the one.'

'Nice-looking house.'

'It's a kind of mixture between art deco and art moderne. The style stems from the 1925 Exhibition Internationale des Arts Decoratifs. In Paris. That's what launched art deco. The geometric patterns on the buildings are meant to echo the Machine Age.'

There was a brief silence. Everyone in the small party turned to stare at Guy.

'Well, that's the longest damn sentence I've heard you come out with since we got here.'

Guy looked down. 'I was interested. I looked it up in the library.'

136

'Looked it up in the library, huh? Good for you, son.' Mr Bancroft lit up another cigarette, shielding his lighter flame with a broad, fat hand. 'See Dee Dee?' he said, after an appreciative puff. 'Told you our boy would be all right without teachers and suchlike. Anything he needs to know he goes and looks it up himself. In the library, no less.'

'Well, I think that's just fascinating, darling. You tell me some more about this house.'

'Oh, I don't think that should be me. Adeline will tell you all about it.'

Lottie watched Mrs Holden flinch slightly at Guy's use of Adeline's first name. There were going to be questions tonight, she could tell.

She could also tell that Mrs Holden was embarrassed by how long it took anyone to answer the door: already on edge, she had stood before the huge white front door clutching her handbag in front of her, raising and lowering it in apparent indecision over whether to knock a second time, in case no one had heard. There were definitely people in – there were three cars in the drive. But no one seemed to be answering.

'They might be out on the terrace,' said Guy. 'I could climb over the side gate and have a look.'

'No,' said Dee Dee and Susan Holden simultaneously.

'We don't want to intrude,' said Susan Holden. 'Perhaps they're . . . perhaps they're gardening.'

Lottie didn't like to mention that the closest thing to greenery on Adeline's terrace was some bread that had been left to moulder down by the big plant pots.

'Perhaps we should have rung ahead,' said Dee Dee.

Then, as the silence became excruciating, the door swung open. It was George, who stood for a second, stared slowly at each member of the little party, and then, with a grin at Celia, made an extravagant sweep of his hand, and said, 'If it isn't Celia and Lottie and a band of merry men. Come on in. Come and join the party.'

'Guy Bancroft Senior,' said Mr Bancroft, holding out a huge hand.

George looked at it, stuck his own cigarette between his teeth. 'George Bern. Delighted. No idea who you are, but delighted.'

He was, Lottie saw, quite drunk.

Unlike Mrs Holden, who stood nervously in the doorway as if reluctant to venture in, Mr Bancroft did not seem remotely perturbed by George's odd greeting. 'This is my wife, Dee Dee, and my son, Guy Junior.'

George leaned back theatrically to take a closer look at Guy. 'Ah. The famous prince of pineapple. I hear you've made quite an impact.'

Lottie felt herself flush and began to walk briskly down the corridor.

'Is Mrs Armand at home?'

'She certainly is, madam. And you must be Celia's sister. Her mother? No, I don't believe it. Celia, you never told me.'

There was just the faintest hint of something mocking in George's voice, and Lottie dared not look at Mrs Holden's face. She walked quietly into the main drawing room, from where the sounds of some discordant piano concerto were filtering through the air. The wind was picking up: in some distant part of the house a door repeatedly squeaked and slammed.

Behind her, she heard Dee Dee exclaiming over some piece of art, and Mrs Holden, in somewhat anxious tones, wondering whether Mrs Armand would mind an unheralded visit, but she *had said* . . .

'No, no. You all come on in. Come and join the circus.'

Lottie could not help but stare at Adeline. She was seated

in the middle of the sofa, as she had been when she had first seen her. This time, however, her air of exotic polish had rubbed off: she had apparently been crying, and sat silently with pale, blotchy cheeks, her eyes lowered, and her hands twisted before her.

Julian had been seated beside her, with Stephen on the easy chair, engrossed in a newspaper. Now, as they approached, Julian stood and strode up to the door. 'Lottie, how delightful to see you again. What an unexpected pleasure. And who have you brought with you?'

'This is Mr and Mrs Bancroft, Guy's parents,' Lottie murmured. 'And Mrs Holden, Celia's mother.'

Julian didn't seem to see Susan Holden. He almost fell upon Mr Bancroft's hand in his eagerness to shake it. 'Mr Bancroft! Guy has told us so much about you!' (Here Lottie noticed Celia's frown as she glanced up at Guy: it was not only Mrs Holden who would be asking questions tonight.) 'Do sit down, sit down. Let us organise some tea.'

'I'm sure we don't want to be any trouble,' said Mrs Holden, who had blanched at a series of nudes on the wall.

'No trouble, no trouble at all. Sit! Sit! We will have tea.' He glanced over at Adeline, who had hardly moved since they arrived, except to bestow a weak smile on her visitors. 'I am very glad to meet you all. I have been entirely remiss in getting to know my neighbours. You'll have to excuse us if we are not quite operational in domestic matters at the moment – we have just lost our help.'

'Oh, I do feel for you,' said Dee Dee, seating herself on a Lloyd Loom chair. 'Nothing worse than being left without help. I say to Guy that having staff is sometimes more trouble than it's worth.'

'It is out in the Caribbean,' said Mr Bancroft. 'You have to have twenty staff to do the work of ten.'

'Twenty staff!' said Julian. 'I'm sure Adeline would be content to have one. We seem to have problems retaining people.'

'Should try paying them occasionally, Julian,' said George, who had poured himself another glass of red wine.

Adeline smiled weakly again. Lottie realised that, with Frances apparently absent, there was no one who was actually going to make the tea. 'I'll make the tea,' she said. 'I don't mind making tea.'

'You will? Splendid. What a delightful girl you are, Lottie.'

'Delightful,' said George, smirking.

Lottie went through to the kitchen, glad to escape the strained atmosphere of the drawing room. As she cast around for clean cups and saucers, she could hear Julian asking Mr Bancroft about his business and, with perhaps more enthusiasm, telling him about his own. He sold art, he told Mr Bancroft. He had galleries in central London, and specialised in contemporary painters.

'Is it popular, this stuff?' She could hear Mr Bancroft walking around the room.

'Increasingly so. The prices certain artists make at auction at Sotheby's or Christie's are, in some cases, trebling by the year.'

'You hear that, Dee Dee? Not a bad investment, huh?'

'If you know what to buy.'

'Ah. That's where you are right, Mrs Bancroft. If you are badly advised, you may end up buying something which, although it may have aesthetic value, has ultimately little monetary worth.'

'We haven't really bought paintings, have we, Guyhoney? The ones we have, I bought because they looked pretty.'

'A perfectly sensible reason for buying something. If you do not love it, it is irrelevant what it is worth.'

There were bills on the kitchen table, several large bills for heating oil, electricity, and some repairs that had been done to the roof. Lottie, who could not help glancing at them, was shocked by the sums involved. And that they were all apparently final demands.

'So what's this one?'

'That's a Kline. Yes. In his work the canvas itself is as important as the brushstrokes.'

'Guess that's one way to save on paint. Looks like a kid could do it.'

'It's worth probably several thousand pounds.'

'Several thousand? Dee Dee? You reckon we could start doing these from home? Give you a little hobby?'

Dee Dee burst into peals of noisy laughter.

'Seriously, Mr Armand. This stuff is worth that kind of money? For that?'

'Art, like all things, is worth what anyone is prepared to pay for it.'

'Amen to that.'

Lottie emerged with the tray. Adeline had stood, and was looking out through one of the huge windows. Outside, the blustery winds had taken on a new force, and bent the grasses and shrubs low in shivering supplication. Below the house, along the beach, Lottie could just make out several tiny figures, battling their way back up the sea path, having finally conceded defeat to the worsening weather.

'Tea, anyone?' she said.

'I'll do it, Lottie dear,' said Adeline, signalling Lottie's release from domestic duties. Lottie, unsure now what to do with herself, chose to stay standing beside the table. Celia and Guy stood awkwardly by the door, until Mr Bancroft scolded his son and told him to sit down and stop looking like he had a broom up his arse. At this Celia had smothered a snort, and Lottie, whose own increasing feelings of doom had been briefly lifted, found again that she dared not look at Mrs Holden's face.

'Have you lived here long, Mrs Armand?' said Dee Dee who, with her husband, seemed unaffected by the various odd behaviours of her hosts.

'Since just before the summer.'

'And where did you live before that?'

'In London. Central London. Just behind Sloane Square.'

'Oh, really, where? I have a friend in Cliveden Place.'

'Cadogan Gardens,' said Adeline. 'It was a rather nice house.'

'So why did you choose to come all the way out here?'

'Come, come,' Julian interrupted. 'The Bancrofts do not want to hear about our very boring domestic history. Now, Mr Bancroft, or Guy, if I may, tell me more about your business. From where did you first have the idea of importing these fruits?'

Lottie watched Adeline, who had closed her mouth and cleared her face of all emotion. She could do that if displeased: she took on the appearance of a little Oriental mask – exquisite, apparently benign in appearance, yet revealing nothing.

Why wouldn't he let her speak? thought Lottie, and felt a sense of foreboding that had nothing to do with the worsening weather. The huge windows revealed it to them in advance; showed them the full magnificence of the darkening sky as the leaden clouds edged across the far horizon. Occasionally some empty paper bag or stray leaf whipped into view and out again. Upstairs the door slammed repetitively and arrhythmically, setting Lottie's teeth on edge. The music had long come to a halt.

And still Julian and Mr Bancroft kept talking.

'So how long will you be staying at the Riviera, Guy? Long enough for me to gather together some works that I think you *will* like?'

'Well, I was planning to head back home in a day or two. But Dee Dee is always on at me to have a little break with her, so we thought we might extend our visit to the Holdens here, and perhaps go a way down the coast. Maybe even nip across to France.'

'I've never seen Paris,' said Dee Dee.

'You're a great fan of Paris, aren't you, Celia?' George, stretched out in the rocking chair, was grinning at her.

'What?'

'You're a great fan of Paris. Paris, France, that is.'

He knows, thought Lottie. He knew all along.

'Yes. Yes, Paris—' said Celia, colouring.

'Wonderful to travel in one's youth.' George lit up another cigarette and exhaled lazily. 'Not many young people seem to get the advantages.'

He was doing it deliberately. Lottie watched Celia begin to stammer a response, and, unable to bear her discomfort, leaped in. 'Guy here has done more travelling than anyone I know, haven't you, Guy? He's told us he's lived absolutely everywhere. The Caribbean, Guatemala, Honduras. Places I'd never even heard of. It's all been terribly exciting, listening to him. He conjures up such wonderful pictures . . . the people and everything. The places . . .' Lottie, aware that she was gabbling, tailed off.

'Yes. Yes, he does,' said Celia, gratefully. 'Lots and I have been simply spellbound. And Mummy and Daddy. I think he must have given the entire family the travel bug.'

'And you, Mrs Armand,' said Dee Dee, 'you have a slight accent. Where's it from?'

The door that had been banging upstairs suddenly slammed

unquestionably louder. Lottie jumped and the party looked up. Frances stood in the doorway. She was wearing a long velvet coat and a striped scarf, and her face was as white as the walls. She stood very still, as if she had not expected the room to be populated. Then she faced Adeline, and it was to her that she spoke. 'Do excuse me,' she said. 'I was just leaving.'

'Frances—' Adeline rose, and reached out a hand. 'Please—'

'Don't. Just don't. George, would you be kind enough to drive me to the station?'

George stubbed out his cigarette and pushed himself out of the chair. 'Whatever you say, dearest . . .'

'Sit down, George.' It was Adeline. Some colour had returned to her cheeks, and she bade him down again in a manner that was almost imperious.

'Adeline—'

'Frances, you cannot leave like this.'

Frances was clutching her holdall so tightly that all the blood had drained from her knuckles. 'George, please—'

The room had fallen silent.

George, his customary smirk temporarily wiped from his face, looked at each of the women, and then at Julian. He shrugged, and then rose slowly.

Lottie became aware of the people around them. Mrs Holden and Dee Dee, seated next to each other and clutching their cups of tea, were both transfixed, so much so that Mrs Holden wasn't even *trying* to pretend not to listen. Mr Bancroft, frowning, was swiftly set upon by Julian who, with an exclamation that he particularly wanted him to see something in the study, bore him away from the scene. Celia and Guy sat by the door, their gestures and blank faces unconsciously mirroring each other. Only Stephen seemed truly oblivious, still reading his newspaper. It was, Lottie noticed, almost a week out of date.

'Please come, George. I would like to catch the quarter past, if possible.'

Adeline's voice rose to an uncomfortable pitch. 'No! Frances, you cannot leave like this! This is ridiculous! Ridiculous!'

'Oh, ridiculous, is it? Everything is ridiculous to you, Adeline. Everything that is honest, and real, and true. It is ridiculous because it makes you uncomfortable.'

'That is not true!'

'You are pitiful, you know? You think you are brave and original. But you are just an artifice. An artifice created from flesh.' Frances was wrestling against tears, her long features screwed up in childlike frustration.

'Well.' Mrs Holden had stood up to leave. 'I think we should perhaps . . .' She glanced around and saw that the only route out of the room was blocked by George and the two women. 'It seems we . . .'

'I have told you a thousand times, Frances . . . you ask too much . . . I cannot . . .' Adeline's voice broke.

George, between the two women, lowered his head.

'No. I know you cannot. And that is why I am leaving.' Frances turned, and Adeline reached after her, her face twisted in anguish. George caught her as she missed and placed an arm around her. It was impossible to tell whether it was comforting or restraining.

'I am sorry, Frances!' Adeline shouted after her. 'I am truly *sorry! Please* . . .'

Lottie felt her stomach clench. The world felt out of control, as if all its natural limits had been dissolved. The sound of the door, still banging irregularly, seemed to grow in volume, until all she could hear was Adeline's irregular breaths, and the bang, crash of wood against frame.

Suddenly, Guy was in the middle of the room. 'Let's step

145

outside. Has anyone seen the mural? It's finished, apparently. I'd love to see it finished. Mother? Will you have a look with me? Mrs Holden?'

Dee Dee leaped to her feet, placing a hand on Mrs Holden's shoulder. 'That's a wonderful idea, darling. What a very good idea. I'm sure we'd love to see the mural, wouldn't we, Susan?'

'Yes, yes,' said Mrs Holden gratefully. 'The mural.'

Lottie and Celia brought up the rear, the shock of the previous scene briefly reuniting them. Unable to speak, they raised eyebrows at each other, and shook their heads, their hair starfishing as they stepped outside into the high winds.

'What *was* that?' whispered Celia, leaning right in to Lottie to ensure that she was heard.

'No idea,' said Lottie.

'Goodness only knows what Guy's parents must have thought. I can't believe it, Lots. Two grown women wailing away in broad daylight.'

Lottie felt chilled. Down below them the sea whipped and frothed in a furious frenzy, the mild breezes of summer seemingly forgotten within hours. There would be a storm tonight, without question. 'We should go,' she said, feeling the first spit of rain on her face. But Celia didn't seem to hear. She was walking over to where Guy was standing with the two women, gazing at Frances's handiwork. They were gazing intently at a central figure, exclaiming in lowered voices.

Oh, God, it's Julian, Lottie thought. She'll have done something awful to him.

But it was not Julian they were staring at.

'How fascinating,' said Dee Dee, shouting to be heard above the wind. 'It's definitely her. You can see from the hair.'

'What? Who?' said Celia, pulling her skirt round her legs.

'It's Laodamia. Laodamia. Oh, you know me and my Greek myths, Guy. We don't get a lot of good literature out where we are,' she explained to Mrs Holden, 'so I got kind of interested in the Greeks. Amazing stories, they have.'

'Yes. Yes, we have studied a little Homer at our salon,' said Mrs Holden.

'The painter. He's done her as—'

'She, Mother. It was done by the woman who – the one who's leaving.'

'Ah. Well. Kind of odd, then. But she's painted Mrs Armand as one of the women of Troy. Laodamia was obsessed with a wax image of her missing husband – what was his name? Ah, yes, that was it – Protesilaus. Look, see, she's done his image here.'

Lottie stared. Adeline, apparently oblivious to the people around her, gazed at the crude wax dummy, enraptured.

'Not bad, Mrs Bancroft. Not bad at all. Not the most obvious of references, I would have thought.' George had appeared behind them, a refreshed glass of wine in one hand, his hair blowing upright, as if in shock. 'Adeline as Laodamia indeed. "*Crede mihi, plus est, quam quod videatur, imago.*"' He paused, possibly for effect. '"Believe me, the image is more than it may seem."'

'But Mrs Armand's husband is here . . .' Mrs Holden squinted at the paint, pulling her handbag ever closer to her. 'Julian Armand is here.' She turned to face Dee Dee.

George looked at the image, and turned away. 'They are married, yes,' he said, and wandered back inside, swaying slightly as he went.

Dee Dee raised an eyebrow at Mrs Holden. 'Guy Junior did warn us about these artistic types . . .' She peered back through the terrace doors, holding a hand to her hair as if it might fly away. 'Do you think it's safe for us to go back in now?'

They turned to leave. Celia, who had come out in the thinnest of cardigans, was hugging her arms and stamping impatiently by the door. 'This rain is cold. Really cold. And I haven't brought a coat.'

'None of us has, dear. Come on, Dee Dee. Let's see what they've done with your husband.'

Only Lottie stood still, staring at the mural, hiding the sudden trembling of her hands by ramming them deep into her pockets.

Guy stood several feet away. As she tore her eyes away from the images, she realised that, from the angle at which he was standing, he must have seen it too. On the far left, slightly set apart from the fourteen or so other characters, perhaps a little unfinished in terms of brushstroke and tone. A girl in a long, emerald dress, with rosebuds in her hair. She was leaning in, her expression full of secrets, accepting an apple from a man with the sun on his back.

Lottie looked at the image, then back at Guy.

At the sudden lack of colour in his face.

Lottie had raced home ahead of the others, ostensibly to help Virginia to get the food ready but in fact because she had been overcome by an unstoppable urge to escape. She could no longer force polite conversation; could no longer look at Celia while shielding the raw envy in her eyes; could no longer be near him. Hear him. See him. She had run all the way home, her chest tearing, the air ripping at her lungs, her breathing filling her ears; oblivious to the cold and wind and the wet on her face and the fact that her plait had come out and her hair had snarled into salted strings.

It cannot be borne, she told herself. It just cannot be borne.

She was upstairs, safely running Freddie and Sylvia's bath, when they came in. She heard Vrginia, who had been pleased to be relieved of this particular duty, taking coats, and Mrs Holden exclaiming that she had never been so embarrassed in all her life. Dee Dee was laughing: they had apparently bonded over the strangeness of Arcadia's inhabitants. As the steam rose from the bath, filling the room, Lottie dropped her head into her hands. She felt feverish, her throat dry. Perhaps I am dying, she thought, melodramatically. Perhaps dying would be easier than this.

'Can I bring my cow into the bath?'

Freddie appeared at the bathroom door, already naked and clutching a farmyard toy. His arms were streaked with dirt and dried blood from the dead fox.

Lottie nodded. She was too tired to fight.

'I need a wee-wee. Sylvia says she's not having a bath tonight.'

'Yes, she is,' said Lottie, wearily. '*Sylvia, get in here, please.*'

'I can't reach my flannel. Will you reach me the flannel?'

She would have to leave. She had always known she couldn't stay here for ever; but Guy's presence had brought an urgency to it. For there was no way she could stay here once they were married: they would visit incessantly, and it was too great a cruelty to have to watch them together. As it was, she was going to have to find an extremely good reason to avoid the wedding.

Oh, God, the wedding.

'I need a clean flannel. This one smells.'

'Oh, Freddie . . .'

'It does. Smell. Ow. That water's too hot. Look, my

cow's dead now. You made the water too hot and now my cow's dead.'

'*Sylvia.*' Lottie began to run cold water into the bath.

'Can I wash my own hair? Virginia lets me wash my own hair.'

'No, she doesn't. *Sylvia.*'

'Do I look pretty?' Sylvia had been in Mrs Holden's makeup bag. Her cheeks were heavily rouged, as if she were recovering from some medieval illness, while two blocks of blue shimmer cascaded down over her eyes.

'Oh, my goodness! Your mother is going to tan you. You get that off this instant.'

Sylvia folded her arms. 'But I like it.'

'Do you want your mother to lock you in your room tomorrow? Because I promise you, Sylvia, if she gets one look at you that's what she's going to do.' Lottie was having trouble keeping her temper.

Sylvia's face contorted, and she lifted one lipsticked hand to her face. 'But I want . . .'

'Can I come in?'

Lottie, who was wresting off Sylvia's shoes, looked up and felt her face prickle. He was stooped in the doorway, half hesitant, as if he weren't sure whether to approach. Above the steam and soap, she could smell the clean, cold salt air on him.

'I killed a bear today, Guy. Look! Look at all the blood!'

'Lottie, I – I needed to see you.'

'I wrestled it with my bare hands. I was protecting my cow, you see. Have you seen my cow?'

'Guy, do you think I look pretty?'

Lottie didn't dare move. If she did, she thought she might crack and splinter and all the bits would crumble into nothing.

She was so hot.

'It's Frances,' he said, and her heart, which had briefly allowed itself to quiver, sank. He had come to inform her of some domestic row downstairs. Perhaps he was going to pick Frances up from the station. Perhaps Mr Bancroft was going to buy some of Frances's work.

She looked down at her hands, which were almost imperceptibly trembling. 'Oh,' she said.

'I've got lipstick on. Look! Guy, look!'

'Yes,' he said, distractedly. 'Marvellous cow, Freddie. Really.'

He seemed unwilling to walk into the room. Looked up at the ceiling, and down, as if struggling with something. There was a long pause, during which Sylvia, unnoticed, wiped the makeup from her face with Mrs Holden's good flannel.

'Oh, this is impossible. Look, I wanted to tell you . . .' he rubbed at his hair '. . . that she got it right. On the picture. The mural, I mean.'

Lottie looked up at him.

'Frances saw it. She saw it before I did.'

'Saw what?' Freddie had dropped his cow out of the bath, and was bending perilously over the side.

'I think I'm probably the last to see it.' He was agitated, cast exasperated looks at the two children. 'But she's right, isn't she?'

Lottie ceased to feel hot; could no longer feel the tremor in her hands. She exhaled, a long, shaking breath. Then she smiled, a slow, sweet smile, allowing herself for the first time the luxury of looking at him without fear of what he might see.

'Tell me she's right, Lottie.' His voice, a whisper, sounded curiously apologetic.

Lottie passed Freddie a clean flannel. Tried to convey a world in the slightest of glances. 'I saw it long before the picture,' she said.

Seven

There was, if Mrs Holden said so herself, a definite glow to her cheeks that morning. She might even, she thought, leaning forward as she applied a little mascara (but not too much, it was the Sunday service), allow a suggestion that she looked just a little younger than usual. Her brow looked a little less crumpled; there were perhaps fewer anxiety lines around the eyes. This rejuvenation was partly, it had to be said, down to the success of the Bancrofts' visit. Despite that mortifying argument between the actress and her friend, Dee Dee (extraordinary names, these Americans gave themselves) had thought it all highly amusing, as if it were some touristic attraction they had laid on especially for their visit. Guy Senior had professed himself more than pleased by the paintings he had bought from Mr Armand. They should prove a nice little investment, he said after supper, as he packed them carefully into the car. He had decided he quite liked all that modern stuff. Privately, Mrs Holden would have died rather than have any of those on her drawing-room wall: they looked like something Mr Beans had brought up. But Dee Dee had simply grinned at her in an 'all-girls-together' kind of way and said, 'Whatever keeps you happy, Guyhoney,' and then they had gone, with promises of more fruit and further visits before the wedding.

And there was Celia: she seemed a little less up and down than she had been of late. She was making a bit more of an effort with herself. Mrs Holden had wondered (aloud) whether Celia had neglected Guy a little; perhaps got a bit carried away with the wedding and forgotten about the groom (she had suffered the tiniest pang of guilt that she might have been a contributing factor: one couldn't help getting terribly involved in planning a wedding). But Guy had been a little more solicitous to her daughter, and Celia, in return, was patently doing her very best to look gorgeous and be flirtatious and interesting. Mrs Holden, just to be on the safe side, had given Celia some women's magazines that stressed the importance of remaining interesting to your husband . . . and other things that Mrs Holden still felt a little uncomfortable discussing with her daughter.

She felt better equipped than normal to dish out marital advice: for the past few days Henry Holden had been quite uncharacteristically nice to his wife. He had come home from work on time two days running, had somehow managed not to be called out on any late-night visits. He had offered to take the whole family out to lunch at the Riviera, as an apology for not having been present for most of the Bancrofts' visit. Most importantly, the previous night (here she felt herself pink slightly) he had even made a visit to her bed: the first time he had done so since Celia returned from London, some six weeks previously. He wasn't one of those romantic types, Henry. But it was lovely to get the attention.

Mrs Holden glanced backwards at the pair of single divans, their unruffled candlewick spreads casting discreet canopies over the night's secrets. Dearest Henry. And now that horrid red-headed girl was gone.

Almost unconsciously, she put down her lipstick and lightly tapped the walnut-veneer surface of her dressing-table. Yes, things were going very nicely at the moment.

Upstairs, Lottie lay on her own single bed, listening to Celia and the children downstairs gathering coats in preparation for the walk to church. In Freddie's case, this involved several exclamations and muttered threats, followed by loud protestations of innocence and an eventual slamming of doors. Finally, accompanied by the exasperated cries of his mother, the closing of the front door signified that, apart from Lottie, the house was empty. She lay very still, listening to it stir, hearing the underlying noises more often drowned by the shrieking of children: the tick of the clock in the hall, the gentle, intestinal rumble and hiss of the hot-water system, the distant clunk of car doors shut outside. She lay, feeling these noises seep into her hot head, and wished that she could enjoy this all too rare moment of solitude.

Lottie had been ill for almost a week; she could time it exactly, to the day after the Great Admission, or The Last Day She Had Seen Him, these both being of such momentousness that they required capital letters. The night after Guy had revealed his feelings for her, she had lain awake through the small hours, burning and feverish, her limbs twitching and restless. At first she had thought her delirious, chaotic thoughts were due to her own terrible guilt. But in the morning, examining her throat, Dr Holden had put it down less biblically to a chill and prescribed a week's bed-rest and as many fluids as she could manage.

Celia, while sympathetic, had moved out and into Sylvia's room immediately ('Sorry, Lots, but there's no way I'm getting ill with the whole wedding thing to sort out') and Lottie had been left alone, with only Virginia's regular – and, it had to be said, rather bad-tempered – trays of soup and juice and Freddie's occasional checks 'to see if she's dead yet'.

At times, Lottie had wished she were dead. She had heard herself murmuring at night, terrified in her delirium that she would give herself away. She could not bear that, having finally echoed her own feelings, Guy was now as effectively banished from her as if she had been Rapunzel in a tower with a new haircut. For while normally they might find a dozen reasons to bump into each other around the house, or while out walking the dog, there was no earthly reason why a young man engaged to the young lady of the house should be seen to enter another's bedroom.

After two days, unable to bear his absence any longer, she had made herself go downstairs for water, just to catch a glimpse of him. But she had almost collapsed in the corridor, and Mrs Holden and Virginia, with much grunting and scolding, had carried her back up, a pale arm slung weakly over each of their shoulders. She had only a split second in which to catch his eye, but knew from even that brief look that there was an understanding between them, and that had fuelled her faith for another long day and night.

She had felt his presence: he had brought South African grapes for her, their sweet, taut skins bursting with flavour. He had sent up Spanish lemons to add to boiled water and honey to help her throat, and bruised, fleshy figs to persuade her to eat. Mrs Holden had remarked in admiring tones on the generosity of his family – and, no doubt, kept a few for herself.

But it was not enough. And, like someone dying of thirst and offered a thimbleful of water, Lottie soon decided these small tastes of him made things worse. For now she tortured herself, imagining him, in her absence, rediscovering the many fragrant charms of Celia. How could he not when Celia spent her whole time thinking up ways of winning him over? 'What do you think of this dress, Lots?' she would say, parading a new frock up and down the bedroom. 'Think it makes my bust look bigger?' And Lottie would smile weakly, and excuse herself, on the grounds that she thought she might need a sleep.

The door downstairs opened again. Lottie lay awake, listening to the sound of footsteps ascending the stairs.

Mrs Holden stood at the door. 'Lottie dear, I forgot to tell you – I've left some sandwiches for you in the fridge as we'll probably go straight from church to the hotel for lunch. You've got egg and cress, and a couple of ham, and there's a jug of lemon barley. Henry says you should try to drink it all today – you're still not drinking enough.'

Lottie mustered a grateful smile.

Mrs Holden pulled on her gloves, looking past Lottie at the bed, as if considering something. Then, unsolicited, she walked briskly over and pulled the blankets across, folding them tightly under the mattress. That done, she reached up and felt Lottie's head. 'You're still a little warm,' she said. 'You poor old thing. You've really had a rough time of it this week, haven't you?'

Lottie had not often heard that softness in her voice. When Mrs Holden, having smoothed back Lottie's unwashed hair, then squeezed her hand, she found herself squeezing back.

'Will you be all right by yourself?'

'Fine, thank you,' croaked Lottie. 'Think I'll probably sleep.'

'Good idea.' Mrs Holden turned to leave the room, patting her own hair as she did so. 'I imagine we'll be back by around two. We'll eat early because of the children. Goodness knows how Freddie is going to behave himself seated at a good restaurant. I should imagine I'll be hanging my head in shame before the dessert trolley makes it round . . .' She checked inside her handbag. 'There's two aspirin on the side. Now, don't forget what Henry said, dear. Keep your fluids up.'

Lottie was already feeling the pull of sleep.

The door closed with a gentle click.

She might have been asleep for minutes or hours, but Lottie found that the tapping noise had somehow segued itself from dream into wakefulness, and that as she stared at the door, it was becoming more persistent. More insistent.

'Lottie?'

She must be delirious again. Like the time she had become convinced that all the window-sills were populated by brown trout.

Lottie closed her eyes. Her head felt so hot.

'Can I come in?'

She opened them again. And he was there, glancing behind him as he entered, his blue shirt spattered with tiny spots of rain. Outside, she heard the distant rumble of thunder. The room had dimmed, the daylight smudged and darkened by rainclouds so that it could have been dusk. She pushed herself upright, her face bleary with sleep, uncertain whether she was still dreaming. 'I thought you had gone to the station.' He had said he was going to pick up a crate of fruit.

'A lie, all I could think of.'

The room kept darkening by degrees so that she could hardly see his face. Only his eyes shone out, staring at her with such a burning intensity that she could only think he must be ill, like herself. She closed hers, briefly, to see if he would still be there when she opened them again.

'It's too hard, Lottie. I feel . . . I feel like I'm going insane.'

The joy. The joy that he was. She laid her head back on her pillow, reached out an arm. It glowed white in the half-light.

'Lottie . . .'

'Come here.'

He sprang across the room, kneeling on the floor beside her, and laid his head on her chest. She felt the weight of it on her damp nightdress, lifted a hand and allowed herself to touch his hair. It was softer than she'd expected; softer than Freddie's. 'You're filling up everything. I can't see straight.'

He lifted his head, so that she could see his eyes, amber even in the dim light. She couldn't think coherently: her mind was blurred, swimming. The weight of him held her down; she thought briefly that without it she might float upwards and out of the window into the dark, wet infinity.

'Oh, God, your clothes are soaked . . . you're ill. You're ill. Lottie, I'm sorry. I shouldn't—'

She reached up as he lifted himself away from her, pulled him back down. It didn't occur to her to find excuses for her appearance, her damp, unwashed hair, the musty bouquet of illness: her senses, her sensibility, had lost themselves to need. She held his face between her hands, his lips so close that she could feel his breath. Paused for a fraction of a second, conscious even in her inexperienced state that there was something more precious in the waiting, in the wanting. And then, with a moan of something like anguish, he was upon her; as sweet as forbidden fruit.

Richard Newsome was eating boiled sweets again: she could see him, bold as brass, not even attempting to hide the rustling of the papers as he popped them in, one after another, as if he were sitting in the back row of a cinema. It was disrespectful, and it was definitely lax on the part of his mother, who sat there beside him as if he were nothing to do with her. But then, as Sarah Chilton had often observed, all the Newsomes were like that: never

159

ones to worry about form, or decorum, as long as they were all right.

Mrs Holden shot him a dark look during Psalm 109 but he paid no attention whatsoever. Just methodically unwrapped a purple one, gazed at it with the unconcerned absorption of a cow chewing cud and popped it in.

It was very vexing being so distracted by the Newsome boy and his sweet wrappers: she had particularly wanted to think about Lottie and what she was going to do with her after Celia's wedding. It really was a difficult one: the girl must know she couldn't stay with the Holdens indefinitely, that she would have to decide what she was going to do with her life. She would have suggested enrolling her on a secretarial course, but Lottie had been adamant that she didn't want to return to London. She had once suggested teaching – she was good with the children, after all – but Lottie had greeted this with a look of disgust, as if she had suggested she go and earn her living on the streets. Ideally it would be nice to get her married off: Joe was very sweet on her, according to Celia, but she was such a contrary little thing, it didn't surprise her that they had fallen out lately.

And Henry was no help: the few times she had mentioned her concerns to him, he had got irritated, and said the poor girl had enough to worry about, that she was no trouble, and that she would sort herself out with a proper job in her own time. Mrs Holden couldn't see quite what Lottie had to worry about – she hadn't had to worry about where her food or clothing was coming from for the best part of ten years – but she didn't like to argue with Henry (especially at the moment), so she let it go.

Of course she must stay with us as long as she wants, she had said to Deirdre Colquhoun. We love Lottie as if she were one of our own. Sometimes, such as when she had seen her lying vulnerable and ill on that child's bed, she genuinely thought she believed it. Lottie was much easier to love when she was vulnerable, when those hedgehog spikes dissolved in sweat and tears. But the smallest, most uncomfortable part of Susan Holden told her that this was not true.

She nudged Henry as the collection bag began heading down the row towards them. With a sigh, he reached into his inside pocket, pulled out an unidentified note and put it in. Susan Holden, her new handbag held prominently in front of her, took it from him and passed it on, satisfied that they had been seen to do the right thing.

'Joe? Hey, Joe.' Celia grabbed Joe's arm as he headed out of the church doors and under the brightening sky, where strong breezes blew the last blustering stormclouds off on to the horizon. The pavements were slick with rain, and she cursed under her breath as an unseen puddle sent a splash of dirty water up her shin.

Joe turned, startled at the physical nature of Celia's greeting. He was wearing a pale blue shirt and sleeveless pullover and his hair, usually scuffed with engine oil, had been slicked down in a suitably reverent manner. 'Oh. Hello, Celia.'

'Seen Lottie?'

'You know I haven't.'

'She's not been well.' She fell into step beside him, mindful of her mother's gaze from the gate of the churchyard. It would be nice to get them back together, she had said. Lottie was going to be terribly lonely, after all, with Celia gone.

'Really ill. I mean, with fevers and everything. Seeing things coming out of the walls, she was.'

That stopped him. 'What's wrong?' he said.

'Bad chill, Daddy says. Really bad one. I mean, she might have died.'

The colour drained from Joe's face. He stopped and faced her. 'Died?'

'Well, I mean, she's on the mend now but, yes, it was all very dramatic. Daddy's been terribly worried about her. It's so sad . . .' Celia let her voice fall theatrically.

Joe waited. 'What is?' he said eventually.

'This falling out. With you. And her calling out and all . . .' She stopped abruptly, as if she'd said too much.

Joe frowned. 'Calling out what?'

'Oh, nothing, Joe. Forget I said anything.'

'Come on, Celia. What were you going to say?'

'I can't, Joe. It's disloyal.'

'How is it disloyal if we're both her friends?'

Celia cocked her head to one side, considering. 'Okay. But you mustn't tell her I told you. She's been calling out your name. I mean, when she was at her worst. There I was, mopping her brow, and she would murmur, "Joe . . . oh, Joe . . ." And I couldn't comfort her or anything. Because you and she had fallen out.'

Joe looked at her suspiciously. 'She was calling my name?'

'Endlessly. Well, quite often. When she was really ill.'

There was a long silence.

'You wouldn't . . . you wouldn't be telling lies or anything, would you?'

Celia's eyes flashed, she folded her arms, affronted. 'About my own sister? Or as good as? Joe Bernard, that's the meanest thing I ever heard you say. I tell you, poor old Lottie's been crying out for you and you tell me I must be telling lies. Well, I'm only sorry I said anything at all.' She turned on her stiletto heel and began to walk briskly away from him.

Now it was Joe's turn to grab at her arm. 'Celia. Celia, I'm sorry. Please stop.' He was breathless. 'I suppose it's just a bit hard for me to believe, Lottie calling out and all . . . but

if she's really ill, then that's awful. I'm sorry I wasn't there.'
He looked downcast.

'I haven't told her, you know.' Celia looked levelly at
him.

'Told her what?'

'That you've been stepping out with Virginia.'

Joe blushed. It crept up from his neck as if he were a pink
sponge soaking up water.

'You couldn't expect it to stay secret for long, could you?
She works at our house, after all.'

Joe looked down, kicked at the kerbside. 'It's not as if we're
stepping out properly. I mean, we've just been to a couple of
dances. There's . . . I mean, it's not serious or anything.'

Celia said nothing.

'It's not like Lottie. I mean, if I only thought I had a chance
with Lottie . . .' He tailed off, bit his lip and looked away.

Celia placed a friendly hand on his arm. 'Well, Joe, I've
known her longer than anyone, and all I can say is she's a
funny one, our Lots. Sometimes she doesn't know what she
wants. But I do know that when she spoke from her heart,
when she was genuinely at death's door, it was you she was
calling out for. So. There. It's up to you what you want to
do now.'

Joe was evidently thinking very hard. His breathing had
quickened with the effort. 'Should I come and see her, do
you think?' He looked painfully hopeful.

'Do I? I think she'd love it.'

'When shall I come?'

Celia glanced over at her mother, who was tapping her
watch. 'Look. No time like the present. Let me run over
and tell Mummy I'll be a bit late to the hotel, and then
I'll walk you over there. I'd let you go on your own,' she
explained, laughing, as she half ran, half skipped towards

her mother, 'but I don't think Lottie would appreciate me letting you catch her in her nightdress.'

Lottie's arm was nearly dead. She didn't care: she would have let it fall off rather than unwrap him from around her, move his peaceful, peach-skinned face from its repose, alter the invisible path of his breath from her own. She gazed at his closed eyes as they rested in a brief sleep, at the faint sheen of sweat drying on his skin, and thought she had never felt as truly rested as she did now. It was as if there were no tensions left to feel: she was butter, melted, sweetened.

He shifted in his sleep, and she tilted her head so that she could place a soft kiss on his forehead. He answered with a murmur, and Lottie felt her heart clench with gratitude. Thank you, she told her deity. Thank you for giving this to me. If I died now I would only be grateful.

She felt clear-headed now; her fever had evaporated as rapidly as her own unfulfilled longing. Or perhaps he has cured me, she wondered. Perhaps I was dying for lack of him. She half laughed, silently. Love has made me fanciful and stupid, she thought. But she was not sorry. She was not sorry.

She looked up and away from him. Outside the rain spat meanly on the window, the wind sporadically rattling the panes where Mrs Holden had forgotten to wedge in pieces of felt. They were governed by the weather, here, on the coast. It made all the difference to a day, to its mood, to its possibilities; for the holidaymakers it made and broke dreams. Now Lottie gazed at it with indifference. What could matter now? The earth could crack open and volcanic fire spew forth. She wouldn't care, as long as she could feel his warm limbs around her, as long as she could feel his mouth on her own, the strange, desperate conjoining of their two bodies. Sensations never hinted at by what little Mrs Holden had told them of married love.

I love you, she told him silently. I will only ever love you. And as the rain fell, her eyes filled with tears.

He stirred, and opened his eyes. For a fraction of a second, they were blank, uncomprehending, and then they wrinkled, became warm with remembrance.

'Hello.'

'Hello, you.' He focused, looked more closely. 'Are you crying?'

Lottie shook her head, smiling.

'Come here.' He pulled her to him, and blessed her neck with kisses. She surrendered herself to the sensation, feeling her heart flicker inside her chest. 'Oh, Lottie . . .'

She shushed him with a finger. Met his eyes, as if she could soak him up with looking. She didn't want words: she wanted to absorb him into her bones, to take him under her skin. Some time later he rested his head in the curve of her neck. They lay there in silence, listening to the distant rolling timpani of the wind and departing thunder.

'It's raining.'

'It's been raining for ages.'

'Did I fall asleep?'

'It's all right, it's still early.'

He paused. 'Sorry.'

'For what?' She ran her hand down the side of his face and he clenched his jaw so that she could feel it move.

'You were meant to be ill. And I assaulted you.'

She felt herself giggle. 'Some assault.'

'You're all right, though . . . I mean, I didn't hurt you or anything.'

She closed her eyes. 'Oh, no.'

'Are you still ill? You feel cool.'

'I feel fine.' She turned to face him. 'Actually, I feel better.'

He grinned. 'So that's what you needed. Nothing to do with chills at all.'

'Wonderful cure.'

'My blood is singing. Do you think we should tell Dr Holden?'

Lottie laughed. It came out like a great hiccup, as if it had been waiting, too close to the surface. 'Oh, I think Dr Holden has his own particular version of that cure.'

Guy raised an eyebrow. 'Really? Dr Perfect Husband Holden?'

Lottie nodded.

'Really truly?' Guy looked over at the window. 'Gosh. Poor Mrs H.'

The mention of her name silenced them both. Lottie finally adjusted her arm, feeling the fractious invasion of pins and needles creep upwards. Guy moved his head accommodatingly, and they stared at the ceiling.

'What will we do, Lottie?'

It was the question that had swallowed her up whole. And only he held the answer.

'We can't go back, can we?' He sought her reassurance.

'I can't. How could I?'

He raised himself up on an elbow, rubbed at his eyes. His hair stuck up on one side. 'No . . . It's a mess, though.'

Lottie bit her lip.

'I'll have to tell her sooner rather than later.'

Lottie exhaled. She had needed to hear it, had needed him to say it unprompted. Then she thought of the implications of what he had said, and felt her stomach constrict. 'It's going to be awful,' she said, shivering. 'Really awful.' She sat up. 'I'll have to leave too.'

'What?'

'Well, there's no way I can stay, is there? I don't think Celia's exactly going to want me around.'

'No, I suppose not. Where would you go?'

She looked at him. 'I don't know. I hadn't thought about it.'

'Well, you'll have to come with me. We'll go back to my parents'.'

'But they'll hate me.'

'No, they won't. It'll take a bit of getting used to, and then they'll love you.'

'I don't even know where they live. I don't even know where you live. I know so little.'

'We know enough.' He placed his hands around her face. 'Dearest, dearest Lottie. There is absolutely nothing more I need to know about you. Other than that you were meant for me. We fit, don't we? Like gloves.'

She felt the tears come again. Glanced down, almost afraid to look at him with the magnitude of what she was feeling.

'Are you all right?'

She nodded again.

'Do you want a handkerchief?'

'Actually, I want a drink. Mrs Holden made a jug of lemon downstairs. I'll go and get it.' She slid her feet on to the floor, reached for her nightdress.

'You stay there. I'll get it.' He padded around the room, reaching for his clothes. Lottie watched him as he moved, unselfconsciously, marvelling at the beauty of him, of the way his muscles moved under his skin. 'Don't move,' he instructed. And then, pulling his shirt over his head, he was gone.

Lottie lay, smelling the sea-salt scent of him on her damp

nightdress, listening to the distant sound of the fridge opening downstairs, and the clinking of glasses and ice-cubes. How many times could you listen to the sound of the one you loved moving around before you became inured to it by familiarity? Before it stopped catching in your throat, lodging briefly in your heart?

She heard the sound of his footfall on the stairs, and then a pause as he adjusted himself so that he could push open the door with his hip. 'I'm back,' he said, smiling. 'I was just imagining doing this for you in the Caribbean. We squeezed our juice fresh out there. Straight off the—'

And froze, as they heard the sound of a key in the door.

They glanced at each other in horror, and then, galvanised, Guy leaped for his shoes, pulling them on to his feet and stuffing his socks into his pockets. Lottie, stricken, could only pull the covers around her.

'Hello? Lots?'

The sound of the front door closing, of feet coming up the stairs, more than one set.

Guy, flushing, reached for the tray.

'Are you decent?' Celia's voice, a sing-song, was light, mocking.

'Celia?' It came out as a croak.

'I've got a visit—' Celia's smile slid as she opened the door. She stared, bemused, at the two of them. 'What are you doing in here?'

Oh, God, it was Joe behind her. She could just make out his head as it dipped in embarrassment.

Guy thrust the tray at Celia. 'I was just bringing Lottie a drink. You can take over, now you're here. Never was much good at being nursemaid.'

Celia looked down at the tray. At the two glasses. 'I brought

Joe,' Celia said, still unbalanced. 'To see Lottie.' Behind her, Joe coughed into his hand.

'How – how lovely,' said Lottie. 'But I'm not – I really need to freshen up.'

'I'll go—' said Joe.

'You don't have to go, Joe,' Lottie called. 'I – I just need to freshen up a bit.'

'No. Really. I don't want to be any trouble. I'll come back when you're up.'

'Erm . . . I'd like that, Joe.'

Celia placed the tray carefully on Lottie's bedside table. Then she looked sideways at Guy. She smoothed her hair, an unconscious gesture. 'You look very flushed.'

Guy raised a hand to his cheek, as if surprised. He went to speak, then changed his mind and mutely shook his head.

There was a long, awkward silence, during which Lottie found herself pulling the covers further and further towards her chin.

'I suppose we'd better leave you in peace,' said Celia, opening the door for Guy to exit. Her voice was low, halting. She didn't look at Lottie when she said it. 'You sure you don't want to stay, Joe?'

Lottie heard his muffled affirmation. He would be talking into his chin.

Guy walked out past her. His shirt, Lottie noted anxiously, was untucked at the back.

''Bye Lottie. Hope you feel better soon.' It jarred, that false cheerfulness.

'Thank you. Thank you for the drink.'

Celia, holding the door for him, stopped and turned. 'Where's the fruit?'

'What?'

'The fruit. You were picking up some more fruit from the station. There's none in the hall. Where is it?'

Guy looked briefly blank, then raised his head in acknowledgement. 'Didn't arrive. I waited for over half an hour, and it wasn't on the train. It'll probably come on the two thirty.'

'I hear you've had a fresh coconut,' said Joe, stepping on his own feet at the top of the stairs. 'Strange-looking things, those coconuts. Like people's heads. But without the eyes . . . And things.'

Celia stood very still for a moment. Then, looking down, she walked past Guy and tripped down the stairs.

Almost forty-eight hours later, Lottie stood shivering in number eighty-seven beach hut, once, according to a fallen nameplate, known as Saranda. She pulled her coat round her, hauling Mr Beans's straining figure back on his lead. It was nearly dark and, without lighting, the hut was growing darker and even less welcoming.

She had been waiting there almost fifteen minutes. Several more and she would have to head back. Mrs Holden didn't like her going out at the moment as it was. She had felt her forehead twice before she grudgingly let her go. If she hadn't wanted fifteen minutes alone with Dr Holden Lottie didn't think she would have allowed her to go at all.

She heard the hissing of bicycle tyres along the pathway. The door opened, tentatively, and he was there, hurling himself off his bicycle, sending it crashing into the door. They embraced hurriedly, their mouths clashing awkwardly.

'I don't have long. Celia is stuck to me like glue. I only got out because she's in the bath.'

'Does she suspect?'

'I don't think so. She never said anything about – you

know.' He bent low and patted Mr Beans, who was sniffing at his feet. 'God, this is awful. I hate telling lies.' He pulled her to him, kissing the top of her head. She wrapped her arms around him, inhaling the scent of him, trying to imprint the feel of his hands on her waist. 'We don't even have to tell them. We could just go. Leave a letter.' He spoke into her hair, as if he wanted to breathe her in too.

'No. I can't do it like that. They've been good to me. The least I can do is explain.'

'I'm not sure you can explain.'

Lottie pulled back, looked up at him. 'They will understand, won't they, Guy? They'll have to. That we didn't mean them any harm? That it wasn't our fault? Because we couldn't help it, could we?' She began to cry.

'It's nobody's fault. Some things are just meant to be. You can't fight them.'

'I just hate the fact that our happiness is going to be built on such misery. Poor Celia. Poor, poor Celia.' (She could afford to be generous now that he was hers. The strength of her sympathy for Celia had shocked even her.) She wiped her nose with her sleeve.

'Celia will survive. She'll find someone else.' Lottie felt a faint pang at the matter-of-factness in his voice. 'Sometimes I thought it wasn't even me she was in love with, just the idea of being in love.'

Lottie stared at him.

'I just felt, sometimes, that it didn't particularly have to be *me*, you know?'

Lottie thought of George Bern. Then felt peculiarly disloyal. 'I'm sure she loves you,' she said, her voice small, reluctant.

'Let's not talk about it. Look, Lots, we have to make a plan. We have to work out when we're going to tell them. I can't keep lying to everyone – it's making me really uncomfortable.'

'Give me until the weekend. I'll see if Adeline will have me. Perhaps with Frances gone they'll need help with the housework. I wouldn't mind.'

'Really? I don't suppose it would be for long. I just need to sort things out with my parents.'

Lottie pressed her face into his chest. 'I wish it was done. I wish we were three months on already.' She closed her eyes. 'It feels like waiting for a death or something.'

Guy was glancing out of the doorway. 'We'd better head back. I'll go first.'

He bent his head and kissed her full on the lips. She kept her eyes open, not wanting to miss a moment. Behind him the lights of a ship winked their way across the harbour.

'Be brave, Lottie darling. It won't be like this for ever.'

And then, with a hand to her hair, he was out and pelting back up the dark path towards home.

Celia had moved back into her room. Lottie had groaned inwardly when she had seen Celia's nightdress lying across her bedspread. She had once been an extremely good fibber: now, with all her emotions as raw as if she had been turned inside out, she found she had become useless at it, a blushing, prevaricating incompetent.

She had stayed away from her as far as possible. This had been made easier by Celia's own propensity towards an almost frantic level of activity. If she wasn't out spending her father's money with an almost religious fervour ('Look! These shoes! I *had* to get these shoes!'), she was sorting out her belongings, casting aside anything deemed 'too young' or 'not London enough'. At dinner, safe in company, Lottie was able to retreat into herself, trying again to focus on her food, drawn only half-heartedly into conversation by Dr Holden, who seemed oddly distracted himself. Mrs Holden was determined to engage Guy, bombarding him with questions about his parents, and what their life abroad was like, smiling and fluttering at him as coquettishly as if she had been Celia herself. Lottie and Celia, to Lottie's relief, had collided only once, the previous evening, when Lottie had admired Celia's new feathered haircut, then pleaded that she, too, needed to retire for a long hot bath.

So it was with some shock that Lottie returned from her breathless, preoccupied walk with Mr Beans to find Celia lying on her bed, wrapped in a towel and apparently engrossed in a bridal magazine.

The bedroom seemed to have shrunk in size.

'Hello,' Lottie said, peeling off her shoes. 'I – I was just about to have a bath.'

'Mummy's in there,' said Celia, flicking a page. 'You'll have to wait a while. There won't be any more hot water.' Her legs were long and pale. She had rose-coloured varnish on her toenails.

'Oh.' Lottie sat with her shoes, her back to Celia, thinking furiously of places to go. Once, they had spent hours lying on their beds, stretching the most trivial subjects into hours of conversation. Now Lottie could not face the thought of being alone with Celia for minutes. Freddie and Sylvia had been put to bed. Dr Holden was unlikely to want to talk. I could go and ring Joe, she thought. I'll ask Dr Holden if I can use the telephone.

She heard the slick sound of the magazine flipping shut behind her, and Celia turning to face her. 'Actually, Lots, I need to talk to you.'

Lottie closed her eyes. Oh, God, please, no, she thought. 'Lots?'

173

She turned, forced a smile. Put her shoes carefully on the floor beside her bed. 'Yes?'

Celia was looking at her intently, her gaze unwavering. Her eyes, Lottie noticed, were an almost unnatural blue. 'This – this is a bit difficult.'

There was a brief silence, during which Lottie slid her hands surreptitiously under her seat. They had begun to shake. Please don't ask me, she begged silently. I won't be able to lie to you. Please, God, don't let her ask.

'What?'

'I don't really know how to say . . . look. What I'm about to say . . . must remain absolutely between me and you.'

Lottie's breath had lodged high in her chest. She thought, briefly, that she might pass out.

'What?' she whispered.

Celia's gaze was steady. Lottie found she couldn't tear her eyes away.

'I'm pregnant.'

Eight

Strictly speaking, it had been meant for emergencies; like the afternoon they pulled the missing five-year-old girl from the harbour round at Mer Point. Or when he had to deliver the kind of news that required a seat first; sometimes a stiff whisky helped them bear up a bit better. But Dr Holden, eyeing the bottle of fifteen-year-old malt in his top drawer, believed that there were days when a tipple or two could be considered, in all fairness, medicinal. Not just medicinal but necessary. Because if he allowed himself to think about it, his were not simply the reservations of a father sending his beloved daughter up the aisle. This sense of anxiety and impending desolation was about what he was being left with: a sterile, loveless marriage to a miserable, flapping wife. A life without even the diversion of Gillian, now she had headed off to Colchester. A little blunt, she had been, and she had never let him think he was anything more than a staging post on her unstoppable path, but she had been funny, and enjoyably undeferential, and she had had skin like the alabaster on those marble frescos, smooth, perfect, but warm. Oh, God, yes. Warm. And now she was gone. And Celia, the only other object of beauty in his life, was going. And what did he have to look forward to? Just a slow grind through middle age, with its endless trivial complaints, and its occasional afternoons at the golf-club bar, with Alderman Elliott and his like clapping him on the back and cheerfully informing him that his best years were far behind him.

Henry Holden reached for the little medicine measure on the shelf behind him, then sat and slowly poured himself a couple of fingers of whisky. It was only a little past ten in the morning, and the whisky's fiery path down felt abrasive, almost shocking. But even that small act of mutiny felt reassuring.

She would notice; of course she would. She would reach up to straighten his tie, or whatever else proprietorial fiddling she could think of, and then, catching his breath, she would step back and look at him, her expression registering just the faintest hint of distaste. But she wouldn't say anything. She would just put on that slightly hurt expression that he couldn't stomach, the one that told of crosses borne and endless days of martyrdom. And, without ever mentioning it directly, she would find some subtle way of letting him know that he had disappointed her, that he had let her down again.

He refilled his measure, and downed another two fingers. This time it was easy, and he savoured the afterburn around the inside of his mouth.

Masters of their domain, they called them. Kings of their own castles. What rot that all was. Susan Holden's wants and needs and miseries dominated their marriage as surely as if she had written them in ink and beaten them into him with a flaming cane. There was nothing that escaped her eye, nothing that prompted in her a sense of spontaneous happiness. Nothing that remained of the beautiful, carefree young solicitor's daughter that she had been when they met, with a waist he could fit his two hands round, and a glint in her eye that used to make his stomach turn over. No, that Susan had slowly been eaten by this miserable matron, this anxious, fretting thing whose only obsessions were how things appeared to be, not how they were.

Look at us! He wanted to scream at her sometimes. Look at what we've become! I don't want my slippers! I don't care if Virginia bought the wrong piece of fish! I want my old life back – a life where we could disappear for days on end, where we could make love until dawn, where we could talk, *really* talk, not just this endless prattling that passes in your world for conversation. He had been tempted, once or twice. But he knew that she wouldn't understand: she would just stare at him, wide-eyed in horror, and then, with a barely suppressed shudder, would compose herself and offer him some tea. Or perhaps a biscuit. Something to 'cheer you up a little'.

Other days, he thought perhaps life had never been like that; perhaps in the same way that one remembered child-hood summers as warm and endless, so one remembered love never made, an uncomplicated passion never really felt. So Henry Holden retreated a little further. Closed his mind to what he had lost. Like a mouse on a wheel, just kept moving forward and tried not to look at the view. Most of the time it worked.

Most of the time.

But by the end of today Celia and her sillinesses and her mercurial moods and her laughter would be gone. Please, God, he thought, let her not end up like her mother. Let the two of them escape our fate. He had initially failed to understand Celia's sense of urgency with this wedding, her determination to bring it forward. He didn't altogether believe her when she said that October weddings were all the rage. But then he looked at her sense of panic and irritation when Susan started fussing about doing it next summer, and understood – she was simply desperate to leave. To escape from that stifling household. Who could blame her? Secretly he would love to do the same.

And then there was Lottie, whose melancholy at Celia's

impending departure had left him aching silently on her behalf. Strange, unreadable, watchful Lottie, who still occasionally warmed him with her unguarded smile. She had always saved a special smile for him, even if she hadn't been aware of it. She had trusted him, loved him as a little girl, more so than anyone else. She had followed him around, placed her little hand inside his own. And still, he knew, there was some kind of connection between them. She understood about Susan. He could see it in the way she watched them all; she could see it too.

But Lottie wouldn't be there for long either. Susan was already hinting furiously about plans and futures and what was supposedly best. And then, after Lottie, the children, and then it would just be the two of them, circling each other. Locked in their respective miseries.

Got to get a grip, Dr Holden told himself, best not to think too hard about these things. He shut the drawer.

He sat for a minute, staring out of the window of his office, past the circulation chart and the medical leaflets that some pharmaceutical rep had left the previous morning. Past the framed photograph of Merham's respected doctor with his beautiful wife and children. Then, almost unaware of what he was doing, he opened the drawer again.

With a flourish, Joe gave the bonnet of the dark blue Daimler a final gloss with a chamois leather, then stood back, unable to keep the beam of satisfaction from his face. 'See your face in that,' he said.

Lottie, sitting silently in the back, waiting for him to finish, tried to raise a smile and failed. She kept looking at the pale leather seats, conscious of the status of its next passengers. Don't think, she told herself. Don't think.

'She worried I'd be late, was she? Mrs Holden, I mean?'

Lottie had volunteered; a means of escape from the mounting hysteria of the Holden household. 'You know what she's like.'

Joe wiped his hands on a clean cloth. 'Bet Celia's excited about going.'

Lottie nodded, trying to keep her face neutral.

'They moving straight on, are they? Where is it, down to London?'

'To start with.'

'Then some fancy country abroad, I reckon. Somewhere hot. Celia'll love that. Can't say I envy her, though, do you?'

She could get through almost any conversation now: a month's practice had left her with a face like a poker professional. Nothing revealed, nothing signified. She thought of Adeline's mask: a benign outward appearance, disclosing nothing. Just a few more hours. Just a few more hours.

'What?' She must have said it aloud. She did that, occasionally.

'Oh. Nothing.'

'How's Freddie doing in that pageboy outfit? Mrs H got him into it yet? I saw him in the high street on Saturday and he told me he was going to cut off his own legs so that they couldn't get him into those trousers.'

'He's wearing them.'

'Bloody hell. Sorry, Lottie.'

'Dr Holden's offered him two shillings if he keeps them on till after the reception.'

'And Sylvia?'

'Thinks she's royalty. Waiting for Queen Elizabeth to come and claim her as her missing sister.'

'She won't change.'

Yes, she will, thought Lottie. She will be happy and gay

and carefree, and then some man will come along like a demolition ball and smash her whole life into impossible pieces. Like Lottie's father had presumably done to her mother. Like Dr Holden had to Mrs Holden. There was no lasting happiness to be had.

She thought of Adeline, whom she had seen yesterday for the first time since the Bancrofts had visited. Adeline, too, had been low, lacking her former vibrancy, had wandered around the pale, echoing rooms as if nothing within them were of any interest, as if she could no longer see the bold canvases, the bizarre sculptures, the piles of books. Julian had gone to Venice with Stephen. George had got a grant at Oxford to write some research document on economics. Lottie did not like to ask about Frances. And soon Adeline would herself be gone. She couldn't bear England in the winter, she said repeatedly, as if convincing herself. She was off to the South of France; to a friend's villa in Provence. She would sit and drink cheap wine and watch the world go by. It would be a wonderful holiday, she said. But the way she spoke made it sound neither wonderful nor like a holiday.

'You must come,' she said to Lottie, who was trying to look as if she didn't care. 'I will be all alone, Lottie. You must come and visit me.'

They had walked slowly out on to the terrace, to the mural, where she had reached out a hand and taken Lottie's, very gently. This time Lottie did not flinch.

Lottie had been so deafened by the humming in her ears that she had hardly heard Adeline's next words. 'Things will get better, dearest girl,' she said. 'You must have faith.'

'I don't believe in God.' She hadn't meant it to sound so bitter.

'I am not talking about God. I simply believe that some-times the fates have a future for us which we cannot imagine.

And to enable them, we just have to keep believing that good things will happen.'

Lottie's rock-hard resolve had given a little then, and she had swallowed hard and looked away determinedly from Adeline's intense stare. But that meant her eyes fell upon the mural, and its two incriminatory figures. Her face had crumpled in frustration and anger. 'I don't believe in fate. I don't believe in anything. How can the fates be looking out for us when they – when they deliberately twist things so horribly? It's rubbish, Adeline. Fanciful rubbish. Things aren't made to happen. People, events, they just collide, accidentally, and then history rushes on and leaves the rest of us to struggle out of the mess.'

Adeline was very still then. She lifted her head fractionally and, raising a hand, slowly stroked the side of Lottie's hair. She paused, as if wondering whether to speak. 'If he is meant for you, he will return to you.'

Lottie pulled back, shrugged a little. 'You sound like Mrs Holden and her ruddy apple peel.'

'You just have to be true to your feelings.'

'And what if my feelings are the least important part in all this?'

Adeline was frowning, confused. 'Your feelings are never the least important part, Lottie.'

'Oh, I've got to go. I've got to go.' Lottie, biting back tears, grabbed at her coat and, ignoring the woman behind her, walked briskly through the house and back up the drive.

The following day, when she had regretted her outburst, she had received a letter. In it, Adeline made no mention of Lottie's temper, but instead enclosed an address where she could be reached in France. She asked Lottie to stay in touch, and told her that the only real sin was in trying to be something one was not. 'There is a comfort in knowing you were true to yourself, Lottie. Believe me.' She signed it, peculiarly, 'a friend'.

Lottie felt the letter in her pocket as she sat watching Joe dress the front of the Daimler with white ribbons. She didn't know why she was carrying it around still: perhaps just having an ally gave her some sense of comfort – without Adeline, there was no one she could talk to any longer. She listened to Joe as one did a fly buzzing around a room: with indifference, occasional mild irritation. Celia had been pleasant enough, but the two girls had neither sought out nor prolonged any contact with each other.

And then there was Guy, whose bemused, unhappy face haunted her, whose hands, skin, scented breath invaded her dreams. She could not bear to be near him, had not spoken to him since their meeting in the beach hut several weeks earlier. It was not because she was angry with him, although there *was* anger, it was because if he spoke to her, pleaded with her, she knew it would weaken her resolve. And if he still wanted to be with her, even after all this, she knew she could no longer love him in the same way. How could she love a man prepared to leave Celia in that condition?

He hadn't known when Celia told her, but he must know now. He had stopped following her around, stopped leaving notes in places he knew she would find them, little scribbled pieces of wretchedness shouting, 'TALK TO ME!!' in blunt pencil. It had been easy for her to stay close to Mrs Holden, to ensure they were never alone. He hadn't understood at first. He must understand now: Celia had said she was going to tell, and he no longer even looked at Lottie but turned a little away from her in any gathering, his face closed and joyless, so that neither of them could directly witness the other's misery.

She tried not to think of what might have been. For, painful as it would have been, she could have forced that cruelty on Celia while Celia still had the chance of finding someone else. How could she leave her to disgrace now? How could she bring disgrace on the very family that had saved her from it? And then other days she felt furious with him: she could not believe that Guy could have shared that closeness, felt those things with Celia. They were the only two people in the world to have felt like that, the only two to have glimpsed those secrets. They fitted like gloves – he was the one who had said it. Now, perversely, she felt betrayed.

'Why?' he had whispered to her, when they had been briefly alone in the kitchen. 'What have I *done*?'

'It's not my place to tell you,' she had said, pulling away from him, and quaking internally at the fury and exasperation on his face. But she had to be cold. It was the only way she could get through it. The only way she could get through any of it.

'I'll give you a ride back up, then, shall I? Lottie?'

He was peering through the window at her, one hand resting on the roof. He looked animated, cheerful, at ease for once in his environment. 'You'd best get out at the top of your road, though. Mrs Holden will probably want the car turning up empty.'

Lottie forced a smile, then closed her eyes, listening to the solid clunk of the car door closing, and the well-lubricated hum of the engine as Joe turned the ignition.

Just a few more hours, she told herself, clutching the letter a little tighter in her hand.

Just a few more hours.

All brides were beautiful, the saying went, but Susan Holden was sure that her Celia was the most beautiful Merham had seen in a good while. With her three-layered veil and lined satin dress, tailored precisely around that size-eight figure, she knocked Miriam Ansty and Lucinda Perry's efforts the previous year into a cocked hat. Even Mrs Chilton – at the time a great admirer of Lucinda Perry's rather daring violet-cream-coloured going-away ensemble – conceded it. 'She's certainly easy on the eye, your Celia,' she had said, after the ceremony, her clutch-bag tucked under her bosom and her feathered hat tipped at a daring angle, 'I'll say that for her. She's easy on the eye.'

More than that, they looked a beautiful couple: Celia, her eyes glistening becomingly with tears as she held the arm of her handsome young husband, he looking stern and a little nervous, as they all did. If he hadn't smiled as much as she would have liked, Mrs Holden wasn't surprised: at her own wedding, Henry hadn't smiled properly until they were upstairs by themselves, and even then only after several glasses of champagne.

And Freddie and Sylvia had lasted the whole ceremony without fighting. Well, there had been that surreptitious kick during 'Immortal, Invisible', but Sylvia's dress had camouflaged the worst of it.

Mrs Holden allowed herself her first sip of sherry, sitting carefully on the gilt-backed chair at the top table, looking down on all the tables below them; the great and the good, she liked to think, of their town. Considering how little time they had had to plan the wedding, it had all gone rather well.

'You okay, Susan?' It was Guy Bancroft Senior, leaning over conspiratorially in his chair, a broad grin lighting up his face. 'I meant to mention that the bride's mother is looking particularly fetching this afternoon.'

Mrs Holden bridled elegantly. It was that Autumn Berry lipstick. It had become rather a lucky one for her. 'Well, I think you and Mrs Bancroft look particularly elegant too.'

It was certainly true in Dee Dee's case: she was wearing a turquoise two-piece in shantung silk with little silk slingbacks in the exact matching shade. Mrs Holden had been plucking up courage all afternoon to ask her whether she had had them made specially.

'Ah. Yes . . . Dee Dee always looks well in her finery.'

'Sorry?'

'Looks just as good in a pair of shorts and bare feet, though. A real outdoors girl, is my wife. My son takes after her. Or should I say, *your son-in-law* . . .' He laughed. 'Guess all this is going to take some getting used to, huh?'

'Oh, we already think of you as part of the family.'

If only Henry would look a little happier. He was staring disconsolately out at the sea of friends, picking at his food and occasionally muttering something to his daughter. Far more than occasionally refilling his glass. Please don't let Henry get too drunk, she prayed. Not in front of all these people. Not today.

'I had to congratulate Mr Bancroft on his delightful puddings.' It was Deirdre Colquhoun, breathless and resplendent in an empire-cut coat-dress made of pink damask (Freddie had insisted noisily that he knew the old sofa she had got the fabric from; Susan Holden cast a quick look around to make sure he was nowhere near), gesturing towards the collapsing displays of exotic fruit, and cut-glass bowls of fruit salad. There were no hardened apples, morello cherries or tinned pineapple to be found in these: instead there were sliced kumquats, paw-paw and mango, dissected starfruit and opaque lychee; flesh of a colour and texture unknown to the English guests. (They subsequently gave many a wide berth, sticking to what they knew. Like plum. And orange. 'Real fruit,' as Sarah Chilton muttered surreptitiously to Mrs Ansty.)

'What a marvellous display you have put on,' Mrs Colquhoun murmured admiringly.

'All fresh, all flown in by airplane yesterday morning.' Mr Bancroft leaned back in his chair and lit a cigarette beneficently. 'I might add that they were cut and peeled by Honduran virgins.'

Mrs Colquhoun went quite pink. 'Goodness . . .'

'What are you saying, Guyhoney? I hope you're not being a naughty boy . . .' Dee Dee sat back to see him, exposing a fair length of tanned thigh as she did.

'She never lets me get away with anything.' But Mr Bancroft was smiling.

'You get away with far too much for your own good.'

'With you looking like that, sweetheart, can you blame me?' He blew her a noisy kiss.

'Well . . . Anyway. The displays look wonderful.' Mrs Colquhoun, a hand to her hair, turned unsteadily and made her way back to her table.

Mrs Holden turned to her husband. That was definitely his third Cognac. She watched him swill it around the balloon glass and swallow it with a kind of grim determination. Oh, why did he have to develop one of his moods today?

Lottie, a seated referee between Freddie and Sylvia, realised she had begun to feel unwell again. She had not felt herself for days, which was unsurprising when her whole being wanted to curl up somewhere hidden and quietly die. For the past month she had felt detached, as if she were moving through fog, only hearing and seeing other people from a distance. It had been something of a relief: when she was occasionally forced into feeling – if she happened upon Celia wrapping her arms around Guy's neck, or if she heard her giggling conspiratorially with her mother about something he had said or done – the pain that pierced her felt almost unbearable. It was real: sharp, determined, punishing.

But this was different. She felt physically unbalanced, as if her blood, like the waves, insisted on rushing away from her when she moved. Food she eyed with suspicion. It tasted wrong; held no pleasures. She simply could not look at the gaudy displays of fruit, they were too bright, as if their very cheerfulness were a direct snub to her.

'Look, Freddie. Look.'

Sylvia had opened her mouth wide, revealing the well-masticated contents of her plate.

'*Sylvia.*' Lottie looked away. She heard Freddie's chuckle of delight, and then a return 'Gaaah' as the contents of his own mouth were exposed.

'Pack it in, you two.'

Joe was seated on the other side of Freddie. He wasn't family, but Mrs Holden had evidently decided to put him on their table anyway. Lottie didn't have the energy to feel resentful about it. Over the long afternoon she had begun to feel rather grateful.

'You okay, Lottie? You're looking a bit pale.'

'Fine, Joe.'

She just wanted to go home and lie down on her bed and stay very, very still for a long time. Except home didn't even feel like home any more. Perhaps it never had been home. Lottie gazed around her at the reception, her habitual low-key feeling of dislocation threatening to become something more overwhelming, to swamp her.

'Look, I've poured you some more water. Drink a bit.'

'Sylvia. *Sylvia*. How many grapes can you fit in your mouth?'

'You really don't look good. Hope you're not coming down with another bug.'

'Look, I can get loads more in than you. Look, Sylvia. *Look.*'

'You've hardly touched your food. Go on, have a drink. Make you feel better. Or I could get them to do you a little warm milk – that's meant to settle your stomach.'

'Please don't go on, Joe. I'm fine. Really.'

His speech had been very short. He had thanked the Holdens for their hospitality, and for putting on such a splendid spread, his parents for the wonderful desserts, and for putting up with him for the past twenty-six years, and Celia. For becoming his wife. The fact that he had said this with no huge enthusiasm, or romantic flourish, was of little comfort. She was still his wife.

And Celia. Celia sat there with her bewitching smile spread across her face, her veil becomingly framing her elegant neck. Lottie couldn't look at her, shocked by the depth of hatred she now felt for her. Knowing she had done the right thing was no comfort at all. Being true to herself, as Adeline had put it, was even less. If she could only persuade herself that she hadn't meant what she had felt, then she could move on.

But she had felt it.

Oh, God, she just wanted to lie down. Somewhere dark.

'Shall I help you to a bowl of trifle?' said Joe.

The guests were starting to get restless. It was time, Mrs Holden decided, for the newlyweds to leave in order that some of the older ladies could go home before it got too late. Mrs Charteris and Mrs Godwin were looking a little weary, and the whole back table had already got their coats.

She decided that it should really be Henry's task. He had done very little during the reception – even his speech had been rather perfunctory – and she didn't want anyone making any comments. She excused herself from her chair and made her way up the long table to her husband. He was gazing at the table, apparently oblivious to the merry conversation around him. Mrs Holden smelt the alcohol on him before she was even at arm's length.

'Henry dear, could I have a little word?'

She quailed at the coldness of his gaze when he lifted his head. He stared at her for what felt like an age: the kind of stare that strips one of any sense of self-possession.

'What have I done now, dearest?' he said. The *dearest* was spat out, like something foul-tasting.

Susan Holden glanced around to see if anyone else had noticed. 'You haven't done anything, dear. I just wanted to borrow you for a minute.' She laid a hand on his arm, glancing round at the Bancrofts, who were deep in conversation.

'I haven't done anything.' He looked down, placed both palms on the table, as if to push himself up. 'Well that makes a change, doesn't it, Susan dear?'

Oh, but she had never seen him this bad. Her brain ticked frantically, trying to weigh up the possibilities of getting him out of there without a public row.

'Makes a change that, for once, it all appears to be *satisfactory* to you.'

'*Henry.*' Her voice was hushed, pleading.

'Well, not often we all manage to come up to scratch, is it? Not often we meet the exacting standards of Merham's hostess with the mostest?' He was standing now, and had started to laugh: a sharp, bitter laugh.

'Darling. Darling, please, can we—'

He turned to her in mock surprise. 'Oh, "darling" now, am I? Isn't that lovely? Now I'm your darling. Goodness me, Susan. I'll be *lover*, next.'

'Henry!'

'Mummy?' Celia had appeared at her side. She was looking at her father and back to Mrs Holden. 'Is everything all right?'

'It's all fine, dear,' said Mrs Holden, reassuringly, trying to pat her away. 'You and Guy go and get ready. You should really be off soon.'

'All fine. Yes, Celia dearest. It's *all fine*.' Dr Holden placed his hands heavily on his daughter's shoulders. 'You go off now and have a fine life with your fine young man here.'

'Daddy . . .' Celia was looking uncertain now.

'You go off and stay beautiful and funny and as sweet as you are. Try your best not to nag and pick at him about things that don't matter. Try not to look at him as if he were a mangy dog when he happens to do anything that *he* might want to do . . . anything that doesn't involve sitting nicely and sipping tea and fretting about what *everybody else thinks*.'

'Henry!' Susan Holden's eyes had filled with tears. She raised a hand to her mouth.

Guy was now standing behind Celia, evidently trying to gauge what was happening.

'Oh, spare me the tears, Susan. Spare me another bloody dose of tears. If anyone should be crying in this place it should be me.'

Celia burst into noisy sobs. Around them, the tables were hushing. People were watching, glancing uncertainly at each other, their drinks stilled in their hands.

'Daddy – why are you being so horrible? Please, this is my special day.' Celia attempted to pull him back, away from the table.

'But it's not just about this day, dearest Celia, is it? It's not just about the bloody wedding. It's about *every bloody day afterwards*. Every bloody endless bloody day until death does you part.' He shouted the last part. Susan Holden, with some horror, saw that they were now the main focus of attention.

'Everything okay here?' called Mr Bancroft.

Guy placed his arm around her. 'Fine, Dad. Erm, why don't you come and sit down, Mrs Holden?'

'Oh, don't bother,' said Dr Holden. 'I'm going outside. You can finish your perfectly fine reception without me. Excuse me, ladies and gentlemen, the show's over. Your good doctor is just leaving.'

'You are a brute, Daddy,' sobbed Celia, as he made his way unsteadily out through the tables of the Riviera's dining room. 'I shall never, ever forgive you for this.'

'Cognac,' said Mr Bancroft, 'can get you like that sometimes.'

'Please get a grip, Celia dear,' said Mrs Holden, who was sipping at a restorative sherry, only the trembling of her hands revealing her own lack of composure. 'People are staring.'

There were three winking lights down at the mouth of the harbour. Fishing-boats, Lottie had decided. The lights were too small for any other. Hauling their treasures from the sea-bed, from that cool, inky darkness, pulling them, silently gasping, into the suffocating night. She pulled her cardigan tighter round her against the chill autumnal air, listening to the swell and hiss of the tide dragging the pebbles in its loose-fingered embrace. It was meant to be the most pleasant way to die, drowning. One of the fishermen had told her: apparently once you stopped struggling and opened your mouth, the panic ceased and the water just took you in, enveloped you in its soft, welcoming blackness. A peaceful way to go, he had called it. Curiously, he hadn't been able to swim either. She had laughed when he told her.

But, then, that had been back when laughter had come easily to her.

Lottie shifted on her chair, breathing in the salt air, wondering how different it would feel from water. She gulped aloud a couple of times, as if testing it, but it didn't seem a convincing substitute. The only times she had swallowed seawater it had burnt the back of her throat, left her choking saltily, retching and drooling. The mere thought of it made her feel nauseous again.

No, the only real answer would be to try it. To swallow it wholly, to go willingly into that dark embrace. Lottie winced and closed her eyes, hearing the unheralded pattern of her thoughts. It is not the pain of today that I cannot bear, she thought, her face buried in her hands. It is the thought of all the days to come: the endless repetition of pain, the jolts of unwelcome discovery. For I will have to know everything about them: about their home, their child, their happiness. Even if I moved far from here I would still have to know. I will have to watch him forget that we were ever close, that he was mine. And I will shrivel with it, and die every day.

What was one death compared with a thousand?

Lottie stood up, allowing the wind to pull at her skirt and hair. It was only a short walk from the Riviera's terrace down to the beach. No one would even know she had gone.

She looked down at her feet, curiously dry-eyed. They moved tentatively, one before the other, as if they were not even under her control.

She barely existed as it was: it seemed only the smallest of steps further.

Out at the harbour mouth, the three lights winked into the darkness.

'Who's that?'

Lottie jumped, turned.

A large, stumbling shadow loomed towards her, attempting clumsily to light a match as it came.

'Oh, it's you. Thank God. I thought it was one of Susan's cronies.'

Dr Holden sat heavily on the end of a bench, and finally managed to light his match. He held it to the cigarette in his mouth, then exhaled, letting the flame extinguish in the breeze. 'Escaping too, are you?'

Lottie gazed out at the lights, then turned to him. 'No. Not really.'

She could see his face now in the light from the upstairs rooms. Even upwind of him, she could smell the alcohol on his breath.

'Bloody awful things, weddings.'

'Yes.'

'Bring out the worst in me. Sorry, Lottie. Had a bit too much to drink.'

Lottie folded her arms across herself, wondering if he wanted her to sit down. She perched a few feet away from him, on the end of the bench.

'Want one of these?' He smiled, offering her a cigarette.

It might have been a joke. She shook her head, smiling weakly back at him.

'Don't know why not. You're not a child. Although my wife insists on treating you like one.'

Lottie looked down at her shoes again.

They sat in silence for a while, listening to the muted sound of the music and laughter filtering through the night air.

'What are we going to do, Lottie? You about to be forced into the big wide world, and me desperate to escape back to it.'

She stilled now, conscious of a new timbre to his voice.

'It's a bloody mess, that's for sure.'

'Yes. Yes, it is.'

He turned to her, moved a little way along the bench. Back at the hotel she could hear the sound of muffled cheering, underlaid by Ruby Murray, singing of happy days and lonely nights.

'Poor Lottie, having to listen to the ramblings of a drunken old fool.'

She couldn't think what to say.

'Yes, I am. I'm under no illusions. I've ruined my own daughter's wedding, offended my wife, and now I'm out here boring you.'

'You're not boring.'

He took another drag of his cigarette. Looked sideways at her. 'You don't think so?'

'I've never thought so. You've – you've always been very kind to me.'

'Kind. Kindness. How could I have been anything but? You had a raw deal, Lottie, and you came here and blossomed in spite of it. I was always as proud of you as I was of Celia.'

Lottie felt her eyes prick with tears. She found kindness so much harder to bear.

'Huh. In some ways you've been more of a daughter than Celia has. You're smarter, that's for sure. Don't have your head filled with romantic twaddle, ridiculous magazines.'

Lottie gulped. Gazed back out to sea. 'Oh. I'm sure I'm as capable of romantic dreams as anyone else.'

'Are you?' There was real tenderness in his voice.

'Yes,' she said. 'For all the good it has done me.'

'Oh, Lottie . . .'

And then, without warning, she began to cry.

In a stroke, he was there beside her, enfolding her in his arms, pulling her into him. She could smell the pipesmoke on his jacket, the warm, familiar scents of childhood. And she gave herself up to him, buried her face in his shoulder, unburdened herself of the grief she had had to hide for so long. She felt his hand stroking her back, as one would a baby's. And she could hear him crooning, 'Oh, Lottie, oh, my poor girl, I understand. I do understand.'

And then he shifted, and she looked up at him and saw, in the dim light, an infinite sadness in his face, the weight of unhappiness long borne, and shivered because she saw herself. 'Poor, dear Lottie,' he whispered.

And then, as his head lowered to hers, she recoiled. For as his hands held her face, his mouth met hers and kissed her hungrily, desperately, their tears mingling on their cheeks, the unwelcome taste of alcohol on his lips. Lottie, stunned, tried to pull back, but he just moaned, and held her closer.

'Dr Holden – please—'

It had taken less than a minute. But as she freed herself, she glanced over and met the shocked figure of Mrs Holden, standing in the hotel doorway, and knew it to have been the longest minute of her life.

'Henry . . .' Mrs Holden's voice was low, shaking. And then, as she reached out a hand to the wall, Lottie fled into the darkness.

It had been very civilised, all things considered. Dr Holden, home before she had finished packing her case, had told her she didn't have to leave like this, despite what Susan had said. They had all decided that it would, however, be the best thing if she left as soon as suitable arrangements could be made. He had a friend in Cambridge who needed a help for their children. He knew Lottie would be very happy there. He had seemed almost relieved when she said she already had her own plans.

He had not asked her what they were.

She had left soon after eleven the next morning, the address of Adeline's house in France clutched tightly in her hand, along with a brief letter to Joe. Celia and Guy had already gone. Virginia appeared indifferent. Neither Freddie nor Sylvia cried: they had not been told that she was leaving for good. Dr Holden, awkward and hung-over, had surreptitiously given her thirty pounds and told her that it was towards her future. Mrs Holden, pale and rigid, had barely looked at her when she said goodbye.

Dr Holden had not said sorry. No one had appeared sad to see her go, even after ten years of living as part of their family.

But Dr Holden's embrace had not been the most unfair thing to happen to her. No, she realised, staring at the calendar of her pocket diary, doing the mental arithmetic for the umpteenth time as she sat on the train to London. No, Adeline's fates had a much crueller sense of humour than even she had envisaged.

PART TWO

PART TWO

Nine

'All three lanes are now reopened on the M11, but watch out for that contraflow at the junction with the M25. And we're just getting reports in of a major snarl-up with traffic at a standstill round Hammersmith Broadway and knock-on problems heading on to the M4 and the Fulham Palace Road. Looks like it might be a broken-down vehicle. We'll bring you more on that later. Now it's coming up to nine thirteen and I'll hand you back to Chris . . .'

Swans mate for life. She was pretty sure it was swans. Perhaps it could have been ducks. Or maybe even peahens. Was that really their name, peahens? That would be like being called potato-people. Or, in her case, digestive-biscuit-and-cigarette-people. Daisy Parsons sat very still, staring out of her window as the birds floated benignly under the bridge, the water around them winking brilliantly in the spring sunlight. It had to be swans. Of course it was. No one would care if a peahen mated for life.

She glanced at the clock. She had been sitting there for almost seventeen minutes. Not that time seemed to have an awful lot of meaning at the moment. It either raced by, as if she had hiccuped and swallowed hours at a time, or, more usually, it dragged, stretching itself like cheap elastic, minutes into hours, hours into days. And Daisy sat in the middle of it all, unsure in which direction she should be travelling.

Beside her, in the car seat, Ellie yawned in her sleep, waving starfish fingers in some invisible salute. Daisy felt the familiar pang of anxiety that she might be about to wake up and, leaning forward, lowered the volume of the radio. It was very important not to wake Ellie up. It was always important not to wake Ellie up.

She mentally graded the roar of traffic around her, the sound of thrumming engines, absently monitoring its volume. Too much and the baby would wake again. Too little, and she would be woken by the amplification of a pin dropping. Which was why this shouting outside was really rather annoying.

Daisy dropped her head on to the steering-wheel. And then, when the knocking on the window became too loud, she looked up, sighed, and opened the car door.

He was wearing a motorcycle helmet; took it off to speak. Behind him, she was dimly aware of several angry-looking people. Some had left their car doors open. You should never leave your car door open. Not in London. It was one of the rules.

'Have you broken down, madam?'

She wished he wouldn't shout. It was going to wake the baby.

The policeman looked at his colleague, who had just approached from the other side of her car. They were all staring at her. 'Have you broken down? We need to get you off the road. You're blocking the bridge.'

The swans had reappeared. There they went, floating serenely off towards Richmond.

'Madam? Can you hear me?'

'Look, Officer, can you just move her? I can't wait around here all day.' He would have been a cross-looking man at the best of times. Big red cheeks, overhanging gut, expensive suit and matching car. 'Look at her. She's obviously a bloody headcase.'

'Please step back into your car, sir. We'll all be moving along in a minute. Madam?'

There were hundreds of them. Thousands. Daisy looked behind her, blinking, at the stationary cars, streaming out like a multicoloured fan. All trying to get on to the bridge. All unable, because she and her little red Ford Fiesta were in the way.

'What's the problem?' He had said it to her twice now. She wished he wouldn't shout. He really was going to wake Ellie in a minute.

'I can't—'

'Do you want me to take a look under the bonnet? Look, we just need to push it over here first. Here, Jason. You undo that handbrake, will you? We need to get this thing cleared.'

'You'll wake the baby.' She tensed, seeing this man in her car, at Ellie's face, so vulnerable in slumber. Suddenly she felt herself beginning to tremble, the now familiar panic starting to spread from her chest.

'We'll just push it over to the side. Then we'll get you going again.'

'No. Please. Just leave me—'

'Look, you release your handbrake. I'll lean across if you like and—'

'I was going to my sister's. But I can't.'

'Sorry, madam?'

'I can't go across the bridge.'

The policeman stopped. She saw him exchange another meaningful look with his colleague.

'*Get a move on!*'

'*Stupid cow!*'

Someone was pushing their horn insistently.

She tried to breathe. Tried to clear the noise from her head.

'What seems to be the problem, madam?'

She couldn't see the swans any more. They had disappeared around the bend when she wasn't looking.

'Please just . . . I can't. I can't go across the bridge.' She gazed wide-eyed at the men, trying to make them understand. Realised as the words came that they never would. 'That – that's where he first told me he loved me.'

Her sister was wearing her London coat. It was a brisk, woman-of-a-certain-means type of coat, dark blue wool with naval buttons, armour against a febrile, untrustworthy city. She saw the coat before she saw her, glimpsed it through the partially open door from where the incurious woman police officer had whisked in and out bearing professional understanding and foul-tasting machine coffee. She had drunk it, untasting, before she remembered she wasn't allowed caffeine. Not when you were breastfeeding. It was one of the rules.

'She's in here,' said a muffled voice.

'But she's all right?'

'She's fine. They both are.'

Ellie slept on uncomplainingly in her car seat at her feet. She hardly ever slept this long but, then, she liked the car seat. Liked feeling enclosed and safe, the health visitor had said. Daisy eyed the chair speculatively, enviously.

'Daisy?'

She looked up.

Her sister looked tentative. As if approaching something that might bite. 'C-can I come in?' She glanced at Ellie and then away, as if reassuring herself. Then she sat on the chair beside Daisy and placed a hand on her shoulder. 'What's happened, sweetheart?'

It was like waking from a dream. Her sister's face. Her feathered helmet of auburn hair, which mysteriously never seemed to need cutting. Her eyes, intent and anxious. Her hand. No adult had touched her for almost four weeks. She opened her mouth to speak but nothing came out.

'Daisy? Sweetheart?'

'He's gone, Julia.' It came out in a whisper.

'Who's gone?'

'Daniel. He's – he's gone.'

Julia frowned, then looked down at Ellie. 'Gone where?'

'Left me. And her. And I don't know what to do . . .'

Julia held her for a long time, Daisy burying her sobs in the dark wool coat, trying to stave off, in that embrace, the moment when she had to become an adult again. Outside, she was dimly aware of the sound of feet on linoleum, the sharp smell of disinfectant. Ellie whimpered in her sleep.

'Why didn't you tell me?' Julia whispered, stroking her head.

Daisy closed her eyes. 'I thought – I thought if I didn't tell anyone, he might come back.'

'Oh, Daisy . . .'

The policewoman stuck her head round the door. 'Your car keys are in Reception. We've not impounded the vehicle. If you agree to drive your daughter home, madam, we'll just leave things as they stand.' Neither woman flinched: they were used to it. The age gap between them was twenty years – since the death of their mother it had been a frequent mistake, but they had behaved more like mother and daughter than sisters.

'That's very kind of you.' Julia made as if to stand. 'I'm sorry if we've caused any trouble.'

'No, no, take your time. We don't need the room at the moment. When you're ready, get someone on the front desk to point you to the car park. It's not far.'

With a bland, understanding smile, she was gone.

Julia turned back to her sister. 'Oh, darling. But why? Where has he gone?'

'I don't know. He said he just couldn't cope with it all. That it wasn't what he had expected, and now he's not even sure if it's what he wanted.' She was sobbing again now.

'Daniel said this?'

'Yes. Bloody Daniel. And I told him it wasn't what I'd bloody expected either, but somehow my feelings didn't seem to count. And he said he thought he was having some kind of breakdown and needed some space, and that was it. I haven't heard from him in over three weeks. He didn't even take his mobile.' She had found her voice now.

Her sister shook her head, staring into the middle distance. 'He said what?'

'That he couldn't cope. He didn't like the mess of it. The chaos.'

'But it's always a little difficult after a first baby. And she's only, what, four months?'

'You don't have to tell *me*.'

'It gets easier. Everyone knows it gets easier.'

'Well, Daniel didn't.'

Julia frowned, looked down at her immaculate court shoes. 'Did you still . . . I mean some women stop giving their partners any attention after they have a baby. Were you still . . . ?'

Daisy stared at her incredulously.

There was a brief silence. Julia resettled her bag on her lap, and stared out of the small, high window. 'I knew you should have got married.'

'*What?*'

'You should have got married.'

'That wouldn't have stopped him leaving. There is such a thing as *divorce.*'

'Yes, Daise, but at least he would have had some financial obligation towards you. As it is, he's been able to just swan off into the sunset.'

'Oh, for God's sake, Julia. He's left me in the bloody flat. He's taken virtually nothing from the joint account. He's hardly left me like some disgraced Victorian maid.'

'Well, I'm sorry, but if he's really left you, then you have to be practical about these things. I mean, how are you going to support yourself? What are you going to do about the rent?'

Daisy shook her head in fury. 'I can't believe you're doing this to me. The love of my life has left me, I'm in the middle of a bloody nervous breakdown, and all you can think about is the bloody *rent.*'

The shouting woke the baby, who began to cry, eyes screwed shut against whatever disturbance had interrupted her dreams.

'Oh, now see what you've done.' She unstrapped the baby from the seat and pulled her to her chest.

'No need to get hysterical, darling. Someone has to be practical. Has he agreed to pay the rent?'

'We didn't exactly get as far as that discussion.' Daisy's voice was icy.

'And what about the business? What about that big project you said you were taking on?'

Daisy settled Ellie on to her breast, turning away from the door. She had forgotten about the hotel. 'I don't know. I can't think about that now, Ju. It's all I can do to get through each day in one piece.'

'Well. I think it's time I came home with you and got you sorted out. Then we can have a sit-down and work out what we're going to do about your and my little niece's future. And in the meantime I'll give Marjorie Wiener a call and tell her exactly what I think of her precious son.'

Daisy held on to her baby daughter, waves of weariness sweeping over her. As Ellie finished, pushing Daisy's nipple rudely out of her mouth, Daisy stood up, and pulled down her jumper.

Her sister was staring at her. 'Gosh, you are having problems getting that baby fat off, aren't you, darling? I tell you what, when we've sorted you out at home, I'll enrol you in one of those slimmers' courses. My treat. If you look a bit more together, you'll feel so much better, I promise.'

Daniel Wiener and Daisy Parsons had lived together in their one-bedroom flat in Primrose Hill for almost five years, during which time the area had become almost unbearably trendy and their rent had risen accordingly unbearably. Daisy would have been quite happy to leave: as their fledgling interior-design business grew, she hankered after tall ceilings and french windows, utility rooms and larders. A back garden. But Daniel had insisted they stay in Primrose Hill: the address was better for clients than some more spacious place in Hackney or Islington. Look at their quality of life, he argued. The elegant Georgian houses, the gastropubs and restaurants, Primrose Hill itself for picnics in the summer. And their flat was beautiful: based above a designer shoe shop, it had a huge Regency-style living room, and a bedroom with a tiny balcony that looked out over everyone else's walled and snail-ridden gardens. They had made clever modifications: a washing-machine squeezed into a cupboard, a shower fitted into a corner alcove. A tiny minimalist kitchen with a chic mini-range cooker, and oversized extractor hood. In the summer they had often squeezed two chairs on to the balcony and sipped their wine, congratulating themselves on where they were, how far they had come, bathed in the evening sun and the idea that their home and its surroundings were a reflection of themselves.

Then Ellie had arrived, and somehow the charm had ebbed away as the flat had gradually shrunk, its walls closing in, the remaining space increasingly cluttered with piles of damp Babygros, half-empty packets of wipes, soft toys in garish colours. It had begun with the flowers: bouquet after bouquet, arriving relentlessly, filling up all the shelf space until they had run out of vases and put them in the bath. The blooms became oppressive, the stink of their stale water permeating the flat, Daisy too exhausted and too overwhelmed to address them. And then slowly, creepingly, there was less and less room to move: they waded around the flat, picking their way over piles of unironed clothes or shrink-wrapped boulders of nappies. The high chair that her cousins had sent stood unused in its box, taking up what they had thought of as the library corner, a plastic baby bath stood propped against the wall in the hall, leaning against the baby buggy, which never quite folded enough, while Ellie's cot sat flush next to their bed, squeezed up against the wall: if Daisy wanted to go to the loo in the night she had to either climb over Daniel or slide down towards the foot of the bed. And then, invariably, the sound of the flush would wake Ellie, and Daniel would bury his head under the pillow and rail against the unfairness of his life.

She hadn't cleaned since he'd gone. She'd meant to, but somehow the days and nights had all melded together and she seemed to have spent most of them pinned to their once-pristine beige linen sofa, Ellie feeding in her

arms, and Daisy staring unseeing at the vacuous daytime
television or weeping at the picture of them all, entwined,
on the mantelpiece. And slowly, without Daniel to wash
up in the evening, or take out the rubbish (how was she
meant to carry a bin-bag and a baby down two flights of
steep stairs?), it had all built up around her, and the piles
of pooed-upon white vests and stained dungarees had taken
on a kind of unapproachable quality, had become something
altogether too big to confront. And the detritus had taken
over, become part of the furnishings, so that she started
not even to see it. And faced with this chaos she had worn
the same sweatpants and sweatshirt every day, because they
were slung over the chair and therefore visible, and she had
eaten crisps, or packets of chocolate digestives from the
convenience store, because cooking something would have
meant she had to wash up first.

'Okay. Now I'm worried.' Her sister had shaken her head
in disbelief, the cool smell of her Anaïs Anaïs almost drowned
by the pungent, insanitary one of used nappies, several of
which lay on the floor where they had been removed, their
contents exposed to the air. 'Gracious, Daisy, what have you
done? How have you let it get so bad?'

Daisy didn't know. It felt like someone else's home.

'Oh, my goodness. Oh, my goodness.' The three of them
were inside the front door, Ellie jiggling in her mother's arms,
refreshed and looking around.

'I'll have to phone Don. Tell him I'm staying over. I can't
leave you like this.' She began to move swiftly around the
room, collecting up dirty dishes, tossing baby clothes into a
pile by the coffee table. 'I told him I was only coming in to
buy a couple of new duvet sets for the barn.'

'Don't tell him, Ju.'

Her sister stopped, looked at her directly. 'Don knowing

is not going to make this go away, sweetheart. It seems to me there's been far too much not facing up to things round here.'

She had sent her out in the end, to walk Ellie around the park. When she had said Daisy was getting under her feet, she had known it to be not just a figure of speech. It had given Daisy a little time to breathe: it was as if it were the first time she had known what she was doing in weeks. Not that that helped particularly: the pain just became more acute. 'Please let him come home,' she begged, murmuring the words so that passers-by looked sharply and surreptitiously at her. Just let him come home. By the time she returned, her sister had somehow magicked the flat into order, even filling a vase with fresh flowers and placing it on the mantelpiece.

'If he does return to his senses,' she said, in explanation, 'you want him to think you're doing fine by yourself. You want to look like you're together.' She paused. 'Little shit.'

But I'm not together, Daisy wanted to scream. I can't eat, I can't sleep. I can't even watch television because I'm too busy looking out of the window in case he happens to walk by. Without him I don't know who I'm meant to be. But there was little one could tell Julia Warren about pulling oneself together. After her first husband had died, she had observed a decent period of mourning, then thrown herself into a selection of dating clubs (intimate dinners a speciality), and after a couple of false starts had cultivated and won Don Warren, a Weybridge businessman with his own detached house, a successful printed-label business, a head of thick dark hair and a trim waistline that, in Julia's view, had made him something of a catch. ('They're all bald, by that age, you see, sweetheart. Or with half a ton of blubber hanging over their belts. And I can't be doing with all that.') And the then Julia Bartlett had been something of a catch herself: independently well-off, perennially well turned-out (she had never been seen without her makeup, she liked to say: with both husbands she had risen twenty minutes before them to ensure she looked 'done') and a multiple bed-and-breakfast business in her barn that she refused to relinquish, despite not needing the money, because one never knew apparently. One just never knew.

As had been proven by her sister.

'I've been looking through your bank statements, Daise, and you're going to have to get something sorted out.'

'You did what? You had no right. They're private.'

'If they're private, darling, they should have been filed away, not sitting on your coffee table where anyone could see them. Anyway. With your outgoings I think you've got about another three weeks before you're eating into your savings. I took the liberty of opening a couple of these letters, and I'm afraid your landlord – who sounds like a bit of a moneygrabber to me – is going to put your rent up in May. So you're going to have to think about whether you can afford to keep this place on. It seems frightfully expensive for what it is, I have to say.'

Daisy handed Ellie to her sister. The fight ebbed out of her. 'That's Primrose Hill.'

'Well, you're going to have to think about cutting your cloth. Or else get in touch with that Child Support thingy. The one where they get people to cough up.'

'I don't think it's come to that, Ju.'

'Well, how else are you going to support yourself? The Wieners are loaded. They aren't going to miss a few thou, are they?' She sat down, brushing imaginary crumbs from the sofa and gazing adoringly at her niece.

'Look, darling, I've been having a think while you were out.

If Daniel doesn't come back within another week, we should really bring you home. I'll give you the little self-contained flat in the barn for nothing, just until you're on your feet, and then you've got your privacy. But Don and I will be just at the other end of the garden. And there are lots of interior decorators in Weybridge – I'm sure Don can ask some of his business associates to see if anyone's got an opening for you.'

Weybridge. Daisy pictured herself consigned for ever to pelmeted swags and mock-Tudor executive homes for LWT comedians in golfing shoes. 'It's not really me, Ju. My inspiration is a bit more . . . urban.'

'Your inspiration is more council fly-tip at the moment, Daisy. Well, the offer is there. Now, I'm going to catch the train back tonight, after all, as we've got a dinner. But I'm coming back down in the morning, and I'll take little Ellie off you for a couple of hours. There's a nice man in that hairdresser's across the road who's agreed to fit you in tomorrow for a cut and blow-dry. We'll have you smartened up in no time.'

She turned to Daisy as she knotted her scarf, ready to go.

'You've got to face up to this, darling. I know it's painful but it's not just about you any more.'

A friend of hers had once described it as like waking up with your mother's body. Staring at her post-baby figure in the long mirror, Daisy thought longingly of what she remembered of her mother's neatly contained shape. I'm just spilling out all over, she thought miserably, eyeing the saddlebags of flesh on her thighs, the newly crêpy skin clinging to her stomach. I went to bed and woke up with my grandmother's body.

He had told her once that the moment he saw her he knew he wouldn't be able to relax again until he had her. She had liked that 'had' with its intimations of sex and possession. But that had been when she had dressed her size-eight figure in skin-tight leathers, in fitted tops that showed off her sculpted waist and high breasts. That was when she was blonde and golden and carefree, back when she despised anyone over a size twelve for their lack of self-control. Now those pert breasts looked both swollen and collapsed, blue-veined and apologetic, flesh-coloured Womble snouts, occasionally and inappropriately leaking milk. Her eyes were small pink punctuation points at the top of smudged blue shadows. She couldn't sleep: she hadn't slept for more than two hours at a time since Ellie was born, and now lay restlessly awake even when her daughter slept. Her hair was greasy, scraped back into an old towelling band so that a good two inches of darker roots showed through. Her pores were so open she was surprised she couldn't hear the wind whistling through them.

She regarded herself coldly, with her sister's assessing gaze. It was no wonder he hadn't wanted her. Daisy let a hot, fat tear squeeze its way out and trail a salty path down her cheek. You were meant to get back into shape quickly after having a baby. Pull in your pelvic floor at traffic-lights; run up and down stairs to tone your thighs. It was the rules. She thought back, as she had several thousand times, to the few times he had made advances towards her since Ellie's birth, and her exhausted, tearful refusals. He made her feel like a piece of meat, she had told him crossly on one occasion. There was Ellie pawing at her all day, and now he wanted to do the same. She thought back to the shock and hurt on his face and wished she could turn back the clock. 'I just want my Daisy back,' he'd said, sadly. She'd wanted her too. She still did, torn between the fierce, ovewhelming love for her child, and a desperate hankering for the girl she used to be, for the life she used to have.

For Daniel.

She flinched as the telephone rang in the living room, her very being tensed towards anything that might wake the baby. She grabbed a cardigan and threw it around herself, just making it before the answerphone cut in.

'Mr Wiener?'

It wasn't him. She let out a small breath of disappointment, bracing herself for another conversation.

'No. He's not here.'

'Is that Daisy Parsons? Jones here. From the Red Rooms. We met a few weeks ago about my hotel? Well, I met your partner, anyway.'

'Oh. Yes.'

'It's just that you were going to put a start date in writing for me. And I don't seem to have had anything.'

'Oh.'

There was a short pause.

'Have I called at a bad time?' His voice was gruff, aged by spirits or tobacco.

'No. Sorry . . .' She took a long gulp of air. 'I – it's been a difficult day.'

'Yes. Well. Can you give me a start date in writing?'

'For the hotel?'

He sounded impatient now. '*Yessss*. The one you quoted for.'

'It's just – things have changed a little since we last spoke.'

'I've told you. That price was my absolute limit.'

'No – no, not the costings. Erm . . .' She wondered if she was going to be able to say it without crying. She took a long, slow breath. 'It's just that my partner . . . well, he . . . he's left.'

There was a silence.

'I see. Well, what does this mean? Are you still in business? Are you honouring contracts?'

'Yes.' She had said it on automatic pilot. He didn't know he had been their only one.

He thought for a minute. 'Well, if you can guarantee me the same job, I can't see any problem. You ran through your plans pretty comprehensively . . .' He paused. 'Had a partner walk out on me once, when I was starting out. Never realised till he was gone but it was the making of me.'

He went quiet, as if uncomfortable with revelation. 'Anyway, you've still got the job if you want it. I liked what you had planned.'

Daisy made to interrupt him, then stopped herself. She stared around her at the flat that no longer felt like home. At the home that might not be hers for much longer anyway.

'Miss Parsons?'

'Yes,' she said, slowly. 'Yes, I do.'

'Good.'

'There's just one thing.'

'What?'

'We – I mean, I like to live on site while I'm working. Would that be a problem?'

'It's pretty basic . . . But no, I guess not. You've just had a baby, haven't you?'

'Yes.'

'You might want to make sure the heating's working first. It can still be a bit bracing up there. For another month or so.'

'I'll also need a retainer. Would five per cent be acceptable to you?'

'I can live with that.'

'Mr Jones, I'll put something in the post tonight.'

'Jones. It's just Jones. I'll see you on site.'

Daisy marvelled at the insanity of what she had just done. She thought of Hammersmith Bridge, and Weybridge, and of Don's friends, glad-handing her with patronising eyes. Poor old Daisy. Mind you, not too surprising when you looked at how she'd let herself go. She thought of her sister, 'just popping in' to the barn, to make sure she wasn't comfort-eating her way through another packet of digestives. She thought of the unnamed seaside town, and salt air and clear skies, and not having to wake up every morning in what had been their shared bed. A chance to breathe, away from mess and history. She didn't know how she was going to manage the job singlehandedly. It felt like the least of her problems.

In the next room, Ellie began to cry again, her thin wail swiftly building to a crescendo. But as she went to her, Daisy didn't flinch. For the first time in weeks, she felt something close to relief.

Ten

'You know, I'd never seen underwear like it in my life. Hardly anything to it, just little whispers of lace it was. Well, if I put that on, I thought, it wouldn't be mutton dressed as lamb, it would be mutton tied up in a string bag.' Evie Newcomb laughed, and Camille paused, not wanting to get any cream in her eyes. 'You should see some of the stuff they have in these catalogues. I tell you what, Camille love, you wouldn't want to be wearing it on a cold day. And it's not even the fabric – although you know I used to work in the rag trade and, frankly, the quality left a little something to be desired – it's the ruddy holes they put in everywhere! Holes in places you wouldn't believe. There was one pair of drawers I looked at, and I couldn't have told you which holes you put your legs in, that's for sure.'

Camille smoothed Evie's hair back under the white cotton hairband and began sweeping her hands gently across her forehead.

'As for the accessories, or whatever you call them, well, I looked and looked, but I couldn't work out what half of them were *for*. And you wouldn't want to be doing the wrong thing with them, would you? I mean, you wouldn't want to end up down the hospital explaining that little lot to a doctor. No, I left them well alone.'

'So it wasn't a success, then?' Camille said, when the mask was fully applied.

'Oh, no. I took your advice, love. I bought two outfits

in the end.' Her voice lowered. 'I've never seen Leonard's face like that in thirty-two years of marriage. He thought his ship had come in.' She chuckled. 'I thought I'd killed him afterwards.'

'But he's not talking about getting that cable-television thing any more. The one with the Dutch channels.'

'Nope, or taking up bowls. So you've done me a real favour there, Camille. A real favour. Can I have some of those eye pads again? They were lovely last time.'

Camille Hatton made her way over to the cupboard and reached up to the fourth shelf where she kept her Cooling Eye Pads. She had been busy this morning: normally she didn't have so many appointments, unless there was a wedding or a dance on at the Riviera Hotel. But the summer season was edging closer, and all over town the female inhabitants were treating themselves, priming themselves for the annual influx of guests. 'Do you want the tea ones or the cucumber ones?' she asked, feeling for the boxes.

'Ooh. Tea, please. Speaking of which, Tess couldn't make me a cup, could she? I'm absolutely gasping.'

'No problem,' she said, and called for her young assistant.

'There was one thing that made me laugh, though. Just between you and me. Here, come over here. I don't want to shout it across the salon. Did I tell you about the feathers?'

The onset of the spring months always seemed to make people want to talk more. It was as if the March winds that picked up, blowing in from the sea, quietly shifted away the stasis of winter, reminding people of the possibilities for change. That, and in the ladies' case, the new influx of women's magazines.

When her boss, Kay, had opened the salon, nearly nine

years ago, the women had been shy. They had been reluctant to try the treatments, fearful that it looked in some way overly indulgent. They would sit rigid and silent as she smoothed and pasted, as if waiting for ridicule, or for her to make some dreadful mistake. Then, gradually, they came regularly. And about the time that the Seventh-day Adventists took over the old methodist church, they began to talk.

Now they told Camille everything: about unfaithful husbands, recalcitrant children. About the heartbreaks of lost babies and the joys of new ones. They told her things that they wouldn't have told a vicar, they joked – about lust and love and libidos battered, like Leonard's, into new life. And she never told. She never judged, or laughed, or condemned. She just listened as she worked, and then, occasionally, tried to offer some suggestion to make them feel better about themselves. Your congregation, Hal had joked. But that had been back when Hal still joked.

She bent over Evie's face, feeling the moisturising mask harden under her fingertips. It was a tough environment for skin, a seaside town. The salt and wind blew tiny lines prematurely into a woman's face, aged and freckled it, remorselessly stripping away whichever moisturiser was applied. Camille carried hers in her handbag and reapplied it throughout the day. She had a thing about skin feeling dry: it made her shiver.

'I'll peel that off in a minute,' she said, tapping Evie's cheek. 'I'll let you drink your tea first. Tess is just coming.'

'Oh, I do feel better, love.' Evie leaned back in the seat, making the leather squeak under her considerable bulk. 'I come out of this place a whole new woman.'

'Sounds like your Leonard thinks so, anyway.'

'Here's your tea. You don't take sugar, do you, Mrs Newcomb?' Tess had a photographic memory for tea and coffee requirements. It was an invaluable asset in a beauty salon.

'Ooh, no, that's lovely.'

'Phone, Camille. I think it's your daughter's school.'

It was the school secretary. She spoke in the firm yet oleaginous tones of those accustomed, through a steely charm, to getting their own way. 'Is that Mrs Hatton? Oh, hello, Margaret Way here. We've had a little problem with Katie and we wondered if you could possibly come and pick her up.'

'Is she hurt?'

'No, not hurt. She's just not very well.'

Nothing clenched the heart like an emergency call from the school, Camille thought. For working mothers it held a potent mixture of relief when the child turned out not to be injured, and irritation that they were going to jettison the working day.

'She says she's not felt very well for a few days.' The supposedly offhand remark held a mild rebuke. Don't send your children to school ill, it said.

Camille thought of her appointment book. 'I don't suppose you've rung her father, have you?'

'No, we like to ring the mother first. That's who the child tends to ask for.'

Well, that told me, she thought. 'Okay,' she said. 'I'll be along as soon as I can. Tess,' she said, replacing the handset on the wall, 'I've got to go and pick Katie up. Not well, apparently. I'll try to sort something out, but you may have to cancel some of this afternoon's appointments. I'm really sorry.'

There were only a few ladies who were content to have Tess minister to them instead. They didn't feel they could tell Tess stuff, they told Camille. Too young, somehow. Too . . . But Camille knew what they really meant.

'There's a lot of it about,' said Evie, from under her mask. 'Sheila from the café has been under the doctor almost ten days now. Winter was too warm, I reckon. All the bugs have been breeding.'

'You're nearly done, Evie. Do you mind if I go? Tess will put your tightening moisturiser on.'

'You go ahead, love. I'll be off soon anyway. I promised Leonard a fish supper and I've run out of oven chips.'

Katie had fallen asleep under her rug. She had apologised, with her peculiar mixture of eight-year-old maturity going on twenty-eight, for interrupting her mother's working day, and had then said that she'd like to sleep. So Camille sat there beside her for a while, her hand resting on her daughter's covered limbs, feeling powerless and anxious and vaguely irritated at the same time. The school nurse had said she looked very pale, and asked whether the dark shadows under her eyes meant she was staying up too late. Camille had been affronted at her tone, at the unspoken suggestion that what they politely referred to as Camille's 'situation' meant that she might not always be aware quite how late her daughter was awake.

'She doesn't have a television in her room, if that's what you mean,' she said abruptly. 'She goes to bed at half past eight and I read her a story.'

But the nurse had said that twice this week Katie had fallen asleep during lessons and that she seemed lethargic, lacklustre. And reminded her that she had been ill not two weeks ago. 'Perhaps she's a bit anaemic,' she suggested, and somehow her kindness made Camille feel even worse.

On the slow walk home, Camille had asked if it had anything to do with her and Daddy, but Katie had said irritably that she was 'just ill' in a tone of voice that meant the conversation was closed. Camille didn't push it. She had handled it well, they all said. Possibly too well.

She leaned down and kissed the sleeping form of her daughter, then stroked the silky muzzle of Rollo, their Labrador. He had settled himself with a sigh at her feet, his wet nose brushing against her bare leg. She sat, for some moments, listening to the steady ticking of the clock on the mantelpiece, and the distant hum of traffic outside. She was going to have to ring. She took a deep breath.

'Hal?'

'Camille?' She never rang him at work any more.

'I'm sorry to bother you. It's just I needed to talk about tonight. I was wondering if you'd mind coming back a bit early.'

'Why?'

'Katie's been sent home from school and I need to go out and catch up on a couple of appointments that I had to cancel this afternoon. See if I can reschedule.'

'What's wrong with her?'

In the background she could hear nothing but the sound of a distant radio, none of the hammering, clamping or voices that had once indicated a thriving workshop. 'Just some virus or other. She's a bit low, but I don't think it's anything serious.'

'Oh. Good.'

'The school nurse thinks she might be a bit anaemic. I've got some iron pills.'

'Right. Yes, I suppose she has been a bit pale.' His tone was casual. 'So who are you going to see?'

She had known that was coming. 'I haven't organised anything yet. I just wanted to see if it was possible.'

She could hear him struggling.

'Well, I suppose there's nothing I couldn't bring home.'

'Are you busy?'

'No. In fact it's been dead all week. I've been working out savings on toilet paper and lightbulbs.'

'Well, as I said, I've got nothing fixed. If no one's available, I won't need you back early.'

They were so polite. So solicitous.

'No problem,' he said. 'You don't want your customers getting upset. No point jeopardising our one good business. Just – just ring me if you need picking up from anywhere. I can always get your mum to sit with Katie for five minutes.'

'Thanks, love, that's really kind.'

'No problem. Better go.'

Camille and Hal Hatton had been married for precisely eleven years and one day when she revealed to him that his suspicions about Michael, the estate agent from London, had been correct. Her timing, it was fair to say, stank. They had just woken up after celebrating their wedding anniversary. But, then, Camille was a fairly straightforward person – or, at least, she had thought she was until the Michael episode – and her talent for comfortably carrying other people's secrets did not extend to her own.

They had been happily married: everyone said so. She said so, on the occasions when she said anything. She was not outwardly romantic. But she had loved Hal with a fierce passion that had not, unlike her friends' marriages, gradually dissipated into something more relaxed (their euphemism, her mother said, for sexless). They had made a handsome pair. Hal, it was widely agreed, was 'fit', while she was tall and strong, with thick blonde hair and a chest like a cartoon barmaid. And he, with his university education, prospects and skill at restoring antique furniture – he had been prepared to take her on. Because not everyone would have done, in spite of her obvious charms. And perhaps because of all these things, their evident passion for one another had been so all-consuming and so long-lasting that it had become something of a joke among their friends. (When they joked, however, Camille had always heard a tinge of something else in their voices: something like envy.) It was the best way they had of communicating. When he was silent, and withdrawn, and she felt unable to bridge the gap to him, when they had argued, and she didn't know how to bring him home, the sex had always been there. Deep, joyous, restorative. Undiminished by Katie's arrival. If anything, she had wanted him more as the years wore on.

And that had been part of the problem. When Hal had started up on his own and moved to new premises over at Harwich, the business had taken up increasing amounts of his time. He had to stay late, he would explain in another late-night telephone call. The first year of any new business was crucial. She had tried to understand, but her physical longing for him – as well as the practical problems of not having him around the house – had grown.

Then the recession had struck and furniture restoration had somehow toppled down people's list of priorities. Hal had grown more tense and distant and some nights had failed to come home at all. The faint stench of sweat on his clothes and stubble on his chin told of another night on the sofa at his offices, his grim demeanour of staff laid off, bills unpaid. And he had not wanted to sleep with her. Too tired. Too beaten down by it all. Unused to failure. And Camille, who had never known rejection in her thirty-five years, had felt panicked.

That was where Michael had come in. Michael Bryant, new in town and up from London to capitalise on the growing demand for beach huts and bungalows by the sea. He had wanted her from the start, had wasted no time in telling her so. And eventually, demented with grief at the perceived loss of her husband, bereft of the physical love that sustained her, she had succumbed.

And regretted it immediately afterwards.

And made the mistake of telling Hal.

He had raged, at first, then wept. And she had thought, hopefully, that the expulsion of such passion might be a good sign because it showed he still cared about her. But then he had grown cold and withdrawn, had moved into the spare room and, ultimately, up the road to Kirby-le-Soken.

Three months later he had returned. He still loved her, he said, muttering furiously into his chest. He would never not love her. But it was going to take a while to trust her.

She had nodded, mutely, just grateful for her second chance. Grateful that Katie wasn't going to become another in a long line of depressing statistics. Hopeful that they could rebuild the love they once had.

A year on, they were still tiptoeing through minefields.

'She feeling better?'

In the front room, just out of earshot, Katie sat, eyes glazed, in front of a blistering run of cartoon explosions.

'She says so. We've been stuffing her with iron tablets. I dread to think what it's doing to her digestive system.'

Camille's mother snorted, and placed another pile of plates in a kitchen cupboard. 'Well, she looks like she's got a little more colour in her face. I did think she'd got a bit pale.'

'You as well! Why didn't you say anything?'

'You know I don't like to butt in.'

Camille smiled wryly.

'So what are you going to do about tomorrow? I thought Hal had that weekend in Derby.'

'It's an antiques fair and it's just the day. He's coming home on the late train. But, yes, unless she goes to school, I'll have to cancel my appointments again. Can you see if Katie's egg's done, Mum? My hands are wet.'

'Another minute, I think . . . It's a long way for him to go for just one day.'

'I know.'

There was a brief silence. Camille knew that her mother was well aware of why Hal didn't want to stay away at night. She thrust her hands deeper into the washing-up water, searching for stray cutlery.

'Well, I don't think you should send her back to school for one day. You want to give her a long weekend to get right again. If you want me to take her, I'm free from mid-morning. And I'll still have her Saturday evening, if you want to go out.'

Camille finished the washing-up, placing the last plate carefully on the rack. She frowned, and turned slightly. 'Aren't you going to Doreen's?'

'No. I've got to go and meet this designer person. Hand the keys over. And take the last of my stuff.'

Camille stopped. 'It's really sold?'

'Of course it's sold.' Her mother's voice was dismissive. 'Been sold for ages.'

'It – it just seems so sudden.'

'It's not sudden in the slightest. I told you I was going to do it. This man didn't have to get a mortgage or anything, so there's no point hanging around.'

'But it was your house.'

'And now it's his house. Will she want ketchup?'

Camille knew better than to argue when her mother was

225

using that tone of voice. She pulled off her rubber gloves and began to smooth moisturiser into her hands, thinking about the house that had, in its way, dominated her childhood. 'So what's he going to do with it?'

'Luxury hotel, apparently. Some kind of upmarket place for creative types. He's got a club in London – all writers and artists and entertainers – and wanted something similar by the sea. Somewhere his type could escape to. It's going to be very modern, he says. Very *challenging*.'

'The town will love that.'

'Bugger the town. He's not going to change the outside of the house – so what business is it of theirs?'

'Since when has something not being their business stopped anybody round here? The Riviera will make a fuss. It'll be taking their business.'

Mrs Bernard moved behind her daughter and put the kettle on. 'The Riviera can barely muster enough customers to keep it in doilies. I can't see a hotel for London's movers and shakers making a huge difference to them. No, it'll do this town good. Place is dying. It might help put a bit of life back into it.'

'Katie will miss it.'

'Katie will still be welcome to visit it. In fact, he said he wanted to keep the house's links with its past alive. It's what he liked about it in the beginning – all the history.' She added, with a faint hint of satisfaction in her voice, 'He's asked me to help advise on some of the restorations.'

'What?'

'Because I know how it used to look. I've still got the pictures and letters and things. He's not just some blundering developer. He says he wants to keep the character of the place.'

'You sound as if you like him.'

226

'I do like him. He calls a spade a spade. But he's curious. You don't get many men of that sort who are curious.'

'Like Pops.' Camille couldn't help herself.

'He's younger than your father. But no. You know your father's never been interested in that house.'

Camille shook her head. 'I don't really understand, Mum. I don't understand why, after all these years. I mean, it was the one thing you were always adamant about – even when Pops got fed up—'

Her mother interrupted: 'Oh, you children. You think the world owes you an explanation. It's my business. My house, my business. It's not going to affect any of you, so let's not harp on.'

Camille sipped at her tea, thinking. 'So what are you going to do with the money? You must have got a fair bit for it.'

'None of your business.'

'Have you told Pops?'

'Yes. He made the same silly noises you did.'

'And told you he had a great idea for the money.'

Her mother snorted a laugh. 'You still don't miss a trick, do you?'

Camille dropped her head. Let it slip out apparently innocuously. 'You could take Pops on a cruise. Just the two of you.'

'And I could donate it all to NASA to see if there are little green men on Mars. Now, I'm going to have this tea, then I'm going to nip to the shops. Do you need anything? I'll take that soppy dog of yours while I'm at it. He looks like he's getting fat.'

'You look very pretty. I like your hair like that.'

'Thank you.'

'It's like the way you wore it when you worked at the bank.'

Camille put a hand to her head, feeling the sleek chignon that Tess had put in for her before she left. She had a gift for hair, Tess. Camille suspected that she would be gone within a year – too much talent in her hands for a sleepy seaside beauty salon. 'Yes. You're right. I did.'

It was a thing they did now, this going out together on a Saturday night, heedless of whether they had the money, or were too exhausted to want to. Camille's mother would have Katie – which she loved – and the two of them would make an effort for each other. They would dress up smartly, as if they were still courting, as the counsellor put it. And they would make conversation with each other, away from the sedative of television, the distractions of domesticity. Sometimes Camille suspected that neither of them could face it, that Hal was struggling to come up with the requisite compliment to show he'd noted her appearance. It was hard finding two hours' worth of fresh conversation with someone you had been speaking to all week. Especially when you weren't allowed to spend the whole time talking about your child, or the dog. But sometimes, like tonight, she heard an honesty in his remarks and felt reassured by the routine of it, from her lengthy soak in the tub to the way Hal still pulled out the chair for her before she sat down. The way they just occasionally made love at the end of the night. You had to make time for each other, the counsellor had said. You had to build your routines. And they still had a lot to rebuild.

Hal ordered the wine. She knew which one it would be before he even spoke: a shiraz. Probably Australian. Under the table she gently rested her leg against his, and felt an answering pressure.

'My mother's house sale has finally gone through.'

'The white house?'

'Yes. Not Pops's house.'

'She really went ahead with it then. I wonder why.'

'I don't know. She won't tell me.'

'Why doesn't that surprise me?'

Her antennae were finely tuned for disparaging remarks, but Camille recognised only an acknowledgement of her mother's secretive nature.

'Who's she sold it to?'

'A hotelier. He's going to turn it into a luxury retreat.'

Hal whistled through his teeth. 'He'll have his work cut out. She's had nothing done to it in years.'

'She had part of the roof fixed a few years ago. But I don't think money is a factor.'

'What? He's loaded?'

'I got that impression.'

'I wonder what she got for it. It's a great site. Great views.'

'I think the fact that it was untouched worked in its favour. They all advertise "original features" now, don't they? And I think she sold some of the furniture with it.'

Hal murmured his assent. 'I would have liked to live in that house,' he said.

'Not me. Too close to the cliff edge.'

'Yes. Yes, I suppose it is.'

Sometimes they managed whole stretches of conversation without either of them making reference to or even privately thinking about it. She fought the urge to say something else about the house, just to prolong it. That was the thing they never told you about break-ups: you lost the person on whom you usually just offloaded all those mildly interesting observations you collected throughout the day. Things that weren't interesting enough to merit a phone call to a half-friend or acquaintance, just things you wanted to remark upon. Hal had always been good like that. They had never run out of stuff to say. And she was grateful.

She smelt the duck before it was placed in front of her: hot, fatty, succulent, with the tang of something citrussy in its sauce. She had eaten nothing since breakfast – Saturdays often got her like that.

'Are you going to your mum's house tomorrow?'

'No.'

'So where are you going?' said Camille. She realised as soon as the words were out that they had come out wrong. Some slight inflection had given them an edge she hadn't intended. She backtracked: 'I just wondered if you had any special plans.'

Hal sighed, as if weighing up how to respond. 'Well, I don't know if this really counts as "special", but one of my neighbours from Kirby is holding a lunch party tomorrow and Katie and I are invited. He's got a little girl. A year younger,' he added. 'If it's all right by you I thought we might go. She and Katie got on quite well.'

Camille smiled, trying to cover the sudden discomfort that had enveloped her. The thought of the two of them being invited anywhere without her was painful; the idea that Katie had been making friends, laying down roots at that place where he had lived . . .

'Is that okay?'

'Of course it is. I was just interested.'

'You can come, if you want. I'm sure you'd like them. I would have asked you anyway but you usually like to have your time on Sundays.'

'No . . . no . . . you should go. It's just . . . I know so little about your life over there. It's – it's hard for me to imagine you . . . her . . .'

Hal put down his knife and fork, apparently considering this. 'Yes,' he said, finally. 'You want me to drive you over some time? So you can get an idea of it?'

She didn't. 'No. No, I'm not sure I . . .'

'Look. We won't go. You're uncomfortable. I don't want to make you uncomfortable.'

'I'm not. Really. Just go. It's a fact of our past, and it's good that some good things came out of it. You go.'

One had to be open about what had happened to the relationship, face up to the past in order to move forward. That's what the counsellor said.

They ate in silence for some time. To her right, a couple had begun to argue, urgently, in whispers. Camille kept her face to the front, listening to the strain in the woman's voice. The waiter came, and refreshed her glass.

'The duck looks good,' said Hal. He shifted a little so that he had increased the pressure on her leg. A delicate pressure, but there all the same.

'Yes,' she said. 'Yes, it is.'

Katie was awake when her father looked in to check on her; she was reading a dog-eared paperback that he knew she had read twice before. She refused to read anything new at the moment, just reread four or five of her favourite books in rotation, despite knowing the endings and even some passages by heart.

'Hey, you,' he said, softly.

She looked up, her half-illuminated face clear, guileless. Her eight-year-old beauty made his heart ache for future hurts and heartaches.

'You should be asleep.'

'Did you have a nice time?'

'We had a lovely time.'

She seemed reassured, closed her book, and allowed herself to be tucked in. 'Are we going to Kirby tomorrow?'

'Yes. If you still want to.'

'Is Mummy coming?'

'No, no. She likes us to have some special time.'

'But she doesn't mind?'

'Of course she doesn't mind. She likes you to have new friends.'

Katie lay silently as her father stroked her hair. He did this often, these days, just grateful that he could now, any night he wanted.

She shifted, turned to her father, brow furrowed. 'Daddy . . .'

'Yes.'

'You know when you left . . .'

His chest tightened. 'Yes.'

'. . . did you get fed up of Mummy because she couldn't see?'

Hal stared at her duvet, with its pink pattern of comic cats and plant pots. Then he moved his hand and placed it over his daughter's. She upended hers, so that she could squeeze it back. 'Sort of, sweetheart.' He paused, let out a long breath. 'But it wasn't about Mummy's eyes. It really wasn't about Mummy's eyes.'

Eleven

The traditional seaside town was 'in' again. She had read it in one of the colour supplements and several interiors magazines, as well as a feature in the *Independent*. After a few lengthy decades where the pleasures of windbreaks, gritty sandwiches and mottled blue legs had been superseded by Coppertone tans and cheap package holidays, the tide had begun slowly to turn again and young families especially were returning to traditional seaside towns, trying to recapture the mythical innocence of their youth. The more affluent snapped up run-down holiday cottages or bungalows, while the remainder were buying up beach huts, sending their values soaring to headline-grabbing levels. Sidmouth in place of St Tropez, Alicante supplanted by Aldeburgh; anyone who was anyone was now strolling through some allegedly unspoilt seaside town eating at family fish restaurants and extolling the joys of the good old bucket and spade.

Except no one seemed to have told Merham. Daisy, driving slowly through the little town, her visibility impaired by the travel-cot, high chair and dustbin bags of clothes she had somehow squeezed into the boot of her car, stared at the dusty knitting shop, cut-price supermarket and Seventh-day Adventist church, and felt a sudden sense of foreboding. Primrose Hill this was not. Even bathed in the milky bright light of a spring afternoon the town seemed faded and tired, stuck in an unlovely combination of eras where anything bold or beautiful was deemed 'showy' and unwelcome.

She stopped at a crossing as two old women shuffled across, one leaning heavily on a shopping trolley, while the other sniffed crossly into a patterned handkerchief, her hair pinned down by a clear plastic helmet.

She had driven around for almost fifteen minutes trying to find the house, and during that time had seen only two people under retirement age. The car dealership was dominated by a banner offering 'motability' deals for the physically challenged, while the only visible restaurant stood between a hearing-aid shop and no fewer than three charity shops in a row, each displaying a sad haul of unfashionable crockery, oversized men's trousers and cuddly toys that no one wanted to cuddle. Its only redeeming feature, as far as she could see, was its endless beach, rulermarked by rotting breakwaters, and the manicured, post-Palladian splendour of its municipal park.

On spying a man with a little girl, she wound down her window and called, 'Excuse me?'

He looked up. His clothes betrayed his relatively young age, but his face, behind thin-rimmed glasses, was exhausted, prematurely lined.

'Do you live here?'

He glanced at the little girl, who was clutching a box of batteries, trying fiercely to prise one out. 'Yes.'

'Can you point me in the direction of Arcadia House?'

His head jolted a little in recognition, and he looked at her a little more assessingly. 'You're the designer, are you?'

Oh, God, it was true about these places. She mustered a smile. 'Yes. Or at least I will be if I can find it.'

'It's not far. You want to turn right, head down to the roundabout, and follow the road up all the way past the park. It's set into the cliff. It's the last house you'll come to.'

'Thanks.'

The little girl tugged at her father's hand. 'Dad . . .' she said, impatiently.

'I think you'll find the previous owner's there waiting for you. Good luck,' he added, and suddenly broke into a grin, then turned away before she could ask him how he knew.

The house made up for it. She knew it as soon as she glimpsed it; felt that flicker of excitement, the pleasure of a new canvas, as soon as it laid itself out, broad and white and angular, before her at the apex of the curved drive. It was bigger than she'd expected, longer and lower, with layers of cubed-glass windows and portholes gazing wide-eyed out at the glinting sea. Ellie was still asleep from the journey, so she had opened the car door, peeled herself from the plastic seat and stepped out on to the gravel, her stiffness and sweatiness evaporating as she took in the modern lines, the brave, brutal angles of it, breathing in the fresh salt air. She didn't even need to look inside: set like some great outcrop of rock against the vast curve of the ocean, under a wide open sky, she knew the rooms were generous and flooded with light. Daniel had taken photographs, had brought them back when she was at home with the newborn Ellie, and she had worked on her ideas at night, drawn up her initial sketches from those. But the photographs had not done it justice, had given no hint of its minimalist beauty, its severe charm, and the plans they had had for it already seemed too tame, too mundane.

She glanced behind her, checking that Ellie was still asleep, then ran lightly down to the open gate, which led through into the stepped garden. There was a paved terrace, its whitewash worn and blistered with lichen, while down a series of steps, overhung with lilac, a path led through overgrown walled enclosures to the beach. Above her the breeze murmured meditatively through the branches of two Scots pines, while a colony of overexcited sparrows dived in and out of an unruly hawthorn hedge.

Daisy gazed around her, her mind already a jumble of ideas, each swiftly conjured and discarded as she took in some new feature, some unusual marriage of space and line. She had briefly thought of Daniel, of the fact that this should have been their project, but she pushed away his image. The only way she was going to be able to do this was if she treated it as a new start; as if, like Julia had said, she had pulled herself together. The house helped. She tripped down the stairs, peering into windows, turning to take it in from different angles, seeing its possibilities, its latent beauty. Oh, God, she could make this place magical. It held more promise than anything she had ever worked on before; she could turn it into something that would grace the pages of the hippest style magazines, a haven that would be a draw for anyone who had ever had a notion of what style really meant. It will design itself, she thought. Already it is speaking to me.

'Trying to exercise her lungs, are you?'

Daisy spun round to see Ellie, tearstained and hiccuping, in the arms of a short, elderly woman with gun-metal hair tucked behind her ears in a severe bob. 'Sorry?' She moved forward, up the steps.

The woman handed Ellie to her, several thick bangles colliding on her arms. 'Thought you must be hoping for an opera singer, the way you left her howling.'

Daisy ran a hand gently over Ellie's drying tears. Ellie leaned forward, resting her face against her mother's chest. 'I didn't hear her,' she said, awkwardly. 'I couldn't hear anything.'

The woman stepped forward, looked past the two of them to the sea. 'I thought you girls were all meant to be paranoid about baby-snatchers these days. Afraid to leave them for a minute.' She gazed neutrally at Ellie, who was now smiling at her. 'What is she? Four, five months? You've all got it arse-upwards as far as I can see. If you're not fretting about what you're putting in their mouths, popping them into cars for ten-yard journeys, you're leaving them to scream miles from anywhere. Makes no sense.'

'We're hardly miles from anywhere.'

'Giving them to nannies, then complaining when they get attached.'

'I don't have a nanny. And I didn't leave her deliberately. She was asleep.' Daisy heard the petulant tremor of tears in her voice. They seemed to be permanently there, these days, waiting just under the surface to break through.

'Anyway. You'll want the keys. Jones, or whatever he calls himself, can't get here till the middle of the week so he's asked me to get you settled in. I've left you my granddaughter's old cot – it's got a few bite marks round the top, but it's still sound. There's still some bits of furniture in there, and cooking things in the kitchen, but I left you some bed linen and towels, because he didn't say what you'd be bringing. And there's a box of groceries in the kitchen. Thought you probably wouldn't come with much.' She glanced behind her. 'My husband's going to bring up a microwave later as we couldn't get the range working, so you'll have something for bottles. He'll be here about half six.'

Daisy was unsure how to respond to this swift shift from censure to generosity. 'Thank you.'

'I'll be in and out. I won't get in your way. But there are some things I've still got to remove. Jones said I could take my time.'

'Yes. I – I'm sorry. I didn't catch your name.'

'That's because I didn't give it to you. I'm Mrs Bernard.'

'I'm Daisy. Daisy Parsons.'

'I know.'

As Daisy held out her hand, shifting Ellie's weight on her hip, she noted the older woman's swift glance at her ring finger.

'You'll be staying on your own?'

Daisy looked unconsciously at her hand. 'Yes.'

Mrs Bernard nodded, as if that were to be expected. 'I'll go and check that the heating's working, then I'll leave you to it. You won't need it now, but there's a frost due tonight.' As she got to the gate at the side of the house, she turned and called back, 'There's all sorts already got their knickers in a twist about this place. They'll be along before you know it, telling you where you're going wrong.'

'That's something to look forward to, then,' said Daisy, feebly.

'I shouldn't take any notice. This house has always managed to upset them, one way or another. Don't see as how you'll be any different.'

It was only when Ellie had settled, safely wedged into the double bed with a clutch of pillows, that the tears had come. Daisy had sat in the half-furnished house, fatigued, lonely and, without the distraction of her daughter, unable to escape the mammoth task she had taken on – and that she had taken it on singlehandedly.

She had picked at a microwave meal, lit a cigarette (a renewed habit), and wandered through the decrepit rooms, with their smell of mildewing fabrics and beeswax. Slowly her visions of glossy pages and stark, modernist walls had been overtaken by alternative images: of herself, clutching a screaming baby, faced with recalcitrant workmen and a furious owner while outside a crowd of angry locals demanded she be removed.

What have I done? she thought miserably. This is too big, too far beyond me. I could spend a month on one room alone. But there was no going back: the Primrose Hill flat was empty, her remaining furniture in her sister's barn, half a dozen explanatory messages, apparently unheeded, to Daniel on his mother's answerphone. (Flustered and apologetic, she had said she didn't know where he'd gone either.) If he didn't pick them up, he wouldn't know where to find them. That's if he was planning to find them.

She thought of Ellie, peacefully asleep, unaware that her father had deserted her. How would she cope with the knowledge that he hadn't loved her enough to stay around? How could he not have loved her enough?

She had wept, quietly, considerately, still somehow fearful of disturbing the baby even in this huge space, for almost twenty minutes. And then, at last, the twin narcolepsies of exhaustion and the distant draw and hiss of the sea had brought sleep.

When she awoke, there was another box in the front porch. It contained two pints of full-cream milk, an Ordnance Survey map of Merham and the surrounding area, and a small selection of old, but immaculate, baby's toys.

For a baby who more usually considered being seated at a different end of the sofa sufficient trauma to trigger a lengthy crying fit, Ellie adapted remarkably quickly to her new home. She lay in the middle of her crocheted blanket gazing out of the oversized window and crowing at the gulls that swooped and shrieked rudely through the sky above her. Propped up, she would watch her mother's progress around the room, her little hands fumbling to place any nearby object into her mouth. At night, she often slept four or five hours at a stretch – for the first time in her short life.

Her apparent satisfaction at her new surroundings meant that, in those first few days, Daisy was able to jot down a block of new designs, taking her inspiration from the still-visible sketchings on some of the walls, the almost legible scrawled writings that had lain undisturbed for several decades. She had asked Mrs Bernard about these, curious as to who had placed them there, but the older woman had said only that she didn't know, that they had always been there, and that when, having seen them, her daughter's friend had scribbled on the wall as a child she had whacked him with a broom handle.

Mrs Bernard had turned up every day. Daisy still didn't know why: she seemed to glean no pleasure from Daisy's company, and sniffed dismissively at most of her suggestions. 'Don't know why you're telling me,' she said once, when Daisy appeared disappointed at her response.

'Because it was your house?' said Daisy, weary of her tone.

'And now it's not. No point looking to the past. If you know what you want to do with it, you should just get on with it. You don't need my approval.'

Daisy suspected it sounded more unfriendly than was meant.

The lure, she thought, was Ellie. Mrs Bernard would approach the baby shyly, warily almost, as if expecting to be told that she was really none of her business. But then, with half an eye on Daisy, she would pick her up and, slowly gaining confidence, would carry her around the rooms, pointing things out, talking to her as if she were already ten years older, apparently relishing the baby's responses. Then, 'She likes looking at the pines,' or 'Blue's her favourite colour,' she would announce, the faintest hint of challenge in her voice. Daisy didn't mind: she was grateful to have someone else to care for the baby – it helped her focus her mind on her designs, for already she had understood that trying to refurbish this hotel with a demanding five-month-old in tow was going to be almost impossible.

Mrs Bernard said little about her part in the house's history, and although Daisy was increasingly curious, something in the older woman's demeanour discouraged close questioning. She told her briefly, in conversation, that she had owned it 'for ever', that her husband never came here, and that the reason why the second largest bedroom still housed a bed and chest of drawers was that she had used it as a bolthole for most of her married life. She said nothing else about her family. Daisy said nothing about her own. They existed in a kind of uneasy equanimity, Daisy grateful for Mrs Bernard's interest in Ellie, yet somehow conscious of a kind of latent disapproval, both of Daisy's own situation, and of her plans for the hotel. She felt a little like a prospective daughter-in-law and that, in some way that wasn't going to be explained to her, she didn't quite measure up.

On the Wednesday, however, Ellie's run of unusually amenable behaviour came to an abrupt end. She woke at a quarter to five and refused to be put back to sleep so that by nine Daisy was already cross-eyed with exhaustion, and at a loss as to how to keep her fractious infant happy. It rained, dark, load-bearing clouds scudded across the sky, leaving them confined to the house, the shrubs outside bowing under the weight of the wind. Below them, the sea churned, murky grey and restless, a forbidding vista designed to quell any romantic illusions about the British coastline. And Mrs Bernard picked that day not to turn up. Daisy found herself pacing the floor endlessly, jiggling her child up and down against her chest, as she tried to clear a space in her treacly mind for reclaimed-wood floors and polished steel door handles. 'C'mon, Ellie, *please*, darling,' she murmured ineffectually, and the child wailed louder and harder, as if her request in itself were an affront.

Jones arrived at a quarter to eleven, exactly two and a half minutes after Daisy had finally put Ellie down to sleep, and thirty seconds after she had lit her first cigarette of the day. She gazed around her at the debris-strewn room, replete with half-empty coffee cups and the remains of last night's microwave meal, and wondered which part she had the energy to attack first. He slammed the door behind him, of course, which meant that Ellie, upstairs, immediately rent the air with a scream of outrage and Daisy found herself slaving venomously at her new boss, while he in turn stared incredulously at his less-than-minimalist drawing room.

'Jones,' he said, looking up at the ceiling, whence Ellie's muffled screams could be heard. 'I take it you forgot I was coming.'

He was younger than she had imagined, perhaps approaching middle age instead of exiting the other side, and crosser-looking, two dark brows knitting above a once-broken nose. He was also tall and slightly overweight, giving him the unfinessed look of a rugby forward, but this was offset by a pair of sage wool trousers and an expensive soft grey shirt; the muted wardrobe of the properly rich.

Daisy tried to blot out the noise of her child. She thrust out a hand, fighting the urge to berate him for his noisy inconsideration. 'Daisy. But you know that . . . She – she's a bit challenging this morning. She's not usually like this. Can I get you a coffee?'

He looked at the cups on the floor. 'No, thank you. It stinks of smoke in here.'

'I was just about to open some windows.'

'I'd rather you didn't smoke in the house. If at all possible. You've remembered why I'm here?'

Daisy cast around desperately for some piece of stored knowledge. It was like trying to see through cotton-wool.

'The planning officer. She's due this morning to look at the bathroom plans. And the conversion of the garage? For the staff flats?'

Daisy had a dim recollection of a letter mentioning something similar. She had stuffed it into a carrier-bag, along with her other filing. 'Yes,' she said. 'Of course.'

He wasn't fooled. 'Perhaps you'd like me to fetch my copy of the plans from the car so that we at least look prepared.'

Upstairs, Ellie was reaching new crescendos. 'I am prepared. I know it looks a little chaotic, but I just haven't had a chance to straighten things up this morning.'

Daisy had stopped breastfeeding almost three weeks ago, but the sound of Ellie's prolonged crying, she realised with some horror, was making her leak. 'I'll get my folder,' she said hurriedly. 'It's just upstairs.'

'I suppose I'd better try to straighten this lot up. We at least want her to *think* we're professional, don't we?'

She forced a smile, and ran past him up the stairs to Ellie, muttering expletives as she went. Once in their shared bedroom, she calmed her puce-faced child, then rummaged through her holdall, trying to find something a little more professional-looking to wear. Or something that was not made of sweatshirt material and blotted with baby sick. She found a black polo-neck and long skirt, and wriggled her way into them, stuffing her brassière with tissue paper to soak up any more embarrassing emissions. Then, having scraped her hair back into a ponytail (at least her sister had made her get her roots done), she walked back down the stairs, a pacified Ellie on her hip and the folder of bathroom plans under her other arm.

'What are these?' He was holding up a sheaf of her new designs.

'Just some ideas I had. I was going to talk to you—'

'I thought we'd agreed. On each room. On the costings.'

'I know that. It's just that when I got here the space was so incredible . . . I just got inspired. It made me think of other things—'

'Stick to the plans, okay? We're already tight on timings as it is. I can't afford to start going off at tangents.' He threw down the papers on the old sofa.

Something about the way her drawings fluttered on to the floor made Daisy bristle. 'I wasn't thinking of charging you any extra,' she said, pointedly. 'I just thought you'd want the best designs for the space.'

'I was under the impression I had ordered the best designs for the space.'

Daisy fought to hold his impenetrable stare, determined that, having buckled under everything else, she would not be driven over by this man. He didn't think she was up to it: it was apparent in his demeanour, the way he kept sighing when he walked around the room, the way he interrupted her, the way he looked her up and down as if she were something unpleasant that had just come into the room.

She thought, briefly, of Weybridge. And then Ellie sneezed, grunted audibly, and sent the poisonous contents of her bowels shooting into her clean Babygro.

He left, partially pacified, after lunch, the plans having been approved by the local planning officer, who, Daisy decided, had been so distracted by and enamoured of the now sanitary and beguiling Ellie that she would have conditionally approved a three-lane motorway stretching from the utility room to the garden. 'You know, it's lovely to see this house being used after all these years,' she said, as they finished their tour. 'And a lovely change for me to see something a bit ambitious. Usually I get double garages and conservatories. No, I think it'll be wonderful and, provided you stay within your plans, I can't see any problems with the parish council.'

'I've been told some of the locals aren't too keen on the house being redeveloped.' Daisy intercepted a sharp look from Jones as she spoke.

But the planning officer shrugged. 'Between you and me, they're very backward-looking in this town. And it's been to their cost. The other little resorts have allowed the odd pub or restaurant to grow along their coastline, and now they're thriving all year round. Poor old Merham's been so concerned with keeping everything as it was that I think it's lost sight of what it is.' She gestured out of the window, up along the coast. 'I mean, it's getting a bit run-down. There's nothing for the young people. Personally I think it'll be a shot in the arm if we can get a few new visitors. But don't quote me on that.'

She gave Ellie's cheek another fond tickle, and then she was gone, with a promise to be in touch.

'Well, I think that went rather well.' Daisy, walking back down the hallway, was determined that she should get some credit.

'Like she said, the town needs the business.'

'Still, I'm glad she approved the plans.'

'If you did your job right, there was no reason why she shouldn't. Now, I've got to head back to London.

I've got a meeting at five. When are the workmen due to start?'

There was even something intimidating about the size of him. Daisy felt herself shrink back as he walked past her towards the door. 'The plumbers are in on Tuesday, and the builders start moving that kitchen wall two days later.'

'Good. Keep me in touch. I'll be up again next week. In the meantime you need to sort out some childcare. I can't have you faffing around with a baby when you're meant to be working. Oh,' he glanced downwards, 'you've got toilet roll hanging out of the bottom of your jumper.'

He didn't say goodbye. But he did close the door quietly as he went.

There was always a bed for her in Weybridge. She was not to forget that, her sister had told her on the phone. Some three times now. She plainly thought Daisy was mad for having dragged her baby daughter to some draughty old wreck at the seaside when she could be living in centrally heated splendour in the best room of Julia's barn, with the added bonus of family babysitting thrown in. But she had to deal with things in her own way. At least Julia understood that. 'Just so you know I'm always there to pick up the pieces.'

'I'm not in pieces any more. I'm fine.' Daisy sounded more convincing than she felt.

'Are you counting calories?'

'No. Nor am I exercising. Or blow-drying my hair. I'm too busy.'

'Busy is good. It's good to keep your mind active. And the Scarlet Pimpernel? Heard from him yet?'

'No.' She had given up ringing his mother. It had got embarrassing.

'Well, I know you didn't want it but I have found out the

number for the Child Support Agency, when you're ready.'

'Julia . . .'

'If he wanted to play big boys' games, he should have been prepared for big boys' consequences. Look, I'm not forcing it on you. I'm just telling you I've got it. When you're ready. Just like the barn. It's all here, waiting for you.'

Daisy pushed Ellie along the coastal path in her all-terrain buggy, puffing on her fourth cigarette of the morning. Julia didn't think she was going to make it. Her sister thought she would make some headway into the Arcadia project then admit that it was all too much, give up and come home. She couldn't blame her, considering the state Julia had found her in. And for the last few days, Weybridge had, admittedly, started to look strangely attractive. The plumbers had failed to turn up on Tuesday, as promised, having had to go to a series of apparent emergencies. The builders had started knocking through the kitchen wall, but the supporting steel beam had not been delivered so they had stopped at a car-sized hole 'just to be on the safe side'. They were currently sitting outside on the terrace enjoying the spring sunshine and making bets on the Cheltenham Gold Cup. When she had asked whether there was anything else they could be getting on with, they had blustered on about safety regulations and RSJs. She had set her jaw against tears and tried not to think about how different things might have been had Daniel been there to deal with them. Finally, having spent most of her morning on the phone arguing with various suppliers, she had ventured out to get some air. And pick up some more tea. Considering she was supposedly in charge of the project, she had heard the phrase 'white with two sugars' several more times than she was strictly comfortable with.

It was a shame, really, because if it hadn't been for the stresses of Arcadia, she would have felt almost cheerful this morning. The surroundings seemed to be conspiring to make her feel better, the sea and sky a series of textbook blues, the spring daffodils bobbing merrily along the borders, a soft breeze hinting of the summer months ahead. Ellie squealed and crowed at the gulls that swooped before them, hoping for some scrap of rusk to be hurled from the pram. Her cheeks, in the fresh air, had developed the glow of blushing apples. ('Windchapped,' Mrs Bernard had said, disapprovingly.) The town also looked more cheerful, largely due to the presence of a scattering of market stalls in the little square, their striped tarpaulins and overspilling trays of goods bringing a much-needed hint of life and colour.

'Hey, Ellie,' she said, 'Mummy could splash out and have a jacket potato tonight.' She had given up on microwave meals, and now ate wedges of bread and butter, or finished off Ellie's jars. Quite often she was too exhausted even to do that, and fell asleep where she sat on the one sofa, waking at five with a stomach clawing from hunger.

She paused a while at the fruit and veg stall, loading up with carrots to mash for Ellie and fruit for herself. You didn't have to cook fruit. It was as she collected her change that she felt a tap on her shoulder. 'Are you the girl at the actress's house?'

'Sorry?' Daisy turned from her organic reverie to find a middle-aged woman sporting the kind of quilted green jacket favoured by horse-owners and a burgundy felt hat pulled low over her head. Less conventionally, on her lower legs, she wore dark red leg-warmers and a pair of stout walking-shoes. She was also, like her rather fleabitten Alsatian, standing a little too close.

'Are you the girl at Arcadia House? The one who's ripping it all to bits?'

Her tone was aggressive enough to draw the attention of

several passers-by. They turned, curiously, their intended purchases still in their hands.

'I'm not "ripping it to bits" but, yes, I am the designer who's working on Arcadia House.'

'And is it true you're going to put in a public bar? To attract all sorts of London types?'

'There is going to be a bar, yes. I can't say who the clientele is likely to be because I'm only in charge of the décor.'

The woman's face was getting steadily more pink. Her voice carried in the manner of someone who liked having their opinions heard. Her dog, apparently unnoticed, was edging its nose uncomfortably close to Daisy's crotch. She made a tiny move as if to shoo it away, but it looked steadily at her from blank yellow eyes and moved its nose nearer.

'I am Sylvia Rowan. I own the Riviera. And, I feel obliged to tell you, we don't want another hotel around here. Especially not one that's going to attract all sorts of undesirables.'

'I hardly think—'

'Because it's not that kind of town. You wouldn't know, but we've worked jolly hard to keep this town special.'

'It may be special, but I hardly think you're ring-fencing the Vatican.'

There were at least four other faces drawing closer now, waiting for the next chapter in the exchange. Daisy felt vulnerable with her daughter in front of her, and it made her unusually aggressive in return. 'Anything we're doing at the hotel we're doing with planning permission. And any bar will, no doubt, have the approval of the appropriate licensing authorities. Now, if you'll excuse me . . .'

'You don't understand, do you?' Sylvia Rowan planted herself firmly in front of Ellie's push-chair so that Daisy would either have to steer round her into the growing crowd of onlookers or run her over. The dog eyed her crotch with something that might have been either enthusiasm or malevolence. It was hard to tell.

'I have lived in this town all my life, and we have all fought hard to maintain certain standards here,' Sylvia Rowan brayed, pointing her wallet towards Daisy's chest. 'This includes stopping endless bars and cafés cluttering up the seafront, unlike so many other seaside towns. That way it is still a pleasant place for its residents to live, and a desirable place for visitors to come and stay.'

'And nothing to do with the fact that your hotel runs one of the bars.'

'That is irrelevant. I have lived here all my life.'

'Which is why you probably can't see how run-down it's got.'

'Look, Miss – whoever-you-are. We don't want lowlife here. And we don't want to be overrun with Soho's drunken overflow. It's not that kind of town.'

'And Arcadia House is not going to be that kind of hotel. For your information, the clientele are going to be very upmarket, the kinds of people happy to pay two or three hundred pounds a night for a room. And those kinds of people expect taste, decorum and a lot of bloody peace and quiet. So why don't you just get your facts straight and leave me alone to do my job?'

Daisy wheeled the push-chair round, ignoring the potatoes that toppled out of the carrier-bag, and began to walk briskly back across the market square, blinking furiously. She turned, shouting on the wind, 'And you should train your dog better. It's incredibly rude.'

'You can tell your boss, young lady, that you haven't heard the last of this.' Sylvia Rowan's voice carried back to her. '*We are the people of England . . . and we have not spoken yet.*'

'Oh, bog off, you horrible old bag,' Daisy muttered, and then, safely out of sight of onlookers, stopped, lit her fifth cigarette of the day, inhaled deeply, and burst into tears.

Twelve

Daisy Parsons had grown up into the kind of young woman about whom older people murmur approvingly, 'Lovely girl.' And she was lovely: she had been a sweet child, with the ringleted blonde locks of a Miss Pears model, a ready smile and a desire to please. She had been educated privately, liked by everyone at her school, and had worked industriously to pass exams in architecture, art and design, in which, her tutors said, she had 'a good eye'. Into her teens, apart from a brief unsuccessful experiment with vegetable hair dye, she had done nothing to frighten her parents, or leave them sleepless and frantic in the early hours of the morning. Her boyfriends had been few, carefully selected, and generally nice. She had let them go regretfully, usually with some apologetic tears, so that nearly all looked back on her without rancour, and most usually as 'the one that got away'.

And then Daniel had come: tall, dark, handsome Daniel with his respectable parents, both accountants, Protestant work ethic, and exacting style. The kind of man who made other girls immediately dissatisfied with their own. Daniel had come to protect her at a time when she was starting to weary of having to look after herself, and both had adapted to their respective roles in the relationship with the contented shimmying of a chicken settling down to roost. Daniel was the driving force in the business, the strong, forthright one. The protector. This freed Daisy up to become her perfect version of herself: beautiful, sweet, sexy, confident in his adoration. A lovely girl. Each saw the perfect vision of themselves reflected in the other's eyes, and liked it. They rarely argued: there was little need. Besides, neither of them liked the emotional messiness of argument, unless they knew it to be the snappings of foreplay.

Which was why nothing had prepared Daisy for this new life, thrust permanently into a spotlight of disapproval and almost incessantly in dispute – with builders, townspeople, Daniel's parents – at a time when she felt most vulnerable, and without even her traditional armour of loveliness to fall back on. The plumbers, apparently oblivious to her pleadings, had gone off to work on another job because they couldn't start installing the bathrooms until the builders had finished laying the surface over the new septic tank. The builders couldn't lay the surface as they were waiting for parts. The suppliers had apparently emigrated. Sylvia Rowan, according to talk, was planning a public meeting to object to the desecration of Arcadia House, and the risk to the standards, morals and general well-being of Merham's citizens if the work was allowed to continue.

Jones, meanwhile, had called in a cold fury the day after her confrontation in the market square, and unleashed a verbal torrent on the various ways in which she had already failed to come up to scratch. He could not believe they were already running behind schedule. He could not understand why the RSJ, when it finally arrived, was the wrong width. He had little faith that they were going to be able to open, as planned, in August. And, to be frank, he was very much starting to doubt whether Daisy was committed and possessed the ability to complete the job to his satisfaction.

'You're not giving me a chance,' said Daisy, biting back tears.

'You have no idea how much of a chance I'm giving you,' he said, and rang off.

Mrs Bernard had appeared in the doorway with Ellie. 'You don't want to start crying,' she said, nodding towards the terrace. 'They're not taking you seriously as it is. You start blubbing everywhere they'll have you down as all hair and hormones.'

'Thank you very much, Mrs Bernard. That's really helpful.'

'I'm just saying, you don't want them walking all over you.'

'And I'm just saying, when I want your bloody opinion I'll bloody ask for it.'

Daisy had swept a folder of papers off the table, and marched outside finally to lose her temper with the builders, only the second time she had done so in her life (the first had been when Daniel admitted he had consigned Mr Rabbit to the dustbin on the grounds that he lowered the tone of their bedroom). This time, she shouted so loudly that her voice could be heard as far as the church, as could a choice selection of threats and expletives filtering through air more used to the cry of gulls and avocets. The radio, meanwhile, was seen flying on a rapid trajectory through the air above the cliff path before it shattered on the rocks below. It was followed by a lengthy silence, then the muttering and slow shuffling of feet as six recalcitrant builders found other ways to occupy themselves.

Daisy marched into the house, hands on hips as if resting on a holster, fired up, as the builders would later mutter, and ready to blow again.

This time she was met with silence. Mrs Bernard and Ellie, a smile on both their faces, had disappeared back into the kitchen.

★   ★   ★

'So, how's it going up there?'

Camille folded the plastic layer over the perfumed cream, then placed her mother's hands in the heated mitts. It was the only treatment she'd agree to, a weekly manicure. Facials, body wraps, they were all a waste of time, but her hands she had always taken care of. She had decided a long time ago: if touch was one of the main means by which she would be communicating with her daughter, then that touch should always be a pleasant one.

'It's going.'

'Are you finding it difficult?'

'Me?' Her mother sniffed. 'No. Doesn't make any difference to me what they do to it. But I think the poor girl's struggling a bit.'

'Why?' Camille moved across to the door to shout for a cup of tea. 'Tess said she heard she was on her own with a baby.'

'She is on her own. And a face like a wet weekend half the time. The workmen think she's a joke.'

'Do you think she'll cope?'

'On current form? Probably not. She finds it hard to say boo to a goose. I can't see how she's going to renovate a hotel. She's only got till August.'

'Poor girl.' Camille came and sat down, facing her mother. 'We should go up there to see her. She's probably lonely.' She reached behind her and, without fumbling, located cream, which she began to apply to her own hands.

'I go all the time.'

'You go for the baby. Even I know that.'

'She doesn't want you blundering in. It'll look like I've been talking about her.'

'You have been talking about her. Come on, we'll make it a day out. Katie would love it. She hasn't been in there for ages.'

'Shouldn't Hal be working?'

'Hal is entitled to take a weekend, Mum, just like the rest of us.'

Her mother snorted.

'Look, you don't want her to get too miserable, Mum. If she goes, we'll get some idiot up wanting to install gold pedestals and Jacuzzis and what-have-you. Oh, hello, Tess. White no sugar when you're ready. You'll have satellite dishes off the side of it, and executive conferences there every weekend.'

'You okay, Mrs Bernard?'

'Fine, thanks, Tess. This daughter of mine is trying to stick her nose in up at Arcadia.'

Tess grinned. 'Ooh, Camille, you don't want to go getting involved with that little lot. There's going to be a battle over that hotel. Sylvia Rowan's been in here shouting the odds all morning. "It wouldn't have happened in the old days of the Guest-house Association,"' she mimicked.

Camille placed the cream behind her on the shelf, and shut a cupboard door. 'All the more reason to show the girl a friendly face or two. God knows what she thinks she's let herself in for.'

Mrs Bernard shook her head irritably. 'Oh, all right. We'll go up Sunday. I'll tell the girl to prepare for an invasion.'

'Good. But you've got to bring Pops as well. He's actually quite interested in seeing what she's doing.'

'Yes, well, he would be.'

'What?'

'He thinks that now the house is gone I'll be spending all my time at home with him.'

They all came, in the end. A Bernard family outing, as Camille's father jovially put it, offloading everyone from his beloved Jaguar on to the gravel drive. 'I tell you what, chaps, I can't remember the last time we all went out together.'

Daisy, standing at the door in her one good shirt, Ellie on her hip, eyed Mr Bernard with interest. Mrs Bernard had seemed a solitary character so it was quite hard now to reconcile her with this bluff, gentle man with apologetic eyes and hands the size of hams. He was wearing a shirt and tie, the kind of man who always did at weekends, and highly polished shoes. You could tell a lot about a man from the shine on his shoes, he told her later. The first time he had met Hal and his brown suede numbers, he thought he must be a Communist. Or a Friend of Dorothy.

'Katie's christening,' called Camille, who was holding the car door as Katie and Rollo poured out of the back. She waved in the general direction of the house. 'Hello. Camille Hatton.'

'That doesn't count,' said Hal. 'Hardly an outing.'

'And I don't remember it,' said Katie.

'Mother's Day three years ago, when we took you and Camille to that restaurant over at Halstead . . . What was it?'

'Overrated.'

'Thank you, Mother-in-law. French, wasn't it?'

'The only thing French about that place was the smell of the drains. I've brought some cakes. Didn't want you to go to any trouble.' Mrs Bernard handed Daisy the box that she had held on her lap, then in exchange reached out and took the compliant Ellie from her mother.

'How lovely,' said Daisy, who was beginning to feel invisible. 'Thank you.'

'We had a lovely time,' said Mr Bernard, shaking Daisy's hand warmly. 'I had steak *au poivre*. I still remember it. And Katie had seafood, didn't you, love?'

'I don't know,' said Katie. 'Have you really not got a telly?'

'No. Not any more. You're the man who gave me directions,' said Daisy, as Hal drew nearer.

'Hal Hatton. And you've met Katie.' His face looked younger, more relaxed than the last time they had met. 'Nice of you to have us over. I hear you're on quite a deadline.' He took a step back. 'God, I haven't seen this place in years.'

'There's a few walls knocked through, and some of the smaller bedrooms have become bathrooms,' said Mrs Bernard, following his gaze. 'They all want *en suite* nowadays apparently.'

'Do you want to come through?' Daisy said. 'I found some chairs and I've put them out on the terrace, seeing as it's such a nice day. But we can move in, if you like. Just watch out for rubble.'

It was as she held the door open that she realised the blonde woman couldn't see. Her dog didn't look like a guide dog: it had no frame or harness for her to hold, but it did glance behind itself as if well used to adjusting its own speed, and then, as Camille stepped towards the door, her husband's hand appeared at her elbow, withdrawing discreetly when she had made it past the front step.

'It's straight on, but I suppose you know that,' she said, with a shade of awkwardness.

'Oh, God, no,' said Camille, turning to face her. Her eyes were clear and blue, perhaps deeper-set than usual. 'This was always Mum's house. We never really had much to do with it.'

She didn't look like a blind person. Not that Daisy had a clear idea of how a blind person should look, having never actually met one. She just imagined that she should look somehow dowdier. Perhaps a little overweight. She certainly shouldn't be wearing designer jeans and makeup, and have a waist measurement possibly half the size of her bust. 'Did you not come here much as children?'

Camille called ahead, 'Hal? Is Katie with you?' She paused. 'We did come here occasionally. I think Mum used to get nervous about me being so close to the cliff edge.'

'Oh.' Daisy didn't know what else to say.

Camille stopped. 'She didn't tell you I was blind, did she?'

'No.'

'Plays a lot of cards close to her chest, my mother. But I suppose you've discovered that.'

Daisy stood still for a minute, staring at the smooth, caramel-coloured skin, the abundant blonde hair. Her hand rose unconsciously to her own. 'Do you want . . . I mean, do you want to feel my face or something?'

Camille burst out laughing. 'God, no. I can't stand touching people's faces. Unless I'm working, that is.' She reached forward, tentatively touched Daisy's arm. 'You're quite safe, Daisy. I have no desire to run my hands over anyone's face. Especially beards. I can't stand beards – they make me shudder. I always think I'm going to find food in one. Now, has my dad managed to let go of his car for two minutes? He's become obsessed with the thing since his retirement,' she confided. 'That, and his bridge. And his golf. Likes his hobbies, does Pops.'

They emerged on to the terrace. Hal guided his wife into a seat, and Daisy watched this casual intimacy with a flicker of envy. She missed having a protector.

'Used to be a beautiful house, didn't it, love?' Mr Bernard placed his car keys in his pocket and turned to look at his wife, a strange mixture of emotions flickering over his face.

'Not that anyone round here ever thought so.' Mrs Bernard shrugged. 'Till it started changing.'

259

'I always thought it would benefit from a monkey-puzzle tree.'

Daisy took in the quick glance exchanged by the Bernards, and the uncomfortable silence that followed it.

'So, what do you make of Merham?' said Hal.

Coming from a family that was not so much broken as irrevocably fractured by bereavement, Daisy automatically assumed that all other families were like the Waltons. Daniel had told her so more than once, when she had emerged from one of his family gatherings shocked at the noisy disagreements and simmering resentments that flared up as regularly as the barbecue. But, still, she found it hard to view them dispassionately; found herself unconsciously trying to fit in, to tap into some shared family history. She refused to believe that being part of a large, extended family could be anything other than a comfort.

The Bernards and Hattons, however, had a kind of forced jollity about them, as if they were permanently reassuring themselves of their status as a family, edged by an apparent determination only ever to refer to the good. They exclaimed over the general pleasantness of everything: weather, surroundings, each other's outfits, and addressed each other with fond insults, made references to shared family jokes. Except Mrs Bernard, who smacked down any Waltonesque sentiments with the determined efficiency of a hygienist swatting a fly. Just as a Mother's Day treat was only memorable for the stench of drains, so every reference had to be smothered with a caustic aside, only partially alleviated by occasional wit. Thus the endless beauty of the beach was tempered by the fact that holidaymakers were now staying away – and she didn't blame them; the glossy new family car was so smooth it made her feel sick; Camille's boss at the salon was apparently 'mutton dressed as mutton'. The only exception to this was any reference to Katie, in whom her grandmother took evident pride, and the house, which, perversely, Mr Bernard didn't seem to want to talk about at all.

Daisy, who had looked forward to a visit from the family more than she cared to admit, had found it all curiously wearing. And never having been around anyone blind before, she became awkward with Camille, unsure where to look when she addressed her, dithering over whether she should serve things directly on to her plate, or allow Hal, who had seated himself beside her, to do it for her. She had tripped over the dog twice, the second time eliciting a polite yelp of protest.

'You don't have to put the sandwiches practically into her mouth,' said Mrs Bernard, suddenly. 'She's only blind, not a bloody invalid.'

'Love . . .' said Mr Bernard.

Daisy, flushing, had apologised, and stepped backwards into the laburnum.

'Don't be so rude, Mum. She's only trying to help.'

'Don't be so rude, Granny,' echoed Katie, half-way through a chocolate éclair. She was rocking Ellie's car seat with her foot.

'Let me apologise for my mother,' said Camille. 'She's old enough to know better.'

'I don't like people fussing over you.'

'And I don't like you jumping in over my head. That's what makes me feel like an invalid.'

There was a brief silence. Camille, apparently unperturbed, made a move forward for her drink.

'I'm sorry,' said Daisy. 'I just didn't know how you were going to tell between crab and Marmite.'

'Oh, I just take lots of everything. That way I usually manage to get what I want.' Camille laughed. 'Or I get Hal to get them for me.'

'You're more than capable of looking after yourself.'

'I know that, Mother.' This time there was an edge to Camille's voice.

'I don't know how you cope with having her under your feet all day, Daisy,' said Hal. 'The sharpest tongue on the east coast.'

'Mummy says Granny can cut paper with her tongue,' said Katie, prompting an embarrassed ripple of laughter at the table.

Mrs Bernard, however, was suddenly quiet. She gazed at the contents of her plate for a minute, then looked over at Hal, her face blank. 'How's the business?'

'Not great. But there's an antiques dealer over at Wix who has promised to put some work my way.'

'I guess it's a bit like mine,' said Daisy. 'When things get tight, people don't spend money on the insides of their houses.'

'You've been talking about that dealer for weeks. You can't hang around waiting for ever. Shouldn't you wind it down now? Try to get a job somewhere?'

'Come on, love . . . not here.' Mr Bernard reached an arm towards his wife.

'Well, there must be places need people who can do carpentry. Furniture warehouses and suchlike.'

'I don't make factory furniture, Ma.' Hal was struggling to maintain his smile. 'I restore individual pieces. It's a skill. There's a big difference.'

'We had terrible trouble getting work in our first couple of years,' said Daisy, quickly.

'Hal's got some things in the pipeline,' said Camille, her own hand sliding under the table towards her husband's. 'It's been a quiet time for everyone.'

'Not that quiet,' said her mother.

'I'm taking it one day at a time, Ma, but I'm good at what I do. The business is a good one. I'm not quite ready to give up on it yet.'

'Yes, well, you want to make sure you don't go bankrupt. Or you'll drag everyone down with you. Camille and Katie included.'

'I've got no intention of going bankrupt.' Hal's face had hardened.

'No one ever has any intention of going bankrupt, Hal.'

'That's *enough*, love.'

Mrs Bernard turned to her husband, her face childishly mutinous.

There was a prolonged silence.

'Anyone want something else to eat?' said Daisy, trying to fill the gap. She had found an old hand-thrown bowl in one of the downstairs cupboards, and filled it to the brim with glistening fruit salad.

'Have you got any ice cream?' said Katie.

'I don't eat fruit,' said Mrs Bernard, standing to clear the table of plates. 'I'll make us all a pot of tea.'

'Don't take Mum's comments too much to heart,' said Camille, appearing at her side in the kitchen, as she cleared the plates. 'She's not really nasty. It's all a bit of a front.'

'A cold front,' joked Hal, who appeared behind her. He followed her everywhere, Daisy had noticed. She was increasingly uncertain whether he was being protective or just needy.

'She's all right underneath. She's just always been a bit – well – sharp, I guess. Would you say sharp, Hal?'

'Your mother makes a steel blade look cuddly.'

Camille turned to face Daisy. Daisy focused on her mouth.

'Actually, you're okay. She likes you.'

'What? She said so?'

263

'Of course not. But we can tell.'

'It's the way she hasn't been baying for your blood at midnight, her fangs dripping saliva.'

Daisy frowned. 'It doesn't feel . . . You surprise me.'

Camille smiled brightly at her husband. 'It was her idea that we all come today. She thought you might be lonely.'

Daisy smiled, her faint pleasure that Mrs Bernard liked her after all dampened by the idea that she was now an object of pity. She had spent twenty-eight years being a girl whom everyone envied; the sympathy mantle did not sit comfortably. 'It was nice. Of you all. To come, I mean.'

'A pleasure,' said Hal. 'To be honest, we were keen to see the house.'

Daisy flinched at his choice of words, but Camille didn't seem to notice. 'She never really welcomed visitors up here, you see,' she said, reaching down for Rollo's head. 'It was always her little bolthole.'

'Not so little.'

'We only came up on the odd occasion. And Dad never really liked it here, so it's not like it was ever a family home.'

'So you won't miss it?'

'Not really. Most houses I don't know are just a series of obstacles to me.'

'But didn't you mind? Her always coming away from you all?'

Camille turned to face Hal. She shrugged. 'I guess it's only what we've always known. Mum has always had to have her own space.'

'I suppose all families have their eccentricities,' said Daisy, whose family didn't.

'Some more than most.'

★   ★   ★

Several hours later, Hal and Camille strolled back through Merham arm in arm, Rollo a few paces ahead, Katie skipping backwards and forwards, apparently involved in some complicated negotiation with the edges of the paving slabs. Occasionally she would run back and thrust herself pleasurably between them, demanding to be swung upwards, even though she was too tall and too heavy now. It was beginning to lighten up in the evenings, the dog-walkers and evening travellers looking rather less resolute and windblown, walking with their heads up instead of braced against the wind. Hal nodded hello to the owner of the newsagent's, who was just closing up for the evening, and they turned the corner into their own street. Katie ran on ahead, shrieking at some friend she had spied at the top of the road.

'Sorry about Mum.'

Hal put his arm around his wife. 'It's okay.'

'No. It's not okay. She knows you're working as hard as you can.'

'Forget it. She's just worried about you. I guess any mother would be the same.'

'No, they wouldn't. They wouldn't be so rude, anyway.'

'That's true.' Hal stopped to adjust Camille's scarf. One end had started to work its way towards her feet. 'You know, maybe she's right,' he said, as she rebuttoned her coat collar. 'That dealer's probably stringing me along.' He sighed, loudly enough for Camille to hear.

'Is it that bad?'

'We've got to be completely honest now, haven't we?' He smiled mirthlessly, mimicking the counsellor's words. 'Okay . . . it's not good. In fact, I've been thinking I should start working out of the garage. Silly paying for the workshops when . . . when there's nothing in them . . .'

'But Daisy said she might be able to find—'

'It's that, or pack in the business altogether.'

'I don't want you to give it up. It's important to you.'

'You're important to me. You and Katie.'

But I don't make you feel like a man, thought Camille. I still somehow make you feel diminished. The business is the only thing that seems to keep you upright.

'I think you should give it a while longer,' she said.

Daisy, settling down for the evening with a sheaf of fabric samples, felt a little better. Camille had invited her to come to the salon for a treatment. Her treat, she said. As long as she could do something adventurous. Mrs Bernard had agreed to look after Ellie on a more regular footing, hiding her evident pleasure under a tart litany of conditions. Mr Bernard had told her not to let the buggers get her down, with a wink in the direction of his wife. And Ellie, unusually, had gone to sleep without a murmur, exhausted by the unaccustomed levels of attention. Daisy had sat on the terrace, wrapped up against the evening chill, looking out to the sea and smoking a leisurely cigarette as she worked, feeling, briefly, not lonely. Or not as lonely. It might well have lasted a few days. So it had seemed doubly unfair when the fates, in the shape of her long-silent mobile phone, had conspired to destroy her temporary equilibrium.

First Jones rang and told her (not asked, she noted) that he wanted to meet the following evening for A Talk. Words guaranteed to place a clammy hand around her heart. Seven weeks and three days ago Daniel had told her he wanted A Talk. 'We'll go out somewhere. Away from . . . distractions,' Jones said. He had meant Ellie, she knew.

'I'll babysit,' Mrs Bernard had said approvingly, the following day. 'Good for you to get out a bit.'

'As the hangman said to the condemned man,' muttered Daisy.

And then, on Monday, shortly before he was due to arrive, the phone rang again. This time it was Marjorie Wiener to tell her, breathlessly, that she had finally heard from her son. 'He's been staying with one of his old friends from university. He says he's been having a bit of a breakdown.' She sounded flustered. But, then, Marjorie Wiener always sounded flustered.

Daisy's initial heartstop had been replaced by a slow, simmering anger, which rose swiftly to the boil. A breakdown? Surely if you were having a nervous breakdown, you couldn't be together enough to recognise it? Wasn't that what *Catch 22* was all about? And how easy for him to have a breakdown, with no child to look after. Because as far as she was concerned a breakdown was a luxury – she didn't have the time or energy for one.

'So, is he coming back?' She was having difficulty keeping her voice level.

'He just needs some time to work things out, Daisy. He's really in a state. I've been quite worried about him.'

'Yes, well, you can tell him that he'll be in even more of a bloody state if he comes anywhere near us. How does he think we've survived without him? Without even a bloody five-pound note from him.'

'Oh, Daisy, you should have said if you were short. I would have sent some money . . .'

'That's not the fucking point, Marjorie. It's not your responsibility. It was Daniel's responsibility. *We were Daniel's fucking responsibility.*'

'Really, Daisy, there's no need for language like—'

'Is he going to ring me?'

'I don't know.'

267

'What? He asked you to ring me? Six years together and a baby and suddenly he can't even speak to me in person?'

'Look, I'm not particularly proud of him at the moment, but he's not himself, Daisy. He's—'

'Not himself. He's not himself. He's a father, now, Marjorie. Or he's meant to be. Is it someone else? Is that it? Is he seeing someone else?'

'I don't think there's anyone else.'

'You don't think?'

'I know. He wouldn't do that to you.'

'Well, he seems to have had no trouble doing pretty well everything else to me.'

'Please don't go getting yourself in a state, Daisy. I know it's hard but—'

'No, Marjorie. It's not bloody hard. It's bloody impossible. I've been left alone with barely a word of explanation by someone who can't even bring himself to talk to me. I've had to leave our home because he didn't think about the fact that me and *our* baby had no money to support ourselves. I'm stuck in a building site a million miles from nowhere because Daniel took on a bloody job that he had no intention of completing—'

'Now, that's hardly fair.'

'Fair? You're going to tell me what's fair? Marjorie, no offence, but I'm going to put the phone down. I'm going to . . . No, I'm not listening. I'm putting the phone down now la la la la la—'

'Daisy, Daisy dear, we'd really like to see the baby—'

She had sat, trembling, her dead phone in her hand, Marjorie's feeble request buried under her burgeoning sense of outrage. He hadn't even thought to ask how his daughter was. He hadn't seen her for more than seven weeks, and he hadn't even wanted to make sure she was okay. Who was this man she had loved? What had happened to Daniel? Her face crumpled, and she dropped her head on to her chest, wondering how the pain could continue to manifest itself so physically.

And even as she fought to contain her sense of anger and injustice, a creeping voice asked whether she should have lost her temper at all. She didn't want to do anything to put him off coming back, did she? What would Marjorie say to him now?

Conscious, suddenly, of another presence in the room, she turned to find Mrs Bernard standing very still in the doorway, Ellie's dirty clothes in the crook of her arm. 'I'll take these home with me this evening and put them through the wash. Save you walking all the way to the launderette.'

'Thank you,' said Daisy, trying not to sniff.

Mrs Bernard still stood there, looking at her. Daisy fought the urge to tell her to go away. 'You know, sometimes you just have to move on,' the older woman said.

Daisy looked up sharply.

'To survive. Sometimes you just have to move on. It's the only way.'

Daisy opened her mouth as if to speak.

'Still. As I said, I'll take these home with me when I leave. The little one dropped off no trouble. I've put the extra blanket on as it's a bit chilly with that easterly wind.'

Whether it was the wind or the Wieners, Daisy found herself infected with a kind of recklessness. She had run upstairs and pulled on a pair of black trousers – the first time she had been able to do so since Ellie's birth – and a red chiffon shirt that Daniel had bought her for her birthday, back before she had become pregnant and consigned to feminine marquees. The combination of stress and a broken heart might inflict terrible damage on your peace of mind, she thought, her jaw set, but, boy, did it help your figure. She teamed this with a pair of stiletto-heeled boots, and an unusual amount of makeup. Lipstick could do wonders for one's sense of self-worth, her sister had said. But then Julia had never been seen without it, not even in bed with flu.

'You can see your bra through that,' remarked Mrs Bernard, as she tripped down the stairs.

'Good,' said Daisy, spikily. She was not going to be swayed by Mrs Bernard's miserable asides either.

'You might want to tuck the label into your collar, though.' Mrs Bernard smiled to herself. 'People will talk.'

Jones rubbed at his brow as he pulled the Saab into Merham high street and headed towards the park. His head had begun to pound shortly after he passed Canary Wharf and by the time he was half-way along the A12 the slight throb over his eyes had become a full-blown headache. He had fumbled in his glove compartment, on a whim, and located the pills that Sandra, his secretary, had secreted there. A bloody marvel, that woman. He'd give her a rise. If he hadn't already given her one three months ago.

The discovery of the paracetamol was the one high point in a month of lows. Which said something about his month. Alex, his ex-wife, had announced that she was getting married. One of his most senior barmen had almost come to blows with two influential journalists who had decided to play naked Twister on the pool table. It hadn't been the nakedness he had objected to, he protested to Jones afterwards, it had been the fact that they wouldn't move their drinks off the baize. But now there was barely a day when the Red Rooms wasn't mentioned in society or gossip columns as 'past it' or 'failing', while his attempts to woo the journalists with a crate of whisky had come unstuck when they reported the gesture and branded it 'desperate'.

And in a month's time a rival club – the Opium Rooms – was opening two streets away, its proposed membership, ambience and ethos suspiciously close to the Red Rooms' own, its arrival already generating a buzz in the circles Jones called *his* own. That was why this Merham retreat had become so important: you had to stay ahead of the game. You had to find new ways to keep your members close.

And now this bloody girl was screwing it up. He had suspected she wasn't up to it when she kept whingeing on about him calling 'at a bad time'. He should have listened to his gut instinct: in business there were no bad times. If you were professional, you just got on and did the job. No excuses, no prevarication. It was why he didn't like working with women – there was always some period pain or boyfriend that meant they couldn't quite focus on the job in hand. And if you confronted them about it, they usually burst into tears. In fact, apart from his secretary, there were only two women he felt completely comfortable with, even after all these years: Carol, his long-standing PR, who only had to raise a manicured eyebrow to express disapproval, whose loyalty was absolute, and who could still drink him under the table; and there was Alex, the only other woman who wasn't either particularly impressed by him or frightened of him. But Alex was getting married.

When she had told him, his first, childish instinct had been to ask her to marry him again. She had burst out laughing. 'You're incorrigible, Jones. It was the worst eighteen months of both our lives. And you only want me now that someone else does.' Which, he had to admit, had been partially true. Over the years since, he had made the occasional pass at her, which she gracefully refused (he was secretly glad), but they had each valued their continued friendship (to the annoyance, he knew, of Alex's new partner). But now she was moving on, and things were going to change. And the seal on their past would be absolute.

Not that there weren't distractions. It was very easy to get laid running a club. When he had started out, he frequently slept with the waitresses, usually tall, slender wannabe actresses or singers, all hoping to rub up against some producer or director while serving drinks. But he had soon discovered that that led to rivalries, tearful demands for pay-rises, and eventually the loss of good staff. So for the last year and a half he had led the life of a monk. Well, a mildly promiscuous monk. Occasionally he would meet a girl and take her back, but it seemed to give him less and less satisfaction, and he always offended them because he could never remember their names afterwards. Half the time it wasn't worth the aggro.

'Jones. It's Sandra. Sorry to bother you while you're driving, but the date has come through for your licensing appearance.'

'And?' He fiddled to get the hands-free set to his ear.

'It's the same time as your trip to Paris.'

He spat out an expletive. 'Well, you'll have to ring them. Tell them to reschedule.'

'What? Paris?'

'No. The court appearance. Tell them I can't make that date.'

Sandra paused. 'I'll ring you back,' she said.

Jones pulled the Saab up the hill and on to the gravel driveway that led to Arcadia. Problems, problems, problems. Sometimes he felt that he spent his entire time sorting out other people's messes rather than getting on and doing what he did best.

He switched off the engine and sat for a minute, his head still painful, his brain too full of stress and clutter to appreciate the silence. And now there was more. The girl was going to have to go. It would be for the best. He was a great believer in cutting a situation off before it got too bad. He would go with the other firm, the one based in Battersea. Just, please, don't let her burst into tears.

Jones reached into the glove compartment and shovelled another handful of headache pills into his mouth, wincing as he swallowed without water. He sighed, got out of the car and walked up to the front door. It was opened, before he could ring the bell, by Mrs Bernard. She stood there with that steady gaze, the one that suggested she knew quite what you were all about, thank you.

'Mr Jones.'

He could never quite bring himself to correct her.

'I wasn't expecting to see you.' He stooped to kiss her cheek.

'That's because you've never had children.'

'What?'

'Someone has to babysit.'

'Oh.' He stepped in, glancing around at the half-stripped walls, the piles of builder's debris. 'Yes.'

'Things are warming up.'

'So I see.'

She turned and walked down the hallway, neatly sidestepping the empty paint trays. 'I'll tell her you're here. She's just on the phone to the plumbers.'

Jones sat on the edge of a chair, and took in the half-finished drawing room, with its musty smell of drying plaster and newly repaired floor. In the corner of the room stood an aluminium pyramid of Farrow and Ball paints while swathes of fabric ran like rivers over the back of the tatty old sofa.

Arterial gullies dissected the room, revealing where electrics had been stripped out and replaced. On the floor a sheaf of catalogues offered light fittings in 'Miami', 'Austen' and 'Blink'.

'That was McCarthy and his boys. They're starting on the front two bathrooms tomorrow.'

Jones looked up from the catalogues to see a woman he didn't recognise striding across the room, mobile telephone still in hand.

'I've told him any more delays and we start deducting money. I said we had one per cent for every day lost written into the small print of the contract.'

'We do?' said Jones.

'No. But I figured he's too lazy to check, and it obviously put the frighteners on him. He said he'd cut short the other job he's on and be with us by nine a.m. Are we going, then?' She grabbed her wallet and keys and a large folder from a bag on the floor.

Jones fought the urge to search the house for the girl he remembered, the rather soggy-looking one wearing shapeless old clothes with a baby attached to her hip. This one did not look flaky and tearful. This one would not have looked out of place in his club. This one's shirt revealed a black bra and what appeared, underneath, to be a compelling pair of breasts.

'Is there a problem?' she said, waiting. Her eyes glittered, held something that could have been either challenge or aggression. Either way it made his balls tighten unexpectedly.

'No,' he said, and walked after her up the drive.

They chose the Riviera – partly, Jones said, to suss out the opposition, but in the main because there were no pubs or bars in Merham. Those who wanted to drink socially did so at the hotel, or at one of the two licensed restaurants in the town, or went further afield. In normal circumstances – or as much as any of her circumstances could be considered normal at the moment – Daisy would have felt pretty uncomfortable going in there at all. But something about the evening, and her red chiffon blouse, and the fact that she knew she had already unbalanced Jones, for all his bluff and bluster, made Daisy bullish, so that she positively sauntered when they walked together into the bar.

'Can I see your wine list?' Jones leaned his considerable bulk on the bar. It was staffed by a pale, pustular young man who barely filled his shirt collar and broke off from whispering to a giggling waitress with barely concealed irritation. There were two other couples in the bar: one elderly, contentedly watching the sea in silence, the other, possibly business partners, arguing over some figures on a pad.

Daisy gazed around the room, with its french windows and sea views, as Jones muttered at the wine list. The sun was setting, but there was nothing to transform the bar into a place where one might want to snuggle up and listen to the sea as it darkened to ink. In fact, it might have been a beautiful room, were it not frilled and fancied to within an inch of its life. The same apricot-themed floral material occurred everywhere: on the curtains, pelmets, seat coverings, even surrounding the plant pots. The tables were white, over-wrought iron. It looked less like a bar than a tea room. Then, thought Daisy, judging by the clientele, it probably sold more tea than alcohol.

'Seventeen quid for the equivalent of Blue Nun,' murmured Jones, as she turned back to him. 'No wonder it's not exactly buzzing in here. Sorry, did you want wine?'

'No,' Daisy lied. 'But it'll do.' She fought the urge to light a cigarette. It would have given him the moral advantage somehow.

They seated themselves at a corner table. Jones sat at an angle to her, poured them both a glass of wine, then studied her occasionally from the corner of his eye, as if trying to work something out.

'Awful décor in here,' she said.

'First place I came when I viewed the house. I wanted to see what was on offer. People who decorated it ought to be shot.'

'Pebbledashed into submission.'

He raised an eyebrow.

Daisy looked back down at her drink. So he was not in the mood for a joke. Sod him. She thought, briefly, of Ellie, wondered if she was sleeping through for Mrs Bernard. Then she pushed the thought aside, and took a long sip of her wine.

'I guess you know why I'm here,' he said, eventually.

'No,' she lied again.

He sighed. Looked at his hand. 'I've not been happy about the way things have been going up here.'

'No, nor have I,' she interrupted. 'In fact, I'd say it's only in the last few days that we've got back on track. By the end of the week I reckon we'll have made up our lost ground.'

'But it's not really good enough—'

'No. You're right. And I've told the builders I'm not happy.'

'It's not just the builders—'

'No, I know. It's been the plumbers too. But they're sorted now, as I told you. And I think I should be able to work a bit off their bill, so we may come in under budget.'

He was silent for a minute, looking at her from under dark,

suspicious brows. 'You're not going to make this easy for me, are you?'

'No.'

They stared at each other, unblinking, for a minute. Daisy was very still. She had never held out on anyone like this, even Daniel. She had always been the one to capitulate, the one to smooth things over. It was the way she was made.

'I can't afford to let this get behind, Daisy. There's a lot riding on it.'

'For me too.'

He rubbed at his forehead, thinking. 'I don't know . . .' he muttered. And then again. 'I don't know.'

Then suddenly, unexpectedly, he raised his glass. 'Ah, hell. Seeing as you have evidently acquired a pair of bollocks since we last met, I guess I'll have to hang on to mine. For the time being.' He waited for her to pick up her glass, then clashed them together. 'Right. God help us. Don't let me down.'

For a bottle of gnat's piss, as Jones delicately put it, it seemed to go down remarkably easily. To Daisy, who had drunk nothing stronger than Irn Bru since giving birth, the raw kick of alcohol seemed to signify a welcome return to her old self, an indicator that another Daisy was waiting to emerge.

It also made her swiftly drunk, so that she forgot to be inhibited by the man opposite, and began to treat him as she would have treated any man before Ellie's birth. She tried to flirt with him. 'So what's your real name?' she said, as he ordered a second bottle.

'Jones.'

'Your first name.'

'I don't use it.'

'How . . . modern of you.'

'You mean how pretentious.' He grunted.

'No. Well, yes. It is a bit, though, just giving yourself one name. Like Madonna?'

'You try growing up in South Wales with a Christian name like Inigo and see where it gets you.'

Daisy almost spat out her drink. 'You're kidding,' she said. 'Inigo Jones?'

'My mother was keen on architecture. She said I was conceived at Wilton House in the West Country . . . Problem was, they've since decided that Inigo Jones didn't even design the bloody thing. His nephew did.'

'What was he called?'

'Webb. James Webb.'

'Webb,' she tried it out. 'Webby. No, it doesn't have quite the same ring to it.'

'No.'

'Ah. Oh, well, at least it explains why you've got such good taste in buildings.' She was shameless. But someone was going to bloody like her. If it killed her.

He looked up at her from under lowered brows. One of them might have raised.

'It's going to be fabulous,' she said, determinedly.

'It'd better be.' Jones emptied his glass. 'And it won't be if you insist on having those new windows made by hand. I had a closer look at those figures yesterday. It's too much for bathroom windows.'

Daisy looked up sharply. 'But they have to be hand-made.'

'Why? Who's going to be looking at a bathroom window?'

'It's not that. It's the style, for the house. It's particular. You're not going to pick them up in Magnet and Southern.'

'I'm not paying for hand-made.'

'You agreed the costs. You okayed them several weeks ago.'

'Yes, well, I hadn't had time to look at the small print.'

'You're making it sound like I was trying to deceive you.'

'Don't be so melodramatic. I've just had a closer look, and I can't see why I'm paying for hand-made windows in a place where no one's going to be looking at them anyway.'

The faintest hint of warmth had rapidly evaporated. Daisy knew it, and knew that she should back off, in order to save it. But she couldn't help herself. The windows were important. 'You *okayed* them.'

'Oh, come on, Daisy. Change the record. We're meant to be working in partnership. It's not going to work if you start bleating on about keeping things to the letter.'

'No, it's not going to work if you start going back on things you've already agreed.'

Jones reached inside his jacket and pulled out a packet of tablets, popping two into his mouth. 'I take it you weren't the entertainment and hospitality half of your partnership.'

Daisy was stung. Her voice was cold and level as she said, 'Yes, well, you didn't hire me for my interpersonal skills.'

There was a long silence.

'Ah, come on. I can't face bickering like this. Let's go and get something to eat. I've never yet found a woman I could argue with on a full stomach.'

Daisy bit her tongue.

'Okay, Daisy. You know the area. Take me somewhere nice. Somewhere you think I might like.'

Arcadia's terraces folded out in steps, their bleak angles softened by the overgrown shrubs around them, their paved floor illuminated by the soft light from the windows. Below, on the sea path, people strolled by on their way down to or home from the beach, barely noticing the brutal building above them.

'House looks good from here,' said Jones, cramming a handful of chips into his mouth. 'Always good to see it from another angle.'

'Yes.'

'Not quite the angle I expected, admittedly.'

He was not, she observed, as they sat on the sea wall, the most cheerful of men. But fed, watered and headache-free, he was less confrontational company. She found herself working to make him laugh, forcing him to admire her. Men who gave nothing up always affected her like that.

Daniel was his polar opposite: he let all his feelings show – his neediness, his passion, his explosive temper – and she had been the one to hold back. Until Ellie, that was. Everything was until Ellie. Daisy looked at the light across the bay, at the house where her child (hopefully) lay sleeping, and wondered, not for the first time, what would have happened if they had never had her. Would he have stayed? Or would something else have pushed him away?

She shifted slightly, conscious that the cold of the sea wall was seeping through the seat of her trousers. She was drunk, she realised, and getting maudlin. She pushed herself upright, trying to pull herself together. 'Have you got children?'

He finished his chips, rolled the paper into a ball and put it beside him. 'Me? No.'

'Never been married?'

'Yes, but no kids, thank goodness. It was enough of a disaster without them. Those fish and chips were good. Haven't had skate for years.'

Daisy was silent. She looked straight down at the sea, lost for a second in the gentle lapping of the waves.

'So what happened to you?' he asked, a few moments later.

'What?'

'I'm assuming it wasn't immaculate . . .'

'What? Oh, er, no. The old story, I suppose. Boy meets girl, girl has baby, boy decides he is having an early mid-life crisis and buggers off into the sunset.'

He laughed. Daisy didn't know whether to feel pleased, or to berate herself for having reduced her life's tragedy into a comic soundbite.

'Actually, that's not fair,' she found herself saying. 'He's just having a difficult time at the moment. I don't want to . . . I mean, he's a good person. I think he's just a bit confused. A lot of men find it difficult, don't they? The whole adjustment thing?'

A dog appeared out of the darkness, sniffing at Jones's empty wrappings. His owner, walking along the sea path behind them, called him away.

'He was the man you ran your business with? Daniel, was it?'

'That's the one.'

Jones shrugged and looked out to sea. 'That's tough.'

'It's more than tough.' The bitterness that crept into her voice surprised even her.

There was a lengthy silence.

Daisy shivered in the evening air, wrapping her arms around her. The chiffon shirt was not the warmest of tops.

'Still . . .' Jones said, his face breaking into a tender smile, only partially visible in the moonlight.

Daisy's heart leaped into her mouth as his hand reached out. And pinched one of her untouched chips.

'. . . you're doing okay. Looks like you're doing okay.'

He stood up, hauled her to her feet. 'C'mon, Daisy Parsons, let's get another drink.'

⋆　　⋆　　⋆

Mrs Bernard already had her coat on when they arrived back at the house, Jones tripping over two piles of rubble in the hallway. 'I heard you coming down the drive,' she said, raising an eyebrow. 'Nice time, was it?'

'Very . . . productive,' said Jones. 'Very productive, wasn't it, Daisy?'

'I bet your business meetings in London don't involve fish and chips and sitting on people's walls,' said Daisy. The second bottle of wine had gone from being an extremely bad idea, to an entirely necessary one.

'And alcohol,' said Mrs Bernard, eyeing them both.

'Oh, no,' said Jones. 'They always involve wine. But not . . .' here he and Daisy looked at each other and both began to giggle '. . . quite this vintage.'

'For someone who thought it was so grim, you did drink an awful lot of it,' she said.

Jones shook his head, as if trying to clear it. 'You know, for a crap wine, it had some alcohol content. I actually feel a bit drunk.'

'You look drunk,' said Mrs Bernard. She might have been disapproving. Daisy was beyond caring.

'But I don't get drunk. I never get drunk.'

'Ah,' said Daisy, holding a finger aloft, 'you don't get drunk . . . unless you eat lots of headache pills at the same time. Then you probably get very drunk.'

'Oh, Christ . . .' Jones rummaged around in his trouser pockets and pulled out a packet. '*Not to be taken with alcohol.*'

Mrs Bernard had disappeared. Daisy sat down heavily on the chair, wondering if she'd gone up to Ellie. She hoped Ellie wasn't crying: she wasn't sure she'd make it up the stairs. 'I'll get you a coffee,' she said. And struggled to get up.

'I'll be off, then,' said Mrs Bernard, who had reappeared in the doorway. 'See you soon, Mr Jones. Daisy.'

'It's . . . er . . . yes, yes, Mrs Bernard. Thanks again. I'll see you out.'

The door closed quietly. A moment later Jones walked back into the room. Daisy was suddenly acutely aware of his presence. She hadn't been alone with a man since . . . since the police officer had driven her car over Hammersmith Bridge. And that had made her cry.

The room still smelt of drying plaster, the sofa in the middle of the room covered in dust-sheets, and a single lightbulb providing the room's only light. For a building site, it was suddenly uncomfortably intimate.

'You okay?' he said. His voice was low.

'Fine. I'll make the coffee,' she said, and on the third attempt managed to stand.

Almost a third of it had sluiced out of the cup between the kitchens and the drawing room, but Jones did not seem to notice that his was a rather meagre drink. 'I can't find my car keys,' he had said, swaying and repeatedly patting his pockets, as if they might suddenly reappear. 'Could have sworn I put them on that table when we came in.'

Daisy cast around the room, trying to keep the horizontals from swimming up and unbalancing her. She had felt increasingly less stable during her time out of the room, and her anxiety about Jones's increasing attractiveness had been overtaken by anxiety about her ability to stay upright. 'I haven't seen them.' She had put the cup down on a paint-splattered packing-case.

'We didn't take the car out, did we?'

'You know we didn't. We passed it in the drive as we came back in. You stroked it, remember?'

'That's middle age for you,' he muttered. 'You start seeing beauty in your car. It'll be leather jackets next.'

'And hair dye. And prepubescent girlfriends.'

He had been a bit quiet after that.

Daisy left him searching the room while she tried to locate her mobile phone, which she had found bleeping in her jacket. No one would ring this late. Unless it was Daniel. She flung her jacket around, trying to get into the right pocket, feeling curiously fearful as she did so that Daniel might guess she had a man in the house.

'Hello?'

'It's me.'

Daisy's face fell.

'You can tell Mr Jones I'll bring his car keys back tomorrow. I didn't think it was a good idea for him to drive, and I didn't think you were in a position to tell him. Working for him and all.'

She slid down the wall, the phone only half to her ear.

'I'll be round about eight-ish. Ellie's bottles are made up in the fridge.'

'But where's he going to sleep?'

'He can walk back down to the Riviera. Or kip on the sofa. He's a big boy.'

Daisy turned off her phone, pushed herself upright and walked back into the drawing room. Jones had given up on his search and was slumped on the dust-sheeted sofa, his legs stretched out in front of him.

'Mrs Bernard took your keys,' she said.

It took some seconds to register.

'Not by mistake,' she added.

'Bloody woman. Oh, Christ,' he said, rubbing at his face. 'I've got a bloody meeting at seven forty-five. How am I meant to get back to London now?'

Daisy felt suddenly very tired: the convivial, fluid atmosphere had somehow dissipated with the telephone call. She had not been up later than ten p.m. for weeks, and it was now edging towards midnight.

'She suggested you get a room at the Riviera.' Daisy sat on the edge of the chair, gazing at the sofa opposite. 'Or you could stay here. I'm quite happy on the sofa.'

He looked at it.

'I don't think you'd quite fit on it,' she added. 'Ellie gets up early, so we could wake you.' She yawned.

He looked at her, a more sober, level kind of look. 'I'm not going knocking on the door of the Riviera now. But I can't turf you out of your bed.'

'I can't let you sleep on this sofa. You're twice as long as it is.'

'Do you never stop arguing? If you sleep on the sofa, and I sleep in your room, what happens if the baby wakes up in the night?'

She hadn't thought of that.

He leaned forward, and dropped his head into his hands. Then he lifted it, and grinned, a broad, piratical grin. 'Christ, Daisy. What a pair of drunken fools, eh?' His smile changed his whole face: he looked mischievous, somebody's reprobate uncle. She felt herself relax again. 'I came up here to bloody fire you. Now look. What a pair of drunken fools . . .'

'You're the boss. I was only following orders.'

'Only following orders. Yes . . .' He got up, lumbered towards the stairs. 'Look,' he said, turning, 'tell me if I'm out of line here, but there's a double bed, right?'

'Yes.'

'You go one side, I'll go the other. No funny stuff, both of us keep our clothes on, and tomorrow morning we'll say no more about it. That way we both get a decent night's sleep.'

'Fine,' Daisy said, yawning again so that her eyes watered. She was so tired she would have agreed to sleep in Ellie's cot.

'One thing,' murmured Jones, as he collapsed on to the bed, his shoes kicked off, his tie loosened.

Daisy lay on the other side, knowing his presence should have made her feel uncomfortable and self-conscious, but too drunk and tired to care. 'What?' she muttered into the dark, remembering, and not entirely caring that she had forgotten to take off her makeup.

'As my employee, you get to make the coffee in the morning.'

'Only if you agree to the hand-made windows.'

She heard a muffled expletive.

Daisy grinned, shoved her hands under the pillow, and passed out.

Once upon a time, she had thought that Daniel's return would cause her to burst, that on seeing him, she would literally explode with relief and joy, that she would fizz like a catherine wheel, send shimmering sparks skyward, like a rocket. But now Daisy knew it wasn't like that at all: Daniel's presence back in her life felt like the return of a deep peace, the stemming of an ache that had embedded itself into her bones. It was like coming home. That was how someone had once described finding love to her, and Daisy, now resting in his arms, knew it to be true also of its restoration. It was like coming home. She shifted, and the arm, wrapped tightly around her so that its fingers entwined with her own, moved accommodatingly. She had longed to feel that weight on her. When she had been pregnant it had felt too heavy, almost intrusive, and she had kept to her own side of the bed, propped and supported by pillows. After Ellie, it had been a reassuring reminder that he was still there. That he was still there.

But Daniel wasn't there.

Daisy's eyes opened, allowing the blurred shapes to segue slowly into focus, trying to adjust to the chill eastern light of morning. Her eyes felt dry, gritty, and her tongue had swollen to fill her mouth. The room, she knew, swallowing arduously, was hers. A few feet away Ellie stirred in her cot, speeding the too-short journey from deep sleep towards wakefulness, the daylight winking through the crack in the curtains on to her blankets. Outside a car door slammed, and below on the path someone called out. One of the builders, probably. Daisy lifted her head and noted that it was a quarter past seven. The hand slid down her side and, finally, dropped away.

Daniel wasn't there.

Daisy pushed herself upright her brain joining her a split second later. Beside her, a dark head lay on the pillow, its hair thatched in sleep. She sat very still and stared at it, at the rumpled shirt attached to it, struggling to think back, piecing together the jumble of words and images. And slowly, with the inevitable force of a slow-motion punch, it hit her. It wasn't Daniel. The arm hadn't been Daniel's. He hadn't come back.

The peace wasn't hers.

And abruptly, noisily, Daisy burst into tears.

It was obvious what had happened, Mrs Bernard thought, as, in a bad-tempered spray of gravel, the rear of the Saab disappeared down the drive and towards London. You didn't have to be a brain surgeon to work it out. The two of them had been barely able to look at each other when she came in, Daisy clutching the child in front of her like a shield, all tear-stained and pale. He had looked fed up and anxious to get away. And

287

like a man with an extremely bad hangover, which, of course, with all those silly headache pills, was what he was.

There had been all that electricity between them the night before, all that conspiratorial joking, as if they had known each other years, not days. And the sofa, she noted as soon as she walked in, had not been slept on.

'Always a price to pay for mixing business with pleasure,' she had said to him, as she handed him his keys. She meant the drinking, but he had given her a hard look – the kind of look he probably used to intimidate his staff. Mrs Bernard just smiled. She was much too tough a bird to be frightened of the likes of him. 'See you soon, Mr Jones,' she said.

'I doubt it'll be soon,' he had replied and, with hardly a glance in Daisy's direction, had climbed into his car and left. As he started it, it was possible that he had mouthed 'Women!' to himself.

'What a daft mummy you've got,' she told Ellie quietly, as they walked round the garden and back towards the house. 'I think she took my advice a bit too literally, don't you? No wonder she's in such a mess.'

A shame, really. For in his drunken state, as he saw her out of the house the previous evening, Jones had confided in the older woman that Daisy was a bit of a revelation to him, not the sad sap he'd had her down as, or even the ballbreaker she'd tried to present herself as, simply, as he put it, shaking his head in surprise, 'a lovely girl'.

Thirteen

Camille smoothed the algae wrap over Mrs Martigny's bulk, running her hands along her stomach and back to ensure even coverage. In places it had already started to dry, and she pushed more of the muddy unguent around, like someone smearing tomato sauce on to unbaked pizza dough. Swiftly, she pulled off a length of clingfilm, smoothed it over the top of Mrs Martigny's stomach, and around each thigh, then covered her with two warm towels, still fresh enough to smell of fabrio-conditioner. The movements had a languorous, precise rhythm, and Camille's hands were sure and swift. It was a job she could have done in her sleep. Which was just as well, because her mind was far away, still locked into a conversation she had had several hours earlier.

'Do you need any help?' said Tess, poking her head round the door so that the looped tape of whale noises and electronic relaxation music oozed in through the gap. 'I've got ten minutes before Mrs Forster's highlights have got to come out.'

'No, we're fine. Unless you want some tea or coffee. A drink, Mrs Martigny?'

'Not for me, Camille dear. I'm just drifting off nicely under here.'

Camille did not need help. What she was going to need was a job. She closed the door on Mrs Martigny and her twenty-minute anti-cellulite wrap, digesting Kay's apologetic words of earlier that morning, feeling the black clouds that she had staved off for so long gather ruinously around her head. 'I'm really sorry, Camille. I know you love this place – and you're one of the best beauticians I've ever worked with. But John has always wanted to move back to Chester, and now he's retired, I don't feel I can say no. To be honest, I think the change will do us good.'

'When are you selling up?' Camille had tried to keep her face blank, her manner upbeat.

'Well, I haven't told Tess or anyone else yet, but I was going to put it on the market this week. And, hopefully, we can sell it as a going concern. But between us, Camille, I don't think Tess will stick around for long. She's got itchy feet. You can tell.'

'Yes.' Camille attempted a smile. Neither of them said the unspoken, about her own job prospects.

'I'm sorry, love. I've dreaded telling you.' Kay's hand reached out and touched Camille's arm. An apologetic gesture.

'Don't be silly. You must do what you think is right. No point hanging around here if you'd rather be somewhere else.'

'Well, my son's up there, as you know.'

'It's good to be near your family.'

'I have missed him. And now his Deborah's expecting. Did I tell you that?'

Camille had made the right encouraging noises. She heard her voice from far off, as if it belonged to someone else, approving, exclaiming, reassuring, all the while making frantic internal calculations about what this was going to mean.

It couldn't have come at a worse time. Hal had told her the previous night that if he didn't get a commission in the next ten days he would have to admit defeat and wind up the business. He had said it in a curiously flat, unemotional tone, but when she had reached for him that night, had attempted to comfort him, he had pushed her gently away, his rigid back a silent rebuke. She did not persist. She never did now. Let him come back to you at his own pace, that was what the counsellor had said. She didn't say what Camille should do if he didn't come back.

Camille sat very still outside the treatment room, only half hearing the sounds she usually found a comfort: the muffled explosions of the blow-dryer, soft-soled shoes shuffling along the wood floor, the broken rhythms of human chatter.

Her losing her job would not be his fault, but he would use it as another stick with which to beat himself, another brace with which to widen the gap between them. I can't tell him now, she thought. I can't do that to him.

'You all right, Camille?'

'Fine, thanks, Tess.'

'I've just booked Mrs Green in for an aromatherapy facial on Tuesday. You were a bit busy so I offered to do it myself, but no, I wouldn't do . . . She said she wanted to have a word with you about something.' She laughed good-humouredly. 'I'd love to know what these women tell you, Camille. I reckon one day you're going to make a fantastic source for the *News of the World*.'

'What?'

'All their affairs and stuff. I know you're very discreet, but I bet this town is a right old hotbed of bad behaviour underneath.'

A quarter of a mile along the coast, Daisy sat on a small turfed outcrop, a few feet above a shingly cove, Ellie sleeping beside her in her push-chair. The sky was bright and still, the waves bobbing politely, tiptoeing their way backwards and forwards across the beach. In her hand she held the letter.

You're probably furious with me. And I wouldn't blame you. But, Daise, I have had time to think while I've been here, and one of the things I've realised is that I never actually had a chance to *want* a baby. I was pretty well presented with one. And although I do love her, I don't love the way she affected us, or our lives . . .

She didn't cry. She felt too cold to cry.

I miss you. I really do miss you. But I'm still so confused. I just don't know where my head is at the moment. I can't sleep properly, I've been put on antidepressants by the doctor, who has suggested I see someone to talk it all through, but that feels like it would be too painful. I feel torn about seeing you . . . but at the moment I'm not sure us seeing each other would make things any clearer.

He had enclosed a cheque for five hundred pounds. It was signed off his mother's account.

Just give me some time. I'll be in touch, I promise. But I do need more time. I'm really sorry, Daise. I feel like a complete shit, knowing I've hurt you. Some days I just hate myself . . .

It was all about him. All about his trauma, his struggle. There wasn't a single question mark in it – how was his daughter? Was she eating solids yet? Sleeping through the night? Holding things in her little pink fingers? How was *she* coping? His only reference to Ellie was in his own confusion. His selfishness, Daisy thought, was matched only by his lack of self-awareness. I wanted you to have a father, she told her daughter silently. I wanted for you the paternal adoration that should have been a right. And instead you got a self-obsessed jellyfish.

And yet in his written words there was an echo of the way he spoke, a ghostly echo of that emotional urgency she had loved for so long. And an honesty that she wasn't sure she was ready to feel. He hadn't known if he was ready for a baby. He had been quite frank about that for some time. 'When the business is up and running, babe,' he'd say. Or: 'When we've got a bit of money behind us.' He had been furious, she suspected, when she told him she was pregnant, although he had hidden it well. He had been outwardly supportive, gone to all the classes and scans, said the right things. It wasn't her fault, after all, he had told her more than once. They were in this together. 'It takes two to tango,' Julia had added.

But it didn't, always, did it?

Daisy sat on the grass and, for the first time, guiltily allowed herself to think back. Not to Ellie. To a pill packet, glanced at and discarded. To fourteen months before.

'They've finished the two front rooms. Want to take a look?'

Mrs Bernard lifted the newly awake Ellie from her push-chair as Daisy returned, closing the big white door behind her. 'The beds are coming tomorrow, so they'll start to look almost done. And that man rang about the blinds – he's going to call back this afternoon.'

Daisy, chilled and tired, peeled off her coat and laid it over what would become their reception desk. It was a 1930s piece she had found in Camden, which she had kept in its protective bubble-wrap since its delivery last week. She had wanted to show Jones, but they had not spoken directly in the ten days since they had last met. Mrs Bernard, looking uncommonly cheerful, motioned her along behind her. 'And look, they've started doing the gardens. I was going to ring you, but I thought you'd be back soon enough.'

Daisy looked down at the stepped terraces, where a selection of trees and shrubs were being dug into freshly composted earth. Some of the more overgrown plants, the lilac and wisteria, had been cut back diplomatically so that the hint of wildness and magic remained. But the terraces, scrubbed and repaired, now stood stark and clean against the organic forms around them, the smell of sage and thyme from the new herb garden mixing with the buddleia, whose spindly limbs were now bowed with heavy blooms.

'Makes a difference, doesn't it?' Mrs Bernard was beaming, pointing things out to Ellie.

She liked to do that, Daisy had noticed. She supposed, with a pang, that she hadn't been able to with Camille. 'It's coming on,' she said, gazing around her, a rare sense of achievement and pleasure germinating inside her, displacing the black hole that seemed to suck out everything that was good. They were still behind schedule, but it was coming together.

The rooms that needed to be knocked through were open and bright, while a newly installed electronic shutter allowed light to come in through the oversized skylight when required, while saving them from the blinding heat of midday. At least three of the bedrooms were now only awaiting their furniture, their replastered walls giving off an intoxicating smell of new paint, while newly waxed herring-bone floors settled under a layer of builders' dust that wouldn't disappear until they did. The banks of stainless-steel units had been installed in the kitchens, along with the industrial-sized fridges and freezers, and all but one of the bathrooms had their sanitaryware. The basics done, Daisy was now thinking about the detail. That was what she had always done best, happily spending hours researching a single piece of antique fabric, or looking through reference books to see exactly how pictures were hung or books stored. Next week, she told herself, she would sit down with Mrs Bernard's albums of the place. They were a treasure she had not allowed herself until 'Daniel's' side of the work, as she saw it, had been completed.

'Oh, I meant to tell you. They're ripping out that corner seat. Apparently the wood has rotted too far. But the chippie reckons he can make you one just like it. I didn't think it was worth troubling the listings people about. And that jasmine up the side is going to need thinning out as it's strangling the guttering. But I said that was okay. I put it in myself when Camille was small.' She explained: 'The smell, you see. She liked things that smelt nice.'

Daisy frowned at the older woman. 'Don't you mind?'

'Mind what?'

'All this ripping out. This was your house for years, and now I'm demolishing it and remaking it as I see it. It's not going to be anything like it was.'

Mrs Bernard's expression closed over. 'Why should I mind?' she said, her irritated tone at odds with her elaborate shrugging. 'No point looking backwards, is there? No point hanging on to things that aren't there.'

'But it's your history.'

'Would you rather I was upset? Snivelling around, telling you, "Oh, it wasn't like this in my day"?'

'Of course not – it's just—'

'It's just old people are meant to be forever harping on about the past. Well, I don't have a blue rinse, or a bus pass, and I couldn't give a stuff whether you paint the walls yellow with blue spots . . . So you do what you want, as I keep telling you. And stop looking for everyone's approval.'

Daisy knew when a conversation was closed. She bit her lip, and walked back into the house to make tea. Aidan, the foreman, was already in the kitchen, the tinny sounds of a radio burbling behind him.

'She told you about the meeting, has she?' He was squeezing the bag out with his fingers, his gaunt face speckled with pale turquoise Farrow and Ball paint.

'What meeting?'

'Your woman down in the hotel there. She's calling a meeting about the hotel. Wants the council to stop your works.'

'You're kidding me, right?'

'I kid you not.' He dropped the bag into the plastic carrier that doubled as a rubbish bin and leaned back against the new stainless-steel units. 'You'd better get down there tonight. I'd get the auld boss along as well. You know what they're like in this sort of place. Those women can be terrifying.'

'She frightened the pants off of me.' Trevor, the plumber, stuck his head in, searching for biscuits. 'Late fifties with a dog attached, right? Buttonholed me down at the newsagent's when I was buying some fags and started having a right old go. Told me I didn't know what I was doing and I was opening some Pandora's box or something.'

'It's the bar,' said Aidan. 'They don't want a bar.'

'But how can you have a hotel without a bar?'

'Don't ask me, love. I'm just telling you what they're all whingeing about.'

'Oh, hell. What are we going to do now?' Daisy's fractured sense of self-possession, barely netted together, now disintegrated again.

'What do you mean *do*?' Mrs Bernard stood in the door,

296

Ellie balanced on her hip. 'There's nothing *to* do. You'll go down there, listen to what she has to say, then stand up and tell them they're all a load of backward-looking fools.'

'That'll go down well,' said Trevor.

'So tell them what it's really like. Win them round.'

'Speak in public?' Daisy's eyes had widened. 'I don't think so.'

'Well, get Mr Jones up here. Get him to do it.'

Daisy thought back to the two conversations they had had since he left. He had resurrected his previous opinion of her, she could tell: flaky, over-emotional, not to be trusted with anything. His manner, when talking to her, was cautious and dismissive. He ended telephone calls prematurely and abruptly. When Daisy, still feeling stupid about her outburst, had asked him in what she thought was a conciliatory manner when he would be coming up again, he had asked why? Didn't she think she could handle it by herself?

'No,' she said, furiously. 'I don't want to get him up here.'

'Sounds like he'd handle it better than you could.'

'We won't go. We'll leave the hotel to speak for itself.'

'Oh, that's brave. Give Sylvia Rowan a clear way to badmouth you to everyone.'

There was something profoundly annoying about Mrs Bernard's scornful tone. Daisy felt she had heard it too often. 'Look, I don't do speaking in public.'

'That's stupid.'

'What?'

'You won't speak up for your own work. You won't ring Jones because you made a fool of yourself with him. So you'll sit here and let everyone walk all over you. That's stupid.'

Daisy had had enough. 'Oh, and I suppose you never did anything wrong in your life, did you? You married a decent man, had your family, grew up to be an upstanding member of the community. Never suffered a moment's self-doubt. Well, bully for you, Mrs Bernard.'

'Which shows how much you know. I'm just saying, in your circumstances, you need to stick up for yourself a bit more.'

'My circumstances? I don't wear a bloody scarlet letter on my forehead, Mrs Bernard. Outside Stepfordwivesville, there are people bringing children up on their own, who aren't considered to have "circumstances", as you put it.'

'I am quite well aware—'

'I never chose this, you know? I thought I was creating a family. I didn't think I was making myself a single parent. You think it was on my life plan to spend my life living in a building site with a baby whose father doesn't know what she looks like any more? With a load of disapproving bloody battleaxes? You think that's what I wanted?'

Trevor and Aidan exchanged glances.

'There is no need to get hysterical.'

'Well, stop bloody getting at me.'

'Don't be so sensitive.'

There was a brief pause.

'And what do you mean I made a fool of myself with Jones?'

Mrs Bernard glanced at the men. 'I'm not sure I should say.'

'Say what?'

'Oh, don't mind us.' Aidan settled back against the units, mug of tea in hand.

For the first time, Mrs Bernard looked unbalanced. 'Well. You probably thought you were doing the right thing . . . moving on . . .'

'What on earth are you talking about?'

'You and him. The other morning.'

Daisy frowned, waited.

The men were very still, listening.

'I suppose young people are different nowadays . . . things are different . . .'

'Oh, God, you think I slept with him, don't you? Oh, I don't believe it . . .' Daisy laughed joylessly.

Mrs Bernard walked past her and began to point out something of intense interest to Ellie through the window.

'For your information, Mrs Bernard, not that it is any of your bloody business, Mr Jones and I have not laid a bloody hand on each other. He stayed here because you took his car keys, no other reason.'

'He's a lovely man, though,' interjected Trevor.

'Lovely. I'd go out with him. If I was a girl.' Aidan grinned.

Mrs Bernard turned and walked past them all. 'I never said anything of the sort,' she said. 'I just thought you shouldn't have been drunk around him, that's all. Him being your boss and all. But I won't offer my opinion if you don't want it.'

'I don't want it. In fact, I just want to be left alone.'

'Well, that's easy enough. Here, take the baby. I've got to go and get some shopping.' She pushed past Daisy, thrust her daughter at her and left the house.

'Daisy? Is everything all right?'

'No. Yes. I don't know. I just needed to hear a friendly voice.'

'What's the matter, darling?'

'Oh, you know. Just house hassles.' She traced the receiver with her finger. 'And Daniel wrote.'

'That's a shame. I was hoping he was dead. To say what?'

'That he's confused. Not happy.'

'Oh, poor Daniel. Well, that's big of him. So what's he going to do now?'

Julia, Daisy realised, was not the best person to ring.

'Nothing. He's – he's sorting himself out.'

'Which leaves you where, exactly?'

'Forget it, Ju. Let's not talk about it. Anyway, Ellie's fine. She's doing well with her solids, and she can almost sit up by herself. She's getting a real seaside glow in her cheeks. When things aren't so busy, and it's warmed up a little, I'm going to take her for a paddle.'

'Bless . . . Shall I come up and see you both? I miss my little babycakes.'

It really was the most irritating word. 'Let me get past this week. I'll ring you.'

'You don't have to do this, you know, Daise. You can come home to us. Any time you like. Don's told me I shouldn't have let you go there on your own.'

'I'm fine.'

'But you'll think about it. If it all gets too much. I don't want you feeling you're on your own.'

'I'll think about it, Ju.'

'Besides, Daise, it's *Essex*.'

The Alderman Kenneth Elliott Community Centre had cancelled its regular bingo night, and the few pensioners who had arrived for their game were not best consoled by the prospect of a planning meeting. Some stood outside exclaiming disconsolately at each other over their handbags, as if unsure now whether to stay or return home, while several others sat inside on their moulded plastic chairs, their cards at the ready, just in case. The bingo-caller, a former DJ who was hoping to make his way on to the cruise-ship circuit, stood outside smoking furiously and thinking of the fifteen pounds that would now not be his. All of which might have gone some way towards explaining the prematurely bad-tempered mood among those of Merham's inhabitants who had braved the sudden showers – to come.

It was a low, kidney-coloured building, erected in the late 1970s apparently with no aesthetic considerations either inside or out, merely a badly heated shell in which Merham's One o'Clock Club, Tuesday social, bingo and few mothers and toddlers fought politely for days and space in which to arrange the chairs and serve orange squash, cheap biscuits and tea from its temperamental oversized urn.

On the walls of its entrance lobby, photocopied sheets of A4 paper advertised a dial-a-bus service, a confidential drugs-advice line and a new play session for children with mental or physical handicaps. Plus a smaller notice, unseen by the former DJ, noting that this Thursday's bingo evening would be cancelled. Dominating all of these was a new poster, more than twice the size of the others, with 'SOS – Save Our Standards' stencilled on it in lilac ink. The residents of Merham, it exhorted, needed to call a halt to the damaging development of what it inexplicably called the 'actress's house' to protect its young people and Merham's traditional way of life.

Daisy looked at this, at the audience of largely middle-aged people with their backs to her, shuffling into seats and looking expectantly at the stage, and fought the urge to turn round and head back for the relative safety of Arcadia. She was only prevented by the equally terrifying prospect that both Jones's and Mrs Bernard's visions of her were right: that she was weak, spineless, flaky. Not up to it. She hauled Ellie, simultaneously stripping her of Mrs Bernard's perennial multitude of layers, out of her push-chair, tucked it into a corner then sat as unobtrusively as she could at the back of the hall, while the local mayor, a short, broad man who took evident pleasure in handling his chain of office, with a minimum of fuss, introduced Sylvia Rowan.

'Ladies and gentlemen, I'll keep this short as I know you're all anxious to be home.' Mrs Rowan, resplendent in a red boxy jacket and pleated skirt, stood at the head of the hall, her hands clutching each other under her bosom. 'I'd like to thank you for such a splendid turnout. It just goes to show that community spirit is not dead in some parts of our beloved country!' She smiled, as if waiting for applause, but then, sensing only the dullest murmur of agreement, ploughed on. 'Now, I've called this meeting because, as you know, we have spent many years protecting Merham from going the way of Clacton and Southend. We have, despite considerable opposition, always managed to restrict the circumstances in which alcohol can be sold publicly in this town. Some may think us backward, but I like to think we in Merham have kept a certain family feel, a certain standard to our little town, by not allowing it to become just another row of pubs and nightclubs.'

She smiled at a muffled 'Hear hear' from the back. Daisy jiggled Ellie gently.

'Merham, I feel, is simply one of the most pleasant seaside towns in England. For those who wish to drink there are the restaurant run by Mr and Mrs Delfino here, the Indian restaurant, and ourselves at the Riviera Hotel. That has always been more than sufficient for our town's inhabitants, and kept away the – shall we say? – rougher elements that are traditionally attracted to seaside towns. But now . . .' she looked around the room '. . . we are under threat.'

The room was quiet, with only the occasional scrape of a shoe or shrill ring of a mobile phone to break the silence.

'We are all glad, I'm sure, to see one of our finest buildings being renovated. And I am told by the district planning officer that everything being done to the house is in keeping with its history. Those of us who know the house's history will be wondering quite what that means!' She let out a nervous little laugh, echoed by some of the older people in the room. 'But as you know, this is not going to be for private use. The actress's house, as we long-standing residents know it, is going to become a hotel for Londoners. Created by the owner of a nightclub in Soho, no less, who wants a place for his type to stay outside the city. Now, some of us may question whether we really need Soho types headed down here and using Merham as their private playground, but as if that were not bad enough, the new owner is applying for permission for . . .' she checked a piece of paper in her hand '. . . a helipad. So you can imagine the noise if we have helicopters landing at all hours of the day or night. And not just one but *two* bars, with extended opening hours. So that all sorts can wander around the grounds as drunk as you like, and quite possibly bringing drugs and who knows what else into our little town. Well, ladies and gentlemen, I for one am not willing to stand for it. I think we should lobby our local MP, and our planning officer, and get them to withdraw permission for a hotel here. Merham doesn't need it, and it certainly doesn't want it!' She ended with a flourish, waving the crumpled sheet of paper above her head.

Daisy glanced around her at the noddings of approval, and her heart sank.

The mayor stood at the front, thanking a flushed Mrs Rowan for her 'passionate words' and asking if anyone present had something to add. Daisy's hand rose, and two hundred expectant pairs of eyes turned to her. 'Erm, I'm Daisy Parsons, and I'm the designer who's—'

'Speak up!' came a call from the front. 'We can't hear you.'

Daisy moved into the walkway between the two banks of chairs, and took a deep breath. The air was smoky, charged with the mingling of several inexpensive perfumes. 'I'm the designer renovating Arcadia House. And I've listened carefully to what Mrs Rowan has to say.' She kept her eyes focused just above their heads, so that she didn't have to see anyone. If she noted their expression, she knew she would grind to a halt.

'I understand you feel strongly about the house, and that's admirable. It's a beautiful house, and if anyone wants to come—'

'Louder! We still can't hear you!'

Daisy continued. 'If anyone wants to come and see what we're doing, you'd be more than welcome. In fact I'd love to hear from anyone who knows the house's history, or its previous inhabitants, because we want to build elements of its past back into the new décor. Although it's not listed, we really are being incredibly sympathetic to the ethos behind its design.'

On her hip, Ellie shifted, her eyes bright and round as glass buttons.

'Mrs Rowan is right, there is an application in for a helipad. But that would be hidden from the town's view, would only operate within a limited time-frame and, frankly, I don't think we'll end up building it anyway. I'm sure most visitors will come by car or train.' She looked around at the unmoved faces. 'And, yes, we have applied for licensing for two bars, one inside and one out. But the kinds of people who are going to come to Arcadia are not drunken yobs, they're not going to get drunk on cheap cider and have fights down on the seafront. These are wealthy, civilised people who just want a gin and tonic and a bottle of wine with their meal. You probably won't even know they're here.'

'Noise carries from that house,' interrupted Sylvia Rowan. 'If you've got a bar outside there'll be music and all sorts, and if the wind is blowing the right way the whole town will have to listen to it.'

'I'm sure we can sort something out, if you tell the owner your concerns.'

'What you don't understand, Miss Parsons, is that we've seen it all before. We've had parties and all sorts up at that house, and we didn't like it then.' A murmur of agreement crossed the room. 'And that's without the impact it will have on our existing restaurants.'

'It will bring more trade to them. To the town.'

Ellie, unaccountably, began to wail. Daisy shifted her to her other hip and tried to focus on the argument above the abrasive sound of her crying.

'And draw existing trade away.'

'I really don't think they're the same sort of market.' Standing in the middle of the hall, Daisy hadn't felt so alone before in her whole life.

'Oh? And what are you saying our sort of market is, then?'

'Oh, for goodness' sake, Sylvia, you know very well that the kind of people who come for Sunday tea at your precious hotel are hardly going to be playing drum and bass or whatever it's called at some modern bar.'

Daisy glanced to her left to see Mrs Bernard standing up several rows away, her husband on one side of her, Camille and Hal on the other. The older woman turned, taking in the faces of those people around her. 'This town is dying,' she said slowly and deliberately. 'This place is on its last legs and we all know it. The school is under threat, half the shops in the high street are boarded up or given over to charities, and our market is shrinking by the week because there's not enough custom here to keep the stallholders afloat. Even our bed-and-breakfasts are vanishing. We need to stop looking backwards, stop opposing every prospect of change, and start letting in a bit of fresh air.'

She looked over at Daisy, who had stuck her little finger into Ellie's mouth and was rocking backwards and forwards on the balls of her feet.

'We might not feel comfortable having newcomers in our midst, but we're going to have to attract someone if our businesses are to survive, if our young people can build a future here. And better wealthy people from London than no people at all.'

'Wouldn't have happened if the Guest-house Association had still been here,' said an elderly woman in the front row.

'And what happened to the Guest-house Association? It died because there weren't enough guest-houses to make an association worthwhile.' Mrs Bernard turned and looked scornfully at Sylvia Rowan. 'How many of you have seen your takings or your earnings go up in the last five years? Well, come on!'

There was a general murmuring and shaking of heads.

'Exactly. And this is because we've become backward-looking and unwelcoming. You ask the landladies – we don't even have enough charm to attract families any more, our lifeblood. We need to embrace change, not reject it. You go away and think about that before you start trying to pull the rug from under our new businesses.'

There was a faint spattering of applause.

'Yes, well, you would say that, wouldn't you?'

Mrs Bernard turned to face Sylvia Rowan, who looked her straight in the eye. 'That developer has probably paid you enough for the house. And, by all accounts, he's paying you still. So you're hardly going to be impartial.'

'If you don't know me well enough by now, Sylvia Holden, to know that I know my own mind, then you're an even sillier woman than you were a girl. And that's saying something.'

There was some surreptitious laughter at the back of the hall.

'Yes, well, we all know what kind of a girl—'

'Ladies, ladies, that's quite enough.' The mayor, per-haps fearful of menopausal fisticuffs, placed himself firmly between the two women. Daisy was shocked by the naked enmity in their faces. 'Thank you, thank you. I'm sure you've both given us plenty to think about. I think we should take a vote now—'

'You don't think we've forgotten, do you? Just because no one talks about it any more doesn't mean we've forgotten.'

'Mrs Rowan – please. We'll take a vote and see which way the land lies before we move on to anything else. Hands up all those who are against – or not entirely supportive of the Arcadia redevelopment.'

'You need to stop living in the past, you silly woman.' Mrs Bernard, her voice a stage whisper, took her seat next to her husband. He whispered something, and patted her hand.

Daisy held her breath and gazed around the room. Almost three-quarters, by her reckoning.

'Those for?'

She walked over to the pram and placed her protesting daughter inside. She had done what she had promised. Now it was nearly Ellie's bedtime, and she wanted to be at the place she had begun, in the absence of anywhere else, to think of as home.

★   ★   ★

'You're not letting yourself get even more bloody miserable, are you?' Mrs Bernard was in the drawing-room doorway, a sheaf of folders under her arm.

Daisy had been lying on the sofa, Daniel's letter in her hand, listening to the radio and indeed feeling even more bloody miserable, as Mrs Bernard put it. Now she pushed herself upright and made room for the older woman to sit down. 'A bit, I guess,' she said, raising a vague smile. 'I didn't know there was quite so much opposition.'

'Sylvia Rowan's against it.'

'But there's a lot of bad feeling. It's actually a bit unnerving . . .' She took a deep breath.

'You're wondering if it's all worth it.'

'Yes.'

'You don't want to worry about that lot,' Mrs Bernard scoffed. 'Don't forget, it was only the local busybodies turned up. And those who thought it was the bingo. All those who stayed away probably couldn't give a stuff one way or the other. And they'll have a job withdrawing permission once it's been granted, whatever that silly woman thinks.' She looked at Daisy, her expression briefly questioning. The casual observer might even have said concerned.

She studied her hands meditatively. 'First time I've spoken to that family in getting on forty years. You'd be surprised at how easy that is, even in a small town. Oh, they all talk to Camille, of course, but she knows I'm not interested so she keeps it to herself. Anyway . . .' she let out a sigh '. . . I just wanted to say you don't want to go jacking it all in. Not now.'

There was a short silence. Upstairs, Ellie moaned in her sleep, the sound sending a ripple of coloured lights over the baby monitor.

'Maybe not. Thanks . . . And thanks for coming and speaking up. It . . . it was good of you.'

'No, it wasn't. I just didn't want to let that misery think she had it all her own way.'

'She's got a lot of support, though. They really don't like the prospect of outsiders coming in, do they?'

The older woman was chuckling now. Her face was wry, its features softened. 'Things never change,' she said comfortably. 'They never change.' She reached for one of her folders. 'Tell you what, you go and get me a glass of wine, and I'll show you what this house used to be like. Then you'll see what I mean.'

'The pictures.'

'Decent wine. French. If it's that Blue Nun or whatever you and Mr Jones were talking about the other night, then you can forget it. I'll go right now.'

Daisy got up to fetch a glass. She halted in the doorway to the kitchens, and turned. 'You know, I hope it's not too nosy or anything, but I have to ask . . . How did you end up owning this place? If it wasn't anything to do with your husband, I mean. There aren't many women who end up with an architectural masterpiece to use as their own private bolthole.'

'Oh, you don't want to go getting into all that.'

'Yes, I do. I wouldn't have asked otherwise.'

Mrs Bernard traced the top of her folder with her finger. 'I got left it.'

'You got left it.'

'Yes.'

'Left it.'

There was a lengthy pause.

'And that's all you're going to tell me?'

'What else do you need to know?'

309

'I don't *need* to know anything . . . but do you have to keep everything so close to your chest? Come on, Mrs Bernard. Thaw a little. You know a damn sight more about me than I know about you. It doesn't all have to be a state secret. I'm not going to say anything. I've got no one to tell, have I?'

'I'm showing you the pictures, aren't I?'

'But they're not about you. They're about the house.'

'It might be the same thing.'

'I give up.' Daisy disappeared into the kitchens, then came back, shrugging good-humouredly. 'I know when I'm beaten. Let's talk fabrics, then.'

The older woman sat back and gave her a long, steady look. Something had shifted in her this evening, Daisy thought. There was an air about her, a kind of 'Well, if we've come this far . . .'.

She waited, saying nothing, as Mrs Bernard turned back to her folders, and then, finally, opened one, face up, on her lap. 'All right. If it bothers you so much,' she said. 'I'll tell you how I got it, as long as you promise me you're not going to go blabbing to everyone. But first I need a drink. And enough of this Mrs Bernard nonsense. If I'm going to have to tell you all my "state secrets", you can call me by my first name. Lottie.'

Fourteen

Dear Joe

Thank you for your letter, and the photograph of you with your new car. It certainly looks very smart, and a very nice shade of red, and you look quite the proud owner. I have put it on my little table, near the one of my mother. I don't have many pictures, so it was a bit of a treat.

There is nothing much to report here. I am having a break from housework and reading a book which Adeline has lent me. I like the art-history ones best. She says she is going to turn me into a Reader. Like she is getting me to practise my painting so that I can give Frances a surprise when she gets here. I am not very good – my watercolours tend to run into each other, and I get more charcoal on my fingers than the paper. But I quite like it. It's not like we did it at school. Adeline keeps going on about me learning to 'express myself'. When Julian comes he says I am 'expanding my vistas', and that one day he'll frame one and sell it for me. I think this may be his idea of a joke.

Not that there are many jokes here. In the village you are evidently considered a fast sort if you dare to put a brooch on with your dress and it's not a Sunday. There is one woman – she runs the bread shop (the bread is in sticks as long as your leg!) – who is very cheerful and chats away to us. But Madame Migot, who is a sort of doctor, always looks very severe at her. Then again, she looks severe at everyone. Me and Adeline especially.

I don't know if I told you where our village was. It is half-way up a mountain, Mount Faron, but it's not like the mountains in books with snow at the top. This one is very hot and dry and has a military fort, and when George drove Adeline and me up the narrow path to the top the first time I was almost sick with fright. Even at the top I had to hang on to a tree. Did you know they have pines here? Not the same as the ones at home, but it did make me feel better. Adeline sends her love. She is picking herbs in the garden. They smell very strong here in the heat, not like Mrs H's old garden at all.

I hope you are well, Joe. And thanks for keeping on writing. Sometimes I have been a bit lonely, truth to tell, and your letters have been a comfort to me.

Yours, etc.

Lottie lay on her side on the cool flagstones, her hips supported by a cushion, another under her neck, waiting for the moment when her bones would start to complain about the uncompromising solidity of the floor below. Her joints didn't last long now: even on her soft feather-bed upstairs they would begin twingeing within minutes of her settling into any position, demanding that she find new pressure points upon which to lie. She rested, feeling the first hints of discomfort creeping up her left thigh, and closed her eyes in irritation. She didn't want to have to move: the floor was the coolest place to be – in fact, the only cool place in a house of simmering heat, scratchy fabrics and huge, buzzing airborne creatures that crashed into furniture and mumbled angrily against the windows.

Outside, she could see Adeline, under an oversized straw hat, moving slowly around the yellowing, overgrown garden, picking herbs and sniffing them before laying them in a little basket. As she strolled back towards the house the baby kicked hard, and Lottie muttered bad-temperedly, pulling the silk kimono so that she didn't have to look at her swollen stomach.

'Do you want a drink, Lottie dear?' Adeline stepped over her and made for the sink. She was used to Lottie lying on the floor.

She was also used to her cheerlessness.

'No, thank you.'

'Oh, bother, we're out of grenadine. I hope that wretched woman comes from the village soon – we're out of nearly everything. And we need the linen laundered as well – Julian is returning this week.'

Lottie pushed herself upright, and fought the urge to apologise. No matter how many times Adeline scolded her for it, she still felt guilty that in these last weeks of pregnancy she was fat and slow and useless. For the first few months after her arrival, Lottie had managed the housework and cooking ('We had a woman from the village, but she was such a misery'), gradually hauling the ramshackle French house into an orderly shape, moulding herself on a hybrid of Mrs Holden and Virginia, her role as housekeeper her payment for Adeline's hospitality. Not that Adeline wanted payment, but Lottie felt safer that way. If you earned your keep, it was harder for people to ask you to leave.

Adeline, meanwhile, had seemed to consider it her mission to persuade Lottie (against all available evidence, as far as Lottie could see) that there were things to be gained from leaving Merham. She had become a sort of teacher, encouraging her to be 'brave' in what she attempted to portray for herself. Initially self-conscious and unwilling, Lottie had been surprised that, as someone who no longer appeared to exist anywhere, she could leave such solid images on a page. Adeline's praise brought a rare sense of achievement to her – Dr Holden had been the only person to praise her for anything – a sense that there might be some other purpose to her life. And slowly, gradually, she had had to admit a creeping interest in these new worlds. They offered opportunities for escape from her existing one if nothing else. But now she was huge. And good-for-nothing. If she stayed upright for too long she felt dizzy, and fluid pooled in her ankles. If she moved too much, she broke into a fine sweat, and the bits of her body that now rubbed against each other became pink, sore and chafed. The baby moved restlessly, sending her stomach into impossible shapes, pushing against its inelastic confines, leaving her sleepless by night and exhausted by day. So she sat, or lay on the floor, sunk deep into her own misery, waiting for the heat, or the baby, to drop.

Adeline, thankfully, said nothing about her depression and ill-temper. Mrs Holden would have got cross, and told her that she was affecting everybody's moods with her black dog. But Adeline didn't mind if Lottie didn't want to talk, or participate. She just kept on, apparently impervious, humming, moving around her and asking without rancour whether she would like something else to drink, another cushion, or to help her compose another letter to Frances. Adeline wrote a lot of letters to Frances.

She didn't seem to get any replies.

It was almost six months since Lottie had left England, seven since she'd left Merham. For all the distance between them it might have been ten years. In her initial state of shock, Lottie had, perhaps naïvely, gone to her mother, who, her hair now fiercely lacquered into a kind of helmet and her mouth a vivid shade of tangerine, had told her not to bother thinking she could bring it home. She couldn't believe, she said, waving a cigarette, that Lottie hadn't learned by her own example. Lottie had wasted all the opportunities God had given her, which were a damn sight more than *she* had ever been given, and she had left the Holdens with them thinking she was no better than she was.

Besides – and here her mother had become curiously coy, almost conciliatory – she had made a life for herself now, was courting a nice widower. He was a moral type, he wouldn't understand. He wasn't like the others, she said, with a glance towards Lottie that might have been something like a guilty acknowledgement. He was *decent*. Before her cup of tea was half drunk, Lottie understood that not only was she not being invited to stay but, just as in Merham, she no longer appeared to exist.

Her mother had not told this man she had a daughter. There had been a few pictures of her around the house when she had lived there; now there were none. Over the mantelpiece, where there had stood one of her and Auntie Jean, her mother's late sister, there was now a framed picture of a middle-aged couple, arm in arm outside a country pub, squinting, his bald pate shining in the sunlight.

'I wasn't asking for anything. I suppose I just wanted to see you.' Lottie gathered her things, unable even to summon up the energy to feel hurt. Compared to what she had been through, this woman's rejection felt like a curiously minor thing.

Her mother's face had looked pinched, as though she were holding back tears. She batted at her face with a sponge from a powder compact, then reached out a hand and clutched Lottie's arm. 'You let me know where you are. You write, now.'

'Shall I sign it Lottie?' Lottie turned sulkily towards the door. 'Or would you prefer "your good friend"?' Her mother, tight-lipped, had stuffed ten shillings into her hand as she left. Lottie had looked at it and almost laughed.

Lottie did not love France, despite all Adeline's best efforts. She didn't much like the food, apart from the bread. The rich stews with their garlic undertow and the meats with their heavy sauces made her long for the comforting blandness of fish and chips and cucumber sandwiches, while her first whiff of strong French cheese in the market had her retching by the side of the road. She didn't like the heat, which was much fiercer than Merham's but without the benefit of the sea and its incoming breezes, or the mosquitoes, which attacked her remorselessly, like whining divebombers, at night. She didn't like the scenery, which seemed arid and unfriendly, the soil parched and the vegetation curling surlily under the heat of the sun, or the crickets, which clattered away incessantly in the background. And she hated the French: the men who eyed her steadily, speculatively, and, as she grew, the women, who did the same but this time with disapproval and, in some cases, open disgust.

Madame Migot, who acted as the local midwife, had come to see her twice, at Adeline's request. Lottie hated her: she would manipulate her stomach roughly as if she were kneading bread, then take her blood pressure and bark instructions at Adeline, who would sound inexplicably calm and unapologetic in return. Madame Migot never once said anything to Lottie; she barely met her eye. 'She's a Catholic,' Adeline would murmur, as the older woman left. 'It's to be expected. You, of all people, should know what they're like in a small town.' But that was it. Despite everything, Lottie missed her own small town. She missed the scent of Merham, that mixture of sea-salt and Tarmac, the sounds of the Scots pines in the sea breeze, the open, orderly greens of the municipal park and the rotting breakwaters stretching off into infinity. She liked the smallness of it: the way one knew its limits, and that they were unlikely to be exceeded. She had never had Celia's wanderlust, her desire to push out for new horizons; she had just been grateful for her tenure in the pleasant, well-ordered town, perhaps presciently aware that it was unlikely to last.

Most of all, she missed Guy. During daylight hours she had steeled herself against thoughts of him, had erected a barrier in her mind whereby, with a stiff determination, she could force his image away as if she were pulling a curtain across his face. At night, though, he ignored her pleas for peace and wandered in and out of her dreams, his lopsided smile, his slim brown hands, his tendernesses both calling to her and taunting her with their absence. Sometimes she woke up calling his name.

Sometimes she wondered how it were possible to be so far from the sea and still feel as if she were drowning.

Spring became summer and visitors came and went, sitting outside on the terrace under straw hats, drinking red wine and sleeping in the heat of the afternoon. Often with each other. Julian came, far too polite to mention her increasing girth, or to ask her how it had come about. He was relentlessly cheerful, dangerously extravagant. He was, apparently, making money again. He gave Adeline the Merham house, and a fearfully expensive bust of a woman that, to Lottie, looked like ants had been at it. Stephen came twice. A poet called Si came, and in a strong public-school accent told them all repeatedly that he was 'cranked', said he was only 'hanging' till he could find a 'gig' and thought Adeline the 'most' for 'laying on' a room. He was, George said mockingly, a Beat by way of Basingstoke.

George came and stayed; it was only then that Adeline

seemed to come alive, engaging in vehement whispered conversation with him, while Lottie tried hard to pretend she wasn't there. She knew they were talking about Frances.

Once, drunk, he had looked at Lottie's stomach and made some joke about fruits and seeds and Adeline had actually hit him.

'You know, I quite admire you, little Lottie,' he told her, when Adeline was out of earshot. 'You were probably the most dangerous thing ever to happen to Merham.'

Lottie, hiding under an oversized hat, gave him a dark look.

'I always thought it would be your sister who got herself into trouble.'

'She isn't – wasn't my sister.'

George didn't appear to hear. He lay back on the grass, nibbling at a piece of the mouldering, pungent salami that he liked to buy at the market. Around them, the crickets kept up their whirring chorus, breaking occasionally in the afternoon heat, as if they were a motor for the day itself.

'And you the serious one. Doesn't seem just, somehow. Were you just curious? Or did he promise that he would be yours for ever? The *apple* of your eye perhaps? A bit of a *peach*? Gosh, Lottie, I don't suppose Madame Holden ever heard you using language like that . . . Very *ripe*, I should say . . . All right, all right . . . Now, are you going to eat any of those figs, or can I have them?'

Whether it was her misery or her detachment from her old life, any life, Lottie found it hard to feel any joy, or any sense of tender anticipation towards this baby. Most of the time she found it hard to think of it as a baby. Sometimes, at night, she felt a terrible guilt that she was bringing it into the world with no father; into a place where it would be eyed distastefully by the Madame Migots, and with suspicion by anyone else.

Other times she felt a searing resentment of it: its existence meant she would never be free of Guy's presence, of the pain that went with it. She didn't know what frightened her more: the prospect of not loving it because of him, or loving it for the same reason.

She hardly thought about how, practically, she was going to cope. Adeline told her not to worry. 'These things sort themselves out, darling,' she said, patting her hand. 'Just stay away from the nuns.'

Lottie, huge and weary and tired of just about everything, hoped she was right. She didn't cry or rage. Since the first few weeks, when she had discovered her predicament, she hadn't bothered. It wasn't going to change anything. And it felt easier to deaden her emotions, to contain them, rather than have them raw to the touch, as they had been. As the pregnancy progressed, she became dozy, detached, simply sat for hours in the overgrown garden watching dragonflies and wasps as they hovered around her, or when it became too hot, lay inside on the cold floor, like a kimono-clad walrus sunning itself on the rocks. Perhaps she would die in childbirth, she thought. And was perversely comforted.

Perhaps cognisant of the fact that Lottie's depression was growing at an inverse rate to the days remaining before the birth, Adeline began forcing her to come out with her on what she called 'adventures', even though they rarely contained any more adventurous activity than the ordering of red wine or pastis, or perhaps the purchase of an apple tart, or sweet, custardy *Tropézienne*. Shunning the sticky, traffic-fumed city heat of nearby Toulon, Adeline made George drive them further along the coast to Sanary. Lottie missed the sea, she reasoned aloud. The palm-fringed seaside town, with its shaded cobbled streets and cheerful, pastel-shuttered houses, would be a welcome tonic. It was famous for its artists and artisans, she said, sitting Lottie at a pavement café, close to the soothing burble of a stone fountain. Aldous Huxley had lived here, while writing his *Brave New World*. The whole of the southern coast had provided inspiration for artists over the years. Frances and she had travelled from St Tropez to Marseille one year, and by the end of the trip there had been so many canvases in the boot of the car that they had been forced to drive with their luggage on their laps.

George, pleading an appointment inside at the bar, had whispered something to Adeline and left them.

Lottie, ignoring the black-skirted woman who placed a basket of bread in front of her, said nothing. This was partly because she had fallen asleep in the car on the way there, and sleeping, along with the heat, left her sluggish and stupid for some time after she had woken. It was also in part because the baby made her self-absorbed. She had gradually whittled down her persona to a few simple symptoms: swollen feet, sore, stretched belly, itchy legs, misery. So it was an effort to move beyond these things to notice anyone else, or that Adeline, opposite, who had finally left her to her thoughts in order to read a letter, had not changed position for some time.

Lottie took a sip of her water, and studied Adeline's face. 'Are you all right?'

Adeline didn't answer.

Lottie heaved herself upright, and glanced around at the people seated at the tables, who seemed content to spend hours doing almost nothing. She tried not to spend any time in the sun: it made her feel nauseous and overheated. 'Adeline?'

She was holding the letter, half open, in her hand.

'Adeline?'

Adeline looked up at her, as if she had only just become aware of her presence. Her face, as ever, was impassive, aided by a pair of neat dark sunglasses. Her raven hair had fallen forward on her wet cheek. 'She has asked me not to write any more.'

'Who?'

'Frances.'

'Why?'

Adeline looked out across the cobbled courtyard. Two dogs were snapping at each other over something in the gutter. 'She says . . . she says I have nothing new to say.'

'That's a bit harsh,' said Lottie, grumpily, adjusting her sun hat. 'It's hard finding new things to put in letters. Nothing happens here.'

'Frances is not harsh. I don't think she means . . . Oh, Lottie . . .'

They had never spoken about personal things. When Lottie had arrived, she had begun tearfully, apologetically, to explain about the baby, but Adeline had just waved a pale hand and told her that she was always welcome. She had never asked anything about her circumstances, perhaps believing that Lottie would volunteer any information she felt compelled to share, and likewise revealed little of her own. Adeline chatted pleasantly, ensured that her friend had everything she needed and, apart from the odd question about Frances, they might have been distantly related, visitors determined to enjoy their stay.

'What am I to do?' She looked so sad, so resigned. There was no one else. 'She should not be by herself. Frances has never been any good by herself. She gets too . . . melancholy. She needs me. Despite herself, she needs me.'

Lottie eased herself back into one of the wicker chairs, knowing it would be imprinted on her thighs within minutes.

She raised a hand against the sun and studied Adeline's face, wondering if Adeline had it the right way round. 'Why is she so cross with you?'

Adeline looked at her, then down at her hands, still clutching the unwelcome letter. She looked up again. 'Because . . . because I cannot love her in the way that she wants me to.'

Lottie frowned.

'She does not think I should be with Julian.'

'But he's your husband. You love him.'

'Yes, I love him . . . But as a friend.'

There was a short pause.

'A friend?' Lottie said, thinking back to the afternoon she had spent with Guy. 'Only a friend?' She stared at Adeline. 'But . . . but how can he bear it?'

Adeline reached down and lit herself a cigarette. It was something Lottie had only seen her do in France. She inhaled, looked away.

'Because Julian loves me as a friend also. He has no passion for me, Lottie, no physical passion. But we suit each other, Julian and I. He needs a base, a certain . . . creative environment a respectability, and I need stability, people around me who can . . . I don't know . . . entertain me. We understand each other like that.'

'But . . . I don't understand . . . Why did you marry Julian, if you didn't love him?'

Adeline put down the letter carefully, and refilled her glass. 'We have skirted around each other, you and I. Now I shall tell you a story, Lottie. About a girl who fell hopelessly in love with a man she couldn't have, a man she met during the war, when she was . . . living another life. He was the most beautiful creature she had ever seen, with cat's eyes of green, and a sad, sad face because of the things he had endured. And they both adored each other, and swore that if one died the other could no longer bear to live, so that they could be joined somewhere else. It was a violent passion, Lottie, a terrible thing.'

Lottie sat, her aching limbs, her encroaching heat rash, temporarily forgotten.

'But you see, Lottie, this man was not English. And because of the war he could not stay. And he was sent to Russia, and after two letters this girl never heard from him again. And, dearest Lottie, it drove her mad. She was like a mad thing, tearing her hair and shouting at herself and walking the streets for hours, even when bombs were falling all around.

'And eventually, a long time after, she decided that she had to live, and that to live she had to feel a little less, suffer a little less. She could not die, much as she wanted to, because somewhere out there he might just still living. And she knew that, if the fates intended it, she and her man would find each other again.'

'And did they?'

Adeline looked away and exhaled. The smoke, in the still air, came out as a long, even whisper. 'Not yet, Lottie. Not yet . . . But, then, I don't expect it to be in this life-time.'

They sat in silence for a while, listening to the lazy humming of the bees, the conversation around them, the distant dull ringing of some church bell. Adeline had poured Lottie a watered-down glass of wine, and Lottie sipped at it, trying not to look as nonplussed as she felt. 'I still don't understand . . . Why did Frances paint you as that Greek woman?'

'Laodamia? She was accusing me of hanging on to some-thing false – an image of love. She knew I would rather live within the safety of marriage to Julian than risk loving again.

Seeing Julian always used to upset her. She said it was a reminder of my ability to lie to myself.'

She turned to Lottie, her eyes wide and wet. She smiled, a slow, sweet smile. 'Frances is so . . . She believes I have killed off my capacity to love, that I find it safer to be with Julian and love something that cannot be there. She thinks that because she loves me so much she can bring me back to life, that by sheer force of her will she can make me love her too. And you know, Lottie, I do love Frances. I love her more than any other woman I know, anyone but him . . . Once, when I was feeling very low, I did . . . she was so sweet . . . but . . . it would not be enough for her. She is not like Julian. She could not live with a half-love. In art, in life, she demands honesty. And I can never love anyone, neither man nor woman, as I loved Konstantin . . .'

Are you sure you don't love her? Lottie wanted to ask, thinking back to Adeline's numerous letters, her uncharacteristic desperation at Frances's continued absence. But Adeline interrupted her. 'This is why I knew, you see, Lottie.'

Adeline reached out and held her wrist, an insistent hold. Lottie found herself shivering, despite the heat.

'When I saw you and Guy together, I knew.' Her eyes burned into Lottie's. 'I saw myself and Konstantin.'

Dear Joe
Excuse me if this letter is short, but I am very tired and do not have much time to write. I had my baby yesterday, and she is a little girl, very beautiful. In fact she is the most darling thing you can imagine. I will get some pictures done and send you one, if you are interested. Perhaps when you are less sore with me.

I just wanted to tell you I am sorry you had to find out about my condition from Virginia. I did want to tell you, really, but it was all a bit complicated. And no, it is not Dr Holden's baby, whatever that spiteful cow says. Please believe that, Joe. And make sure everyone else knows it too. I don't mind what you say.

    Will write soon,
    Lottie

It had not been a good night to have a baby. Not, Lottie thought afterwards, that there would ever be a good night to have a baby. She had not known that pain so great could be endured and lived through; she felt corrupted by it, as if there were innocent Lottie and Lottie who had known something so terrible that she had been rent out of shape, warped for ever after.

She had not started the evening rent out of shape, merely irascible, as Adeline had fondly put it. Fed up with heaving her bulk around in the heat, lumpen and exhausted, unable any longer to fit comfortably into anything but Adeline's bizarre, floating dressing-gowns and George's forgotten shirts. Adeline, by contrast, had been in a better mood the previous three days. She had sent George to find Frances. Not just to hand her a letter, but to find her and bring her to France. Adeline believed she had found a way to restore Frances to them, a way to make her feel loved without compromising Adeline's own immutable love for Konstantin. 'But you have to talk to me,' Adeline wrote. 'You may leave for ever if you still feel I have nothing to say, but you have to talk to me.'

'George will not take no for an answer,' she exclaimed, satisfied. 'He can be a very persuasive man.'

Lottie thinking of Celia, muttered sourly, 'I know.'

George hadn't wanted to return to England. He had wanted to stay for the Bastille celebrations. But, unable to refuse Adeline anything, he had determined that he should at least have a vicarious presence at the festival; he had eyed Lottie for some minutes, then, perhaps deterred by her sticking out her tongue, asked Si, the beat poet, to take photographs for him with his new Zeiss Ikon camera. ('Cool,' said Si.) 'It will be worth it,' said Adeline, kissing George goodbye. Lottie had been slightly taken aback to note that it was full on his lips.

Seventy-two hours later, Lottie thought she would never be taken aback by anything again in her life.

Now she lay in her bed, dimly aware of the heat, the mosquitoes attracted by the animal scents of blood and pain still lingering in the room, her eyes fixed on the tiny, perfectly formed face in front of her. Her daughter looked as if she was sleeping – her eyes were closed – but her mouth shaped small secrets into the night air.

She had never known anything like this: the wrenching joy that came from indescribable pain, the disbelief that she, plain old Lottie Swift, a girl who no longer even existed, could have created anything so perfect, so beautiful. A reason far greater than anything she could have imagined to live.

She looked like Guy.

She looked like Guy.

Lottie bent her head to her daughter's, and spoke so quietly that only she could hear: 'I will be everything to you,' she said. 'You will miss nothing. You will feel the lack of nothing. I promise I will make sure I am enough for you.'

'She has skin the colour of camellias,' Adeline had said, her eyes filled with tears. And Lottie, who had never fancied Jane, or Mary, or any of the other names suggested by Adeline's magazines, had named her daughter.

Adeline didn't go to bed. Madame Migot had left just after midnight, George was coming in the morning, perhaps with Frances, and she would not be able to sleep. They sat together through that first, long night, Lottie wide-eyed and wondering, Adeline dozing gently in the chair beside her, occasionally waking to stroke either the baby's impossibly soft head or Lottie's arm, in congratulation.

At sunrise, Adeline raised herself stiffly from the armchair, and announced that she would make tea. Lottie, still holding her baby in her arms, and long-craving a hot, sweet drink, was grateful: every time she moved her body ached and bled, new obscene pains shooting through her, cramps an echo of the terrifying hours before. Bleary-eyed and blissful despite everything, she thought she might as well stay in this bed for ever.

Adeline opened the shutters, letting in the luminous blue glow of the dawn and stretching in front of it, both arms raised in salute. The room was subtly filled with the gentle lights and sounds of their surroundings, cattle making their way slowly up a hillside, a cockerel crowing and, underlying them all, the crickets whirring like tiny clockwork toys.

'It is cooler, Lottie – can you feel the breeze?'

Lottie closed her eyes and felt it caress her face. It felt, briefly, like Merham.

'Things will be better now, you'll see.'

Adeline turned to her and, for a moment, perhaps because she was weakened by childbirth and exhaustion, Lottie thought her the most exquisite thing she had ever seen. Adeline's face was bathed in a phosphorescent glow, her sharp green eyes softened and made uncharacteristically vulnerable by what she had just witnessed. Lottie's eyes filled with tears; unable to express the love she suddenly felt, she could only reach out a trembling hand.

Adeline took it and kissed it, holding it to her cool, smooth cheek. 'You are lucky, dearest Lottie. You have not had to wait your lifetime.'

Lottie glanced down at her sleeping daughter, and allowed the tears of grief and gratitude to drop heavily on to the pale silk shawl.

They were interrupted by the sound of an approaching car, their heads raising like startled, feral animals. As the door slammed, Adeline was already upright and alert. 'Frances!' she said and, Lottie temporarily forgotten, made a brief attempt to straighten her crumpled silk dress, to smooth her unruffled hair. 'Oh, my goodness, we have no food, Lottie! What will we give them for breakfast?'

'I – I'm sure she won't mind waiting a bit . . . once she knows . . .' Lottie couldn't have cared less about breakfast. Her baby stirred, a tiny hand curling around the air.

'No, no, of course you are right. We have coffee, and some fruit from yesterday. And the *boulangerie* will be open soon – I can walk down once they are settled. Perhaps they will want to sleep, if they have travelled all night . . .'

Lottie watched Adeline whirling around the room, her customary stillness abandoned for a kind of childish nervousness, an inability either to sit or to focus on any task in hand.

'Do you think I am fair to ask this of her?' said Adeline, suddenly. 'Do you think I am selfish to make her come back to me?'

Lottie, dumbstruck, could only shake her head.

'Adeline?' George's loud voice broke through the silence of the house like a gunshot. Lottie found herself flinching, fearful already of waking her baby. 'Are you there?' He appeared in the doorway, dark and unshaven, his customary linen trousers crumpled like old cabbage leaves. At his appearance a sense of foreboding shot through Lottie, the sweetness and silence of the new dawn already swept away by his presence.

Adeline, oblivious, ran to him. 'George, how marvellous. How *marvellous*. Have you brought her? Is she with you?' She raised herself on tiptoe to look over his shoulder, stilled as she strained for the sound of further footfall. She stepped back, examined his face. 'George?'

Lottie, looking at the blackness of George's eyes, was chilled.

'George?' Adeline's voice was quieter now, almost tremulous.

'She's not coming, Adeline.'

'But I wrote – you said—'

George, apparently oblivious to Lottie and the new baby, placed his arm around Adeline's waist, took her hand in his. 'You need to sit down, dearest.'

'But why? You said you would find her – I knew that after this letter she couldn't—'

'She's not coming, Adeline.'

George sat her on the chair next to Lottie. Knelt down. Held both her hands.

Adeline searched George's face, and slowly saw what Lottie, unencumbered by her own desperate needs, had already seen. 'What is it?'

George swallowed. 'There's been an accident, darling girl.'

'Is it driving? She is such a terrible driver, George. You know you should not let her behind a wheel.'

Lottie heard the growing terror behind Adeline's gabbling and began to tremble, unnoticed by the two people beside her.

'Whose car is it this time? You will sort it out, George, won't you? You always sort it out. I will get Julian to pay you back again. Is she hurt? Does she need anything?'

George lowered his head on to Adeline's knees.

'You shouldn't have come, George! You shouldn't have left her! Not by herself. You know she is no good by herself – that is why I sent you to get her.'

His voice, when it came, was gruff, broken. 'She – she's dead.'

There was a lengthy pause.

'No,' said Adeline, firmly.

George's face was hidden, buried in her lap. But his hands clutched hers tighter, as if preventing her from movement.

'No,' she said again.

Lottie struggled to hold back her tears, clamped her hand across her mouth.

'I'm so sorry,' George croaked, into her skirt.

'No,' Adeline said, then louder: 'No. No. No.' And her hands had broken out of George's own, and she was batting at his head, swatting at him in a frenzy, her gaze unseeing, her face contorted. 'NO NO NO NO' in an endless, determined shouting. And George was weeping and apologising, and clutching at her legs, and Lottie, now lost in her own tears, her eyes blurred and stinging so that she could barely see, finally found the energy to drag herself and her baby out of the bed, uncaring of the pain that was only physical. Leaving a silent trail of blood and tears, she made her way slowly across the room and closed the door.

It was not an accident. The coastguard knew this because he was among those who had seen her, shouted to her. Some time later he was one of the three men it took to pull her out. But mainly they knew because of Mrs Colquhoun, who had been present for the whole thing, and who was still suffering attacks of the vapours almost a week later.

George told Adeline several hours after his arrival, when

330

both had been fortified by Cognac and Adeline, wearily, said she wanted to hear everything, every detail that he knew. She asked Lottie to sit with her, and even though Lottie would much rather have hidden upstairs with her baby, she sat, rigid-faced and tense with apprehension, as Adeline gripped her hand, and periodically, violently, shook.

Unlike in life, in death Frances had been rather orderly. She had left Arcadia so uncharacteristically tidy that it had been easy for Marnie, who identified her, to tell she had been staying there. There, she had put on her awkward long skirt, the one with the willow pattern, pulled her long dark hair into a neat bun, and her elongated face was set and resigned as she walked along the path towards the seafront. 'I am so sorry,' she wrote in a letter, 'but there is an emptiness just too great to be borne. I am so sorry.' Then, head held high, as if she were looking upon some distant point on the horizon, she had walked, fully clothed, into the sea.

Mrs Colquhoun, realising this was no ordinary early-morning swim, had shouted – she knew Frances had heard her as she had glanced up and over at the cliff path – but then Frances had simply increased her pace, as if aware that it might lead to an attempt to stop her. Mrs Colquhoun had run all the way to the harbourmaster's house, trying to keep an eye on her all the time, watching Frances as she waded up to her waist, her chest. As she got deeper, some of the waves had got larger, one almost knocking her off her feet and her bun into long, sodden strands. But she kept walking. Even as Mrs Colquhoun, her heel broken and her voice hoarse from shouting, banged upon the front door, she kept walking, a distant figure on some invisible course through the water.

The noise alerted two lobstermen, who had pitched out after her in a boat. By this time a small crowd of people, drawn by the noise, had assembled and were shouting at

Frances to stop. There was some concern afterwards that she might have thought they were angry and hastened her journey, but the coastguard said, no, she had been determined to do it. He had seen them like that before. You could pull them out, but you'd find them hanging from a beam two days later.

At this point George had wept, and Lottie had watched as Adeline held his face, as if offering absolution.

Frances hadn't flinched as her head went under. She just kept walking, and then one wave came, two waves, and suddenly you couldn't see her any more. By the time the boat was far enough out in the harbour, she had been caught by the current. They found her body two days later in the estuary at Wrabness, her willow-patterned skirt wound round with entrails of weed.

'I was meant to meet her for dinner, you see, but I had to stay up at Oxford. I rang her to say I'd been invited out by this Fellow, and she said I should go, Adeline. She said I should go.' His chest heaved, great snotty sobs wetting his clenched hands. 'But I should have gone down, Adeline, I should have been there.'

'No,' said Adeline, her voice distant. '*I* should have been there. Oh, George, what have I done?'

It was only in retrospect that Lottie realised Adeline's accent had changed during the telling of George's story. She had stopped sounding French. In fact, she seemed to have no accent at all. Perhaps it was shock. Mrs Holden used to say it could get you like that. She had known a woman whose brother had been killed in the war and had woken up with every hair on her head turned grey. (And not just her head, she had added, blushing at her own audacity.)

Lottie barely had time to recover from the birth before, in

effect, she had become a mother of two. In the first weeks of her child's life, Adeline seemed to die a little. At first she had refused to eat, wouldn't rest, walked the gardens of the house weeping at all hours of the day or night. Once she walked the entire dusty road to the top of the mountain, and was brought down, dazed and sun-scorched, by the old man who ran the refreshment stall at the summit. She cried out in her sleep, on the few occasions that she slept, and looked frighteningly unlike herself, her sleek hair unkempt, her porcelain complexion muddied and spoiled by grief. 'Why didn't I trust her?' she would cry. 'Why didn't I listen? She had always understood me better than anyone.'

'It wasn't your fault. You weren't to know,' Lottie would murmur, knowing that her words were inadequate, mere platitudes that didn't touch the surface of what Adeline was feeling. Adeline's pain made her uncomfortable: it was too close to her own, a raw wound that she had almost managed to cover.

'But why did she have to prove it to me this way?' Adeline would wail. 'I didn't want to love her. I didn't want to love anyone. She should have known it was unfair to ask.'

Or perhaps Lottie was just too emotionally exhausted by the demands of her baby. She was a 'good baby', as they were called. But, then, she had to be. Holding a desperate Adeline in her arms, Lottie could not always get up in time to comfort a crying newborn; if she was trying to cook and clean around her grieving friend, Camille had to fit in with Lottie's tasks, button-eyed within her improvised sling, or sleep through the noise of rugs beaten and kettles whistling.

As the weeks went past, Lottie became increasingly exhausted, and despairing. Julian came, but couldn't cope with the emotional mess of it all. He signed some more money over to his wife, gave Lottie the keys to his car, and left for an art fair in Toulouse, taking the pale, silent Stephen with him. The other visitors dried up. George, having stayed the first two days and drunk himself into a coma, left with promises to return. Which he failed to keep. 'Look after her, Lottie,' he said, his eyes bloodshot and a half-established beard covering his chin. 'Don't let her do anything stupid.' She didn't know whether his evident fear was for her welfare or his own.

At one point, when Adeline had cried for a whole day and a night, Lottie had frantically searched her bedroom, hopeful of finding some reference to Adeline's family, someone who could come and help lift her out of her depression. She flung her way through the rows of brightly coloured outfits, her nostrils filled with the scent of oil of cloves, her skin brushed by feathers, silks and satins. It was as if she, like Lottie, barely existed: apart from one theatre programme, which showed that several years ago she had appeared in a minor role in a theatre in Harrogate, there was nothing – no photographs, no letters. Except for those from Frances. Lottie thrust them back into their box, shivering at the thought of having to be party to Frances's last, futile emotions. At last, in the suitcase in the wardrobe, she found Adeline's passport. She rifled through it, thinking that perhaps it would reveal a family address, or some clue at least where help might be found to assuage her grief. Instead she came across Adeline's photograph.

She had a different haircut, but it was unmistakably her. Except the passport called her Ada Clayton.

The mourning lasted one day short of four weeks. Lottie woke one morning to find Adeline in the kitchen, cracking eggs into a basin. She had not mentioned the passport: people's lives were best left, like sleeping dogs, undisturbed.

'I am going to Russia,' Adeline said, not looking up.

'Oh,' said Lottie. She wanted to say, What about me? What she said was 'What about the atomic bomb?'

Dear Joe
No, I am sorry but I'm not coming home. Not to Merham, anyway. It's a bit complicated, but I think I may go back to London and try to get myself a job. I have been doing housekeeping for Adeline, as you know, and she has some artist friends there who are looking for someone like me and don't mind the baby. Little Camille will grow up with their children, which will be nice for her and, despite what you said, there is no reason why I shouldn't support myself, after all. I will let you know when I am settled and perhaps you will come and visit.

Thank you for the things for the baby. It was nice of Mrs Ansty to choose them for you. I am painting a picture of Camille, who looks very fine in the bonnet especially.

Yours, etc.

Three days before Lottie and Adeline were due to leave the French house, Madame Migot had come for her final kneading session of Lottie's womb. Or undignified peering at Lottie's undercarriage. It was hard to know which particular pleasure she would choose for that visit. Lottie, despite feeling rather less proprietorial of her body now that it had played host to another human being, none the less still felt invaded by the frank pulling and prodding that the older woman employed, as if she were some piece of stretched-out skinned rabbit hanging up in the market. The last time she had come, supposedly to check that Camille was feeding properly, she had, without any reference to Lottie, reached a hand inside Lottie's loose blouse, taken hold of her breast and with a swift roll of finger and thumb sent a jet of milk spraying across the room before Lottie had a chance to protest. Apparently satisfied, she had muttered something to Adeline, and moved on without explanation to check the baby's weight.

This time, however, she had made only cursory fumblings at Lottie's abdomen before picking up Camille with an expert grasp. She had held her for some time, chuckling to her in French, checking her umblicus, her fingers and toes, exclaiming at her in tones far softer than she ever used towards Adeline or Lottie.

'We're leaving,' said Lottie, holding up a postcard from England. 'I'm taking her home.'

Ignoring her, Madame Migot had grown quieter and, eventually, silent.

Then she had walked over to the window and studied Camille's face for some time. She barked something at Adeline, who had just walked into the room, clutching a map. Still apparently rooted somewhere deep in her own thoughts, it took Adeline some minutes to comprehend. Then she shook her head.

'What now?' said Lottie, irritably, fearing that she had done something else wrong. The colour of her towelling napkins had apparently been a village disgrace, the manner of their pinning a matter for Gallic hilarity.

'She wants to know if you've been ill,' said Adeline, frowning as she tried to listen to Madame Migot. 'Julian's friend in the embassy says I will have to get some sort of visa to go to Russia, and that it's almost impossible without diplomatic help. He thinks I should come back to England to sort it out. It's too, too annoying.'

'Of course I'm not ill. Tell her she'd look like this too if she had a baby keeping her up half the night.'

Adeline said something back in French, then, after a pause, shook her head again. 'She wants to know if you have a rash.'

336

Lottie was about to say something rude, but was silenced by the expression on the Frenchwoman's face.

'*Non, non*,' the woman was saying, making a sweeping motion towards her stomach.

'Before you had a bump, she means. She wants to know if you had a rash before you became . . . heavy . . . ? Early in your pregnancy?' Adeline, her attention captured, looked quizzically at the midwife.

'A heat rash?' Lottie thought back. 'I've had lots of heat rashes. I don't cope very well with this heat.'

The midwife wasn't satisfied. She fired off more questions in urgent French, then stood looking at Lottie expectantly.

Adeline turned.

'She wants to know if you felt ill. If you had a rash when you were newly pregnant. She thinks . . .' She said something in French to the older woman, who nodded in reply. 'She wants to know if there is any possibility you could have had German measles.'

'I don't understand.' Lottie fought an urge to reach out for her daughter, to pull her protectively close to her. 'I had a heat rash. When I first got here. I thought it was heat rash.'

The midwife's face softened for the first time. '*Votre bébé*,' she said, gesturing. '*Ses yeux* . . .' She waved her hand in front of Camille's face, then looked up at Lottie, and did it again. And again.

'Oh, Lottie,' said Adeline, her hand to her mouth. 'What are we to do with you now?'

Lottie stood very still, an unseasonal chill seeping into her bones. Her baby lay peacefully in the woman's arms, her fair hair forming a feathery halo, her seraphic face illuminated by the sun.

She hadn't blinked.

★   ★   ★

'I came back to Merham when Camille was ten weeks old. The London family didn't want me once they knew. I wrote and told Joe, and he asked me to marry him as I stepped off the train.'

Lottie sighed, placed her hands in front of her on her knees. 'He had told everyone that the baby was his. It caused a scandal. His parents were furious. But he could be strong, when it counted. And he told them that they would be sorry if they made him choose between us.' The last of the wine was long gone. Daisy sat, oblivious to the late hour, to the fact that her feet had gone to sleep under her.

'I don't think his mother ever forgave me for marrying him,' Lottie said, lost in the distant memory. 'She certainly never got over me landing her precious son with a blind daughter. I hated her for that. I hated her for not loving Camille like I did. But I suppose, now I'm old, I can understand a little better.'

'She was just trying to protect him.'

'Yes, yes, she was.'

'Does Camille know this?'

Lottie's face closed over. 'Camille knows that Joe is her father.' Her voice held a note of challenge. 'They've always been very close. She's a daddy's girl.'

There was a brief silence.

'What happened to Adeline?' Daisy whispered. She said it with a kind of dread, fearful of what she might hear. She had found herself weeping at the story of Frances's suicide, remembering her own darkest days just after Daniel had left.

'Adeline died almost twenty years ago. She never came back to the house. I used to keep it clean for her, just in case, but she never came. After a while she didn't even write. I don't think she could bear to be reminded of Frances.

She loved her, you see? I think we all knew it even when she didn't. She died in Russia. Near St Petersburg. Quite wealthy, she was, even without the things Julian had given her. I liked to think she was there because she'd found Konstantin.' Lottie smiled shyly, as if embarrassed by her own romanticism. 'And then when she died she left me Arcadia in her will. I always think she felt bad about me marrying Joe.' Lottie stirred, began to gather her things around her, placing her glass on the floor by the chair. 'I think she thought she let me down by disappearing when she did.'

'Why?'

Lottie looked at her as if she were stupid. 'If I'd had the house and the money then, I wouldn't have needed to get married at all . . .'

I cried for six whole days on my honeymoon. Peculiar, Mummy said afterwards, for someone who had been so desperate to leave home, especially as a married woman. And more so when you think of our wonderful cruise ship, with our beautiful first-class cabin, paid for by the Bancrofts.

But I was terribly sick, so much so that Guy had to spend hours wandering around on his own while I lay in our cabin feeling wretched. I still felt miserable about Daddy. And, strangely, I felt absolutely rotten about leaving Mummy and the children. You see, I knew nothing was going to be the same again. And although you might think you want that, when it actually happens it feels so dreadfully final.

We didn't behave like honeyspooners at all, really, not that I would have told the parents or anyone. No, my postcards were full of the amazing sights and the terrific dinner dances and dolphins and sitting at the captain's table – and I told them about our cabin, which was absolutely stacked with walnut and had a huge dressing-table with lights all around the mirror and free shampoos and lotions, which they refilled every day.

But, then, Guy wasn't himself for a lot of it. He told me it was because he preferred open spaces to water. I got a bit upset at first, and told him he'd have wasted a lot less of both of our time if he'd told me beforehand. But I didn't like to push him too hard. I never did. And he came round in the end. And as that nice Mrs Erkhardt said, the one with all the pearls, simply all couples argue on their honeymoon. It's one of those things that no one ever tells you. They never tell you about other things, either. But she wasn't so specific about those.

Besides, it was fun in parts. When they first realised we were on our honeymoon the band struck up 'Look At That Girl', you know, that tune by Guy Mitchell, every time we entered the dining room. I think Guy got rather sick of it after the third go. But I rather liked it. I just liked everyone knowing he was mine.

I heard from Sylvia, some time later, about Joe. Mummy was surprisingly cool on the whole thing. She didn't even want to know whether the baby really was his, which surprised me. I would have thought she'd be simply mad to know. In fact, she got positively shirty when I brought the subject up. But I think she had her hands full with Daddy's drinking at the time.

I didn't tell Guy. Women's gossip, he said once, when I started telling him about Merham. I never mentioned it again.

PART THREE

PART THREE

Fifteen

Daisy had worried for almost ten days about how to apologise properly to Jones; how to find ways to convey that her look of horror, her abject tears that morning, had not been a reaction to him, but to who he was not. She had thought of sending flowers, but Jones didn't seem like a flowers man; and she didn't know what the individual blooms were supposed to convey. She thought of just ringing, and saying it, in blunt terms, his terms: Jones, I'm sorry. I was embarrassing and crap. But she knew she would not be able to leave it at that, that she would blather and bleat and stammer her way through a messy explanation that he would despise even more. She thought of sending cards, messages, even getting Lottie, as she was now brave enough to address her, to do it for her. He was scared of Lottie.

She did nothing.

Fortuitously, perhaps, the mural did it for her. One afternoon, as she waded, pen-sucking, through lists of specifications, Aidan had approached her to tell her that one of the painters had been scraping lichen from the outside terrace wall, and had found colour underneath the whitewash. Curious, they had chipped away a little more, and found what appeared to be the image of two people's faces. 'We didn't like to do any more,' he said, leading her outside into the bright sunlight, 'in case we ended up pulling off the paint underneath.'

Daisy stared at the wall, at the newly revealed faces, one

of whom she could just make out to be smiling. The painter, a young West Indian man called Dave, sat smoking a cigarette on the terrace. He nodded his interest at the wall.

'You want to get a restorer in,' said Aidan, stepping back. 'Someone who knows about them. It might be worth a bit.' He had pronounced it 'muriel'.

'Depends who it's by,' said Daisy. 'It's nice though. Kind of Braque-ish. Do you know how far it goes across?'

'Well, there's a patch of yellow in this left-hand corner, and blue up there to the right, so I wouldn't be surprised if it's a good six feet. You want to ask your woman there what she thinks. She might have been around when it was painted. She might know something about it.'

'She never mentioned anything,' said Daisy.

'There's a surprise,' said Aidan, rubbing at dried plaster on his trousers. 'Mind you, she never mentioned anything about nappies on site and no drilling during sleepy bye-byes either.' He grinned slyly and leaned back, as Daisy turned to go inside. 'Here, you're not putting the kettle on, are you?'

Lottie had been out with Ellie so Daisy rang Jones, initially planning to tell him, eager to have him associate her with something good.

'What's the problem?' he said, bad-temperedly.

'No problem,' said Daisy. 'I – er – I just wondered if you were coming up on Thursday.'

'Why Thursday?' In the background, she could hear the sound of two telephones ringing, some woman having an urgent conversation. 'Tell him I'll be down in a minute,' he yelled. 'Give him a glass of wine or something.'

'Health and safety. About the kitchens. You said you wanted to be there.'

'Well, give him a coffee! Hello? Oh, Christ, I did, didn't I?' He groaned, and she heard him place his hand over the receiver and shout something at what she assumed was his secretary. 'What time are they coming?' he said, a moment later.

'Half eleven.' She took a deep breath. 'Look, Jones, stay for lunch afterwards. I'd like to show you a couple of things.'

'I don't eat lunch,' he said, and put the phone down.

She had rung Camille, remembering that Hal was something artistic but not wanting to call him directly. It was the kind of thing you had to worry about when you were a single woman. But Camille had been enthusiastic, had said Daisy should speak to him straight away. She didn't need to get a restorer, Hal could do it. He had done all sorts of courses on restoration back at art school, not just furniture, Camille was sure. Hal himself sounded less convinced, uncertain that his knowledge was up to date enough.

'But you could find out about any new techniques. I mean it's not a canvas, it's only an outside wall.' Daisy had gauged from Camille's tone how much this job might mean to them both. 'It can't be that important if they've slung a load of whitewash over it.'

Hal had seemed hesitant at first, then cautiously enthusiastic, as if he couldn't believe he was being thrown a lifebelt, albeit a small, potentially leaky one. 'I've got a friend over in Ware who still does a bit. I could ask him. I mean if you don't mind that I'm not a professional.'

'If you do a proper job on it, I couldn't care less if you were a professional mud-wrestler. But I need you to start now. I want a good part of it visible by Thursday.'

'Okay,' said Hal, sounding like someone who didn't want to show quite how pleased they were. 'Right. Great. Well, I'll make a few phone calls and dig out some kit, then head over.'

This was her chance, Daisy thought, as she went out to

the garden. This would show Jones that she was capable not just of renovating the interior of this building by herself but of rising above this persona that these people seemed to think of as her: the Daisy she pitied and despised. It was a ridiculous trait, Daniel had once told her, this desperate need for everyone to approve of her, but she felt it regardless. The evening that Jones had come she had felt satisfied that he had seen a newer, better side of her. Because, she cautiously admitted to herself, she was beginning to approve of that person too, instead of solely mourning the loss of Old Daisy. She was stronger now, not quite so bowed by the events of the recent months. Babies do that, Lottie had said, when Daisy asked her how she had coped alone. You have to be strong.

Daisy, thinking back to Primrose Hill, had disagreed but understood that, in some small way, she had slowly, through some form of osmosis, perhaps, acquired a little of Lottie's own thick skin. She had thought endlessly about how the young Lottie had given birth, almost unsupported, in a country far from home, and how she had refused to be cowed when, disgraced and penniless, she returned. She had watched how Lottie the elder now sliced through life like a breadknife, generating respect from those around her simply by virtue of her own confidence and acerbic wit. She expected people to accord her her due, that things would go the way she desired. And what was she, when it came down to it? A pensionable housewife, wife of a garage-owner in a small town, mother of a disabled daughter, who had never had a job, a career, anything. Not that she would dared have described Lottie like that to her face. Daisy, meanwhile, was still the Old Daisy she had been (albeit a slightly more generously built version) – she was still attractive, still intelligent, just about solvent, and now, as her accountant put it, she was a sole trader. 'I am a Sole Trader,' she had said aloud to herself after she put the phone down. It sounded so much better than Single Parent.

She did miss him. Still cried occasionally. Still considered it an achievement if she could get through a couple of hours without thinking of him. Still found herself occasionally checking his horoscope in case it offered some clue as to his return. But almost three months after he'd gone, Daisy could at least envisage a time, maybe a year ahead, give or take a month or two, when she would get over him.

She tried not to think about whether Ellie would ever feel the same way.

The hours Hal worked on the 'muriel', Aidan said, it was no wonder his business was on the floor. You couldn't do hours like that at a fixed price, he told Daisy, as they sat drinking tea in the kitchens, watching through the window as Hal, bent double against the wall, painstakingly brushed at a tiny section of worn paint. Daisy of all people should know. Small-businessmen couldn't afford to be perfectionists.

Small-businessmen couldn't afford to be anything if they didn't get the upstairs corridors finished by Tuesday, like they'd promised, Daisy said pointedly, but Aidan had affected not to hear.

'Now, if your man there were paying him by the hour . . .'

'I think he's enjoying it,' said Daisy, ignoring the fact that most of the time Hal looked rather agonised.

'Is this okay?' he would ask her three or four times a day, as she came out to admire the increasingly distinct images. 'You don't want to employ a professional?' He never looked particularly convinced when Daisy said she didn't.

But Camille, who came up twice a day, bringing tea and sandwiches between appointments, said that when he got home he was buoyant. 'I think it's exciting,' she said, not seeming to mind her husband's lengthy absences. 'I like the thought that it's been hidden. I like the thought that it's Hal who is bringing it back to life.' They held hands when he thought no one was looking. Daisy, somewhat enviously, had caught sight of Hal explaining the images to his wife then breaking off to pull her to him, and kiss her.

The only person apparently not pleased about the mural was Lottie. She had been to town on one of her mysterious errands. (She would never tell anyone where she was going, or what she was doing. If asked, she would tap her nose with her finger, and tell people to 'mind your own'.) On arriving back, when she caught sight of Hal working on the exposed images, she had exploded, and demanded that he stop immediately. 'I painted over it! It wasn't meant to be shown,' she said, gesturing wildly at Hal. 'Paint it back again.'

Daisy and the workmen, who had been examining some guttering, had stopped what they were doing to see what the shouting was.

'It's not meant to be shown!'

'But it's a mural,' said Hal.

'I told you! You shouldn't be taking the paint off. Just stop, do you hear me? I would have told you about it if it was meant to be seen.'

'What's under there?' murmured Aidan to Dave. 'The plans of where she buried the bodies?'

'I can't stop the renovation now,' said Daisy, perplexed. 'Jones is coming specially to see it.'

'It's not yours to show.' Lottie was uncharacteristically, weirdly, agitated.

Camille, who had been bringing Hal tea when Lottie arrived, stood holding the mug, blank incomprehension on her face. 'Mum?'

'Hey, what's the matter, Ma? What's upset you so much?' Hal had reached out a hand to Lottie's shoulder.

She had shrugged him away furiously. 'Nothing's upset me. Yes, it has – you wasting your time uncovering some piece of rubbish has upset me. You should be concentrating on your business, not fannying around on some worthless piece of graffiti. Why don't you do something useful, like try to save your business, eh?'

'But it's beautiful, Lottie,' said Daisy. 'You must have seen that.'

'It's rubbish,' said Lottie. 'And I shall tell that stupid boss of yours it's rubbish. And I'm the historical adviser, or whatever you call it, on this house, and he will agree with me.' And she had walked off, her back bristling her displeasure, leaving them all open-mouthed and halting.

But Jones didn't agree.

Daisy, sneakily, brought him to see it while Lottie was out. 'Shut your eyes,' she told him, as he stepped on to the terrace. He raised his eyes to heaven as if she were an imbecile and he was forced to indulge her. She took his arm, and steered him round the pots of paint to where Hal had recently stopped work.

'Now open them.'

Jones opened his eyes. Daisy's did not leave his face. Beneath his dark, beaten-down brow, he blinked in surprise.

'It's a mural,' said Daisy. 'Hal here's restoring it. The builders found it under some whitewash.'

Jones looked at her, apparently forgetting to be irritated, and moved closer, peering at the images. He was, she noted, wearing the most appalling pair of corduroy trousers. 'What is it?' he said, after a minute. 'Some kind of Last Supper?'

'I don't know,' said Daisy, glancing guiltily behind her for

351

the sound of the push-chair. 'Lottie – Mrs Bernard – won't tell me.'

Jones kept peering, then stood up. 'What did you just say?'

'She's a bit unhappy about us uncovering it,' she said. 'She won't say why, but it seems to have upset her.'

'But it's beautiful,' said Jones. 'It looks great out here. Gives the terrace a focus.' He turned, and walked to the far end of the terrace to examine it from a distance. 'We're going to have chairs here, aren't we?'

Daisy nodded.

'Is it old?'

'Definitely this century,' Daisy said. 'Hal thinks it must be forties' or fifties'. Certainly no earlier than the thirties. Perhaps she covered it up during the war.'

'I had no idea . . .' Jones was speaking to himself now, one hand raised to the back of his head. 'So . . . can I ask how much I'm paying for this? The restoration, I mean.'

'A damn sight less than it's worth.'

He smiled slowly at her, and she grinned in response. 'Don't suppose you've found any priceless antiques hanging around while you're at it?'

'Nah,' said Dave, appearing behind them, lighting another cigarette. 'She's out buying milk for the babby.'

It was over. Hal sat in his car outside Arcadia, looking at the latest sheaf of bills that wouldn't begin to be covered by the mural money, and felt something peculiarly like relief that it was now out of his hands, that the thing he had known for weeks, possibly months, was inevitable had become a reality. The last bill, the one he had put off opening until lunchtime, had been so huge that it had left him no choice. He would wind up the business, and then, once the mural restoration was over, he would set out to find a job.

He closed his eyes for a minute, letting the hope, the tensions of the last weeks finally ebb away, to be replaced by a kind of dull, grey mist. It was just a business. He had repeated those words to himself like a mantra. And if the disposal of its assets meant that he could stave off bankruptcy, then at least they all had a future. But, then, they *did* have a future. He and Camille – the past few weeks had convinced him of that.

Focus on the good stuff, that was what the counsellor said at their last session, wasn't it? Be grateful for the things that you have. He had a wife and a daughter. Health. And a future. His mobile phone broke the silence, and he fumbled in the glovebox, trying to blink away what felt suspiciously like tears.

'It's me.'

'Hi, you.' He leaned back against his seat, glad of the sound of her voice.

Nothing urgent. She just wanted to find out what time he might be home, whether he would like chicken for supper, to tell him that Katie was going swimming; the comforting minutiae of domestic life. 'Are you okay? Sound a bit quiet.'

'I'm fine,' he said. 'I'll bring some wine home, if you like.'

She sounded a little unconvinced, so he tried to make himself sound more animated. He didn't tell her what she needed to hear – that could wait – but instead the things she liked to hear: what had happened 'at work' that day. What he had uncovered. The latest *bons mots* from the builders. He told her how her mother now barely spoke to him while he was working on the wall, and yet as soon as they left

Arcadia she would chat to him as if nothing had happened. 'Maybe you should ask her. Find out what's bothering her about it.'

'There's no point, Hal. You know there's no point asking her anything. She won't tell me,' said Camille, sounding sad and cross. 'I don't know what's wrong with my mother sometimes. Do you know it's their anniversary next week and she said she's needed at Arcadia? Dad's so disappointed. He'd booked the restaurant and everything.'

'I suppose they could go another night,' he said.

'But it's not the same, is it?'

'No,' he said, thinking back. 'No, it's not.'

'Better go,' she said, brightening. 'Mrs Halligan's complaining about her pickling.'

'What?'

She moved closer to the phone. 'It's what happens to your skin after you've been waxed. She's got pickling in an unfortunate area and now she can't put her tights back on.'

Hal laughed. It felt like the first time he'd done so in months. 'I do love you,' he said.

'I know,' she said. 'I love you too.'

Daisy walked Jones into the rooms that would one day be known as the Morrell Suite, but were, for now, known among the builders as Blue Bog after the colour of the bathroom. It was the most traditional bedroom in the house, and it was finished. The bed, like all the others had come from a contact in India who specialised in old colonial furniture. Next to it stood a military chest, its clean, angular corners squared off in brass, its aged mahogany veneer glowing against the pale grey of the walls. At the end of the room, which was really two rooms knocked through, were two comfortable chairs and a low, carved table. On this, Daisy had placed a cloth, with plates of crab sandwiches, a bowl of fruit and a bottle of water. 'I know you don't eat lunch,' she said, as he stared at the arrangement, 'but I thought if you really weren't hungry, I'd have your half for supper.'

He was wearing odd socks. She found it curiously reassuring.

He walked once, slowly, around the room, taking in the décor, its contents. Then he stopped and stood in front of her.

'Actually, I – I wanted to say sorry,' she said, her hands pressed together in front of her. 'About that morning. It was daft. Well, more than daft. I can't explain it except to say that it was nothing to do with you.'

Jones looked down at his feet, and shuffled uncomfortably.

'Oh, go on. Sit down, please,' she said, helplessly, 'or I'm going to feel really stupid. Worse, I'm going to start wittering. And you don't want that. Almost as bad as crying.'

Jones stooped towards the sandwiches. 'You know, I'd hardly even thought about it,' he said, with a sideways look at her, and sat.

'I wouldn't normally offer lunch in the bedroom, but it's the only room that's quiet,' she said, after they had started to eat. 'I would have liked to set this up on the terrace, near the mural, but I thought we might get flecks of paint or turps in our sandwiches.' She *was* wittering. It was as if she had no control over what came out of her mouth. 'Plus Ellie's asleep next door.'

He nodded, giving little away. But he looked relaxed, she thought. 'I'm surprised you went ahead without me,' he said, eventually. 'The mural, I mean.'

'I knew you'd be pleased if you just saw it. If I'd asked you

355

whether to go ahead you would have found reasons to fret about it.'

He paused, his sandwich half-way to his lips, then lowered his hand and looked at her properly. Really looked, so that she found herself prickling with the beginnings of a blush. 'You're a strange one, Daisy Parsons,' he said. But it wasn't unfriendly.

She relaxed then, told him the history of each piece of furniture, the decisions behind each choice of paint and fabric. He nodded, his mouth full, taking it all in while committing himself to little in the way of responses. Daisy struggled not to ask him what he thought, whether he was pleased. If he wasn't pleased, she told herself firmly, he'd tell her.

Gradually, she found herself embellishing some of the stories, telling jokes, determined to unbend him a little. It was good to have company; urban company. Someone who knew their Gavroche from their Green Street. Someone who could talk about more than paint charts or the state of the neighbouring B-and-Bs. She had even put on makeup for his visit. It had taken her forty minutes to locate her makeup bag.

'. . . and the reason they sent the big one at a discount was that it was so large they'd had it three years and never had room to take it out of the warehouse.' She laughed, pouring herself another glass of water.

'Has Daniel been in touch?' he said.

Daisy halted, flushed.

'Sorry,' he said. 'Shouldn't have asked. None of my business.'

Daisy looked at him, put down the bottle. 'Yes,' she said. 'Yes, he has. Not that it makes much difference.'

They sat in silence for a minute, Jones intently studying the corner of the table.

356

'Why do you ask?' she said, and for a few seconds the air in the room became a vacuum, and she was aware that his answer had suddenly become crucial to fill it.

'I met an old friend of his who wanted to speak to him about something . . .' Jones looked up at her. 'I thought you might have the number.'

'No,' said Daisy, feeling inexplicably cross. 'I don't.'

'Right. No problem, then,' he said, into his collar. 'They'll just have to sort themselves out.'

'Yes.'

Daisy sat for a minute, unsure why she felt so unbalanced. Outside, through the open window, she heard her name being called. Aidan's voice. Probably a paint query. 'I'd better see what he wants,' she said, almost grateful for the interruption. 'I'll only be a moment. Eat some fruit. Please.'

When she returned, some minutes later, she stopped in the doorway at the sight of Ellie in Jones's arms. Flushed with sleep, the baby was sitting upright against him, blinking. When Jones saw Daisy, he became awkward, and made as if to thrust the baby at her. 'She woke up while you were gone,' he said, a little defensively. 'I didn't like to leave her to cry.'

'No,' said Daisy, staring. She had never seen her baby held by a man before, and it jolted her, plucked at previously undiscovered heartstrings. 'Thanks.'

'Friendly little soul, isn't she?' Jones walked forward and handed her over, managing somehow to tangle his hands with Ellie's limbs as he did so. 'Considering I'm not used to them. Babies, I mean.'

'I don't know,' said Daisy, truthfully. 'She only gets held by me and Mrs Bernard.'

'I've never held one before.'

'Nor had I. Till I had one, I mean.'

He was looking at Ellie as if he had never *seen* a baby before. Suddenly aware that Daisy was watching him, he touched Ellie's head lightly and stepped backwards again. ''Bye, then,' he said to the baby. 'I suppose I'd better get off.' He glanced towards the door. 'The office will be wondering where I am. Thanks for the lunch.'

'Yes,' said Daisy, adjusting Ellie's weight on her hip.

He made towards the door. 'It's looking good,' he said, turning to face her. 'Well done.' He forced a smile, looking strangely unhappy. He's got thumbnails like Daniel's, Daisy thought. 'Look. Next week,' he said abruptly. 'I think you should come to London. I need to talk to you about the opening arrangements somewhere where I've got all my files and things around me, and I thought maybe we could go to that reclamation yard while we're at it. The new one you were talking about. For the outdoor stuff.'

He cocked his head to one side. 'I mean – are you free to come to London? I'll buy you lunch. Or dinner. At my club. You can see what it's like.'

'I know what it's like,' said Daisy. 'I've been in there.' She grinned. An Old Daisy grin. 'But yes. That sounds great. You name the day.'

Pete Sheraton wore the kind of shirt that trading-floor dealers had worn in the eighties: boldly pinstriped, white-collared, starched white cuffs. It was the kind of shirt that spoke of money, of deals in smoky rooms, the kind of shirt that always made Hal wonder if Pete was less satisfied with his lot as a provincial bank manager (staff: three cashiers, one trainee manager and Mrs Mills who cleaned Tuesdays and Thursdays) than he liked to admit.

The cuffs that steered Hal into his office that afternoon

were pierced with two tiny just-visible naked women. 'The wife's idea,' he said, glancing at them as Hal sat down opposite. 'She says it stops me becoming ... too bank-managery.'

Hal smiled, tried to swallow.

He and Pete had known each other for years, since Veronica Sheraton had paid Hal to frame a portrait of the two of them together for Pete's fortieth birthday. It was a truly dreadful thing, revealing Veronica in a puff-sleeved ballgown and soft focus, and Pete, behind her, as several feet taller than he was with a complexion like burnt toffee. Their eyes had met at its 'unveiling', and one of those peculiar, uncontrivable male bonds was formed.

'You've not come to book a game of squash, I take it?'

Hal took a deep breath. 'Sadly, not this time, Pete. I – I've come to talk to you about winding up the business.'

Pete's face fell. 'Oh, Christ. Oh, Christ, mate, I'm sorry. That's bad luck.'

Hal wished Pete could look a bit more objective about the whole thing. Suddenly the old-fashioned, stiff, unfriendly bank manager felt like an easier option.

'You're absolutely sure? I mean, you've talked to your accountant and everything?'

Hal swallowed. 'Not to tell him the final verdict, no, but let's say it won't come as a surprise to anyone who's seen my bottom line.'

'Well, I knew you weren't exactly in takeover and acqui-sitions mode . . . but still . . .' Pete reached into his drawer. 'Do you want a drink?'

'No. Best to keep a clear head. I've a lot of calls to make this afternoon.'

'Well, listen, don't worry about anything this end. Any-thing I can do, let me know. I mean if you want to consider a loan or something, I'm sure I can get you a preferential rate.'

'I think we're beyond loans.'

'It's such a shame, though, when you think of all that money . . .'

Hal frowned.

There was a brief silence.

'Oh, well. You know best.' Pete stood, and walked back round the desk. 'But listen, Hal, don't make any decisions tonight. Especially if you haven't talked to your accountant. Why don't you have a think, and come back and see me tomorrow? You never know . . .'

'It's not going to change, Pete.'

'Whatever. Think about it anyway. Things all right with you and Camille? Good, good . . . And little Katie? That's what counts, eh?' Pete placed his arm on Hal's shoulders, then turned towards his desk. 'Oh, I nearly forgot. Look, I know it's probably not the time, but would you mind giving this to your missus? It's been sitting in my drawer for ages – I kept meaning to give it to you at our next game of squash. I know it's not quite the rules, but it is you . . .'

Hal held the stiffened envelope. 'What is it?'

'It's just the braille template for her new chequebook.'

'But she's got one.'

'Not for the new account.'

'What new account?'

Pete looked at him. 'The one with . . . Well, I assumed it was some insurance policy or something you'd cashed. That's why I was a bit surprised when you said about the business . . .'

Hal stood in the middle of the room, shaking his head. 'She's got money?'

'I assumed you knew.'

360

Hal's mouth had dried, the high-pitched ringing in his head an echo of a year before. 'How much?'

Pete looked anxious. 'Listen, Hal, I've obviously said too much already. I mean, I just assumed that with Camille's sight and all . . . Well, you normally handle most of her financial stuff.'

Hal stared at the envelope in front of him. He felt as if someone had slowly let the air out of his lungs. 'A separate account? How much?'

'I can't tell you that.'

'It's me, Pete.'

'And it's my job, Hal. Look, go home, talk to your wife. I'm sure there's some obvious explanation.' He began almost physically to propel Hal towards the door.

Hal stumbled across the room. 'Pete?'

Pete glanced out through the open doorway into the branch office, then back at his friend. He took out a piece of paper, scribbled a figure on it and flashed it at Hal. 'It's not far off that, okay? Now go home, Hal. I can't say a thing more.'

Sixteen

It wasn't hard to work out where the money had come from – they had all wondered how Lottie was going to divvy up Arcadia's proceeds. The thing that haunted him, that left his stomach in toxic knots, his food like ashes on his tongue, was that she had kept it silent, hidden, while watching his business crumble around him. That she had comforted him, even, while all the time she had held the wherewithal to make it better, the one thing she had said she believed in; the one thing they both knew he could do. Given time. And a bit of luck. That she had lied to him again made him feel sick. It was worse than the discovery of her infidelity because this time he had allowed himself to trust her again, had forced himself to overcome his fear, his distrust, and placed himself in her hands. This time it could not be ascribed to her dejection, her insecurities. This time it was about what she thought of him.

If she'd wanted him to know about it, she would have told him. That was the incontrovertible fact that Hal returned to, hour after feverish hour, the fact that stopped him confronting her, demanding answers of her. If she had wanted him to know, she would have said something. God, he had been such a fool.

She had been reserved around him over the last few days, a new wariness imprinted on her face. Being unable to see the nakedness of other people's expressions, she had never

362

thought to hide her own. He had watched her, barely able to hide his frustration and fury.

'You okay?' she would say, meaning, was he all right with the end of his business? Was he in need of a hug? A kiss? Things that were *supposed to make it all right*. He looked at her uncertain expression, at the hint of guilt it conveyed, and wondered how she could speak to him at all.

'Just fine,' he would answer. And, with another wary glance in his direction, she would shepherd Katie out, or turn back to making the supper.

Worse still was what it all meant. For the money, and her decision to keep it from him, could mean only one thing. He knew they had not had the easiest year, that things still felt artificial, stilted. He knew he had rejected her on occasions when he need not have done so, that some small, mean part of him was still punishing her. But he thought she might have given a hint that things were coming to this . . .

Then, what hint would he have expected? This was a woman who had been unfaithful at a time when he was on his knees, when his business was dying, when it was as much as he could do to hold himself together. So unexpected had her confession been that on the morning she had told him he had felt such a sharp, shocking pain in his chest he had briefly wondered if he was dying. She had given no clue then either.

And yet he still loved her. The last weeks he had felt a growing ease, a sense that something precious was being restored to them. He had, if not forgiven her, begun to see the possibilities for forgiveness; that, in the clichés of that bloody counsellor, a marriage could become stronger.

Provided you were honest.

She had nodded at that. Taken his hand and squeezed it. It had been their last session.

Hal shifted himself further towards the edge of the bed, dimly conscious of the plastic template, glowing, radioactive, in his jacket pocket, of the dawn light slowly illuminating their room, heralding another night lost to thought, another day of furious indecision and dread ahead.

Camille's hand, in sleep, slid off his side and fell uselessly beside her.

From now on, the announcer said, the train was Liverpool Street only, repeating himself for good measure. Daisy leaned towards the window as the flat marshlands of the Lee valley gradually melded into the grimy and unlovely suburbs of East London. After two months in the little world that was Arcadia, and Merham, she felt curiously provincial, almost anxious at the prospect of returning. London seemed inextricably bound up with Daniel. And thus with pain. She was safe in Merham, free of history and association. It had only been as the train headed towards the city that she realised that the house had given her greater peace of mind than she had thought possible.

Lottie would have told her she was being stupid. 'Lovely day out you'll have,' she said, spooning sweetened porridge into Ellie's gaping mouth. 'Do you good to get away from here. You might even find time to catch up with your friends.' Daisy found it hard to think of any. She had always described herself as more of a boys' girl, while conscious that that was the kind of thing girls say when other girls' men find them a little too attractive. Perhaps she should have made more of an effort, for there was only really her sister ('Have you called the CSA yet?'), Camille ('I can hardly feel any stretchmarks. You're fine'), and now Lottie, who, since revealing a little of her past, had become more relaxed with her, her fierceness, her stringent opinions more often tempered with humour.

'I hope you're going to put something smart on,' she'd said, as Daisy went upstairs to get changed. 'You don't want to look like a sack of spuds. He might take you somewhere smart.'

'It's not a date,' said Daisy.

'Closest you're going to get,' Lottie shot back. 'I'd make the most of it, if I were you. Besides, what's wrong with him? He's not married, he's not bad-looking. He's obviously got a fair bit of money behind him. Go on, wear that top that shows your underwear.'

'I've just come out of a big relationship. The last thing I need is another man.' She stopped on the stairs, tried to hide her blush.

'Why?'

'Well. Everyone knows. I mean, you shouldn't go straight from one thing into another.'

'Why not?'

'Because – well, you know, I might not be ready.'

'But how will you know?'

'I don't know . . . It's a rebound thing. You're meant to wait a while. A year or something. Then you're carrying less emotional baggage.'

'Emotional baggage?'

'You just have to be in a state where you're ready to meet someone else. When you've got closure on your last relationship.'

'Closure?' Lottie rolled the unfamiliar word around her mouth. 'Close your what? Who says?'

'I don't know. Everyone. Magazines. Television. Counsellors.'

'You don't want to be listening to them. Haven't you got a mind of your own?'

'Yes, but I just think it would be a good idea for me to

hold off for a while. I'm not ready to let anyone new into my life yet.'

Lottie threw up her hands. 'You young girls, you're so picky. It's got to be the right time. It's got to be this, it's got to be that. No wonder so many of you end up single.'

'But, look, none of this applies to me anyway.'

'No?'

Daisy looked straight at Lottie. 'Because of Ellie. And Daniel . . . I mean, it's only fair on her if I give him some time to come back. So she has the chance to grow up with her father.'

'Oh, yes? And how long are you going to give him?'

Daisy shrugged.

'And how many good men are you going to turn down in the meantime?'

'Oh, come on, Mrs Ber— Lottie, it's only been a few months. And they're hardly beating down the door.'

'You've got to move on,' Lottie said vehemently. 'No point hanging on to the past, baby or no baby. You've got to make a life for yourself.'

'He's Daisy's father.'

'He's not here.' Lottie sniffed. 'If he's not here, he forfeits the right to be anything at all.'

Lottie had never, Daisy realised, told her who Camille's father was. 'You're a harder woman than I am.'

'Not hard,' Lottie had said, turning away towards the kitchen, her face suddenly closed again. 'Just realistic.'

Daisy looked away from the train window, leaned down and rubbed her sandalled foot on the back of her leg. She didn't want another man. She still felt damaged and raw, her nerve-endings exposed. The thought of anyone seeing her post-baby body naked filled her with horror. The prospect of being left again was too awful to contemplate. And then

366

there was Daniel. She had to leave the door open for him, for Ellie's sake.

If he ever decided to use the bloody thing.

'Camille?'

'Oh, hi, Mum.'

'I'm nipping out to the supermarket lunchtime. Me and little Ellie here. Do you need anything?'

'No. We're fine . . . Is Hal there?'

'Yes, he's outside. Just having a cup of tea. Do you want me to get him?'

'No. No . . . Mum, does he seem all right to you?'

'All right? Why? What's wrong with him?'

'Nothing. I think nothing. He's just . . . he's just been a bit odd lately.'

'What do you mean, odd?'

Camille was silent. Then she said, 'He's off with me. It's like he's . . . he's retreated into himself. He doesn't want to talk to me.'

'He's just wound up his business. He's bound to be feeling a bit sore.'

'I know . . . I know . . . It's just . . .'

'What?'

'Well, we knew it was going badly before. We knew he was going to have to close it. And things were really good between us. The best they've been for ages.'

Her mother paused. 'Well, he's been fine with me . . . It's not . . . There's nothing you're not telling me, is there?'

'What do you mean?'

'What happened before. With the two of you. There's been no . . . no recurrences.'

'No, Mum, of course not. I wouldn't do anything . . . We're fine. We're past all that. I was just worried because

367

Hal . . . wasn't quite himself. Look, forget it. Forget I mentioned anything.'

'You haven't spoken to him about it?'

'Forget it, Mum. You're right, he's probably just upset about the business. I'll give him a bit of space. Look, better go, I've got to go and take off Lynda Potter's algae wrap.'

Lottie glanced down at her bag, suddenly reassured that she had done the right thing. She wouldn't tell Camille about the money yet: she would wait until she definitely needed it, until she confided in her again. It sounded like that time might not be as far away as Lottie had hoped.

'You know what he needs?'

'What?'

'Closure. That'll make him feel better.'

There were eighteen empty mints packets littering the foot-well of Jones's car. It was hard to count them all without manoeuvring too obviously: many were partially obscured by other pieces of automobile detritus, such as roadmaps, scribbled directions and old petrol receipts. But Daisy had plenty of time to locate every one, given that for the first seventeen minutes of their journey, as they crawled through the city traffic, Jones had shouted almost constantly – and bad-temperedly – into his mobile telephone. 'Well, you tell him. He can send in who he bloody likes. All the kitchen staff have had cross-contamination training. We've got records of delivery temperatures, we've got recorded storage temperatures, delivery quality, everything to do with that bloody party. If he wants to send in the bloody Food Standards tell him I've got eighteen bloody individual frozen portions in those freezers – one for every single dish we served. So we can bloody send those away for analysis . . .' He motioned to Daisy, waving towards the glovebox, signalling for her to open it. 'Yes, we do. There's not a paragraph in that food-hygiene training that my staff don't know off by heart. Any of them. Look, he says he had the duck. The duck, right?'

As she opened it, several tapes fell out, along with a wallet, a bag of mints and several unidentified electrical cords. Daisy stuck her hand into the remaining mess, fishing around and hauling out items for Jones's inspection.

'No. No, he didn't. I've got two members of staff say he had the oysters. Hold on a minute.' He broke off to wave at the glovebox. '*Headache pills*,' he mouthed. 'You there? Yes. Yes, he did. No, you're not listening to me. Just listen to me. He had the oysters, and if you look at his bar bill, he had at least three measures of spirits. Yes, that's right. I've got the till records.' He grabbed the packet from Daisy's hand, punctured the foil bubbles and popped them directly into his mouth. 'Food poisoning, my arse. He just didn't know not to drink spirits with them. Bloody imbecile.'

Daisy looked out of the passenger window at the simmering traffic, trying to fight the irritation that had originated with Jones's casual, one-handed mimed greeting and grown with each of the three telephone conversations he had continued since she had got into the car. 'Sorry. Be right with you,' he had said, initially, and then hadn't.

'I don't give a flying f—' he shouted, and Daisy closed her eyes. Jones was a big man, and somehow, coming from him in the enclosed space of his car, the effect of his expletives was unhappily magnified. 'You tell him to send his f—' Here, he turned and caught Daisy's pained expression. 'You tell him to send his lawyers, Health and Safety, whoever he wants to me. I'll sue his arse right back for defaming my establishment. Yes. That's right. Any records they want to see, they know where to find me.' He pressed a button on his dashboard, then ripped the earpiece from his face.

'F—' He pursed his lips. 'F— bl— ruddy man. Ruddy salesman trying it on for compensation. That's all it is. He eats the bloody oysters, drinks a load of spirits, then wonders why he's got guts-ache the next day. So it's got to be my fault. Send round Health and Safety and shut me down until they've swabbed us from here to kingdom come. God, they really get my goat.'

'Evidently,' said Daisy.

He hadn't even seemed to notice her. He had made more noise, been more animated than at any other time since they had first met, but none of it was directed at her. There she was, possibly looking better than at any time since she'd had the baby, wearing a new T-shirt and skirt, her skin glowing from Camille's salt scrub, her legs smoothed and defuzzed by Camille's torturous waxing, looking if not exactly Old Daisy, then at least Fairly Rejuvenated Daisy and he'd noticed what, precisely? When looking at her long, brown legs? That she was stepping on the directions for how to get to the salvage yard.

'It's his girlfriend put him up to it,' said Jones, signalling right and leaning forward over the wheel. 'We've had her in before, trying it on. Sprained her ankle in the toilets, I think it was, last time. No medical evidence, of course. I'd ban her if she was a member. But I wasn't in that night.'

'Oh.'

'It's the Americans have done this. Bloody litigation culture. Everyone wants something for nothing. Everything's got to be someone else's fault. God!' He banged his fist on his steering-wheel, making Daisy jump.

'If I had that little shit in again, I'd give him food poisoning, all right. What's the time?'

'Sorry?'

'Eldridge Street, Minerva Street . . . It's somewhere along here. What's the time?'

Daisy looked at her watch. 'Twenty-five past eleven.'

'Salvage. That's it. Just there. Bloody little . . . Now, where am I going to park?'

Daisy's good mood of the previous hour had dissolved faster than Jones's headache pills. Finally losing patience, she stomped out of the Saab and into the architectural salvage yard, the cool bestowed by the air-conditioned interior now swamped by the heavy heat of a city summer.

Daisy was not used to being ignored. Daniel had always made a point of telling her she looked nice, of offering suggestions on what she wore, touching her hair, holding her hand. He took care of her when they were out, too, checking that she was warm enough, that she had enough to eat, drink, that she was happy. But, then, this wasn't a date, was it? And Daniel hadn't hung around to check that she was okay when it counted.

Men. Daisy found herself using a silent expletive worthy of Jones's own, then hating herself for becoming the kind of bitter and twisted man-hater that she had always despised.

The yard was huge, and tired-looking, vast timbers piled up on oversized storage shelves, slabs of stone in forbidding towers, graveyard statuary staring unseeing past her. Beyond the corrugated-iron of the entrance, the London traffic seethed, belching purple fumes and angry horns up into the fuggy air. Ordinarily, a trip to a new architectural salvage yard would have given her the same sense of anticipation and pleasure as that of a starlet in the front row of a catwalk show. But Daisy's mood was tarnished by Jones's filthy temper. She had never been able to disassociate herself from men's moods: she would try to jolly Daniel out of his temper, fail, hate herself for failing, then eventually succumb to it too. He, perversely, had never been affected by hers.

'Couldn't find a bloody meter. It's on a double yellow.'

Jones strode through the gates towards her patting his pockets, waves of discontent radiating from him. I'm not going to talk to him, Daisy thought crossly, until he snaps out of it and speaks to me nicely. She turned away and began walking towards the windows and mirrors section, her arms folded across her chest, her head low on her shoulders. A few yards away, she heard the ring of his mobile phone echo through the yard, and his explosive response. The only other visible occupant of the yard, a middle-aged man in thin spectacles and a tweed jacket, turned to see the source of the noise and she glowered in response, as if she were nothing to do with the perpetrator.

She kept walking until she was in the covered-shed area, as far away from his voice as she could get, barely noticing the Victorian sanitaryware, the engraved mirrors around her, furious that she had let herself be so affected by Jones's lack of attention. She felt herself, with what she secretly knew to be the southerner's deep-rooted sense of superiority, write him off silently as ignorant and ill-mannered, in the same way that her sister might. It didn't matter how much money you were worth if you couldn't behave properly in company. 'Look at Aristotle Onassis,' Julia would say. 'Didn't he belch, and fart like a navvy?' Perhaps all rich men were rude, Daisy rationalised, unused to having to modify their behaviour to suit others. It was hard to tell: Jones was the only seriously rich person she knew.

She stopped in front of a small stained-glass window, upon which was inlaid a grinning cherub. She loved stained glass: it was hard to find, but almost always worth using as a feature. Her bad mood briefly forgotten, she pondered where she might put it, running through an internal list of doorways, dressing-room windows, outside screens. It took her some minutes to realise she didn't want it for Arcadia. She wanted it for herself. She had bought little for herself, apart from toiletries and food, for months. Once, Daisy had thought shopping as necessary to her well-being as food or air.

She reached forward and examined the glass, squinting to see it properly in the dim light of the shed. None of the segments was broken, none of the lead missing; unusual in a piece this size. She knelt and searched for a price. When she found it, she stood up, then let the window rest back gently on its supporting frame.

'Sorry,' said a voice behind her.

Daisy turned. Jones was standing at the entrance to the covered area, his telephone still in his hand. 'Been a bit of a morning.'

'So I see,' said Daisy.

'What's that, then?'

'What?'

'What you were looking at.'

'Oh, just some stained glass. Not suitable for Arcadia.'

He looked down. 'What's the time?' he said, eventually.

Daisy sighed, looked at her watch. 'Five past twelve. Why?'

'No matter. Just didn't want to be late for lunch. Got a table booked.'

'But it's your club.'

'Yes . . .' He looked at the floor for a few minutes, then glanced around him, his eyes adjusting to the shadow. 'Sorry, anyway. For the journey. And everything. You shouldn't have had to listen to all that.'

'No,' said Daisy. She stood up and walked out into the light.

There was a short delay, as Jones apparently realised she was not waiting for him. 'Are you upset about something?' He was half a pace behind her, reaching for her elbow.

Daisy stopped. 'Why should I be?'

'Ah, don't do that. Don't do that female thing. I haven't got time to play twenty questions guessing what the matter might be.'

Daisy felt herself redden with fury, made worse by the suspicion that what she was feeling might sound ridiculous. 'Forget it, then.' She carried on walking, a lump rising inexplicably to her throat.

'Forget what?'

She wasn't, she realised, entirely sure.

'Ah, c'mon, Daisy . . .'

She faced him, furious. 'Look, Jones, I didn't have to come here, today, you know? I could have stayed at the house in the sun, and worked and played with my daughter and had a nice time. You're the one telling me I haven't got time to spare, after all. But I thought we were going to have a good buying session and a nice lunch. I thought it might be . . . useful for both of us. I didn't think I'd spend my day stuck in an overheated scrapyard listening to the rantings of an ignorant pig with Tourette's.'

It was fair to say it hadn't sounded quite that harsh in her head.

There was a brief silence.

Daisy contemplated the temporarily obscured fact that he was her boss.

'So. Daisy . . .' He stood squarely in front of her. 'Still trying to spare my feelings, then?' She looked up at him.

'Truce? If I turn my phone off?'

She was not a girl to hold a grudge. Not usually, anyway. 'You don't have another hidden in your jacket?'

'What kind of man do you take me for?' He reached into his inside pocket, and pulled out a second mobile telephone. Which he turned off.

'Bloody Welsh,' she said, looking steadily at him.

'Bloody women,' he said, and held out his arm.

From then on, Jones's mood lightened considerably, elevating her own with it. He became increasingly relaxed, and gave his full attention to her suggestions, offering little resistance even to her more fanciful choices and proffering his credit card with gratifying frequency.

'Are you sure you don't mind spending all this?' she said, as he agreed to buy an obviously overpriced pharmacy cabinet for her to put in one of the bathrooms. 'It's not the cheapest yard.'

'Let's just say I'm enjoying today more than I expected to,' he said. He didn't ask the time again.

Shortly before they left, perhaps infected by Jones's own apparent carelessness with his credit card, Daisy made a decision about the stained-glass window. It was too expensive. She didn't even have a house to put it in. But she wanted it, knew that if she didn't buy it it would haunt her for months afterwards. In the same regretful manner that friends reminisced about lost boyfriends, she still thought back to a Venetian chandelier she had lost at auction.

She walked over to Jones, who was settling up at the payment cubicle and organising delivery. 'I'll just be five minutes,' she said, pointing towards the shed. 'I want to get something for myself.'

She nearly cried when they said it had been sold. She should have known to buy it as soon as she saw it, she berated herself: anything that was good should be pinned down immediately. If your eye couldn't see its worth clearly enough to make a decision, you didn't deserve it. She stared at the cherub, wanting it more keenly now that there was no chance of it becoming hers.

She had rescued a sofa once, had managed to locate the dealer who had bought it from under her nose while she perused a junk shop, and offered to buy it from him. He had charged her almost double the original price, and although she hadn't cared at the time, had just been desperate to have it, as the months went on she found that its price had somehow spoiled it for her. That when she looked at it she no longer saw a hard-won antique, but an inflated sum she had been shoehorned into paying.

'You okay?' said Jones, standing by a stack of unstripped doors. 'Get what you want?'

'No,' said Daisy, leaning casually against one with frosted-glass panels. She was determined not to whinge. She could keep things in perspective now. 'Missed my moment,' she said. Then yelped and collapsed sideways as, with a huge crack, the glass went straight through.

They spent two hours and forty minutes at A and E, where she received twelve stitches, a gauze sling, and several cups of sweetened machine tea. 'I don't think we'll make lunch,' said Jones, as he helped her to the car afterwards, 'but I think a couple of stiff drinks are probably in order.' He placed a packet of painkillers in her good hand. 'And yes, you can drink with these. First thing I checked.'

Daisy sat silently in the passenger seat of Jones's car, her new outfit splattered with blood, feeling hopeless and chaotic and rather more shaken up than she cared to admit. Jones had been surprisingly good about the whole thing: he had sat patiently with her in a succession of waiting rooms as triage nurses, then doctors had mopped her up and restored her arm to something not dissimilar to that of a patchwork doll. He had left twice, to make telephone calls outside, one of which, he said in the car, had been to Lottie, to tell her that Daisy would be later home than expected.

'Is she cross?' said Daisy, looking in horror at the browning bloodstains on his pale leather interior.

'Not remotely. Baby's fine. She says she's going to take her home with her as she's promised a meal with her husband tonight. And you won't be able to drive.'

'Mr Bernard'll be pleased, then.'

'Look, it's an accident. People have them. Don't worry about it.'

He had been like that all afternoon, mellow, reassuring, as if he had all the time in, and none of the cares of, the world. It had been curiously intimate, having to lean on him, having him wrap her arm and sit beside her on the plastic chairs of the hospital corridor. He had lowered and softened his voice to talk to her, as if she were sick as well as injured. She had wondered, periodically, whether he was even the same person who had picked her up from Liverpool Street station that morning.

'Have I ruined your day?'

He laughed at that and, his eyes on the road in front, shook his head.

Daisy, trying to ignore the throbbing in her arm, stopped talking.

His mood hardened when they reached the Red Rooms, partly because there was no one on the front desk when they walked in; a sackable offence, he said later, when she asked why it should be a problem. 'Everyone who comes in here should be greeted like an old friend. I pay them to know the names, the faces. I don't pay them to be taking a late lunch.'

He had held her good arm as she made her way up the many flights of wooden steps, past bars where people sat around under whirring fans, surreptitiously craning their necks at new arrivals who might turn out to be more notable than themselves, waving or exclaiming too-hearty greetings in Jones's direction. Once, she might have thought a bit of rubbernecking fun. But when he said he had arranged for them to have a table on a terrace outside his office she had been relieved, fearful at the thought of her bloodied clothes, her sling, being exposed to the sharp, assessing eyes of London's bar crowds.

Because, suddenly, being back felt overwhelming. She felt intimidated by the thudding roar of Soho's traffic, its reverberating roadworks, its braying, shouting people. She felt hemmed in by the height of the buildings, had forgotten how to walk through a crowd, and found herself hesitating, ducking the wrong way. She felt a sudden, unanticipated ache for her child; a deep discomfort when she calculated the number of miles that now separated them. Worse, she kept seeing men who looked like Daniel, and found her stomach clenching, an uncomfortable, reflexive action.

Jones had begged five minutes 'to take care of some business'. The girl who served her drink, an Amazonian beauty with a deep tan and long black hair scraped back artistically into a knot, had eyed her speculatively.

'Fell through a door,' explained Daisy, mustering a smile.

'Oh,' said the girl, uninterestedly, and sauntered off, leaving Daisy feeling stupid for saying anything.

'Jones, I'm really sorry, but I think I'd like to go home,' she said, when he finally emerged on to the terrace. 'Could you give me a lift to Liverpool Street?'

He had frowned, and sat down slowly opposite her. 'Not feeling good?'

'Just a bit wobbly. Think I'd be better back at . . .' She tailed off, realising how she had referred to the hotel.

'Have something to eat first. You've eaten nothing all day. Probably why you're feeling shaky.' It was an instruction.

She raised a half-smile, holding up her hand to shield her eyes against the light. 'Whatever.'

She ordered a piece of steak, and had to sit, uncomfortably, as he took the plate from her and sliced it into pieces that she could spear one-handed. 'I feel like an idiot,' she said, periodically.

'Just eat something,' he said. 'You'll feel beter.' He did not, muttered something, a little embarrassed, about trying to shed a few pounds. 'Spend my whole life entertaining, you see,' he said, glancing down at his stomach. 'Don't seem to burn it off like I once did.'

'It's your age,' said Daisy, downing her second spritzer.

'You're feeling better, then,' he said.

They talked about the mural, and the faces that Hal had painstakingly and meticulously brought forth into the light. Lottie, Daisy told him, was still not happy about having it restored. But having accepted that she was not going to get her way, she had started, albeit gracelessly, to identify some of the figures. One of them, Stephen Meeker, lived a few miles along the coast in a hut on the shingle. (They were not friends, she had said, but he had been very sweet to her when Camille was born.) The day previously she had shown Daisy which was Adeline, and Daisy had stood in front of her, marvelling at this woman staring at what looked like a doll, feeling the decades strip away, making scandalous the behaviour that was now considered the norm. She had identified Frances, too. But Frances's face had been partially rubbed away. Daisy wondered whether they might try to find a picture of her somewhere, from some artists' archive, perhaps, to restore her to the pictorial bosom of her friends. 'It doesn't seem fair that she, of all people, should be absent from it,' she said.

'Perhaps she wanted to be absent from it,' he said.

She didn't tell him about the previous evening; how she had glanced out of the window to catch Lottie standing very still in front of the mural, lost in something unseen. Or how she had slowly reached out her hand, as if to touch something on it, and then, abruptly, as if she were scolding herself, how she had turned and walked stiffly away.

He told her about his plans for the opening of the hotel, showed her several files with details and photographs of previous openings he had held. (In nearly all, she noted, he was flanked by tall, glamorous women.) 'I want to do something a bit different with this, something that reflects the house. But I can't think what,' he said.

'Will it be a celebrity bash?' said Daisy, feeling curiously invaded.

'There'll be a few faces,' he said, 'but I don't want your bog-standard canapé do. The whole point about the hotel is that it's meant to be different, a bit above all that, if you like,' he concluded awkwardly.

'I wonder if any of them are alive,' said Daisy, staring at the folder.

'Who?'

'The people. On Frances's mural. I mean, we know Frances and Adeline aren't. But if it was painted in the fifties, there's a good chance that a lot of them are still around.'

'So?'

'We find them and get them together. At your hotel. For the opening. Don't you think that would be a fantastic publicity stunt? I mean, if these people were the *enfants terribles* of their age, as Lottie says, it would mean fantastic press. You've got the image there, of the mural . . . I think it would be great.'

'If they're still alive.'

'I'm hardly going to invite them otherwise. But it might mollify the locals a bit as well, a reference to their history.'

'I suppose it could work. I'll get Carol on to it.'

Daisy looked up from her drink. 'Carol who?'

'She's my party planner. Runs a PR company, and organises all my dos.' He frowned at Daisy. 'What's the problem?'

Daisy picked up her glass and took a good swig. 'I suppose . . . I suppose I'd like to do it.'

'You?'

'Well, it was my idea. And I did – we did find the mural. I feel sort of attached to it.'

'But how are you going to find the time?'

'It's only a few phone calls. Look, Jones,' almost unconsciously, she reached a hand across the table, 'I think this mural is really special. It might even be important. Don't you think it's the kind of thing that would be best kept secret, for now at least? You'd get more coverage if it doesn't leak out in dribs and drabs. And you know what PR people are like – they can't keep their mouths shut. I mean, I'm sure your Carol is very good but if we just kept the mural between us for now, just till the painting is finished – well, the impact would be greater when it finally came out.'

She had thought he had black eyes, but she saw now that they were a really, really dark blue.

'If you think it's not too much extra work,' he said, 'by all means. Tell them I'll put them up, pay for their transport, whatever. But don't get your hopes up. Some of them may be too frail, or sick, or senile.'

'They're not much older than Lottie.'

'Yesssss.'

They smiled at each other then. An unguarded, complicit smile. And half-way through it, Daisy discovered she felt much better, and stopped because, somehow, she felt like she shouldn't.

He was going to drive her back to Merham. No arguments, he said. It would only take him an hour or two, now the rush-hour was over – and, besides, he wanted to see the mural.

'But it'll be dark,' said Daisy, who had drunk so much that her arm had stopped hurting. 'You won't see much.'

'So we'll turn all the lights on,' he said, disappearing into his office. 'Give me two minutes.'

Daisy sat on the illuminated terrace, her cardigan round her shoulders, listening to the distant sounds of revelry and traffic below. She didn't feel so out of place now. She no longer felt awkward around Jones, as if she were constantly trying to prove something to him, to convince him that he was just not seeing the best side of her. And it was different here, watching him in his own environment, moving easily through a sea of deferential, eager faces. Awful how power made people more attractive, she observed, fighting at the same time a covert sense of anticipation at the idea that the two of them would again be alone in the house together.

She pulled her mobile phone from her bag to check on Ellie, and swore softly when she found that the battery was flat. She hardly used it at Merham – it had probably been flat for weeks.

'You all finished, then?' The waitress began collecting the empty glasses from her table.

'Yes, thank you.' It might have been the alcohol, or Jones's attentions, but Daisy felt less awed by her now.

'Jones said to tell you he'll be another five minutes. Got

caught on the phone.' Daisy nodded understandingly, wondering if when he was finished she could borrow it to call Lottie.

'Meal all right?'

'Lovely, thanks.' Daisy reached forward and pinched a final piece of chocolate torte from her pudding plate.

'Jones looks better anyway. God, he was in a filthy mood this morning.' The girl was stacking plates with the swift, expert touch of someone to whom it had become second nature. She popped used napkins into glasses and balanced them on top. 'It's good that he found a distraction for today.'

'What? Why?'

'His wife. His ex-wife, sorry. Got remarried today – midday, I think. He didn't know what to do with himself.'

The chocolate torte had somehow got stuck to the roof of Daisy's mouth.

'Oh, sorry. You're not going out with him, are you?'

Daisy swallowed, smiled up at the girl's concerned face. 'No. God, no. Just doing the décor on his new place.'

'The one at the seaside? Lovely. Can't wait to see that. Just as well, anyway.' The girl stooped low, glancing in the direction of the door. 'We all love him to death, bless him, but he's a complete slag. I reckon he must have slept with at least half the girls in this place.'

Jones stopped trying to make conversation somewhere past Colchester. He asked if she was tired, and when she said yes, he told her he'd leave her to sleep if she liked. Daisy turned her face away from him and gazed out at the sodium-lit roads speeding past, wondering how she could accommodate so many conflicting emotions in one small, rather worn-out frame.

She liked him. She realised she had probably known it from the moment he had picked her up, and infuriated her by failing to pay her any attention. She had begun to admit it to herself when he had been so uncharacteristically tender and solicitous when she had cut her arm. He had gone white when he saw how much she was bleeding; and the urgency with which he shouted at the yard staff and rushed her to hospital had made her feel protected in a way that she hadn't since Daniel left. (There was still a huge part of Daisy that needed to feel protected.) But the waitress's remark about the remarriage had hit her with the force of a sledgehammer. She had been jealous. Jealous of the ex-wife for having been married to him; jealous of anyone who could still get him that rattled. And then she had mentioned the other girls.

Daisy shuffled lower in her seat, feeling both furious and despondent. It was inappropriate. *He* was inappropriate. It was pointless getting hung up on someone who was, as the waitress had so eloquently put it, a complete slag. Daisy looked at him surreptitiously. She knew the type: 'car-crash men', Julia called them. 'Strangely compelling, but you really don't want to get involved. Just drive past and thank God you're not stuck in the middle.' Even if she had wanted to get involved, which she obviously didn't, Jones would be wrong, even for a rebound. His lifestyle, his history – it all pointed to Serial Infidelity and Avoidance of Commitment.

Daisy shuddered, as if afraid that he could hear her thoughts. Because all this was predicated on the idea that he even liked her, which, frankly, she was not sure that he did. He liked her company, yes, and her ideas, but there was a whole genetic scale between her and that waitress, the slim-thighed, even-tanned girls that populated his world.

'You warm enough? My jacket's in the back if you want it.'

'I'm fine,' said Daisy curtly. Despite the late hour and the renewed throbbing in her arm, she wished that she had caught the train. I can't do this, she thought, biting her lip. I can't allow myself to feel anything. It's too painful and too complicated. She had been healing until she had spent time with Jones. Now she felt all opened up again.

'Mint?' said Jones. She shook her head, and finally he left her alone.

They arrived back at Arcadia at a quarter to ten, the car crunching loudly on to the gravel and leaving a louder silence when it stopped. There was a clear sky, and Daisy breathed in the clean, salt air, hearing the distant rush and roar of the sea below.

She felt rather than saw Jones look at her, and then, evidently deciding to say nothing, he climbed out of the driver's door.

Daisy fumbled across herself trying to open the passenger side, her physical incompetence bringing her dangerously close to tears. She was determined not to cry in front of him again. That would just about top her day.

Mrs Bernard had left some of the lights on – to make the house seem less unwelcoming – and they sent pools of yellow light on to the gravel. Daisy looked up at the windows, feeling acutely the fact that she was about to spend yet another night on her own.

'You okay?' said Jones, beside her. His earlier cheerfulness had been displaced by something more contemplative. He looked, she thought, as if he were on the verge of saying something grave.

'Fine,' said Daisy, swinging her legs out of the car as she held her arm protectively close to her chest. 'I can manage.'

'When's Mrs Bernard bringing the baby?'

'First thing tomorrow.'

'Want me to go and get her for you? It'll take five minutes.'

'No. You get back. You're probably needed in London.'

He had looked at her hard then, and she had blushed at her tone, grateful that in the badly lit driveway he could probably not see the colour in her face.

'Thanks, anyway,' she said, forcing a smile. 'Sorry – sorry about everything.'

'It was a pleasure. Really.'

He was standing in front of her, too big a presence to move past. She stared at her shoes, wishing he would just go away. But he seemed reluctant to move.

'I've upset you,' he said.

'No,' said Daisy, too quickly. 'Not at all.'

'You're sure?'

'I'm just tired. The arm's hurting a bit.'

'You okay by yourself?'

She glanced up at him. 'Oh, yes.'

They stood a few feet from each other, Jones tossing his car keys uncomfortably from one hand to the other. *Why don't you just go?* Daisy wanted to scream.

'Oh,' he said. 'You left something in the boot.'

'What?'

'Here.' He moved round the car and, with a blip of his remote device, opened the back.

Daisy walked after him, her cardigan hauled round her shoulders. Her sling was rubbing the back of her neck, and she reached with her good hand to try to adjust the knot. When she had finished, Jones was still looking into the boot. She followed his gaze downwards. There, on a large grey blanket, lay the stained-glass window, its image just visible in the shadow cast by the boot lid.

Daisy stood still.

'I saw you looking at it.' Jones looked embarrassed now. He shifted his feet. 'So I bought it for you. I thought . . . I thought it looked a bit like your little girl.'

Daisy heard the sound of the breeze in the Scots pines, and the dull whispering of the grass on the dunes. They were almost drowned by the ringing in her ears.

'It's a thank-you,' he said gruffly, still looking into the boot. 'For what you've done. The house and everything.'

Then he lifted his head and looked at her properly. And Daisy, her bag held loosely in her good hand, stopped listening. She saw two dark, melancholy eyes, and a face whose coarseness was offset by the sweetness of its expression. 'I love it,' she said, quietly. Her eyes still on his, she moved a step closer to him, her bandaged arm lifting almost involuntarily towards his, her breath tight in her chest. And stopped as the front door swung open, sending an arc of light splaying across the drive on to them.

Daisy turned towards it, blinking as her eyes adjusted to the silhouette that stood in the doorway, the silhouette that shouldn't have been and didn't seem to be Lottie Bernard's. She shut her eyes and opened them again.

'Hello, Daise,' said Daniel.

Seventeen

'She's really gone and done it this time.'

Lottie was building Ellie a tower of bricks, gazing out at the two figures on the terrace. She turned to Aidan, then stood up. 'Who has?' She had forgotten how much time was spent getting down on to the floor and up again with small children. She hadn't remembered everything aching so much with Camille. Or even Katie. 'Your woman down the road, Mrs Leg-warmers or whatever her name is. Have you seen this?' He walked over to the rug and passed her a copy of the local paper, pointing to the letters page. 'Wants all right-minded people to picket the hotel. To stop auld Jonesy serving alcohol.'

'She what?' Lottie studied the newsprint, absently thrusting coloured bricks at Ellie as she did so. 'Damn fool woman,' she said. 'As if a few decrepit pensioners with placards are going to make a difference. She wants her head tested.'

Aidan picked up a mug of tea from the sideboard, his plaster-covered fingers apparently oblivious to its heat. 'Won't be good publicity, though, for your man. Not quite the image he'd be wanting to project – fighting his way through a line of blue-rinse rebels.'

'It's ridiculous,' said Lottie, dismissively, passing the newspaper back to him. 'As if anyone round here is going to give two hoots about a few gins and tonics.'

Then he leaned backwards, his eye caught by the sight of Daisy with an unidentified man outside. 'Aye-aye,' he began. 'Our Daisy's got a new one on the night shift, has she?'

'Haven't you got anything better to do?' said Lottie, sharply.

'That'd be a matter of opinion,' he said, waited just long enough to get Lottie bristling, then sauntered off.

It was the baby's father. No doubt about it: she had known as soon as he appeared at the door the previous evening, his dark hair and deep-set brown eyes an echo of Ellie's.

'Yes?' she had said, knowing full well what he was about to say.

'Is Daisy Parsons here?' He had been clutching an overnight bag. Something of a presumption in the circumstances, Lottie had thought. 'I'm Daniel.'

She had looked deliberately blank.

'Daniel Wiener. Daisy's . . . Ellie's father. I was told she was here.'

'She's out,' said Lottie, taking in his strained eyes, his fashionable clothes.

'Can I come in? I've just caught the train up from London. I don't think there's a pub round here I can wait in.'

She had wordlessly shown him inside.

It was none of her business, of course. She couldn't tell the girl what to do. But if it had been up to her, she would have told him to sling his hook. Lottie clenched her hands beside her, conscious that she felt inappropriately angry with this man on Daisy's behalf. That he could leave her and the baby to face everything all alone, then think he could just saunter back in as if nothing had happened. Daisy had been doing all right: anyone could see that. She looked across at the baby, who was meditatively gnawing at the corner of a wooden brick, then out at the terrace, where the two figures stood stiffly, several feet apart, she

389

apparently absorbed in the distant horizon, he in something on his shoes.

I ought to wish you a life with your father, Ellie, she said silently. Me of all people.

Daisy sat on the bench under the mural, in a space between several jars of different-sized brushes, as Daniel stood with his back to the sea, looking up at the house. She kept glancing at him surreptitiously, trying to take him all in, and awkward, in case she should be seen doing so.

'You've done a great job,' he said. 'I wouldn't have recognised it.'

'We've been working hard,' she said. 'Me, the team, Lottie, Jones . . .'

'Nice of him to give you a lift back from London.'

'Yes. Yes, it was.' Daisy sipped her tea.

'What happened to you? To your arm?' he said. 'I wanted to ask last night, but . . .'

'I cut it.'

He blanched.

She caught his thoughts a moment after. 'No, no. Nothing like that. I fell through a glass door.' She felt a brief flush of annoyance that he still imagined himself so vital to her existence.

'Does it hurt?'

'A little, but they've given me some painkillers.'

'Good. That's good. Not your arm, I mean. The painkillers.'

It had not begun this stiffly. On seeing him, the previous evening, she had thought, briefly, that she might faint. Then, as Jones discreetly offloaded the stained-glass window and swiftly made his excuses, she had walked inside and, catching hold of the banister, burst into uncontrollable tears. He had placed his arms around her, apologising, his own tears mingling with hers, and she had cried harder, shocked at how his body against hers could feel so familiar and strange at the same time.

His arrival had been so unexpected that she hadn't had time to work out what to feel. The evening with Jones had brought everything to the surface, then suddenly she was confronted with Daniel, whose absence had coloured almost every minute of the last months, whose presence now prompted so many conflicting emotions that all she could do was look at him and cry.

'I'm so sorry, Daise,' he had said, his hands clutching hers. 'I'm so, so sorry.'

A long time later she had pulled herself together and, one-handed, poured them both a large glass of wine. She lit a cigarette, noting his look of surprise as she did so and the efforts he made to hide it. Then she had sat looking at him, unsure what to say to him, what she should dare to ask.

He looked, at first glance, exactly the same: his hair was cut the same way, his trousers, his trainers those he had worn on the weekend before he left. He had the same mannerisms: he ran his hand repeatedly over the top of his head, as if reassuring himself that it was still there. But as she looked more closely, he appeared different: older, perhaps. Certainly more worn. She wondered if she looked the same.

'Are you better?' she had asked. It seemed like a safe question.

'I'm not . . . I'm not so confused, if that's what you mean,' he said.

Daisy had taken a long swig of wine. It tasted acidic: she had drunk too much already. 'Where are you staying?'

'With my brother. Paul.'

She nodded.

His eyes never left her face. They were anxious, blinking. The half-light revealed deep crevices under them. 'I didn't know you were actually living here,' he said. 'Mum was under the impression that you were staying with someone in the town.'

'And who would that be?' she said sharply – the anger was too close to the surface. 'I had to leave the flat.'

'I went there,' he said. 'There's someone else living in it.'

'Yes, well, I couldn't afford the rent.'

'There was money in the account, Daise.'

'Not for the whole time you were gone. Not to support me as well. Not when you took into account the rent rise Mr Springfield landed on me.'

Daniel's head dropped. 'You look well,' he said, hopefully.

She stretched her legs, rubbing at a spatter of browned blood on her left knee. 'Better than when you left, I suppose. But, then, I had only just pushed a whole human being out of my body.'

There was a long, complicated silence.

She looked at the thick dark hair on top of his head, thinking of the times she had cried on waking because it wasn't there beside her. How she had lain in bed remembering what it had felt like entwined in her fingers. She had no urge to touch it now. She felt only this cold fury. And underneath it, curdled with it, fear that he was going to leave again.

'I'm so sorry, Daise,' he said. 'I – I don't know what happened to me.' He shifted forward on his seat, as if preparing to make a speech. 'I've been on these antidepressants,' he said. 'They've helped a bit, in that I don't feel like everything's as hopeless as I did. But I don't want to stay on them too long. I don't like the thought of being dependent on them, I guess.' He took a gulp of his wine. 'I also saw a psychiatrist. For a bit. She was a bit clogs-and-lentils.' He glanced up at her, gauging the reception of an old, shared joke.

'So what did she think? About you, I mean?'

'It wasn't like that, really. She asked me lots of questions and sort of expected me to work out the answers.'

'Sounds like a good way to earn a living. And did you?'

'To some things, I think.' He didn't elaborate.

Daisy was too exhausted to delve into what that might mean. 'So. Are you staying tonight?'

'If you'll let me.'

She took another long drag of her cigarette, and tamped it out. 'I don't know what to say to you, Dan,' she said. 'I'm too tired and it's all too sudden, and I can't think straight . . . We'll talk in the morning.'

He had nodded, still watching her.

'You can sleep in the Woolf Suite. There's a duvet still in its box. Use that.'

The possibility of him sleeping anywhere else had evidently occurred to neither of them.

'Where is she?' he said, as she went to leave the room.

Oh, you're finally interested, are you? she thought. 'She'll be back first thing,' she said.

She hadn't slept. How could she, when she knew he lay, probably awake too, on the other side of the wall? At one point she had berated herself for her response to him, for the fact that she had effectively sabotaged what might have been a glorious reunion. She should have said nothing tonight, simply pulled him to her, loved him, brought him home again. Other times she wondered why she had let him stay at all. The anger felt like a cold, hard thing inside her, sporadically throwing up questions like bile: Where had he been? Why had he not rung? Why had it taken him almost an hour to ask where his daughter was?

She rose at six, bleary-eyed and headachy, and splashed cold water on her face. She wished that Ellie was there: it would have given her a focus, a practical series of things to do. Instead she moved silently around the house, conscious of its familiarity, the feeling of safety that it had bestowed. Until now. Now she would be unable to think about it without Daniel in it; the areas that had been free of him now held him imprinted upon them. It took her several minutes to understand that she felt unbalanced by this because she was expecting him to leave again.

He woke after Lottie arrived. She had handed back Ellie, who looked distinctly unperturbed by her unorthodox evening, and asked Daisy if she was all right.

'Fine,' said Daisy, burying her face in Ellie's neck. She smelt different: of someone else's house. 'Thank you for looking after her.'

'She was no trouble.' Lottie had observed her for a time, raising an eyebrow at Daisy's arm. 'I'll make tea, then,' she said, and went off to the kitchen.

A few minutes later Daniel had come down the stairs, his sore eyes and grey complexion testament to his own unrestful night. He had stopped when he saw Daisy and Ellie in the hall, his foot still resting on the step behind.

Daisy felt her heart skip a beat at the sight of him. She had wondered, several times, whether the previous night she had seen an apparition.

'She – she's so big,' he whispered. Daisy fought back the sarcastic response that came to her lips.

He walked slowly down the stairs and came towards them, his eyes still on his daughter. 'Hello, sweetheart,' he said, his voice cracking.

Ellie, with a child's unfailing ability to defuse a moment, gave him the briefest of glances and promptly smacked Daisy's nose repeatedly, cawing to herself as she did so.

'Can I hold her?'

Daisy, trying to save herself from the harder of Ellie's swipes, looked at the tears in Daniel's eyes, at the raw longing on his face, and wondered why, at this moment, the moment she had thought about for months, the moment she had longed almost physically to see, her overriding instinct was to hold her daughter to her. Not to hand her over at all.

'Here,' she said, holding Ellie towards him.

'Hello, Ellie. Look at you!' He brought her to him slowly, tentatively, like someone unused to holding children. She fought the urge to tell him that he was holding Ellie in a way she didn't like, tried to ignore Ellie's arms reaching out towards her. 'I've missed you,' Daniel was crooning. 'Oh, sweetheart, Daddy's missed you.' Then, overcome by a mass of conflicting emotions, and unwilling for Daniel to see any of them, she walked briskly away from them and off to the kitchen.

'Tea?' said Lottie, not looking up.

'Please.'

'And . . . him?'

Daisy looked at Lottie's back, ramrod straight and neutral, as she moved deftly along the kitchen surface, sorting teapots and teabags.

'Daniel. Yes, he will. White, no sugar.'

White no sugar, she thought, holding on to the work surface to stop her hands trembling. I know his likes better than I know my own.

'Want me to take it out to him? When he's finished with the baby?'

There was an edge to Lottie's tone. Daisy knew her well enough now to hear it. But she no longer resented it. 'Thanks. I'll take mine out on the terrace.'

He had emerged eleven minutes later. Daisy had been unable to prevent herself timing him, monitoring how long he lasted with his child before the periodic squawks of frustration or a crying jag unsettled him so much that he handed her over. He had lasted longer than she'd expected.

'Your friend's taken her upstairs. Said she needs a nap.' He brought his tea out and stood opposite her, looking at the sea below.

'Lottie looks after her for me while I'm working.'

'That's a handy arrangement.'

'No, Daniel, it's a necessary arrangement. The boss didn't like me trying to deal with planning officers and suchlike with a baby on my hip.'

It was always there: this anger, bubbling under, just waiting to spit out at him, to scald him. Daisy rubbed at her brow, exhaustion making her irritable and confused.

Daniel stood in silence for some minutes, sipping his tea. The smell of the jasmine in full bloom was almost overpowering, a faint breeze sending it across the terrace towards them. 'I didn't expect to be welcomed back with open arms,' he said. 'I do know what I've done.'

You have no idea what you've done, she wanted to shout at him. What she said was: 'I really don't want to discuss this while I'm meant to be working. If you can stay another night, we'll talk this evening.'

'I'm not going anywhere,' he said, smiling apologetically.

She smiled back. But his last words had not reassured her.

The day passed, and Daisy was grateful for the distractions of her work, of door-handles wrongly affixed, windows that didn't shut, their irritating mundanity restoring to her a sense of normality and equilibrium. Daniel walked into town, supposedly to get a newspaper but largely, Daisy suspected, because he was finding it as difficult as she was. Aidan and Trevor watched her with interested eyes: some domestic drama of epic proportions was being played out in front of them, distracted them even from the opening matches of some football tournament on the radio.

Lottie just watched, and said nothing.

She had offered, that morning, to relinquish day-to-day care of Ellie to Daniel 'for as long as he's there'. She had offered to show him how to do things like prepare her food, bolt her into her high chair, the way she liked her blanket tucked under her chin as she slept. 'She doesn't want someone faffing around with her, unsettling her,' she said. Something about the look on Lottie's face as she said this persuaded Daisy it might not be the best idea to let her be the one to do this, not if Daisy was serious about Daniel coming home.

Camille came up at lunchtime and, after a quick chat with her mother, asked Daisy discreetly if she was 'doing okay'. 'Stop by at ours for a head massage or something this evening, if you like. Mum will mind Ellie. They're great for stress.' If it had been anyone else, Daisy would have told them to get lost. Having grown up with a Londoner's natural sense of anonymity, she hated the goldfish-bowl element of village life, the way that Daniel's reappearance apparently entitled everyone to an opinion. But Camille seemed uninterested in gossip: perhaps she heard so many sensational tales in her everyday work that she had become inured to its pleasurable possibilities. She just wanted to make her feel better, Daisy thought wonderingly. Or perhaps she wanted company. 'Don't forget, stop by,' said Camille, as she left with Rollo. 'To be honest, when Katie's out with her friends I could do with someone to talk to. Hal seems to prefer his painted ladies to me, these days.' She said it jokingly, but her expression was wistful.

Hal was the only one apparently uninterested in Daisy's romantic situation. Probably, she thought, because he was now deeply engrossed in the mural, which was almost three-quarters revealed. He was absorbed, monosyllabic. He no longer took a lunch break, accepting his sandwiches from his wife without the romantic flourishes of previously. Half the time he forgot to eat them.

Jones didn't call.

She didn't ring him. She wouldn't know what to say.

Daniel stayed on. That second evening, they didn't talk: it was as if the fact that they had both thought of little else all day meant that by the time they had the house to themselves they were exhausted, their arguments already run through countless times in their heads. They ate, listened to the radio, went to their separate beds.

The third evening, Ellie had cried almost incessantly, victim of some internal grumble or emerging tooth. Daisy had walked her round the upper floor of the house: unlike in their flat in Primrose Hill, Ellie's screams, which had always tautened some invisible cord running through her to breaking point, did not prompt in her here a simultaneous anxiety that she was disturbing everyone – her neighbours, upstairs and downstairs, people out in the street, Daniel. She had become accustomed to the space, and the isolation. 'In Arcadia,' she told her daughter fondly, 'no one can hear you scream.'

She walked the corridors, Ellie's sobs diminishing with the various changes of room, trying not to think too hard about Daniel's response downstairs. This, after all, was what had driven him away before: the noise, the chaos, the unpredictability of it all. She half expected him to be gone when she crept back down the stairs.

But Daniel had been reading the paper. 'Is she all right?' he asked, relaxing when Daisy nodded. 'I didn't . . . I didn't like to interfere.'

'She just works herself into a bit of a state,' she said, reaching for her glass of wine and sitting down heavily opposite him. 'She needs to blow herself out a bit before she can fall asleep again.'

'I've missed so much. I'm so far behind you in terms of knowing what she wants.'

'It's not nuclear science,' said Daisy.

'Might as well be,' he said. 'But I'll learn, Daise.'

She had gone to bed shortly afterwards. As she left the room, she had had to fight the unexpected urge to kiss his cheek.

'Julia?'

'Hello, darling. How are tricks? How's my lovely baby-cakes?'

'Daniel's back.'

There was a short silence.

'Julia?'

'I see. When did this little miracle take place, then?'

'Two days ago. He just turned up on the doorstep.'

'And you let him in?'

'I was hardly going to tell him to catch the train home. It was nearly ten o'clock at night.'

Her sister's grunt told Daisy what *she* would have done.

'I hope you didn't—'

'There are eight suites here, Julia.'

'Well, that's something, I suppose. Hold on.' Daisy heard a hand placed over the receiver, followed by a muffled cry: 'Don? Can you turn the potatoes down for me, darling? I'm on the telephone.'

'Listen, I won't keep you. I just wanted to let you know, I guess.'

'Back for good?'

'What? Daniel? I don't know. He hasn't said.'

'Of course not. How silly to expect him to tell you what his plans are.'

'It's not like that, Ju. We – we haven't talked about it yet. We haven't really talked about anything.'

'That's convenient for him.'

'It's not necessarily down to him.'

'When are you going to stop defending him, Daisy?'

'I'm not. I'm really not. I guess I just want to see what – to see what it's like us all being around each other. Whether it even works any more. Then we'll have the serious discussions.'

'And has he offered you any money?'

'What?'

'Well, for his keep. Because he doesn't have anywhere to live, now, does he?'

'He's not—'

'He's living in a luxury hotel. In a suite. Rent free.'

'Oh, Julia, give him some credit.'

'No, Daisy. I'm not prepared to give him any credit whatsoever. Why should I give him any credit after what he's put you through? You and his own child? He's a waste of skin as far as I'm concerned.'

Daisy snorted, unable to help herself.

'Don't just let him walk in and take over again, Daisy. You've been doing fine without him, remember? You've got to keep that thought in your head. You came out the other side.'

Did I? Daisy thought afterwards. She had been less help-less, certainly. She had managed to mould Ellie into a routine of hers, rather than the other way round. She had rediscovered something of herself, something better, she occasionally thought, than Old Daisy. In renovating Arcadia, she had achieved something momentous and unexpected by herself. But she had been lonely. She was not really a girl to whom living alone came naturally.

'You've changed,' Daniel said. He had said it quite unexpectedly, watching her at work.

'How?' she had asked, warily. As far as Daniel had been concerned, all her changes had so far been for the worse. 'You're not as fragile as you were. Not as vulnerable. You seem better able to cope with everything.'

Daisy had glanced outside, to where Lottie was blowing on a foil windmill, making Ellie shriek with delight. 'I'm a mother,' she said.

On the fourth day, Carol the PR woman arrived, exclaiming about the beauty of the house, taking Polaroid photographs of every room, setting Daisy's teeth on edge and sending Lottie's eyebrows into orbit. 'Jones told me about your idea. Very good idea. *Very* good,' she said, conspiratorially. 'It'll make a great feature for one of the glossies. I have *Interiors* in mind. Or maybe *Homes and Gardens*, bless you.' Daisy's irritation that Jones had confided in this woman had been mollified by the idea that her talents might be recognised in print.

'Until then, however, we must keep *schtum*.' She pulled a finger across her lip, theatrically. 'Novelty is everything, after all.' She thought she might break a personal rule, she said, and hold a theme party: a 1950s day out at the seaside. They could be *wonderfully vulgar* and have donkeys and ices and silly postcards. She hadn't seemed to hear Daisy when she pointed out that it wasn't a 1950s house.

'Is Jones coming up again? Before the opening?' Daisy said, as she saw Carol back into her low-slung car, privately marvelling that any fifty-something woman could still fancy herself in a Japanese two-seater.

'He was going to try to get up this afternoon, to meet us,' Carol said, punching her mobile phone for messages, 'but you know what he's like, bless him.' She rolled her eyes skywards, a gesture Daisy was starting to recognise as familiar among Jones's female colleagues. '*So* lovely to meet you, Daisy. And I'm *so* thrilled that we're going to be working together. It's going to be *such* a wonderful party.'

'Yes,' Daisy said. 'See you soon, then.'

Other people had begun to invade. There was a solemn young photographer who said he did all of Jones's brochures, and drove the builders mad, banning them from rooms and using their power cables for his arc-lights. There was the chef, from Jones's London club, who came to check out the kitchens and ate three packets of pork scratchings for his lunch. There was a random planning officer, who turned up unannounced, and left without seemingly checking a thing. And there was Mr Bernard, who appeared that evening to see if Hal wanted to come for a drink. He had knocked on the front door and waited, even though it was open and everyone else walked in and out without breaking their stride.

'Lottie's not here, Mr Bernard,' Daisy said, when she spotted him. 'She's taken Ellie into town. Do you want to come in?'

'I know that, dear, and I didn't want to disturb you,' he said. 'I just wondered if my son-in-law was around.'

'He's out the back,' she said. 'Come on through.'

'If I'm not disturbing anyone. That's very kind.'

He looked a little uncomfortable even walking through the house, his gaze largely fixed in front of him as if he didn't want to appear to be nosy. 'Going well, is it?' was all he would say, and nodded, pleased, when Daisy affirmed that it was. 'Looks like you're doing a lovely job. Not that I'd know much about it.'

'Thank you,' said Daisy. 'I'm glad there are a few people who think so.'

'You don't want to take any notice of Sylvia Rowan,' he confided, as she brought him through to the terrace. 'That family always had a bit of a thing about Lottie. It's probably about her, all this unpleasantness, more than anything else. Grudges do tend to get held a long while out here.'

He patted her arm, and walked off towards Hal, who was washing out his brushes. Daisy watched him go, remembering the evening when Lottie had told her about Camille's birth. Joe, slightly stooped, and wearing his tie and collar even in high summer, was a rather unlikely knight in shining armour. Several minutes later, as Daisy hung and rehung a selection of old photographs in the hallway, he reappeared in the doorway.

'He's a bit busy tonight. Another time, perhaps,' he said. 'Mustn't hold up the schedule, after all.' He looked as if he had become accustomed to many years of disappointment, and that he merely accepted it.

'He doesn't have to work late, if you've got something planned,' said Daisy.

'No. To be honest, Lottie wanted me to have a word with him.'

Daisy waited.

'Oh, nothing to worry about, nothing to worry about,' he

said, walking towards his car, one hand raised by his head. 'It's just this winding up of his business. I think he's taken it very hard. Just wanted to make sure he was all right, you know. Anyway, best be on my way. See you, Daisy.'

She waved him off down the drive.

In the end she went to Camille's. She told Daniel she had an appointment, which was partially true, that he would have to babysit, which made Lottie blanch, and walked the short distance to Camille's house. As she strolled through Merham's sunlit streets, weaving her way round exhausted parents and small children wobbling on unstable bicycles, she realised that, apart from her trip to London, she had barely left the house and its grounds for weeks. Daniel had not looked as frightened as she had thought he might: he had looked rather pleased, as if being allowed to babysit his own child were a privilege, bestowed as one might a badge of honour for good behaviour. She would give him till nine p.m. before she called: she fully expected him to be begging her to return by then.

Camille and Hal's house was large and semi-detached, with generous windows and a 1930s porch, through which she could just make out the joyfully barking figure of Rollo. She heard, then saw Camille making her way surprisingly swiftly down the hall.

'It's Daisy,' she called, to spare Camille the indignity of having to ask.

'Perfect timing,' said Camille. 'I've just opened a bottle of wine. Have you come for the full head?'

'Sorry?'

'The massage.' She closed the door carefully behind Daisy, and made her way back up the hall, her left hand trailing along the wall.

'Oh. If you like,' said Daisy, who'd really just come for the company.

It was a better-decorated house than she'd expected. Then, in retrospect, she wasn't sure what she *had* expected – not the lightness and airiness, though. Not pictures on the walls, perhaps. Definitely not the hundreds of framed photographs dotted around on surfaces, most in ornate antique silver frames. There were Hal and Camille on a wetbike, hiking somewhere mountainous, Katie on a pony, all three dressed up for some gathering. On the mantelpiece, there was a large one of Hal and Camille on their wedding day. The way he was looking at her, that mixture of pride and tenderness on Hal's youthful face, made Daisy's briefly wistful.

'Lovely pictures,' she said.

'The little watercolour is of me. Mum did it, believe it or not, when I was a baby. Shame she doesn't paint any more. I think it would do her good to have a hobby.'

'It's lovely. And the photographs.'

'Are you looking at our wedding pic?' Camille seemed to know from the direction of her voice where Daisy was. She moved fluidly towards the mantelpiece, and picked it up. 'That's my favourite,' she said, fondly. 'It was a really good day.'

Daisy couldn't help herself. 'How do you know?' she said. 'What's in the picture, I mean.'

Camille placed it on the mantelpiece, checking that its base was well back from the edge. 'Katie mainly. She loves pictures. Tells me what's in every one. I could probably talk you through most of our albums as well.' She paused, a half-smile on her lips. 'Don't worry, I'm not going to. Come through to the kitchen. I've got my old treatment chair in there. Katie likes to sit in it.'

She hardly knew Camille, not really *knew*, in the way that

friends knew each other's histories, each other's likes and dislikes, a shared emotional shorthand. If anything, Camille was too reserved for Daisy's comfort: she felt easier around people who laid themselves out in front of her, who spilled out their emotions, like Daniel. But there was something about her that seemed to put Daisy at ease. She didn't feel competitive, in the way she often secretly did with other attractive women. And it wasn't because of Camille's lack of sight. There was just something accepting about her, something calm. Some kind of intrinsic goodness that managed not to be nauseating, or make Daisy feel inadequate for the lack of her own.

Or perhaps it was just the head massage: the alternating pressures of thumb and fingers around her head and neck loosening her thoughts along with her physical tensions. Here, she didn't have to think about Daniel. Here, she didn't have to think at all. 'You're very good at this,' said Daisy, dreamily. 'I think I could fall asleep.'

'You wouldn't be the first.' Camille took a sip of her wine. 'I had to stop doing it for the men, though. Sometimes it had a different sort of effect.'

'Oh. Ah. Not a reputation you want as a masseuse.'

'They think that because you can't see you can't tell. But you can, you know. Just from the breathing.' She put her hand to her chest, and imitated the increased rapidity of desire.

'Really? Oh, my God. What did you do?'

'Called Rollo out from under the table. A big smelly old dog usually did the trick.'

They laughed companionably.

'Your dad was up at the house this evening.'

'Dad? Why?'

'He invited Hal out for a drink.' Camille's hands stilled.

'I think Hal wanted to keep going on the mural. He – he's terribly conscientious.'

'Dad invited Hal out for a drink?'

'That's what he said. Oh, God, have I put my foot in it?'

'No, don't worry.' There was a new steeliness in Camille's voice. 'It's not Dad. That's Mum, interfering again.'

The pleasurable haze of the past minutes evaporated.

'It might just have been a drink,' Daisy ventured.

'No, Daisy, with Mum it's never just a drink. Mum wants to know what's wrong with Hal, why he's taking the whole business thing so badly.'

'Oh.'

'She was on his case to wind it up, and now she's on his case again because he's not handling it as well as she thinks he should be.'

'I'm sure she means well,' said Daisy, weakly.

'I know she means well. But she can never just leave me and Hal to sort things out ourselves.' She sighed, a well-worn expression of exasperation.

'Only child?'

'Yup. Which doesn't help. I think Dad would have liked more, but Mum had quite a rough time with me and it put her off. No drugs in those days.'

'Ouch,' said Daisy, thinking of her own epidural. 'Sorry if I've said the wrong thing. I guess I shouldn't have said anything.'

'Oh, don't worry, Daisy. It's not the first time. No doubt it won't be the last. Comes of living so close to one's parents, I suppose. Perhaps Hal and I should have moved away when we first got married, but we didn't, and then with Katie and everything . . . I needed the help.'

'I know that feeling. I don't know what I would have done without your mum.'

Camille's hands had started moving again, a gentle, repetitive pressure. 'You're quite tense, aren't you?' she said. 'I suppose it's no surprise, with the hotel opening so close and everything. I don't know how you've done it.'

'I haven't yet.'

'Is it easier with Ellie's father here?'

It was subtly done. Daisy toyed with the idea that Lottie had sent Camille to enquire about her relationship too. 'Not really, if I'm honest. I'm sure Lottie told you, he left us when Ellie was a few months old. I haven't got used to him being back yet.'

'So you're back together?'

'I don't know. He's here, I guess.'

'You don't sound convinced.'

'I suppose I'm not. I don't know what to feel, really.'

She was grateful that Camille didn't try to offer any solution, any course of action. Julia could never hear a problem without feeling obliged to fix it, and was usually mildly offended at Daisy's failure to take her recommendations to heart.

'If Hal ever did anything really bad to you, if he ever just walked out, for example, would you be able to take him back? With open arms?'

Camille's hands stopped, and rested, palm down, on Daisy's forehead. 'Hal never does anything wrong,' she said drily. 'But I suppose, if it came down to it, with a child involved and all, I guess it depends on the greatest degree of happiness. If you're all going to be that much happier by being together, even though it's difficult, then it's probably worth fighting for.'

Daisy felt her hands move, as if Camille were shifting her weight.

'I don't know,' she went on. 'When you're young, you tell

yourself you won't put up with anything, don't you? That if your marriage isn't passionate enough, or if he doesn't live up to expectations, you'll just leave, and find someone else. And then you get older and the thought of starting again . . . the sheer awfulness of it all . . . Well, I guess I'd put up with quite a lot before I pulled it all apart. The family, I mean. Maybe you just get used to compromise.' She seemed to be speaking to herself.

She paused. When she spoke this time, Daisy heard a different timbre to her voice. 'That said, if it's impossible to make someone happy, whatever you do, I suppose in the end you just have to admit defeat.'

Lottie placed her bag on the chair in the hall, noting with irritation that Joe's coat was hanging on the peg. 'I thought you were going out for a drink,' she called, hearing the radio in the living room.

Joe emerged, and kissed his wife's cheek. 'He didn't want to come.'

'Why? He can't spend *all* his time working on that painting.'

Joe took Lottie's coat by the shoulders as she slid out of it. 'Can't make him come, love. You can lead a horse to water and all that . . .'

'Yes. Well. Something's up with him. He's been funny for days. And that boyfriend of Daisy's has been hanging around all day, lounging around as if he owns the place.'

Joe held open the living-room door for his wife. She could see he wanted to place his arm over her shoulders. She had told him several months ago that it had always made her feel uncomfortable.

'He is the child's father, love.'

'Well, it's a bit late for him to start realising that now.'

'That's for Daisy to decide. Let's leave that for a moment, shall we?'

Lottie looked at him sharply. Her husband looked down, and then up at her. 'This house stuff . . . I . . . I don't like it, Lottie. It's stirring everything up again. Getting you all agitated.'

'No, it's not.'

'You pitching yourself against Sylvia Rowan when you've spent the last God knows how long steering well clear of the lot of them.'

'I didn't ask her to start causing trouble.'

'And all that business with the mural. It's not that I mind, love, you know that. I've never said anything against you heading down there. But you've not been yourself these last couple of weeks. I don't like to see you getting yourself in a state.'

'I'm not in a state. It's you getting me in a state, going on about everything. I'm fine.'

'Well, all right. But either way I just wanted us to have a little chat. About after.'

Lottie sat down. 'After what?' she asked suspiciously.

'The hotel, and everything. After it opens. Because Daisy will go back to London, won't she? With or without her man friend. And you won't be needed up there any more.'

Lottie looked at him blankly. She hadn't thought about life after Arcadia reopened its doors. She felt chilled. She had never thought about what she would do without it.

'Lottie?'

'What?' She saw her life stretching ahead of her: the Round Table dinner-dances, the small-talk with neighbours, the endless evenings in this house . . .

'I got us some brochures.'

'What did you say?'

'I got us some brochures. I thought we could make it an opportunity, you know, to do something a bit different.'

'Do what?'

'I thought we could go on a cruise or—'

'I hate cruises.'

'You've never been on one. Look, I thought we could even take a trip round the world. You know, stop off in lots of places. See some sights. It's not like we've ever been very far, and we'll have no responsibilities now, will we?'

He didn't say the words 'second honeymoon', but Lottie felt them hanging in the air, and it made her snap. 'Well, that's just like you, Joe Bernard.'

'What?'

'No responsibilities, indeed. Who's going to look after Katie, eh, while Camille's at work? And who's going to help Camille?'

'Hal will help Camille.'

Lottie snorted.

'They're fine now, love. Look at how he was with her over this mural business. Like a pair of lovebirds, they were. You told me yourself.'

'Well, that just shows how much you know. Because they're not fine at all. In my view he's five minutes off leaving her again. And that's exactly why I wanted you to take Hal out tonight and find out what's going on in his damn-fool head. But, oh, no, you're too busy thinking of cruises and suchlike.'

'Lottie . . .'

'I'm going to have a bath, Joe. I don't want to discuss it any further.'

She trod heavily up the stairs towards their bedroom, wondering as she did why tears had sprung so easily to her eyes. It was the second time this week.

★   ★   ★

The noise of the bath running had deafened her, so she didn't hear Joe's footfall as he came up the stairs. His unannounced appearance in the doorway made her jump.

'I do wish you wouldn't sneak up on me,' she yelped, her hand to her chest, furious that he had caught her unguarded.

Joe was stalled momentarily by his wife's tearful face. 'I don't often disagree with you, Lottie, but I'm going to say one thing.'

Lottie stared at her husband, noting that he was standing straighter than normal; that his voice held just a touch more authority.

'I'm going to take a trip. After the hotel opening. I'm going to book a ticket, and take a trip round the world. I'm getting on a bit, and I don't want to get old and feel like I've done nothing, seen nothing.' He paused. 'Whether you come with me or not. Obviously I'd prefer it if you did, but just for once I'm going to do something I want.'

He breathed out, as if his short speech had been the product of some huge internal effort.

'That's all I'm going to say,' he said, turning back to the door, and leaving his wife silenced behind him. 'Now, call down when you want me to put the chops under the grill.'

On the fifth evening, Daniel and Lottie talked. They took Ellie for a walk down on the beach, tucking her firmly into her buggy and swaddling her with a cotton blanket, even though it was a still, balmy evening. Daisy found it difficult to think straight in the house these days, she had told him. She saw it now not as a home, or even a hotel, but as a list of problems that needed solving: a loose window-catch, an unsecured floorboard, a faulty plug socket, a deadline ticking away. Outside, in the fresh air, she found she could gradually clear her head.

This is what I wanted, Daisy thought, seeing them as if from the outside: a handsome young couple and their beautiful child. A family unit, tight, encompassing, exclusive. She hesitated, and then took his arm. He had pressed it to him, so that her hand was warmed, enclosed on both sides.

And then Daniel began to talk.

He had first known there was something wrong when one of his old colleagues had shown him a picture of his own baby, convulsed with pride, and Daniel had realised that not only was he not carrying a photograph he didn't feel a tenth of what his colleague evidently felt.

He had, painfully, allowed himself to admit that he felt hemmed in. Trapped in a situation that was not of his making, his beautiful girlfriend vanished and in her place this tearful blob – he didn't say 'blob', but Daisy knew what he meant – and this squalling child. There seemed to be no beauty, no order in his life any more. And beauty and order were vital to Daniel. This was a man, after all, who had once been unable to sleep because a picture rail had been affixed at a fractionally wrong angle. Daisy had woken at four in the morning to find him meticulously pulling it off the wall, and replacing it with the aid of two spirit levels and several pieces of string. But babies did not care about order. They didn't care that their stink and their noise and their nappies polluted Daniel's little haven. They didn't care that the demands they made ripped their mothers away from the larger, stronger arms who needed them just as much. They didn't care what time they woke you up, or that you needed four hours' sleep together just to be able to earn the money to live. 'And the thing is, Daise, you're not allowed to complain, are you? You're meant to just accept it, and believe everyone when they say, "It'll get easier," even when it feels like it's getting worse, that you'll love them blindly when actually you look at these rather ugly, screaming trolls and you just can't believe they're anything to do with you. If I'd said – if I'd said what was in my thoughts in those early weeks, the real truth, I'd probably have been arrested.'

It had been the vest that finally did it. He had stumbled into the living room one morning, half delirious through lack of sleep, and trodden on a discarded vest that squelched. He had sat, his unclean foot resting on their once pristine rug, and known that he just could not do it any more.

'But why didn't you say something? Why did you bottle it all up inside?'

'Because you didn't look like you could bear it. You were barely coping yourself. How could you cope with hearing that your baby's father had decided she was a big mistake?'

'I could have coped with it a lot better than having my baby's father disappear on me.'

They sat down on a sand dune, noting that Ellie had fallen asleep in her pram. Daniel leaned forward and tucked her blanket more firmly under her chin. 'Well, I know that now. I know a lot of things now.'

He felt restored to her then, the ugly truth of what he was saying bringing forth a kind of sweetness in her. Because he loved Ellie now: that was apparent in everything he did . . . 'I need to know if we can try again,' he said, taking her hand. 'I need to know if you're going to let me in. If we can put it behind us. I really missed you, Daise. I missed her.'

Down on the sand, a shaggy black dog raced backwards and forwards in overexcited circles, leaping and twisting into the air to catch pieces of driftwood thrown by its owner, leaving long, complicated patterns in the sand. She leaned against Daniel, and he placed his arm around her. 'You still fit, then,' he said, into her ear. 'In there.'

Daisy leaned in, trying to clear her head, trying to focus on the sensation of being close to him again. Trying not to listen to the complications.

'Let's go home, Daisy,' he said.

Jones watched the couple with the pram strolling back along the sea path, the man's arm protectively over his girlfriend's shoulder, their baby lost from view in slumber, the evening sun glinting off the wheels.

He sat for some minutes, waiting until they were out of sight, then turned his car round. It was a two-hour drive back to London. Some might say he was mad to come all this way without even stretching his legs. But he had missed the meeting with Carol, he told himself, pulling past the driveway to Arcadia and back down towards the railway station, his eyes unblinking on the road ahead. There was no point in hanging around. That was the only reason he had come, after all.

'It's often meant to be difficult after you have a baby.'

'I suppose it'll take time for us to get used to each other again.'

'Yes.'

They lay side by side, both awake, staring into the dark.

'We're probably a bit tense. I mean, it's been a strange few days.' Daniel reached for her, and she rested her head on his chest.

'You know what, Dan? I don't think we should even talk about it too much. It kind of makes it into an issue . . .'

'Oh. Okay.'

'But you're right. I mean, I think I am a bit tense.'

He reached for her hand, and she lay there, his fingers entwined in hers, trying not to think too hard about the previous half-hour. She would have liked to get a drink, but she knew that he needed the reassurance of her being there, that any attempt by her to move would be misinterpreted.

'Actually, Daise?'

'Yes.'

'There is something I need to talk to you about. Now we're being honest and everything.'

For some reason, an image of Jones flashed into her head, as fragile and opaque as stained glass. 'Okay,' she said, trying not to sound as guarded as she felt.

'I think we need to get everything out into the open before we can put the past behind us.'

She said nothing, hearing his attempts at casualness fall flat and feeling a sense of foreboding, like the distant whistle of an approaching train.

'It's about what happened while we were apart.'

'Nothing happened,' said Daisy. Too quickly.

He swallowed audibly. 'That's what you might want to believe. But it did.'

'Says who?' It would have been Lottie, of course. She knew Lottie thought they shouldn't get back together.

'It was just a kiss,' he said. 'Nothing major. It was when I was at rock bottom, when I didn't know whether I was going to come back.'

Daisy let go of his hand, pushed herself upright on one elbow. 'What did you say?'

'It was only a kiss, Daise, but I thought I should be honest about it.'

'You kissed someone else?'

'While we were apart.'

416

'Hang on, you were meant to be having a nervous breakdown about coping with a new baby, not putting yourself about round North London.'

'It wasn't like that, Daise—'

'Wasn't like what? So there I was with your mother telling me you were practically throwing yourself under a bus, not even well enough to talk to me, and all the while you were snogging for Britain. Who was she, Dan?'

'Look, don't you think you're overreacting just a bit? It was one kiss.'

'No, I don't.' She swept the duvet around her and climbed out of bed, unwilling to admit to herself that the ferocity of her response might have been linked in any way to her own buried guilt. 'I'm going to sleep in the other room. Don't follow me, and don't start padding around the corridors,' she hissed. 'You'll wake the baby.'

Eighteen

The bungalow, clad in bleached white clapperboard and surrounded by a little garden of rusting sculptures, stood on the shingle an unneighbourly hundred or so feet away from its cluster of neighbours. 'I like it like that,' said Stephen Meeker, as they looked out of the window at the uninterrupted view of the shore. 'People don't have an excuse to just pop in. I do hate it when people feel they can do that. It's as if, when you're retired, you should be grateful for any interruption in your dreary old day.'

They sat over tea in the sparsely decorated living room, whose walls were hung with paintings of a quality at odds with the furniture and upholstery around them. Outside, the sea, glinting under an August sky, was empty, the families and holidaymakers tending to stay up the coast in Merham's sandier stretch of water. It was the second time in a week that Daisy had interrupted his dreary old day, but she had been welcomed, partly for the selection of magazines she had brought him as a gift and partly because the time she wanted to talk about was one of the few periods of his life, he said, during which he had been truly happy. 'Julian was rather a lot of fun, you see,' he said. 'Terrifically naughty, especially when it came to finances, but he had this knack for collecting people, in much the same way as he collected art. He was like his wife, in that way. A pair of magpies.'

He had loved Julian for ever, he said, with a rapture that sat oddly on a stiff old man. In the 1960s, when Julian and

418

Adeline had divorced, they had moved into a little place in Bayswater together. 'We still told people we were brothers. I never minded. Julian always got much more worked up about that kind of thing than I did.' Several of the paintings on the wall had been gifts from Julian: at least one was by Frances, who had achieved a belated notoriety after being 'claimed' by a feminist art historian.

Daisy, who had been privately taken aback when she saw the signatures on the other canvases, noted with dismay the stained corners, the paper curling into the salt air. 'Shouldn't they be . . . in a safe somewhere?' she asked tactfully.

'No one to look at them there,' he said. 'No, dear, they will stay in my little hut with me till I pop off. Sweet lady, Frances. Terrible shame, all that business.'

He had become rather animated when she'd shown him the Polaroids of the near-finished mural, wistfully admiring the beauty of his younger self, and pointing out names of those people he could remember. Julian, he told her sadly, would not be available for the party. 'There's no use contacting him, dear. He lives in a home in Hampstead Garden Suburb. Totally ga-ga.' Minette he had last heard of in a commune in Wiltshire; George was 'something eminent' in economics at Oxford. 'Married some viscountess or other. Terribly posh. Oh, and there's Lottie's young man. Or perhaps he was her sister's . . . I forget. "The prince of pineapple", George used to call him. I'll remember his name if you bear with me.' Daisy had been shocked to see the exotic, long-haired goddess of the mural named as Lottie. 'She was rather a looker in those days, in an unconventional way, of course. A bit of a temper but, then, I think some men found that rather attractive. Between us, I don't think anybody was particularly surprised when she got herself into trouble.' He put his cup down on the table and chuckled to himself. 'Julian always said, "*Elle pet plus haut que sa cul . . .*" Do you know what that means?' He leaned forward, conspiratorially. 'She farts higher than her arse.'

Daisy walked slowly back along the beach towards Arcadia, her bare head hot under the midday sun, her feet, like the waves, pulling back from their intended path. The morning had been a pleasant diversion from the increasingly tense atmosphere at Arcadia. The hotel was gearing up for its finish, its rooms restored to their original, stark grandeur, the new furnishings placed and re-placed until their aesthetics satisfied. The building almost hummed now, as if itself anticipating new life, a blood system of new visitors.

So, among its people, one might have expected there to be an air of excitement or achievement as the work drew to a close, but Daisy had rarely felt more miserable. Daniel had barely spoken to her in forty-eight hours. Hal had finished the mural and disappeared without a word. Lottie had been jumpy and bad-tempered, like a dog listening for the approach of a thunderstorm. And all the while, outside, came the distant rumblings of dissent from the village. The local paper had now promoted what it called the 'Red Rooms Hotel Row' to its front pages, from where it had been picked up by several nationals, and reprinted as a typical plucky-villagers-fight-against-impending-change story, and illustrated with pictures of scantily clad female Red Rooms members. Daisy had referred several calls to Jones's office, half wishing, as she did so, that she had been brave enough to speak to him herself.

Not that Jones's London clientele was helping matters. A few of his closest drinking buddies, two of them actors, had come up to 'lend some support'. When they discovered that not only was the hotel not yet ready to offer overnight accommodation but that Jones's bar was not yet stocked, they had been directed by one of the decorators to the Riviera where, several hours later, Sylvia Rowan had ejected them for what she described later in the newspapers as 'lewd and disgraceful behaviour' towards one of her waitresses. The waitress, who seemed somewhat less perturbed, sold her story to one of the tabloids, and promptly handed in her notice, saying she had made more that way than the Rowans paid her in a year. The same tabloid had printed a picture of Jones, at some bar-opening in central London. The woman who stood next to him had her hand clamped over his arm, like a talon.

Daisy paused for a breather and gazed out at the pale blue arc of the sea. With a pang, she remembered that soon it would be her view no longer. That she would have to return with her beautiful, bonny child to a city of fumes and fug, noise and clatter. I haven't missed it, she thought. Not as much as I expected to, anyway.

London still felt inextricably tied up with foreboding and unhappiness, a skin she had almost shed. But a life in Merham? Already she could envisage a time when its sociable confines would become stifling, when the neighbourly interest of its inhabitants would feel like intrusion. Merham was still locked into its past, and she, Daisy, needed to look forward, to move forward.

She thought suddenly of Lottie, then turned back towards the house. She would think about leaving, she decided, after she had sorted out the party. It was a pretty efficient way of not having to think about what she would be returning to.

She had found Daniel in the Sitwell bathroom with one of the builders. He was holding a tile up against the wall, with a piece of dark paper behind it. The builder, Nev, a young man with Titian curls, was gazing disconsolately at a pot of white grouting. She stopped in the doorway. 'What are you doing?' she asked, as neutrally as she could manage.

Daniel glanced up. 'Oh, hi. They were putting white grouting with these tiles. I told them it should be black.'

'And why would you do that?' Daisy stood very still, as Nev glanced backwards and forwards between them. Daniel straightened, and placed the tile carefully behind him.

'The original plans. These shaped tiles were going to have black grouting. We agreed that it looked better, if you remember.'

Daisy felt her jaw clench. She had never disagreed with him, had always capitulated to his vision. 'Those plans have long since been changed, and I think it would be better for everybody if you didn't get involved with matters that no longer concern you, don't you?'

'I was trying to help, Daise,' he said, glancing at the other man. 'It's stupid me sitting around day after day with nothing to do. I just wanted to lend a hand.'

'Well, don't,' Daisy snapped.

'I thought we were meant to be a partnership.'

'Gosh. So did I.'

Daniel looked startled: it was Daisy's second mutiny of the past few days and visibly swept away other certainties. 'I can't keep apologising. If we're going to move this on, we need to separate what happened between us from what happens with the business.'

'It's not that simple.'

'Oh, come on, Daise . . .'

She took a deep breath. 'The company you were part of no longer exists.'

Daniel frowned. 'What?'

'Wiener and Parsons. I wound it up when I took this job. It no longer exists. I'm a sole trader, Daniel.'

There was a long silence. Nev began to whistle nervously, examining the dried paint on his hands. Outside, scaffolding was being dismantled, poles periodically falling to the ground with a muffled crash.

Daniel moved his head from side to side, then looked at her, his mouth set in a grim line. He wiped his hands on his jeans. 'You know what, Daisy? I think you've made that perfectly clear.'

Camille sat in the front of the battered old Ford, listening to the sounds of Merham in high summer filter through the passenger window, mingling with Katie's only half-heard chatter in the back and the smells of fuel and warm Tarmac rising in waves off the road. Rollo sat in the footwell, wedged between her knees, his preferred mode of transport, and Hal, beside her, sat still enough not to make the old leather interior squeak, his silence burning into her bones. She was going to have to tell him about the job. Three more weeks, Kay had said, and less than a month's money in payoff. No one had come forward to buy the business and, sorry though Kay was, she was not sorry enough to keep the damn thing open.

Camille felt the weight of it like a cold stone in the pit of her stomach. She could have coped with the idea that they were going to struggle: she'd find work eventually, as would he. Their meagre savings, along with the mural money, would see them through. But he'd been so difficult lately, so locked into himself. Any innocent query was greeted by a fierce denial, or some biting, sarcastic response, so that she was left feeling at best unhelpful, and at worst stupid.

Because she couldn't understand what was going on. She knew what the business had meant to him, that it was always going to be hard for him to let it go. But she had thought, had hoped, that he would lean on her a little, that it would be something they could go through together. Instead he had made her feel redundant, a feeling she had chafed against her whole life, from the years at school when she had sat on the sidelines embroidering netball strips, because of Lottie's insistence that she should be included in everything, to now when she had to ask shop assistants whether the clothes Katie had chosen for herself were suitable or, as they occasionally had been, for someone ten years older. With a nice sideline in 'extras'.

The car stopped. She heard Katie scramble for the door, then back, and a cool, hurried kiss was plastered on her cheek. ''Bye, Mum.' She leaned back, touching the place with her hand, too slow to catch her quicksilver daughter, who was already out and running up the garden path of her schoolfriend.

'Hello, Katie, go on through. She's in her room.' She heard Michelle at her door, then Hal's impatient jangling of the keys as she came towards the car. 'Hi, Camille. Thought I'd just say hello. Sorry I missed you at school last week – I've been away on a training course.' A light touch on her shoulder. Michelle's voice came at Camille at head height: she must be crouching by the car door. She smelt vaguely of vanilla.

'Anywhere nice?'

'Lake District. Rained every day. I couldn't believe it when Dave said it had been beautiful here.'

Camille smiled, acutely aware that Hal hadn't said a word in greeting. She heard a question in Michelle's silence, and tried to fill it. 'We're just off to the shops.'

'Anything nice?'

'Just to get a new dress for this hotel opening. Hal's been working there, along with Mum . . .'

'I can't wait to see it. I can't see what everyone's getting so worked up about. It's not like half of them will ever set foot inside it anyway.' Michelle sniffed. 'That said, Dave's mum's very anti. She says if we let the Londoners in, we'll have the asylum-seekers here next . . . Silly old bat.'

'They'll get used to it. Eventually.'

'You're right. I'd better let you go, then. Aren't you lucky? I could never get Dave to come shopping with me . . .' Michelle's voice tailed away awkwardly, as she remembered why Hal might be going too.

'Oh, Hal only does it under sufferance,' Camille joked. 'I have to buy him lunch afterwards. And grovel a lot.'

They separated with arrangements to pick up Katie at six, and a promise of coffee later in the week. Camille heard her voice as if from a long way away. She smiled as she heard Michelle's footfall disappearing up the path, and then, as Hal restarted the engine, she reached out her hand and stilled his. 'Okay,' she said, into the silence. 'I can't do this any more. Are you going to leave me?'

She hadn't meant to ask, hadn't even known that it was the question.

She felt him turn to face her. This time the seat squeaked.

'Am *I* leaving *you*?'

'I just can't tiptoe around you any more, Hal. I don't know what I'm doing wrong, and I don't know what's wrong with you, and I can't keep grovelling. I can't keep trying to make things all right.'

'*You*'re trying to make things all right?'

'Well. Not very well, obviously. For God's sake, I just need you to talk to me. Whatever it is. We said we were past this, didn't we? That we were going to be honest?'

'So you'll be perfectly honest?'

Camille withdrew her hand.

'Of course I will.'

'Even about your bank account?'

'What bank account?'

'Your new bank account.'

'I don't have a new bank account. What's that got to do with anything?' She waited for him to say something. 'Oh, for God's sake, Hal, I don't know what you're talking about. You see the printed copies of all my statements, for crying out loud. You know all my bank accounts. You'd be the first to know if I opened one.'

There was a different tenor to his silence somehow. Then, 'Oh, Christ.'

'Christ what? Hal, what is this?'

'Lottie. It's your mother.'

'My mother what?'

'She's set up an account in your name. She's given you two hundred thousand pounds.'

Camille turned so sharply she made Rollo yelp. 'What?'

'From the sale of Arcadia. She's set up this account in your name and I thought – oh, God, Camille, I thought . . .' He started to laugh. She felt him shaking with it, sending tiny, rhythmic vibrations through the car. It sounded almost like he was in tears.

'Two hundred thousand pounds? But why hasn't she told me?'

'It's obvious, isn't it? She doesn't think we're going to last. She wanted to make sure you were secure, even while I went down the drain. The useless husband who can't even keep his own business going . . . How's he meant to look after her little girl?'

He sounded so bitter. But it held a twisted kernel of truth. She shook her head, which was sunk into her hands, thinking of what he must have thought, and how close they had come . . . 'But she . . . the money . . . Oh, God, Hal, I'm so sorry . . .'

Below her feet, Rollo whined to be allowed out. Hal reached an arm around her, pulled her close to him, his other arm reaching round to hold her. She felt his breath in her ear. 'No, sweetheart. I'm sorry. I'm so sorry. I should have talked to you. I've been such an idiot . . .'

They sat like that for some time, both oblivious to the curious glances of the people walking by, of the inquisitive – and perhaps reassured – gaze of Katie and her friend Jennifer from the upstairs window, from where, eventually bored, they tore themselves away.

Camille slowly, reluctantly, also peeled herself away, feeling the beginnings of perspiration where their bodies had welded themselves firmly together.

'Still want to hit the shops?' Hal squeezed her hand, as if unwilling to relinquish his hold on her.

Camille lifted a strand of hair from her face, and tucked it behind her ear. 'No. Drive me to Arcadia, Hal. I've had just about enough of this.'

Daisy checked off the walls and floor of the main lounge, the bar area, the bedroom suites and the kitchens. Then she checked every set of curtains, that they were hung correctly and that their folds fell evenly and without creases, and the light-fittings, to see that they all worked and that every bulb was in place. Then she drew up a list of those jobs that had not yet been completed, those that had been completed wrongly, those items delivered and those that needed to be returned. She worked quietly, methodically, enjoying the cool of the fans – they had decided against air-conditioning – and the breeze that flowed freely through the many open windows. There was a kind of internal peace to be found in order, in routine. It made her understand a little better Daniel's fierce need for things to be balanced and harmonious around him.

He had made her a mug of tea, and they had been civil with each other, managing to discuss Ellie's preference for white over brown bread and the best method of peeling her grapes without any reference to their earlier exchange. He had taken his daughter into town, managing without prompting to remember her nappy bag, her water and some rusks, and to slather her in sun-cream. Ellie had squealed at him then gnawed voraciously at a wooden stick with bells on, and he had chatted comfortably to her while crouching down and deftly fastening her into the push-chair.

They are building a relationship, thought Daisy, watching from the door, and wondered why her happiness in it felt so complicated.

'Where's he taking her?' Lottie was apparently finding it less easy to relinquish her charge.

'Just to town.'

'He doesn't want to take her through the park. There's dogs everywhere.'

'Daniel will look after her.'

'It's stupid, people letting them run around without leads like that. Not when there's so many children about. I don't know why people want to bring them on holiday.'

She had not been herself these last few days. She had snapped at Daisy when she had asked her about her image on the mural, interested to know about the symbolism of their clothes, what they were holding. Daisy didn't tell her what Stephen Meeker had said about temptation and the Old Testament. That he said the imagery had all been quite fitting when you knew that she had tried to seduce the father of the family she was evacuated to. Or that among his old photographs was one of a young Lottie, heavily pregnant, sleeping half naked on a stone floor.

'You wanted some of these old pictures and things for framing.' Lottie held out the box she had been carrying under her arm.

'Well, only ones you're happy to let go. I don't want any that have emotional significance for you.'

Lottie shrugged, as if that were an alien concept. 'I'll sort them upstairs. Where it's quiet.'

She had tucked the box back under her arm, and Daisy had listened to her footsteps echo along the corridor, then turned when Aidan yelled her name from the lobby. 'Someone to see you,' he said, two nails sticking out of the corner of his mouth, his hands thrust deep into his suede apron. As she passed him he raised an eyebrow, and she fought a sudden internal lurch at the prospect of Jones.

Almost unconsciously, she raised a hand to her hair, attempting to smooth it away from her face.

But it wasn't Jones.

Sylvia Rowan stood on the doorstep, her brightly coloured jacket and leg-warmers dominating the pale space around her. By her feet, drooling unpleasantly, sat her blank-eyed dog.

'I've told your man there he might want to stop,' she said, smiling in the manner of a duchess waving at crowds.

'I beg your pardon?' said Daisy.

'Your builders. They need to stop.'

'I think I'll be the judge of—' Daisy was halted by Sylvia Rowan's brandishing of a piece of paper. A little too close to her face.

'Building preservation notice. Your hotel is now spot listed, and subject to an emergency listing. That means you are effectively a listed building for the next six months, so any building work has to be halted.'

'What?'

'It's to stop you spoiling the building any more than you already have. It's legally binding.'

'But the work is practically finished.'

'Well, you'll have to apply for retrospective planning permission for it all. And reinstate anything that the planning people aren't happy with. The odd wall, perhaps. Or some of those windows.'

Daisy thought in horror of the guests already lined up to stay. About the prospect of them unloading their bags to the sound of demolition work. 'But I haven't applied for listed status. Nor has Jones. The fact that it didn't have any was one of its attractions.'

'Anyone can apply for a spot listing, dear. In fact, it was you who gave me the idea when you stood up and said what you were doing to the place. Still, it's in all our interests to preserve our architectural heritage, isn't it? Here's your paperwork, and I suggest you ring your boss and tell him that he might as well postpone his opening.' She eyed Daisy's bandaged arm. 'I might ring Health and Safety while I'm at it.'

'Vindictive auld cow,' said Aidan. 'I'm surprised she didn't eat your baby too.'

'Oh, hell,' said Daisy, reading through the myriad clauses and subclauses of the paper in front of her. 'Look, Aidan, do me a favour.'

'What?'

'Ring Jones. Tell him I'm out or something. But you tell him for me.'

'Ah, come on, Daisy, that's not my job.'

'*Please.*' She tried to look endearing.

430

Aidan raised an eyebrow. 'Lovers' tiff, eh?'

She needed it too badly to swear at him.

She hadn't looked at these since Adeline had died. The fact that she had stared at the top of the box for almost ten minutes suggested a certain reluctance to do so now. Stirring everything up again. Wasn't that what Joe had called it? Memories of Arcadia, of her summer there, like the others, bright sparks turning in an orbit around a peacock-feathered sun. Easier not to look, thought Lottie, sighing, her hand resting on the lid. Easier not to awaken old feelings that had long been better buried. She had proven very good at keeping things buried. But now Daisy wanted to bring everything out into the open, just like she'd uncovered the mural. And in a moment of weakness, when she'd been distracted by Camille and Hal, or her thoughts of cruises and how to avoid them, she'd said she would get the damn things out. Daisy wanted to frame as many photographs and sketches as she could and line the wall opposite the bar with them: a pictorial reminder that guests here were once part of the great tradition of an artistic retreat.

Artistic retreat, thought Lottie wryly, opening the box. Apart from Frances, there had been hardly an artist among them. No, she chided herself, remembering Ada Clayton. The artistry had been in their reinvention of themselves. In camouflage, and cleverness, and in creating people they were not.

She marvelled that the simple act of taking a lid off a box could make her feel as giddy as if she were standing on a precipice. Ridiculous old woman, she told herself. They're only pictures.

But her hand, as she reached in, was shaking.

On the top, now slightly sepia-tinted with age, stood

Adeline, dressed as the Rajah of Rajasthan, her eyes glittering from under a turban, her boyish figure bound in a man's silk jacket. Frances sat beside her, calm, but a slight knowingness around her eyes perhaps betraying some awful knowledge of her destiny even then. Lottie laid it on the newly buffed wooden floor. Next was one of Adeline and Julian, laughing at something, followed by Stephen, and some unnamed man she didn't recognise. A charcoal drawing, probably by Frances, of an upturned dinghy. Another, cracked and yellowed where it had been folded, of George, asleep on some grass. They, and the others, were laid out in neat rows on the floor. A painting of her own, of the French house. She had been so heavily pregnant at the time that she had been able to balance her paintbox on her stomach.

Then Lottie. Her eyes looking sideways up from under a sheet of dark hair lightly sprinkled, as if she were some edible delicacy, with rosebuds.

Lottie stared at her young self, feeling an indelible sadness, like a wave, wash over her. She lifted her head and gazed towards the window, blinking back tears, then turned back to the box.

And quickly shut it. Too late to have missed the lithe, strong limbs, the too-long chestnut hair granted a metallic sheen by the sun.

She rested her hands on the lid, listening to the irregular sound of her heartbeat, her gaze averted from the box as if even looking at it could reimprint on her the image she had not wanted to see.

There were no thoughts in her head, just images, as random and snapshot as those in the box.

She sat motionless and silent. Then, like someone emerging from a dream, she placed the box on the floor beside her and stared at the photographs laid out on the wooden floor.

She would give the whole thing to Daisy. Let her do what she wanted with them. After next week she wouldn't be coming back, after all.

Lottie had got used to the population of builders and decorators who popped up without warning in different parts of the house so she barely looked up when the door opened. She had got down on her knees, ready to start picking up the pictures and putting them back in the box.

'Mum?'

Lottie glanced up, to be met by the delighted face of Rollo.

'Hello, love.' She sniffed and wiped her face. 'Just give me a chance to get up, will you?' She leaned forward stiffly, in order to lever herself upright on the arm of the chair.

'What did you think you were doing, Mum?'

Lottie had been about to stand up but instead sat back heavily on her heels. Her daughter's face was rigid, taut with some awful internal effort. 'Camille?'

'The money, Mum. What on earth did you think you were doing?' Camille stepped forward, so that one foot was on two of the photographs. Lottie's protest lodged in her throat – Camille's hand was trembling at the end of her dog lead. 'I've never argued with you, Mum. You know I've always been grateful for everything you've done, with Katie and all. But it's too much now, okay? This money thing – it's too much.'

'I was going to tell you, love.'

Camille's tone was glacial. 'But you didn't. You just steamed right in and tried to organise my life like you always do.'

'That's not—'

'Fair? True? You want to talk about truth? You've spent my whole life telling me I can do anything by myself –

anything that a sighted person could do – and all the while you never believed it. All the while you were just planning safety-nets for me.'

'It's got nothing to do with your sight.'

'The hell it hasn't.'

'Any mother would do the same.'

'No, Mum. No.' Camille stepped forward, leaving Rollo anxiously eyeing the photographs under her feet. 'Any mother might make provision in her will. She might speak to the family. She wouldn't go secretly siphoning off money because she thinks she's the only one who can look after me.'

'Oh, so what if I just want to make sure that you'd be okay, if – if Hal doesn't stick around?'

Camille's frustration exploded. 'Hal *is* around.'

'Just.'

'We're all right, Mum. We're making it work. At least, we were until you stuck your oar in. How do you think this is supposed to make him feel? He thought I was planning on leaving him again, did you know that? He thought I was planning on leaving him, and he nearly left me first.' She breathed out hard. 'God, if you paid half as much attention to your own relationship as you do to everyone else's this family would be so much happier. Why can't you just focus on Pops for a change, huh? Instead of acting like he doesn't bloody exist.'

Lottie's face sank into her hands. When she spoke her voice was muffled. 'I'm sorry,' she said quietly. 'I just want to make sure you were looked after. I just want you to be independent.'

'In case Hal left me. Exactly. Because even though *I* was the one to have the affair, *I* was the one who put our marriage in danger, you still don't trust him to stick around.'

'Why would you think that?'

'Because somewhere, deep inside you, Mum, you don't believe I'm worth sticking around for.'

'No.' Lottie's head shot up.

'You can't believe that anyone would want a blind woman as a partner. That eventually even Hal is going to get fed up.'

'*No.*'

'So how is it, Mum?'

'Camille darling, all I ever wanted for you was a bit of independence.'

'How the hell is you giving me money making me independent?'

'It gives you *freedom.*'

'And what if I don't want freedom? What's so wrong with being married, Mum?'

Lottie looked up directly at her daughter. 'Nothing. Nothing's wrong with being married. As long as you—' She struggled for words. 'As long as you do it for love.'

Daisy sat beside the telephone, conscious of Daniel's brooding presence upstairs. He had not come down for food but sat listening to the radio in his room, telling Daisy politely that he just fancied some time to himself. She suspected he needed a break from it all, from the magnified atmosphere of the house, of the tinderbox of emotions that was their rekindled relationship. She didn't object – she needed a break from it too.

Daisy had never thought of herself as someone for whom work could provide an escape, but she sat working her way through the list of names that Stephen had given her, grateful for the distraction. It was not a very long list. Two dead, one ga-ga, several more unavailable. It was

not going to be quite the reunion she had originally antici-
pated.

George Bern had made his apologies, but had said through
his secretary that he and his wife were already booked that
weekend. The artist Minette Charlerois, a divorcee called
Irene Darling and Stephen had all agreed to come, and
through Minette several other artists of the age who did not
appear on the mural but had apparently visited the house in
its 1950s heyday. She had not told Lottie, having heard her
exclaim that she didn't like parties anyway, so there was only
one person on the mural now unaccounted-for.

Daisy lit a cigarette, swearing to herself that she would
give up after the opening, then choked slightly when, despite
the international connection, the phone was answered more
speedily than she had expected. '*Hola*?' she said, and relaxed
when she heard a British accent. She identified that it was
the right person, and went into her now well-rehearsed spiel
about the celebratory party to mark the new hotel.

The gentleman was very polite. He waited until she'd
finished before he said he was flattered to be remembered,
but didn't think he'd be able to come. 'That – that was a
very small part of my life.'

'But you married someone from Merham, didn't you?' said
Lottie, scanning her notes. 'That makes you an important
part of this . . . We've uncovered this mural, you see, and
you're on it.'

'What?'

'A mural. Painted by Frances Delahaye. You knew her?'

He paused. 'Yes, yes. I remember Frances.'

Daisy pressed her ear closer to the receiver, gesturing into
the air. 'You must see it again. It's been restored and it's
going to be the key feature of the party, and it will be so
wonderful to get all its subjects together again. Please. I'll

send transport and everything. You can bring your wife and children. They'd probably love it too. Hell, bring your grandchildren. We'll pay for them as well.' I'll square it with Jones afterwards, she thought, wincing. 'Go on, Mr Bancroft. It's one day out of your life. One day.'

There was a lengthy silence.

'I'll think about it. But it would just be me, Miss Parsons. My wife, Celia, passed away some time ago.' He paused, cleared his throat quietly. 'And we never had children.'

Nineteen

On the seventh day before the opening of Arcadia House as an hotel, Camille and Hal took the decision to put their house on the market. It was a big house, they told each other, too big for a family of three, and they were unlikely to have more children ('Although it wouldn't be a disaster', said Hal, squeezing his wife). They began looking for somewhere smaller, close to Katie's school, but perhaps with workshops or a double garage so that while Hal took on another job, he could still pursue his restoration business until the economic climate meant he could try again. They made an appointment with an estate agent, tacitly avoiding that which employed Michael Bryant. They told Katie she would be allowed to choose all the furnishings for her new room, and that, yes, of course, there would still be room for Rollo. Then they instructed the bank to close the account opened by Lottie, and return the money to her.

Lottie rang twice. Both times Camille allowed the answerphone to pick up the message.

On the sixth day before the opening of Arcadia the planning people from the Department of National Heritage came to review the building's emergency listing. Jones, who had been warned of this, arrived with his lawyer and an application for a Certificate of Immunity from Listing, which, he said, had been sent off to the Secretary of State during the purchasing process, and which he had been assured by his best sources would go through, thereby protecting them from the financial damage caused by an emergency listing. Despite that, the lawyer said, they were happy for the Department of National Heritage to take a close look at the work that had taken place, to work out a possible time-scale for any reparations, and to speak at length to Daisy, who had in her possession all the relevant information and documentation relating both to the restoration and the condition of the building before it had been accomplished.

Daisy had hardly heard any of this, let alone understood it, as she had been staring at Jones. He had spoken to her only twice, once to greet her and once to say goodbye. On neither occasion did he meet her eye.

On the fifth day before the opening, Camille walked to her parents' house at a time when she knew her mother would be out, and found her father thumbing through holiday brochures. She had gone nervously, afraid that her mother might have repeated to him the awful thing she'd said to her about their marriage, but her father had been unusually chipper. He was thinking of going to Kota Kinabalu, he said, reading out the travel-guide description of the area to her. No, he had no idea where it was, other than in the East. He just liked the sound of it. Liked the thought of coming home and saying, 'I've just been to Kota Kinabalu.' 'That'd shut them up at the golf club, eh?' he said. 'Bit more exciting than Romney Marsh.' Camille, surprised, had asked whether her mother was planning to go too. 'Still working on her, love,' he'd said. 'You know your mother.'

On an impulse she had hugged him so hard that he'd patted her hair and asked her what that was all about. 'Nothing,' she'd said. 'I just love you, Pops.'

'The sooner this hotel opens the better,' he had replied. 'Seems to me like everyone's getting worked up over nothing, these days.'

439

On the fourth day before the opening Stephen Meeker arrived on Arcadia's broad white doorstep, fanning himself under a straw hat, and announced he'd taken the liberty of speaking to a friend of his from Cork Street who was extremely interested in their mural. He was wondering whether he might come along to the opening, and perhaps bring another friend from the *Daily Telegraph* who specialised in stories about fine art. Daisy had said yes, and invited him in to see it privately before the big day. Stephen had stared at it for some time, at his younger self, and at Julian. He had remarked that it looked quite different from how he remembered it. Then he had placed a bony hand on Daisy's arm as he left, and instructed her never to do the things she felt she ought. 'Do what you really want,' he said. 'That way you won't have any regrets. Because by the time you get to my age, my God, you're weighed down by the bloody things.'

Three days before the opening, Carol had arrived with Jones to run through the checklist of celebrity guests, check the status of the kitchens, car parking, facilities for the musicians, and exclaim on the brilliance of just about everything, in a manner that left Daisy scrambling to complete her instructions. Jones had told her he was pleased, but in a manner that left her unsure if he really was, had lined up the new bar and kitchen staff and given them a brief, half-hearted speech, interviewed three cleaners, then left so swiftly that Carol had commented that he was a miserable bugger, bless him. Julia had rung shortly afterwards, to say that she and Don would be coming to the party, and did Daisy want her to bring her something to wear? She didn't imagine there was much to choose from in that little town. In *Essex*, Daisy thought, hearing the italicised subtext. No, she said. She could sort herself out, thanks.

'Is he coming back for it? The opening?' Julia asked, before ringing off.

'He hasn't gone anywhere,' said Daisy, exasperated.

'Yet,' said Julia.

Two days before the opening, the local newspaper ran a story about the mural, with a snatched photograph that Daisy suspected owed something to one of the builders. Lottie, who had been tense and snappy all week, had blamed Sylvia Rowan and had taken some persuading not to go down there and confront the other woman herself. 'What does it matter?' said Daisy, sitting her down on the terrace with a cup of tea, and trying to sound calmer than she felt. 'It's only the local rag.'

'That's not the point,' said Lottie, crossly. 'I just don't like it being broadcast everywhere. I don't like the painting being looked at by everyone. People knowing it was me.' Daisy had decided not to say anything about the man from the *Daily Telegraph*.

In Merham itself, according to local intelligence, the local Temperance Society, along with the Landladies Association and the remaining members of the Seventh-day Adventist Church were preparing to picket the opening of the hotel, egged on by several reporters and a cameraman from the regional television news. Daisy had tried to ring Jones's office, to warn him, but his secretary had passed her on to Carol. 'Oh, don't worry about them,' she had said, dismissively. 'We'll invite them in for a drink and a photograph, bless them. Always works – disarm them with a bit of charm. Failing that, we'll shove them behind the hedge.'

When Daisy had walked into town with Ellie, later that afternoon, a group of elderly women had stopped their conversation and stared at her as she passed, as if she were carrying something unpleasant on her shoes. When she had

441

walked into the newsagent's, the owner had come round the counter to shake her hand. 'Good on you,' he said, glancing around, as if they might be overheard. 'Business breeds business. That's what these people don't understand. Once you're up and running they'll forget about it. They've just spent so many years opposing everything they don't know how to do anything else.'

The day before the opening, after the builders and kitchen staff had gone, after Jones had left with Carol in her ridiculous sports car, and Daisy had taken Ellie up for her bath, Lottie had stayed on. Then, when the house was silent, she had taken a tour of every single room. A more sentimental person might have said she was saying goodbye. Lottie told herself she was simply checking that all things were as they should be. Daisy had her hands full with the baby, the opening and that useless man of hers, after all, and Jones didn't seem to know whether he was coming or going, so someone had to keep an eye on things. She said it twice, as if that would make it more convincing.

She had walked into and around each room, remembering them as they had been, prompted by the group photographs now framed and on the walls, which occasionally she allowed herself to view. The faces, frozen in time, looked back at her with the glassy smiles of strangers; hardly real people any more, she told herself. Just so much interior decoration, there to add an air of authenticity to some rich man's seaside playground.

She left the drawing room until last, her footsteps echoing on the relaid floor. She seated herself in the same position from which, nearly half a century previously, she had first laid eyes on Adeline, poised and feline on the sofa. The house, stark, white and grand, no longer felt like Arcadia, its rooms no longer silent witnesses to her secrets. Its wax polishes and freshly cut flowers stifled the old scents of salt and possibility. Its gleaming kitchen units, pristine upholstery and pale, perfect walls had somehow missed the point, had smothered the spirit of the place.

Still, who am I to say anything? Lottie thought, gazing around her. There was always too much pain here, anyway. Too many secrets. Its future belongs with other people now. She stared around the room, her gaze landing on the photograph of Celia in her flame red skirt, which now tastefully matched the upholstery. She remembered too-knowing eyes meeting hers mischievously from the chair opposite, slender feet always placed as if for flight. My history, like the photographs, thought Lottie. Just so much interior decoration.

Several minutes later, Daisy had emerged from the bathroom with a towel-wrapped Ellie, and headed for the kitchens to warm her milk. She stopped half-way down the stairs, glanced into the drawing room, then turned slowly and walked back up again, shushing Ellie's protest.

Lottie had sat below her, staring into space, lost deep in some internal reverie. She looked diminished, somehow, frail, and very alone.

The evening before the opening, Jones covered the precarious towers of paper on his desk, closed the door of his office against the raucous laughter of the Red Rooms bars, drank the dregs of a cup of coffee, then fished out and rang the work number of his ex-wife. Alex had sounded surprised to hear from him, assuming, perhaps, as he had, that once she had married the intimate nature of their friendship would change.

He let her talk about their honeymoon, she tactfully

restricting it to the beauty of their island setting, her sunburn, the unimaginable colour of the sea. She gave him her new numbers, knowing that he was unlikely ever to ring her new home. Then she asked him if he was all right.

'Yeah. Fine . . . No, no, I'm not.'

'Anything I can help with?'

'It's a bit . . . complicated.'

She waited.

'I don't know if you're the best person to discuss it with.'

There was caution in her 'Oh?'

'Ah, you know me, Alex. Never been much good at expressing myself.'

'That's for sure.'

'Oh . . . look . . . forget it.'

'Come on, Jones. Now you've started.'

He sighed. 'I just . . . I think I've become attached to someone. Who was single but now isn't.'

There was silence at the other end of the telephone.

'I never said anything. When I should have done. And I don't know what to do about it.'

'She was single?'

'Well, yes. And no. I think I've realised what I feel about her, but I don't feel I can make a move now. It's too late.'

'Too late?'

'Well, I don't know. Do you think it is? Do you think it's fair to say something? In the circumstances?'

Another lengthy silence.

'Alex?'

'Jones – I don't know what to say.'

'I'm sorry. I shouldn't have called you.'

'No, no. It's good that we talk about these things. But . . . I'm married now.'

444

'I know that.'

'And I don't think you having feelings for me is . . . well, appropriate. You know how Nigel feels about—'

'What?'

'I'm flattered. Honestly. But—'

'No, no, Alex. I'm not talking about you. Oh, Christ, what have I said?'

This time the silence was embarrassed.

'Al. I'm sorry. I'm not expressing myself very well. As usual.'

Her laughter was speedy and deliberately light. 'Oh, don't worry, Jones. I'm relieved. I just got the wrong end of the stick.' She spoke like a primary-school teacher, firmly and brightly. 'So, who's this latest girl, then?'

'Well, that's the thing. She's not like the others.'

'In what way? Blonde, for a change? From somewhere exotic? Over the age of twenty?'

'No. Someone I've been working with. She's a designer.'

'Makes a change from the waitresses, I suppose.'

'And I think she likes me.'

'You think? You've not slept with her?'

'It's just that the father of her kid has come back on the scene.'

A brief pause.

'Her kid?'

'Yeah, she's got a baby.'

'She's got a baby? You're in love with someone with a baby?'

'I didn't say I was in love. And you don't have to sound like that.'

'After everything you said to me about kids? How do you expect me to sound, Jones?'

He leaned backwards on his chair.

'I don't believe this.' The voice at the other end was sharp, exasperated.

'Alex. I'm sorry. I didn't mean to upset you.'

'You haven't upset me. I'm married now. I'm far beyond you upsetting me. *So* far beyond that.'

'I just wanted some advice, and you're the one person I know—'

'No, Jones, you wanted someone to make you feel better about the fact that you're in love for the first time, and with the wrong person. Well, I'm not that person any more. It's not fair to ask me. Okay? Now I've got to go. I've got a meeting.'

On the day of the opening Daisy woke at an hour more normally associated with sleep and lay in her bed, watching the dawn filter through the hand-sewn linen curtains. At seven, she got up, walked into her bathroom and cried for approximately ten minutes, taking care not to wake her baby by burying her sobs in an Egyptian cotton hand towel. Then she splashed cold water on her face, put on her dressing-gown, picked up the baby monitor and padded next door to Daniel's room.

The room was dark and silent. He was asleep, a musty-smelling mound under the duvet. 'Dan?' she whispered. 'Daniel?'

He woke with a start, turning to face her, his eyes half closed. He pushed himself partially upright and, perhaps from old habit, flipped back the duvet to invite her in. The unconsciousness of the gesture made Daisy's throat constrict. 'We need to talk,' she said.

He rubbed at his eyes. 'Now?'

'There isn't going to be another time. I have to pack up today. We have to pack up.'

He gazed into the middle distance for a minute. 'Can I get a coffee first?' he said, his voice thick with sleep.

She nodded, looking away almost shyly as he climbed out of bed and into a pair of boxer shorts, the sight and smells of him as familiar and strange as a part of one's own body seen from an unfamiliar angle.

He made her a coffee too, passing it to her as she seated herself on the sofa, his hair sticking upwards and outwards like a small boy's. Daisy watched him, her stomach churning, her words like bile in her mouth.

At last, he sat.

Looked at her.

'It's not going to work, Dan,' she said.

At some point she remembered him putting his arms around her, and her thinking how bizarre it was that he should be comforting her when she was telling him she no longer loved him. He had kissed the top of her head too, the scent of him, the feel of him still perversely consoling.

'I'm sorry,' she had said, into his chest.

'This is about me kissing that girl, isn't it?'

'No.'

'It is. I knew I shouldn't have told you. I should have left it behind. I was trying to be honest.'

'It's not the girl. Really.'

'I still love you, Daise.'

Daisy looked up. 'I know. I still love you. But I'm not in love with you.'

'It's too soon to make this decision.'

'No, Dan, it's not. I think I made it even before you came back. Look, I've tried to persuade myself that it's all still there, that it's worth rescuing – because of Ellie. But it's not. It's just not there.'

He let go of her hands then, and pulled back, recognising

some unfamiliar steel in her voice, something irreversible. 'We've been together so long. We've got a child together. You can't just throw all that away.' His voice was almost pleading.

Daisy shook her head. 'It's not throwing it all away. But we can't go back to what we were. I'm different. I'm a different person—'

'But I love that person.'

'I don't want it any more, Daniel.' Daisy's voice was firmer now. 'I don't want to go back to how we were, to how I was. I've done things I never thought I could. I'm stronger. I need someone . . .'

'Stronger?'

'Someone I can rely on. Someone who I know isn't going to disappear when it all gets rough again. That's if I need anyone at all.'

Daniel threw his head into his hands. 'Daisy, I've said I'm sorry. It was one mistake. One mistake. And I'm doing everything I can to make it right.'

'I know you are. But I can't help how I feel. And I'd be looking at you all the time, trying to second-guess you, trying to work out whether you were going to go again.'

'That's not fair.'

'But it's how I feel. Look . . . maybe if Ellie hadn't come along this would have happened anyway. Maybe we would have become different people anyway. I don't know. I just think it's time for both of us to let go.'

There was a lengthy silence. Outside, the sound of car doors slamming and brisk footsteps downstairs heralded the beginning of the working day. The baby monitor let out a low moan, the acoustic warning of Ellie's awakening.

'I'm not leaving her again.' Daniel looked at her, and his voice held a faint note of challenge.

'I'm not expecting you to.'

'I'll want access. I want to be her dad.'

The prospect of a lifetime spent handing over her precious child at weekends had haunted Daisy, the mere thought of it already enough to move her to tears. It had been the one thing that had nearly saved him from this conversation.

'I know you do, Dan. We'll set something up.'

The morning was hot, the air carrying that kind of stillness which is almost a threat, muffling the sound of the kitchen staff as they began their preparatory work, and the cleaners as they waxed and Hoovered the downstairs rooms. Daisy ran backwards and forwards under the whirring fans, tweaking furniture arrangements, supervising the polishing of taps and handles, her limp shirt and shorts heralding a heat that would become fiercer as the day went on. She continued working her way through the last-minute changes, trying to sublimate her mind to work, trying not to think.

Vans came and disgorged their contents on to the drive, disappeared again in a crunch of gear changes and sprays of gravel, arrangements of cut flowers, food, alcohol ferried in and out under the blinding sun, while Carol, her party dress hanging in readiness in the Bell Suite, directed operations; a designer-clad dictator, her throaty voice wheedling, instructing and blessing in equal measures as it echoed around the grounds.

Lottie had arrived to fetch Ellie at nine. She was not coming to the party ('Can't stand them') and had offered to take the baby home with her. 'But Camille's coming, with Hal and Katie. And Mr Bernard,' said Daisy. 'Ellie would be quite happy with you here. Go on. You've done so much here.'

Lottie had shaken her head mutely. She had looked pale,

her usual bite subdued by some unspoken internal struggle. 'Good luck, Daisy,' she said, and her eyes had met Daisy's with a rare intensity, as if there were more to it than several hours apart.

'There's always a drink for you . . . You can change your mind,' Daisy had called. The figure propelling the push-chair resolutely down the drive did not turn.

She had watched her until they both disappeared, one hand shielding her eyes from the sun, trying to persuade herself that, given Lottie's decidedly ambivalent reaction to the mural, her acid responses to everything else, perhaps it was a good thing she wasn't coming, after all.

Daniel walked upstairs, away from the relentless noise and activity, which conspired to make him feel like even more of a spare part, and into the room that held his things. He had decided not to stay for the party; even if it had been possible for him to spend time around Daisy today, it would be too complicated, too humiliating, to explain his presence to those people he had once thought of as contacts. He needed to be alone; to grieve, to think about what had happened, and what he was going to do next. And possibly, once he got home, to get very, very drunk.

He walked along the corridor, dialling his brother's number on his mobile phone, leaving a message on his answerphone to tell him to expect him that evening. He stopped in the doorway, mid-sentence. Aidan was standing on a step-ladder in the middle of the room, his hands fixed on a fan above his head.

'Hi there,' he said, one hand reaching down for a screw-driver on his belt.

Daniel nodded a greeting. He was well used to the lack of privacy imposed by living in a work in progress, but just at this moment it didn't make Aidan's presence any easier to bear. He picked up his holdall, and began to collect up his clothes, fold them and thrust them deep inside.

'You couldn't do me a favour, could you? Just flick that switch there? Not yet – just when I tell you.' Aidan was balanced precariously, easing a fitting back into place. 'Now.'

Daniel gritted his teeth, crossed the room, flicked the switch on the wall, and the fan eased itself into a blur, audibly cooling the room with a soft hum.

'Your woman there said it was making a noise. Seems okay to me.'

'She's not my woman.' He had not brought a lot of stuff. It was almost pathetic the length of time it took to pack it.

'Youse two had a row?'

'No,' said Daniel, more calmly than he felt. 'We've split up. I'm leaving.'

Aidan wiped his hands together and stood down from the ladder. 'Well, now, I'm sorry about that, you being the babby's father and all.'

Daniel shrugged.

'And you'd only just got back together, hadn't you?'

Daniel was already regretting saying anything. He bent down and scanned the space under the bed for stray socks.

'Still,' came Aidan's voice from above, 'can't say as I blame you.'

'Sorry?' It was hard to hear him under the coverlet.

'Well, no man wants to think of another man staying nights, does he? Not even if he is the boss, know what I mean? No, I'd say you did the right thing altogether.'

Daniel stayed very still, his ear remained pressed to the floor. He blinked, several times, and then he stood up. 'I'm sorry,' he said, and his voice was viciously polite. 'Can you repeat what you just said?'

Aidan took a step down the ladder, looked at Daniel's expression and glanced sideways. 'The boss. Staying with Daisy there. I mean, I assumed you . . . that that's what you . . . Ah, hell. Forget I said anything altogether.'

'Jones? Jones was staying with Daisy? Here?'

'It was probably my misunderstanding of the situation.'

Daniel looked at Aidan's awkward expression, and smiled, a tight, understanding smile. 'No doubt,' he said, hauling his bag to him and pushing past. 'Excuse me.'

No matter how smart the occasion, it usually took Camille a matter of minutes to dress. She would feel her way through her wardrobe, her touch acutely attuned to which fabrics denoted which clothes, pull out the chosen item and, with a quick brush of her hair and a slick of lipstick, she would be ready. It was almost indecent, Kay would say, a beautician like herself taking so little time. Gave them all a bad name.

Today, however, they were almost forty minutes in and so late that Hal was pacing the floor in their bedroom. 'Let me do something,' he would say periodically.

'No,' Camille would snap.

And, with a sigh as loud and heartfelt as one of Rollo's, he would begin pacing again.

Part of it was Katie, who had insisted on helping choose her mother's outfit, and who, to Camille's thinly disguised annoyance, had piled up so many clothes on their double bed that it was hard for Camille, whose cupboards were militarily ordered, to tell what was what. Part of it was her hair, which had, for some reason, decided to stick up around her hairline. But most of it was because she knew her mother was likely to be there, and her indecision over whether she wanted to see her was making her fractious and unable to take even the most mundane decision.

'Shall I get your shoes out, Mummy?' said Katie, and Camille could hear the sound of her shoeboxes, all carefully labelled in braille, collapsing into a disorganised heap.

'No, sweetheart. Not until I've sorted out what to wear.'

'Come on, love. Let me help.'

'No, Daddy, Mummy wanted *me*.'

'Oh, I don't want bloody either of you!' shouted Camille. 'I don't even want to go to the stupid thing.'

Hal had sat down with her then, and pulled her to him. And somehow the fact that, even after all this, her husband still had the ability not just to understand but to forgive her made Camille feel the tiniest bit better.

They had left shortly after two p.m., Camille suspecting that Katie had her done up like a dog's dinner, but trusting that Hal wouldn't let her go out in anything too outrageous. They had decided to walk to Arcadia, Hal reasoning that the drive was likely to be blocked in with visitors' cars, and that even in summer one should enjoy a day like this. Camille wasn't so sure. As Katie's hand sweated into one of her hands, Camille slid the other onto Rollo's harness to help her negotiate any crowds.

'I should have put sun-cream on Katie,' she said aloud.

'Already did it,' said Hal.

'I don't know if I locked the back door,' she said, some time later.

'Katie did it.'

Half-way across the park, Camille stopped. 'Hal, I'm not sure I'm in the mood for this. It's just going to be loads of people making small-talk and I think this heat is going to give me a headache. And poor old Rollo's going to boil.'

Hal took hold of his wife's shoulders. He spoke quietly so that Katie wouldn't hear. 'She probably won't even come,' he said. 'Your dad told me she thought she wouldn't bother.

You know what she's like. Come on. Besides, Daisy will probably be leaving straight after, and you want to say goodbye, don't you?'

'The things she said about Dad, Hal . . .' Camille's voice wobbled with the emotion of it. 'I knew it wasn't exactly a match made in heaven, but how could she say she never loved him? How could she do that to him?'

Hal took her hand and squeezed it, a gesture that spoke of comfort, and a certain futility. They walked on, Katie skipping in front, towards the house.

Daisy stood outside the kitchen in the midst of the group of elderly men and women, smiling as the fourth photographer catcalled them into some new arrangement, whispering under her breath to some of the more frail among them to find out whether they were bearing up, whether they might want a drink, or something to rest on. Around them white-clad sous-chefs rushed about clattering plates and metallic pans, arranging savoury confections on oversized platters. Julia caught her eye across the crowd of people and waved, and Daisy smiled back, wishing it felt like less of an effort. It was going well; really well. The woman from *Interiors* had already translated the house into a four-page spread, with Daisy featuring prominently as its designer; several people had asked for her number, and she wished she had thought to make up cards. She had been so busy that she had barely had time to think about Daniel, other than being conscious of a fleeting gratitude that he had not decided to stay. She saw Jones periodically in glimpses across the overcrowded rooms, always talking, always surrounded by people. The host, in a set of rooms he hardly knew.

But Daisy felt miserable. This was always the hardest bit of a job. The vision you had striven to create, for which you had lost nights of sleep, had worked on with dust in your hair and your fingernails caked with paint. It had finally come together, coloured with pain and draped with exhaustion. And then, when it was perfect, you relinquished it. Except this time it was harder to let it go. This time it had been Daisy's home, her refuge in her daughter's first months. There were people she had made her own, and whom, despite best promises, she would probably never see again.

And where was she leaving it for? Weybridge.

Across the terrace, Julia's smile beamed out at her from under her perfectly frozen hair; proud, well-meaning, mis-understanding everything Daisy now knew she was. I thought I had made it, she thought, in a burst of clarity. In fact, I have nothing. When she had arrived at Merham, she had had a home, a job, her daughter. Now she faced the loss of them all – even if only part of the latter.

'Cheer up, darling.' Carol appeared at her elbow, perennial champagne bottle in hand, topping up, posing for photo-graphs, exclaiming at how perfect everything was, laughing off the chanting villagers outside on the drive. She had sent a tray of drinks out to them, and made sure the newspapers had seen her do it. 'Why don't you head off to the ladies'? Perk yourself up a bit. I'll handle things out here.' Her smile was kind, her tone unarguable.

Daisy had nodded, and fought her way through the chattering groups towards the lavatories. She had passed Jones as he talked, so close she could smell the mints on his breath. Her head was down, so she couldn't be sure, but she thought he hadn't even noticed.

He hadn't expected to enjoy himself but, Hal told Camille repeatedly, he was. Endless people had sought him out to congratulate him on the mural, including the elderly Stephen

455

Meeker, who had asked him to visit later in the week and take a look at a couple of Arts and Crafts chairs that needed some work. Jones had told him there would be a bonus on top of his cheque. 'It's made all the difference,' he said, his dark eyes serious. 'We'll have a talk later about some other work I might have for you.' He had met a number of local businessmen, cannily invited by Carol, who didn't seem to care much about the mural, but thought the new hotel was 'just the job'. It would attract, they said, the 'right sort of people to the town'. Hal, thinking back to Sylvia Rowan's comments, had fought the urge to laugh. Camille, he told her, looked beautiful. He kept catching sight of her talking to people, her hair luminous under the sun, her face relaxed and happy, and his heart would constrict, sentimental and foolish with gratitude that they had survived. Katie, meanwhile, darted fleetingly in and out of the house with other children, like brightly coloured sparrows in and out of hedgerows.

'Thanks,' he had said, catching Daisy as she exited the ladies'. 'For the work, I mean. For everything.' She had nodded her response as if only half aware of him, her eyes apparently casting the room for something, or some-one else.

It was a big day for her, he told himself, turning away. The kind of day on which it would be churlish to take offence. If he had learned one thing, it was not to look for meanings where there were none.

He accepted two glasses of champagne from a waiter and stepped back into the sunshine, his heart lifting at the sound of the jazz string quartet, feeling his first real sense of ease and satisfaction for months. Katie ran past him, squealing, a quick tug on his trouser leg, and he walked on, to relocate his wife on the terrace.

He was halted by a light tap on his shoulder.

'Hal.'

He turned to see his mother-in-law, standing very still behind a push-chair. She was wearing her good grey silk blouse, her one concession to party-going. Her eyes, wide and unusually wary, bored into his almost as if she were going to accuse him of something. 'Lottie,' he said, neutrally, his sunny mood evaporating.

'I'm not stopping.'

He waited.

'I just came to say sorry.'

She didn't look herself. As if she had somehow lost her armour. 'I shouldn't have gone on at you the way I did. And I should have told you about the money.'

'Forget it,' he said. 'It doesn't matter.'

'It does matter. I was wrong. I meant well, but I was wrong. I wanted you to know that.' Her voice was tight, and strained. 'You and Camille.'

Hal, who had – especially on recent occasions – felt less than charitable towards his mother-in-law, suddenly found himself wishing for some waspish comment from her, some sharp observation to break the silence. But she said nothing, her eyes on his, searching for a response.

'Come on,' he said, moving towards her, his arm outstretched. 'Let's find her.'

Lottie placed a restraining hand on his arm. 'I said some awful things,' she said, swallowing.

'Everyone does,' he said, 'when they're hurting.'

She looked at him, and some new understanding appeared to pass between them. Then she took his proffered elbow and they walked across the terrace.

He had been so preoccupied that he hadn't even noticed she was there. Carol looked up at him, a sly, knowing glance from under her razor-sharp fringe, and smiled her professional smile out at the sea of people before them.

'I don't know what's holding you back,' she murmured.

Jones tore his glance from across the terrace, and blinked hard.

'What?'

'You both look as miserable as sin. She seems like a bright girl, bless her. What's your problem?'

Jones sighed heavily. Stared at his empty glass. 'I don't want to break up a family.'

'Is there a family?'

The barman was trying to attract his attention, trying to gauge whether they should start topping up champagne glasses for his speech. Jones wiped his brow, nodded at him, then turned back to the woman beside him. 'I'm not going to do it, Carol. I've gone in feet first every time. Left everyone else to pick up the pieces. But I'm not going to do it this time.'

'Lost your nerve?'

'Gained a conscience.'

'Jones as knight in shining armour. Now I know you're done for.'

Jones took a glass off the tray in front of him and put down the empty one. 'Yeah. Guess I am.' He turned towards his guests, motioning to the band to lower the volume. And muttered, so low that even Carol had to struggle to hear him, 'Feels like it, anyway.'

Daniel sat on the steps behind the kitchen, his body half hidden by the towers of crates, and placed his empty glass on the pile of others on the shaded grass beside him. Overhead, the sun had started its slow, peaceful descent into the west, but behind him the kitchen clattered and hummed over the sound of the music, the occasional expletive and shouted instruction testament to the frantic level of activity inside. He knew they thought he was odd, sitting out here by himself all afternoon, not that any of them had the balls to say anything to his face. He couldn't give a toss.

He just sat, occasionally catching sight of Jones on the terrace as he wandered past the gate, glad-handing, nodding, that stupid fake smile plastered on his face. He sat, waited for the waiter to emerge with another drink, and thought back.

Joe was standing outside with Camille and Katie, a broad-brimmed hat covering his head. He had told Jones, Daisy, Camille and several other people that it was, indeed, a 'very nice do', and that he didn't think anyone had ever seen the old house looking so fine. He seemed much more enthusiastic about it now that he knew its influence over his family was ending.

'Tell that to Sylvia Rowan's lot,' said Camille, who was still unsettled by the chanting on the other side of the wall.

'Some people just don't know when to let bygones be bygones, eh, love?' Joe said, and Camille, acutely tuned to the nuances in people's tone, thought she detected something in his. This was confirmed when Hal returned, placed his hand under her elbow, and told her, gently, that her mother was here. 'You never said,' she accused her father.

'Your mother has told me what she did with the money,' said Joe. 'We've all agreed it was a mistake. But you have to understand she meant well.'

'But that's not half of it, Pops,' said Camille, realising as she spoke that she didn't want to have to tell him what the other half was.

'Please, Camille, love. I've apologised to Hal, and I'd like to apologise to you, too.' Camille heard the pain in her mother's voice, and wished, like a child, that she could unhear the things she had heard. 'Will you at least talk to me?'

'Love?' Hal's tone was gentle, insistent. 'Lottie's really sorry. About everything.'

'Go on, Camille,' said her father. A tone she remembered from her childhood. 'Your mother's been big enough to apologise. The least you can do is have the grace to hear her out.'

Camille suspected she had been outmanoeuvred. Her head was filled with the sound of chanting, with the chatter and clink of partying guests. 'Walk me through these people to the house. We'll find somewhere quiet. First I need to get Rollo a bowl of water.'

Her mother, unusually, did not take her elbow. Instead, Camille felt her cool, dry hand slide into her own, as if she herself were seeking reassurance. Saddened by this gesture, Camille squeezed it in response.

Rollo moved forward under the harness as he tried to determine the most obstacle-free path through the moving throng of people. Camille felt his anxiety travel up the harness, and called softly to him, trying to reassure him. He didn't like parties, a little like Lottie. She closed her hands, aware that in some way she was having to reassure both. 'Head for the kitchen,' she told her mother.

Almost half-way across the terrace – it was hard to judge, with all these people – Camille was halted by a hand on her arm. A floral scent: Daisy.

'I'm so hot I think I'm going to melt. I've had to send Ellie indoors with the bar staff.'

'I'll pick her up in a moment,' said Lottie, a little defensively. 'I just wanted a word with Camille.'

'Sure, sure,' said Daisy, who didn't appear to be listening. 'Can I just borrow you for five minutes, Lottie?

There's someone I want you to meet.' Camille felt them all moving forward. Daisy's voice dipped diplomatically, so that Camille had to strain to make out what she said. 'He says he's a widower and he's got no children, and I think he's feeling a bit lonely. I don't think he's really enjoying himself.'

'What makes you think I'll be any good at talking to him?' Her mother, Camille knew, wanted them to be alone.

'Have you all got glasses?' A low woman's voice. Someone Camille didn't recognise. 'Jones is going to do his speech in a minute.'

'He's one of the mural people,' said Daisy. 'I don't know, Lottie. I thought you might know each other.'

Camille, who had been about to protest that Rollo really needed his drink, felt her mother stop abruptly in her tracks and a tiny, almost inaudible sound escape from the back of her throat. Her hand, in Camille's, began to shake, first tremulously, and then uncontrollably, so that Camille, shocked, dropped Rollo's harness to take it with both of her own. 'Mum?'

There was no reply.

Camille, feeling panicked, her mother's hand still shaking in her own, turned round. 'Mum? . . . Mum? . . . Daisy? What's happening?'

She heard Daisy lean across her, an urgent whisper. Was Lottie all right?

Still nothing.

Camille heard the sound of footsteps approaching slowly. Her mother's hand was shaking so hard.

'Mum?'

'Lottie?' A man's voice, elderly.

Her voice, when it came, was a bewildered whisper: '*Guy?*'

★　　★　　★

461

Katie had spilt orange juice all over her dress. Hal was stooping, trying to wipe it off with a paper napkin, telling her, as he had done a thousand times, that it was time she calmed down, took things a little more slowly, remembered she was in company, when some strange change in the atmosphere drew his attention to the far side of the terrace. It wasn't the tiny grey cloud that had managed, in an endless blue sky, to direct its path over the sun, casting the proceedings into a temporary shade. It wasn't the hubbub of conversation, gradually ebbing as Jones stood and prepared to make his speech. Several feet from the mural, with an uncertain Camille clutching at her arm, Lottie was standing directly in front of an elderly man. They were just staring at each other, not speaking, their faces brimful of some emotion. Hal, perplexed by the tableau, stared at the unfamiliar old man, at Camille beside him, unconsciously echoing his stiff-legged stance, then, as if for the first time, at the stubby features of his father-in-law, who was watching, grey-faced and silent, from the doorway of the drawing room, two drinks motionless in his hands.

And then he saw it.

And for the first time in his life, Hal thanked God his wife could not see. And understood that for all the counselling and relationship-guidance guidelines in all the world, for all the saved couples and restored marriages, there were some times in a life when keeping a secret from one's spouse was the right thing to do.

She had watched the two old people as they walked unobtrusively down the stone steps towards the beach. Barely touching, both as self-consciously erect as if they were waiting for some blow to fall, they walked cautiously and in perfect time, like veteran soldiers reunited after a long war. But as she turned, about to try to convey to Camille something of what she'd seen, something of the expressions on their faces, Hal had whisked her away, and Carol had thrust a glass into her hand. 'Stay put, darling,' she commanded. 'Jones is no doubt going to give you a name-check, bless him.'

And then Daisy had briefly forgotten them, had found her attention drawn to him, to his weatherbeaten face, to his oversized frame, which always made her think of one of those Russian bears, forced, against their will, to entertain. And listening to his commanding voice echo out across the early evening, the trace of the valleys offsetting the gruffness with a melodic lilt, Daisy was overcome by a sudden fear that she had discovered too late what she wanted. That she could no longer protect herself against it. That no matter how inappropriate, how hazardous, how ill-timed, she would rather he was her mistake than someone else's.

She watched him gesturing towards the house, heard the polite laughter, heard the people on each side of her, smiling, wanting to approve, ready to admire. She stared at the house, at the building she knew better than her own self, and the view beyond it, the brilliant arc of blue. She heard her name mentioned, and a polite spattering of applause. And then, finally, her eyes met his and, in that split second, as the cloud moved off the sun and re-flooded the space with light, she tried to convey to him every single thing she had learned, everything she knew.

And then, as it finished, and the people turned away, back to their drinks, back to their broken conversation, she watched him step down from the stone wall and make slowly towards her, his eyes still on hers, as if in acknowledgement. And stopped, in horror, as Daniel launched himself out from behind the privet hedge and, without warning but with a terrible, strangulated war cry, punched Jones fully in the face.

Twenty

The noise of the radio filtered downward, permeating the bedroom door, floating down the stairs to where Camille and Hal stood, facing each other with indecision on their faces, the third time in as many hours that they had done so.

He had been there all evening since returning home straight-shouldered and silent, accompanied by their feeble and muted enquiries as to whether he was all right, and harder, unspoken ones about what they had just seen. He had said he didn't want any tea, thank you. Nor did he need any company. He was going upstairs to listen to the radio. Sorry if he sounded inhospitable, but there it was. They were welcome to stay downstairs, if that was what they really wanted. Help themselves, of course.

And that had been it, for the best part of three hours, during which they conversed in whispers, fielded questions from Katie, who, exhausted, was lying in front of the television with Rollo, and tried repeatedly and unsuccessfully to track down his wife.

'Is she going to leave him, Hal? Do you think that's what it is? Is she going to leave Pops?'

The relaxed, sun-filled aspect of Camille's face had vanished, to be replaced by a dark anxiety. And, somewhere in there, anger. Hal smoothed back her hair from her hot forehead, glanced up the stairs. 'I don't know, love.'

He had told her most of what he knew, holding both her hands, like someone breaking bad news. That the man had looked like an older version of the one in the mural; that the briefest measure of the way they had looked at each other had dispelled any lingering uncertainties he might have had about what that meant. He had struggled to convey the way the old man had reached out and touched Lottie's face, the way she had not ducked away from the contact, but had stood like someone waiting to be blessed. Camille had listened, and wept, and made him describe the mural to her again and again, dissecting it for symbolism, slowly building a picture of why her mother's behaviour, far from being inexplicable, was something they could have, perhaps should have, understood long ago.

Several times, Hal had cursed himself for the role he had unwittingly played in uncovering Lottie's history, in bringing it back to life. 'I should have left that painting as it was,' he said. 'If I hadn't brought this whole thing back into the open, perhaps she wouldn't have gone.'

Camille's response had been resigned, an unwilling acknowledgement. 'She's been gone for years.'

At half past nine, when the dusky sky had abdicated to an inky black, when Katie had fallen asleep on the sofa, when they had called everyone they knew, when they had tried Daisy's mobile number for the seventeenth time – and considered, and decided against, calling the police – Camille had turned to her husband, her sightless eyes filled with a bitter zeal.

'Go and find her, Hal. She's done everything else to him. She at least owes him the decency of letting him know.'

Daisy waited for several minutes for the machine to spit out her change, and then, conscious of the bored gazes of those around her, gave up and carried the two plastic cups of coffee over to Jones.

They had been in A and E for almost three hours now; their speedy admission to a triage nurse had falsely raised their hopes that they might be seen, bandaged, and leave. 'No,' said the nurse, pointing them towards X-ray. They would need to get a picture of it first, as well as his head, then Jones would have to wait for the consultant to realign it. 'We'd normally let you go home but it's a bad one,' she said cheerfully, packing his bloodied nostrils with gauze strips and saline. 'Don't want any stray bits of cartilage floating around in there, do we?'

'Sorry,' said Daisy, for the fifteenth time since they had arrived, as they shuffled off to another part of the hospital. She didn't know what else to say.

It had been easier when it had initially happened, when she had helped haul him off the ground, in shock at Daniel's ranting, drunken state and attempted, desperately, to mop up the blood that streamed down his shirt. Then she had taken charge, grabbing Ellie's supply of cotton wool, shouting for someone to move the cars, the protesters, so that she could get him to hospital, fielding off Sylvia Rowan who had descended like some malevolent old crone to crow that there, see?, the drink-related violence had started already. 'It won't work,' the woman had cried triumphantly. 'I'll have the magistrates revoke your licence. I've got witnesses.'

'Oh, get lost, you old bat,' Daisy had shouted, and hauled him into her car. He had been dazed then, having possibly banged his head when he fell, and had followed Daisy almost docilely, obeying her urgent instructions to sit, hold this, to stay awake, stay awake. Now, however, he was possibly too awake, fuelled by bad coffee and the disinfected atmosphere, his dark headachy eyes glowering out over a surgical dressing, his splattered shirt a ruined reminder of her part in the day's events.

'I'm so sorry,' she said, handing him his coffee. He looked almost worse when she came back to him.

'Stop apologising.' His tone was exhausted.

'She won't be able to, will she? Get your licence revoked?'

'Sylvia Rowan? Least of my worries.' He grimaced as he sipped the coffee.

What does that mean? Daisy wanted to ask. But his demeanour, and the fact that he could hardly speak, made it difficult to glean anything else.

As they sat on their plastic chairs, under the fluorescent light, time had appeared to stall, then lost meaning altogether. Men with alcohol-related injuries, as they were described on the sheet, were evidently not a priority. They sat with the other Saturday-night casualties, interest transiently flickering as some new disaster limped through the swishing electronic doors, the gardening punctures and DIY burns giving way to the bloodied heads and knuckles of Saturday night. At around eight one of the bar staff had arrived with Ellie, apologising and saying that they couldn't find Lottie, and no one else was available to stay with her. Daisy had taken her dozy, fractious daughter, not daring to meet Jones's eye. Disturbed and discombobulated, Ellie had wailed and fought sleep, and it had taken Daisy endless circuits of the A and E area and the fracture clinic to finally get her to nod off in her push-chair.

'Go home, Daisy,' Jones said, rubbing at the lump on his head.

'No,' she had said, firmly. She couldn't. It had been her fault, after all.

At a quarter past eleven, just as the waiting-time screen told them that Jones would be seen almost half an hour ago, a clap of thunder announced the arrival of a huge storm. The noise

467

jolted the waiting casualties from their reverie, the whited flash of lightning causing an audible murmur and, after a brief pause, like an indrawn breath, the night sky pulled back and let its deluge pour down in sheets. The sound of it could be heard through the glass doors; the water came in on the soles of people's feet, making the shiny linoleum floor streaky with mud and polish. Daisy, who had almost fallen asleep, watched, feeling something give at the change in atmosphere, wondering in her overtired state that it held the surreal quality of a dream.

The effect of it was apparent almost twenty minutes later, when a male nurse came out to tell Jones that his waiting time was likely to be extended as they were getting reports of a major pile-up on the Colchester Road. The consultant was likely to be tied up for some time.

'So, do I just go home?' said Jones, as intelligibly as he could.

The nurse, a young man with the jaded air of someone who had swiftly had both idealism and innocence battered out of him, eyed Daisy and the baby. 'If you can bear it, you'd be better off waiting. If you can get it reset tonight you've got much less chance of it being bent permanently out of shape.'

''S already bent out of shape,' said Jones. But he said he would stay.

'You go,' he told Daisy, again, as the nurse walked off.

'No,' said Daisy.

'Oh, for God's sake, Daisy, it's stupid, you and the baby sitting here all night. Go and take her home and if you're really concerned I'll give you a ring later, okay?'

Jones had not asked her why Daniel would want to hit him. But evidently he knew it was because of her. His grand opening had descended into farce because of her.

Daisy had reloaded the spent weaponry of the ridiculous, vindictive Sylvia Rowan. All that effort, all those months of work, undermined by a stupid misunderstanding.

Daisy was too tired. She looked at Jones's exhausted, brooding face, the shadows cast into sharp relief by the unforgiving nature of the overhead lights, and felt her gritty eyes sting. She reached down, scooped up her bag and, standing, kicked the brake off the push-chair. 'I thought he'd gone, you know,' she said, barely conscious of what she was saying.

'What?'

'Daniel. He had said he was going.'

'Going where?'

'*Home.*' She heard her voice rising, a querulous quiver of frustration and grief. And before he could see her lose her composure, before she was reduced yet again to the girl she had never wanted to be, Daisy turned and pushed her child out of the waiting area.

He lived in Spain. He had retired there several years ago, after allowing the management of what had once been his father's fruit-importing company to buy him out. He had got out at the right time: the industry was increasingly taken over by one or two huge multinationals. There was little room for family operators like himself. He didn't miss it.

He lived in a large white house, probably too large but helped by a nice local girl who did for him twice a week and occasionally brought her two sons, at his request, to swim in his pool. He didn't think he would return to England. Too used to the sun.

His mother, he said, his voice lowering, had died of cancer, quite young. His father had never really recovered, and had been killed in a chip-pan fire several years later. A stupid, mundane death for a man like him, but he hadn't been the type to cope by himself. Not like Guy. He was used to it. Sometimes he thought he even quite liked it.

He had no firm plans but a lot of money. A handful of good friends. Not a bad place for a man to be. Not at his age.

Lottie listened to these details, but heard few of them. She found herself unable to stop looking at him, translating the boy she had known into this old man so swiftly that already she had trouble picturing his younger self; registering the unfamiliar melancholy in his tone, and suspecting, knowing, that it echoed her own.

It didn't occur to her to feel conscious of her own appearance, of her greyed hair, her thickened waist, of the translucent, parchment skin on her hands. That had never been the point of it, after all.

He gestured behind them towards the house, where the music had stopped and just the echoing sounds of tidying, of chairs being dragged across floors and industrial cleaners echoed down into the bay.

'So that's your daughter.'

There was a momentary pause, before Lottie replied: 'Yes, that's Camille.'

'Good man, Joe,' he said.

Lottie bit her lip. 'Yes.'

'Sylvia wrote. She said you'd married him.'

'And some, no doubt. Probably about him deserving better.'

They both smiled.

Lottie looked away. 'He did, you know.'

Guy's face was questioning. She halted, startled that there could be familiarity in the way he raised an eyebrow, at the youth still visible in his expression. It made her unguarded. 'All these years I've resented him.'

'Joe?'

'For not being you.' Her voice was a little hoarse.

'I know. Celia couldn't help it but she—' He stopped, perhaps reluctant to be disloyal.

He still had the white hairs. They were harder to spot, among the grey, but she could still just make them out.

'She wrote to you, you know. Several times. After you'd gone. Never sent them. I think she found it all . . . more of a strain than any of us realised . . . I don't suppose I was terribly understanding.' He turned to her. 'I've still got them at home. I never opened them. I could send them to you, if you like.'

She couldn't say. She didn't know whether she was ready to hear Celia's voice. Whether she ever would be. 'You never wrote,' she said.

'I thought you didn't want me. I thought you'd changed your mind.'

'How could you ever think that?' She was a young girl again, her face flushed with the desperate unfairness of love.

He looked down. Out at the distant thunderclouds on the horizon. 'Yes, well, I worked it all out afterwards. I worked a lot of things out afterwards.' He looked at her again. 'But by then I heard you'd married Joe.'

Several people trailed past, glowing under the lowering sun, their loose pink limbs and contented weariness testament to the rare combination of heatwave and English beach. Guy and Lottie sat beside each other, watching them in silence, looking out at the lengthening shadows, listening to the lap and draw of the waves on the shingle. In the distance, on the horizon, a light glinted.

'What a mess, Guy. What a mess we've made of these years.'

471

He reached out a hand. It rested on hers, enclosed it. The feel of it made her draw breath. When he spoke, it was without hesitation. 'It's never too late, Lottie.'

They stared at the sea for as long as it took the sun to disappear finally behind them, feeling the air of the evening turn chill, recognising that there were too many questions, too few adequate answers. Old enough to recognise that some things don't need spelling out. Eventually Lottie turned to him, to the face she had loved, the tracing of its lines telling her nearly everything she needed to know about love and loss.

'Is it true,' she whispered, 'that you never had children?'

Afterwards, at least one holidaymaker making their way slowly in small groups back along the sea path, went home with the observation that it was not often you saw an old woman with her head in her hands, crying with the broken-hearted abandon of a young girl

Daisy drove for miles under the dark sky, guided by the sodium lights of dual-carriageways, and the little car's head-lights in winding country lanes, occasionally, unthinkingly, checking in the rear-view mirror the sleeping baby behind her. She drove slowly, methodically because of the rain, but not thinking where she was going, stopping once for fuel, and a cup of bitter, acrid coffee that had burnt her tongue and left her feeling jittery rather than refreshed.

She didn't want to go back to Arcadia. It already felt like someone else's place; would already be housing the first of its guests, echoing with other people's noise and chatter and acquisitive footsteps. She did not want to go back there with her sleeping child and explain about Jones, and Daniel, and her part in the whole sorry mess.

She wept a bit too, largely from exhaustion – she had barely slept in thirty-six hours – but also from the anticlimactic feeling of the end of the party and the end of her time there, and the delayed shock that any exposure to violence brings. And because the man who meant most to her was lost to her again: his bloodied face, his unhappiness, the unintentional, farcical sabotage of his most important day conspiring against any chance she had had of expressing her feelings.

Daisy steered the car to a gentle halt on a gravelly lay-by, listening to the sound of the rain on the roof and the squeaking drag of the wipers on the windscreen. Below her, in the cobalt darkness, she could see the curve of the coastline and, far out to sea, the faintest glow of the dawn.

She laid her hands across the steering-wheel and sank her head on to them, as if it were being pressed there by a great weight. They had sat there, all those hours, and had hardly spoken. She had been close enough to feel him shift his weight beside her, for their hands to brush, for her head to droop unwittingly on to his shoulder during the one point that she had almost fallen asleep. And yet they had not spoken, except to discuss their requirements for machine coffee, and for him to tell her, again, to go home.

I was so close, she thought. Close enough to touch him. Close enough to hear him breathe. And now I'll never be that close again.

Daisy sat very still. She lifted her head, remembering something Camille had said.

Close enough to hear him breathe. To recognise the rapidity of a heartbeat quickening through want, through need.

Daisy let out a great gulp. Then, suddenly galvanised, she turned the ignition, glanced behind her, and wrenched the car round, its wet wheels spinning in the gravel.

There were three ambulances outside A and E, parked

haphazardly, surrounded by wheeling people in luminous waistcoats who carefully jettisoned their charges on to wheel-chairs, stretchers, walked them in, their heads bent low in consultation. A siren had been left on and the noise it made was deafening, hardly muffled by the still torrential rain, or the sound of her engine. She manoeuvred around them, trying to find a parking space, her gaze flickering into the mirror to check that her child did not stir. Ellie slept on, oblivious to the noise, exhausted by the day's events.

And then, as she sat in the blue light, incapacitated by her inability to think straight and the fact that she had come here at all, she glanced up through her blurred windscreen and saw him, a tall, slightly stooped figure, walking resolutely through the rain, towards the taxi rank. Daisy waited for a split second, making sure. Then she threw open her car door and, oblivious to the rain and to the deafening din of the sirens, began to run across the forecourt, half skidding, half stumbling, until she slid to a halt directly in front of him. '*Stop!*'

Jones stopped. He squinted, apparently trying to establish that it was actually her. One hand rose unconsciously to the oversized white dressing across his face.

'You're not my boss any more, Jones,' she shouted, above the sirens, shivering in her crumpled party dress, 'so you can't tell me what to do. You can't tell me to go home.' It sounded angrier than she had intended.

He looked beaten-down, grey-faced. 'I'm sorry,' he said, his voice thickened and bruised. 'I should have been . . . It's just not how I wanted to be . . . Not how I wanted to be seen. On my back and with a fist in my face—'

'Ssh. Just ssh a minute. I don't want to talk about that. I've been driving all night and I need to say something to you and if I stop now I won't get it out.' She was almost delirious with tiredness, the thrumming rain in her ears coursing in cold tears down her face. 'I know you like me,' she shouted at him. 'I don't know if you even know it yet, but you do. Because apart from the fact that we keep somehow injuring each other and the fact that we argue a lot, and the fact that I may have lost you your licence, which I am really, *really* sorry about, we are *good* for each other. We are a good team.' He made as if to speak again, but she shushed him with her hands, her heart in her throat, no longer caring how she appeared. She rubbed her streaming eyes, trying to gather her thoughts. 'Look. I know I've got baggage. I know someone like me is probably not on your agenda, what with a baby and everything, but you've got a ton of baggage too. You've got an ex-wife who you're obviously not over, and a load of women who you've slept with who still work for you – which, frankly, I think is a bit much. And you're a bit of a misogynist, which I can't say I like either.'

He was frowning now, trying to understand, one hand raised over his eyes so that he could still see her through the rain.

'Jones, I'm too tired. I can't say it like I want to say it. But I've worked it all out. Yes, swans mate for life. But they're only one species, after all. Right? And how can they tell, anyway, if they all look the same?' The ambulance siren had stopped. Or perhaps it had gone. And suddenly it was just the two of them, standing in the middle of the car park, in the cold light of daybreak, with only the sound of the rain around them. She was right by him now, could see his eyes, looking directly into hers, his face pained but perhaps, just perhaps, understanding.

'I can't go on, Jones,' she said, her voice breaking. 'I've got a baby in the car and I'm too tired to talk and I can't explain what it is I feel.' And then, before she could change her mind, she reached up, took his face gently in her wet palms, and placed her mouth on his.

He lowered his head, and she felt with a burst of gratitude his lips on hers, his arms pulling her into him with a kind of relief. She relaxed, feeling the tension disappear, knowing it was right. Knowing she had done the right thing. She breathed in the scent of the hospital on his skin, and it made her feel protective, as if she wanted to enclose him, bring him in to her. And then, abruptly and without warning, he was pushing her away, holding her almost at arm's length.

'What?' said Daisy. I can't bear it, she thought. Not after this. Not after everything.

Jones sighed, looking up to the heavens. Then reached forward, enclosed her hand with both of his. They were softer than she'd expected. 'Sorry,' he growled, with an apologetic smile. 'You don't know how sorry, Daisy. But I can't breathe and kiss at the same time.'

The big white house was as still and quiet as it had been on the day Daisy arrived, its skeleton staff asleep in the staff flats over the garages, its cars silent on the gravel; through the windows, the kitchens tranquil and gleaming, their shining surfaces uninterrupted by the clatter of tools and trays. Aside from their footfalls crunching on the gravel, the only sounds to be heard were the birdsong, the gentle murmur of the breeze in the pines and, somewhere below, the distant lapping of low tide.

Jones handed Daisy the keys to the back door, and she fumbled in the new light, dazed and stupid with lack of sleep, trying to locate the right one. He gestured, glancing vigilantly down at the sleeping baby in his arms as he did so. Daisy wrestled with the lock and, finally, the dormant house allowed them entry.

'Your room,' he whispered, and they padded softly along the corridor and up the back stairs, bumping gently into each other as they went, like drunkards returning home after a long night.

Daisy's belongings were packed into a neat collection of bags and boxes; only the cot and several changes of clothes from the previous day were still visible, evidence that this had once been something more permanent than a hotel room. Just twenty-four hours ago the sight of the luggage had made Daisy feel panicked, and alone. Now it produced a flicker of something like excitement, the promise of a new life and new opportunities cautiously revealing themselves before her.

She closed the door quietly behind her, and looked at the man in front of her. Jones walked slowly across the room, murmuring to the prostrate Ellie held close against his chest. He placed her gently in her cot, taking care not to disturb her, sliding his hands out from underneath her soft limbs, and Daisy pulled a light blanket over her child. She barely stirred.

'That all she needs?' he whispered.

Daisy nodded. They stood there for a few seconds, watching the sleeping child, then she took his hand and pulled him towards the bed, still unmade from the previous morning.

Jones sat down, removed his jacket, revealing his rain-wrinkled, blood-spattered shirt, and took off his shoes. Daisy, beside him, pulled her crumpled party dress one-handed over her head, unselfconscious now about the possible exposure of post-baby bulges or stretchmarks, even in the harsh light of morning. She replaced it with her old T-shirt and climbed in, the covers whispering against her bare legs.

The window was open, carrying in the warm scents of the salted summer morning, the curtains swaying languorously in the breeze. Jones eased himself down, facing her, his eyes black with lack of sleep, his jaw greyed and unshaven, yet all the tensions somehow ironed from his brow. He gazed at her, unblinking, his eyes softened, his hand lifting to trace Daisy's bare skin.

'You look beautiful,' he said, from under his gauze dressing.

'You don't.'

They smiled at each other, slow, sleepy smiles.

He lifted his finger and placed it on her lips. She kept her eyes on his, and lifted her own bandaged hand, lightly touching his face, allowing herself the luxury of the touch for which she had ached for so long. Very gently, she placed her fingertip on his bandaged nose. 'Does it hurt?' she murmured.

'Nothing hurts,' said Jones. 'Absolutely nothing.'

And, with a deep sigh of satisfaction, he pulled her to him, wrapped himself around her, buried his big head in that cool, sweet place where her neck met her shoulder. She felt his soft hair and his stubbly jaw against her, the touch of his lips, smelt the distant echo of antiseptic on his skin. For a second she recognised the flicker of desire, and almost immediately felt it swamped by something more pleasurable, a relaxed anticipation, a deep joyous feeling of safety. She burrowed into him, feeling the weight of his arm, his leg, entwined with hers, his limbs already heavy with approaching slumber. And then, finally, pressed against the steady beat of his heart, Daisy slept.

The rain had passed over Merham. It left pavements silvered with water, glowing liquid peach and phosphorescent blue in the early light. Hal's footsteps, steady and even, splashed as he walked his charge towards the gate.

It was Rollo who first saw them coming up the road:

478

through the window Hal saw him leap out from under the coffee table and scramble towards the door, barking. Camille, jolted from a light sleep, rose awkwardly from the sofa to follow him, stumbling as she reached for her cane, and worked out where she was. But Rollo had not been the most alert. By the time Hal reached the gate, his father-in-law was already half-way down the stairs. He walked out of the open door and down the path with the brisk gait of someone half his age, straight past Hal, who stepped aside – and reclaimed his exhausted wife. There was a short silence. Hal stood in the porch, his ears ringing with birdsong, and placed his arms around Camille, grateful after the long, long night simply to feel her there. He answered her whispered question with a nod, close enough that she could feel his head against hers.

Then Camille took a step back, squeezing his hand. 'We'll go now, Pops,' she called, 'unless you want us to stay.'

'Either way, sweetheart.' Joe's voice was rigid, contained.

Camille made to move, but Hal stayed her. They stood in the doorway, waiting, listening. Joe, several feet away, faced his wife like an old prize-fighter. Hal noted that his hands, behind his back, were trembling. 'You must want a cup of tea,' he said.

'No,' said Lottie, smoothing her hair away from her face. 'No, I just had one up at the café. With Hal.' She glanced behind him, then caught sight of the two suitcases in the hall. 'What's this?' she said.

Joe closed his eyes briefly. Breathed out. As if it were an effort. 'You never looked at me like that. Not in forty years of marriage.'

Lottie faced him. 'I'm looking at you now, aren't I?'

They stared at each other for some time. Then Lottie took two steps forward, and grasped his hand. 'I thought I might take up painting again. I might enjoy doing a bit of painting again.'

Joe frowned, looked at her as if she were not in control of her senses.

Lottie glanced down at their hands. 'This silly cruise thing of yours. You're not going to make me play bridge, are you? I can't stand playing bridge. But I don't mind having a go at a bit of painting.'

Joe looked at her, his eyes widening a fraction. Then: 'You know I'd never . . .' His voice broke and he turned away from them all for a minute, his head sunk into his shoulders. Lottie's head dipped, and Hal, suddenly feeling like an intruder, looked away, his hand closing around Camille's.

Joe appeared to compose himself. He hesitated, looked at his wife, then moved forward, just one or two steps, and placed his arm around her shoulders. She moved into him, a small gesture but there none the less, and together, slowly, they walked towards their house.

It was time to make him happy, she had told Hal, when he found her, down at the beach huts, sitting alone in the dawn. It had been enough to know that Guy had loved her, that they would have been together.

'I don't understand,' Hal had said. 'He was the love of your life. Even I could see that.'

'Yes, he was. But I can let him go now,' she had said simply. And although he could normally describe anything to his sightless wife, Hal struggled to convey the sense of release on Lottie's face, the way her expression, engraved with years of pent-up frustration and grief, had cleared.

'Sitting there, talking to him. It made me realise – all these years wasted. Hankering after someone who wasn't there when I should have been loving Joe. He's a good man, you see.' Outside, two lobstermen had unloaded their boats, hauling their catch over the side with a well-practised ease. Along the shore, the first dogwalkers left meandering tracks on the sand, a temporary history.

'He's known. He's always known. But he never resented me for it.'

She had looked at her son-in-law then, and stood, a hand pushing back her greying hair, a girlish, tentative smile. 'I think it's time Joe got himself a wife, don't you?'

Epilogue

I had to stay in a hospital for a while afterwards. I forget how many weeks. They didn't call it a hospital, of course, not when they were trying to persuade me to go there. They just said it would be a visit home to England, a chance to spend some time with Mummy.

A 'little stay' would make me feel better, you see. Lots of girls had the same problem as me, even if no one really talked about it. It wasn't the sort of thing one talked about, even then. They knew that I'd never liked living in the tropics, that if it hadn't been for Guy I would have come home.

I had wanted that baby, you see. Wanted it so much. I used to dream that it was inside me; sometimes if I put my hand on the bare skin of my stomach I could even feel it flutter. I used to talk to it, silently, willing it into life. Although I never told anybody. I knew what they'd say.

Because Guy and I never spoke about it. He was rather good like that, Mummy said. Sometimes the less attention one paid to something the better. Less damage all round. Then, Mummy always was one to turn a blind eye. She never spoke about it either. It was as if I embarrassed her.

When I came out, everyone pretended I hadn't been there at all. They just got on with things and left me to my dreams. I didn't tell them anything. I knew from their faces they didn't believe half of what I said. Why should they?

But you can't escape your past, can you? Just like you can't escape your fate. Guy and I were never really the same afterwards. It was as if he carried it around, rotting inside him, and could never look at me without the smell of it, the taint of it, colouring his reaction. He was as full of it as I was empty.

Eighteen apples I did, the day that I told you. Eighteen apples.

And still they came out the same way.